Torment

CW01652974

by

Kerry Barnes

Copyright

Torment by Kerry Barnes ISBN - 978-1-8380440-1-5

This is a work of fiction. Names, characters, places, and incidents either are the product of the author's imagination or are used fictitiously. Any resemblance to actual persons, living or dead, events, or locales is entirely coincidental.

For more information, address: kerrybarnes999@gmail.com.

Publishers Once Upon A Book

www.authorkerrybarnes.co.uk

Warning

This book contains graphic details of murder, kidnapping, violence and sexual violence.

Acknowledgements

A big thank you to Robert Wood, my editor, who worked exceptionally hard on this book, as he always does. However, his added input was invaluable, especially at a time when I needed the extra help and support. – Epworth Editing.com -

NotRights book club for the endless support and kind words.

Deryl Easton for her advice and support.

To all the readers who have invested their time in reading my books, I am eternally grateful.

To my family, who have put up with my mood swings during the editing process; thank you for not killing me.

Dedication

To Adam Barnes – my brother.

CHAPTER ONE

21st October 2012

The sound of footsteps followed by the door being opened instantly compelled Yalina to cling tighter to her mother.

Shabir, a supposed relative, appeared, dressed in a blue striped shirt, with patches of sweat clearly visible. He wasn't like her father who only ever wore a Pathani suit. Shabir was now a westernised man. As a young child, she recalled him coming to visit her family. He was so different back then. He was respectful and kinder, often arriving with gifts, and his voice wasn't so harsh.

With her head down, Yalina only watched through her long black lashes. The stream of light from the door ajar was enough to make visible the squalid conditions they had been sleeping in. However, they'd been so tired by the time they had arrived in England all the way from Pakistan that even the stained mattress, with its faded threadbare blankets, was a welcome relief.

'You must come with me, Yalina. Now!'

Shyly, Yalina peered up. Her father often reminded her that she mustn't look a man in the eyes as it would give the wrong impression. *You come from a good family, Yalina. Be a good girl: never bring shame on us.*

As her mother stroked her long raven-black hair, which was pulled back into a single plait almost down to her waist, she whispered, 'Go, Yalina. You must do as he says.'

Gripping her mother's hand tighter, Yalina was terrified of letting go. This was a strange place. It was cold, damp, and cramped for space. But her father had told her and her mother that they had little choice.

Shabir was going to find them work in England so that they could earn a very good wage, enough to send home and to pay the rent. The situation was very risky and so they must be separated. Shabir said it was safer that way. They couldn't afford to be found by the police; it would cause a lot of trouble. Shabir had already found work for Anandia, Yalina's mother. She was to be a maid to a Russian man who would pay very well, as long as she was exceptionally good at cleaning and was also invisible.

Shabir tugged Yalina's arm gently, but she resisted and leaned into her mother. 'Please can I go with you? I can cook, clean. You know how well I can clean.'

Her mother cupped her daughter's defined cheeks and stared into her eyes: they looked like round pools of chocolate brown. 'You must do as Shabir says. You know your father will be pleased when Shabir tells him that his daughter has been a good girl.'

'But please, Mother,' begged Yalina.

Anandia looked up at Shabir, silently pleading with him. He dominated the room, with his rotund body and broad shoulders. But when Shabir narrowed his eyes into a scowl, Anandia knew she couldn't push him. She had been warned not to cross the man. Her husband had made it clear that Shabir was their only hope; they were penniless. Shabir was his so-called cousin; he would do right by them and this was a great honour.

'Please, Yalina, you must go. It is too dangerous for us to be together. Shabir will take good care of you,' she said, nodding as if she too wanted to believe her daughter would be safe.

Anandia had to believe she was doing the right thing: to provide for her other two daughters and her husband. It hadn't been an easy decision, but when her husband had said they may have to resort to selling the youngest two daughters to the Chinese as brides, it made the whole idea of coming to England for work the only option she had left.

Even after she had sold all of their jewellery and her best saris, to help pay towards their passage to England, Shabir had informed them that although there were other fees to find, he would cover the costs for now. She and Yalina could work off the debt over time.

The second tug on Yalina's arm was harder, and she knew she had made him cross. Slowly, she allowed him to pull her to her feet. Looking back at her sweet mother, who was now dressed in modern clothes – jeans and a sweatshirt with a Sesame Street motif – she hardly recognised her. Her mother's bright citrus-coloured saris had somehow always defined her. Wiping away a tear that had escaped her eyes, she turned to look at her mother for one last time, hoping to frame the picture of her in her mind. She wasn't sure what feeling was worse – seeing her mother drenched in sadness or her own fear for what the future might hold.

***

As soon as Shabir closed the door behind them, Yalina blinked to adjust to the light that was shining along the long derelict-looking corridor.

Although she didn't know what the building was she was being held in, she had seen enough to realise it was derelict. The smell of mildew and the sounds of dripping taps and rats scurrying along the passageway at night were enough to give her nightmares. She had only managed to sleep when her mother's arms were around her. But during the last week locked in this creepy building, she had felt like a prisoner. The food was scarce, the toilet consisted of a bucket, and the washing facilities amounted to just a bowl of murky water, an old towel, and a cracked bar of soap. Only her mother's words of encouragement and prayers soothed her fears.

Now, having left the relative safety of her mother in another section of this vast building, she knew for some reason she had reached a pivotal moment in her life. She didn't know why. Why didn't matter. But leaving her mother was a huge deal for her. The thought that she would never see her again briefly crossed her mind.

So where was Shabir taking her now? She desperately wanted to ask, but she was so afraid of him. Everything about him was ugly. He had a deep cold rasping voice and dark beady eyes, and when he smirked, she saw the remains of heavily stained teeth. He reminded her of a fat rat and not the generous person he once was, or, as she realised now, had pretended to be.

Even though she was hurrying alongside him, he continued to squeeze and tug at her arm. She assumed he wanted to make her feel as though she was in trouble and was being taken to a place to be chastised.

The light came from the see-through plastic double swing doors at the end, the type seen in a hospital or at the back of a warehouse As she passed the doors on either side of her, she knew something was wrong. Obviously, behind those padlocked doors were others, because she could hear coughing and whispering, and even some crying. Her legs suddenly turned to jelly, and her head felt hot. She realised that everyone here had been locked in their rooms and hidden away from the police. They were being kept prisoner, and Shabir was their captor.

Shabir stopped abruptly and pushed Yalina to the wall, before pulling a ring from his pocket. The ring contained numerous padlock keys, each one having a coloured ring attached to it.

Yalina watched as he matched the colour green with the green sticker on the padlock. While he fiddled with the lock, her eyes were drawn to the open room to the left. There was no padlock but a long bolt that would have slid across the door. She shivered when she saw the handcuffs hanging from a pipe. Suddenly, she wanted to run back to her mother, but she was frozen to the spot, gripped by terror.

Shabir finally managed to open the door, and there inside was a bunk bed, a bucket, and a tray of half-eaten naan bread. The stench in the room was vile.

Yalina assumed that he would push her inside, but, instead, he shouted, 'Come out!'

Two girls appeared, who looked about fifteen years old. They were so skinny. And their huge round sunken eyes were defined by black eyeliner. It was clearly not newly applied since it was smudged into their cheeks. As they stepped into the corridor, neither of them looked her way.

'Come, we must go,' Shabir urged them, as he pushed the two girls ahead of him, before suddenly snatching Yalina's arm again.

Yalina couldn't hold back this time. 'Where are we going, Uncle?' She had been told to call her father's male family members and friends 'Uncle'. She assumed it was a sign of respect.

A swift backhander caught Yalina across the chest. 'You! Shut up! You are here to work, not to ask questions.'

Yalina wanted to cry out in pain, but she held her scream inside and decided to do as he said. Her father had warned her not to ask questions, but it was part of who she was. She loved to learn and she adored school, but she was fifteen, and she knew she was never going back to her village. Her place now was to help the family. That was what her father had told her.

They walked along a corridor lined with huge pipes overhead and up a slight incline until they came to the set of see-through swing doors. However, Yalina couldn't imagine this place being anything medical since it smelled so musty.

At the end of the corridor were two men dressed in black and around their waists were gun belts. They weren't Asian men.

Shabir nodded to them, and Yalina could tell right away that he wasn't their boss.

One stepped aside to allow him to pass.

Yalina watched as he pushed the two girls out through the doors. He then dragged her past the two men, whom she assumed were guards, but not before she heard one of them speak. He sounded Russian, or at least somewhere from that part of the world.

Once outside, she could see so much better; however, she had to blink a few times, to adjust to the bright light after spending so much time in the dark.

First, she noticed the considerable fence surrounding the perimeter. And standing by a set of twelve-foot-high gates were another two guards. There appeared to be just the one road or a drive that led in and out of the place. Beyond the perimeter was a steep hill. As far as her eyes could see, there were no houses or other buildings, merely grass and bushes and the odd tree. It was clear that they were in a hollow, somewhere in the countryside. Briefly looking back at the see-through swing doors, confirmed to Yalina that they were actually being kept underground in a derelict building. That was why her room had a tiny stained window just below the ceiling.

It was evident from the mountains of sand that this was a building site. She tried to look back to where she'd come from again, to register her bearings, but she was prevented from doing so by Shabir shoving her hard in the nape of her neck.

'Get in the van,' he demanded, as a white van drew up in front of them.

The side door opened and another guard held his hand out to help the girls inside. The other two girls did precisely as they were told.

But Yalina stood her ground and looked at Shabir. 'Where am I going, Uncle?'

His eyes widened and he slapped her face. 'I told you once. I will not tell you again. You do as I say. Now, shut up and get in.'

Yalina held her stinging cheek; her eyes twitched as a tear ran through her fingers.

The Russian guard snatched her hand and pulled her into the van. He pointed to a long plank of wood bolted to the side, which was clearly being used as a makeshift bench. She took her seat opposite the two girls. The Russian then jumped down from the van and slid the door shut. Now, they were left in total darkness.

Once the bumpy journey began, Yalina whispered, 'Where are we going?'

'Shh! Keep quiet, or they will beat us.'

Yalina gasped.

'My name is Sana. What's yours?'

'Yalina.'

'And I am Bina,' said the second girl. 'But you must speak quietly. We are not allowed to talk to each other.'

'Where are they taking us?'

'Is this your first time, Yalina?'

'Yes. I have to work to pay for my little sisters and to be a good girl for my father.'

A sudden bang on the partition between the driver and the back of the van made them all jump.

'No talking back there!' bellowed the driver, who was more than likely Russian or Eastern European.

'Yalina, please speak quietly,' said Sana.

'I'm so sorry,' she whispered. 'Where are you from?'

'Pakistan.'

'We all are,' whispered Bina.

'All?'

'Yalina, there are more of us. You will see when you start working.'

'I am worried. They may have misunderstood. My father has sent me here to work for my Uncle Shabir. It is an honour, he said.'

'Shabir is an uncle to all of us, and we are all honoured, as he constantly reminds us,' replied Bina, with a trace of bitterness to her tone.

The bang on the partition made them jump again. 'Quiet or you will never speak again – understood!'

'Please listen,' said Sana, in her quietest voice. 'You must do as they say, or they will hurt you. And don't think the police will help you because they won't. You cannot trust anyone. And when it gets hard, just remember the money you earn will go to your family.'

Filled with so much trepidation, Yalina felt her legs tremble. 'What will I have to do?' she asked, although she had a pretty good idea, and the thought turned her insides out with dread.

'All you have to think about, Yalina, is that the money is going to your family,' replied Bina, in her very childlike voice.

After what seemed like an hour, Yalina began to feel travel-sick. She had never been able to get used to the bumpy roads in her home town, and now she was being thrown around in the back of a van in a country she knew nothing about. By the time they came to a stop, her ears were ringing. She was ready to throw up, but more than anything, she was shaking all over.

***

The narrow alley was only wide enough for the van and not much else. So as the door slid open, there was a small pathway between the vehicle and the two steps that led down to a steel door. Yalina didn't have time to survey her surroundings before the steel door opened.

Shabir came into view. He had arrived ahead of them. He didn't have to speak. His beady eyes glared as he aggressively flicked his head to indicate they should enter. His fat cheeks jiggled like they had their own dance. 'Hurry!' he hollered.

There was something familiar – the spicy aroma that wafted from the doorway. For a split second, Yalina was back at home, stirring a huge bubbling pot, her mouth drooling. This was a reminder of home.

'Get inside, girl. Don't drag your feet. You don't want to look slovenly,' Shabir growled in her ear, before pushing her viciously in the back. She followed the other two girls as she made their way through a small corridor filled on either side with rows of saris wrapped in plastic protective coverings. She guessed she was in the back of a shop. Suddenly, she was filled with a twinge of excitement, hoping that this was where she would be working.

She loved the materials, the sequins, the glass beads, and the stunning shades of every imaginable colour – like the hessian sacks at the market place back in her village in Pakistan filled with an array of coloured spices. She heard the gentle humming of a sewing machine and was sure it was a shop. Or perhaps it was a laundry; either way, she wouldn't mind working here. The thought was so much more appealing compared to what had previously been running through her mind.

***

Finally, having passed through the corridor of saris, they entered a room. It wasn't a shop. In fact, Yalina had never seen anything like it. The area was large enough to hold a small banquet. They were standing on what she could only guess was a platform; behind it was a wall of curtains, all shimmering with metallic gold thread weaved into them. On the makeshift stage were tall colourful feathers in waist-high plant pots. Beautiful silk floor cushions, low tables, and smoking pipes adorned the lower level floor.

Before Yalina could take it all in, Shabir called out and clapped his hands. An older woman, clearly from Southeast Asia, appeared from behind the curtain with a broom in her hand. Yalina guessed, from her gnarly fingers, which were bent back with wrinkled skin, that she was most likely in her seventies. However, her eyes had lost their lustful glow that she assumed they'd had many years ago.

'Fetch Dominica. Now!'

She nodded and shuffled away back behind the curtain. A moment or two later, another woman appeared, possibly in her mid-thirties, although she clearly wasn't Asian.

Yalina noticed how Shabir bowed, showing his respect.

So the tall woman, with broad shoulders, poker-straight bleached blonde hair and smouldering brown eyes was in charge, thought Yalina.

Slowly, the woman approached, looking Yalina up and down until she was just inches away. Gripping her chin with her long painted fingernails, she turned Yalina's face from side to side.

'Hmmm, yes, excellent, very beautiful. Her eyes are so round. They will attract our best clients.' She stared at Yalina as if she were eyeing a juicy apple. 'And her lips are plump like a Bollywood movie star.'

She let go of Yalina's chin and stepped back. 'Yes, yes, very good. Her tiny waist is perfect for this dance, although I think her hair is too long. But can she dance?'

Shabir coughed, clearing his throat. 'She will dance for you, Ms Dominica. It's in her blood. She just needs to be shown. Her father promised me that she is a quick learner.'

'You are a quick learner? Yes?'

Her accent, which suggested she might be from Russia, was tainted with enough menace for Yalina to nod in agreement. Although she could feel her face glowing red with embarrassment.

'Look up. Er . . . What is her name?'

'It is Yalina. She is fifteen years old and a virgin.'

The word 'virgin' jolted Yalina to lift her face and glance from Dominica to Shabir.

'You speak English?'

'Yes, she does, very well,' replied Shabir.

Dominica waved her hands. 'I asked her, not you. Now, go and bring Hulou. I want to see if this girl can dance. I have a client, especially for her. I don't want to be let down. You understand, Shabir?'

He placed his hands together, bowed, and nodded. 'Of course, Ms Dominica.'

'And these spots on her cheeks. Have them covered up. I will return in one hour.'

She glanced back at Yalina. 'And, please, don't look so, what's the word? Hmmm, yes, knowing, er, clever.'

Again, Shabir called out to the old lady – this time for her to bring to him someone called Hulou.

Dominica lit a cigarette. 'And make sure those other two girls are bathed and made up before the guests arrive.' As she marched from the room, she left behind the scent of a strong sweet perfume and a faint plume of smoke that floated like a magic carpet.

Yalina heard the jangle of beads and the swishing sound of a sari sweeping the floor. She looked up and saw a tall woman with a luscious curvy figure who was dressed in the most delicate electric-blue gown, although, shockingly, much of her breasts were spilling over the top. It clearly wasn't the way they wore their saris back at home. Her face was beautiful, like a real Bollywood actress. But although it was heavily made up with colourful cosmetics, it was far from cheery. Her eyes were dull with sadness; they were empty and full of fatigue.

'Ah, good. You are awake! Now, Hulou, you must teach this girl to dance.'

Hulou merely nodded. 'Fine.'

'She must learn the Mujra.'

Again, the woman replied with no expression. 'Okay.'

'In one hour only!' Shabir wagged his finger.

'Impossible, Shabir, and absurd.'

A sharp slap across her face almost knocked her over. 'You will *make* it happen, or you know what will happen to *you*.'

Hulou wiped her mouth with the back of her hand and then peered at the blood before glaring back at Shabir. 'I won't look good with a fat lip, and if Yuri sees me like this, he will—'

She stopped when Shabir clamped his hand around her mouth. 'You shut up. I manage you, so you do as I say. You must teach the girl to dance. Now!'

He walked towards the corridor where all the saris were. When he glanced back, his face was cloaked in darkness.

'I can replace both of you, and your fathers will still owe a debt. Your passage to England wasn't cheap.'

He glared over Hulou's shoulders at the old woman with the broom. 'And your mother will have to work all her life for your insolence.'

As soon as he was out of sight, Hulou huffed and grumbled under her breath.

'Okay, so show me how you dance,' said Hulou, as she stepped back with her hands on her hips.

Yalina shrugged her shoulders. 'I don't dance. My father would never allow it. It's not right to dance. I am only fifteen.'

'Ha, only fifteen, eh?'

Yalina nodded.

'I was eleven when I first came here. I was made to dance for hours, or suffer at their hands. Now that you are in England, remove any thoughts of your own, because you are not allowed to have them. And there is no point. They own you, Yalina. They bloody own you, now.'

'No, you have it wrong. I don't owe Shabir very much. My mother will work hard and pay the remaining fee that it cost to come here, that's all.'

'Dear child, you must forget your mother. You will probably never see her again. And to be clear, the money you earn will never pay off your fee for passage. The interest is way too high. You will be fed and clothed, but you will never, ever, be free.'

Yalina spun around and looked at the other two girls, hoping for reassurance that she could work her debt off.

'And if you try to escape, the police will beat you so badly, you won't even look like your passport photo, and they will bring you back to be beaten by Yuri, and he can be a cruel man.' She turned her back and removed the fabric covering her shoulder, to reveal a nasty scar from having been burned.

Yalina gasped and felt her eyes fill up with tears. ‘But I can’t do this. I cannot dance.’

‘Well, Yalina, you must, or we will all be beaten, including my mother. They will break her fingers again, so, please, for her, for me, for all of us, learn to dance.’

CHAPTER TWO

As the music began, Hulou started to dance. 'You copy me.'

Yalina was reluctant to sway her hips, let alone shake the top half of her body. Not that her breasts were very well developed, as yet.

'No, no, Yalina. Watch me. You put your legs slightly apart, roll your hips, stick your booty out, and sway. See, watch how I am doing it.'

Feeling embarrassed, Yalina instantly cupped her face and began to cry.

Hulou looked around, making sure no one could see them, and then ripped Yalina's hand away from her face. 'If you don't dance, Yalina, they will have no use for you. They will kill you.' She let go of Yalina's wrist. 'And me, for not being a good teacher.'

'But I cannot dance like this. My father would be ashamed! I will bring shame on the family. He told me I had to be a good girl.'

'You silly girl, you must understand that there is no family honour, Yalina. Your father knew this is the work you would be doing. So when he said you must be a good girl, this is what he meant. Now, we have little time. Please, you must learn this dance now.'

Yalina stamped her foot. 'No, you are wrong, Hulou. My father would never do this to me. He taught me how to be a good girl, a good wife, modest and kind, and—'

'Stop, Yalina, just stop. Your father wanted you to be all those things, including being a virgin because you are worth more. These men want a good dancer, but they want a shy girl in the privacy of their room even more, and a virgin will bring bidders from far and wide for you.'

The blood drained from Yalina's face. Every word that Hulou said brought unbelievable fear. She shook her head as tears rolled down her cheeks. 'No, but he loves me. My father is a good man.'

'There is no such thing as a good man, Yalina. All men are greedy, disgusting pigs, but you must listen to me. If you want to live, then dance. Dance, as they say, as if your life depends on it, because, believe me, Yalina, it does.'

Shaking her head, Yalina sobbed. 'I would rather die.'

Hulou put her arm around her shoulders. 'Yes, we all would, but it may not be you they will kill but your mother.' She flicked her head in the direction of the old lady with the broom. 'My mother is the weapon they have. They beat her if I don't do as they say. She even tried to take her own life to free me.'

Yalina gasped, throwing her hands to her mouth.

'But they saved her, and so I just do as I am told. Now, do you understand?'

Yalina nodded. Her heart, which had been beating so fast, seemed to have suddenly turned to stone, and a veil of darkness slipped over her body.

***

An hour later, on the dot, Dominica entered the room. Instead of sitting on a cushion, she dragged a chair from the back of the room and placed it in front of the stage.

She clapped her hands. 'I want to see what you have for me!'

Yalina was behind the curtain and feeling every hair on her skin stand on end. She had to remember the moves, and right now, she wasn't sure how she could even dance in the new clothes that Hulou had dressed her in. The bra she had been given had forced her small breasts to push up and over the beaded top. The slim fitted skirt that touched the floor was heavy with sequins and only allowed for limited movement. But Hulou had told her that she must lift the skirt, as it would bring in good money. The thought turned her stomach, but she had to hold down the vomit, and the only way she could do that was by thinking about her dear mother. She could not bear to have anyone hurt her mother. She was the sweetest person she knew.

Once Hulou dressed her and applied her heavy make-up, she walked her over to a tall mirror. ‘Look, see, Yalina. You are a different person. When you are on stage, try to remember this isn’t really you. You’re back in Pakistan in your home village.’

Yalina could understand what Hulou saw because she didn’t recognise herself at all. A momentary smile curved her lips. She looked beautiful, but the thought dissipated like a cloud vanishing. She wasn’t vain; she’d never been interested in her looks, and she only wanted to study to be a doctor, not a dancer or a Bollywood actress.

After a quick hug from Hulou, she was ready to go on stage. She peered behind the curtain and saw Dominica sitting on the chair with her legs apart like a man would sit, her shoulders back, with every part of her projecting confidence.

‘Come, Yalina. Stand in the middle. I want to see you!’

Hulou gave Yalina a quick shove, and Yalina hurried to the centre of the stage.

‘Look up. I must see your face.’

Yalina lifted her chin and stared Dominica straight in the eyes. Suddenly, she wasn’t the shy girl from the small village in Pakistan. She was someone else.

‘Yes, very beautiful. Turn the music on! I want to see how you dance.’

The music they had been dancing to suddenly filled the room, and Hulou came on, winding and rolling the top half of her body while her hands were above her head. Sana and Bina followed suit, and Yalina took a deep breath, knowing this was all or nothing.

Visions of her mother in that ridiculous sweatshirt and the desperate look on her face brought the reality of the situation to the forefront of her mind. The more she thought of her mother, the more she rolled her body and twerked her booty, as Hulou called it. Her long hair was up, and in one quick movement, she removed the pin, lowered her head between her knees, and flicked her head back. Her hair became loose and fell around her face. She suddenly found the dance easy. The more she rolled her hips and shook her backside, the more Dominica clapped. She wondered if she herself was enjoying the applause or if she was using the dance moves to discharge her anger. Perhaps that was it. While the music allowed her freedom from her grief and pain, at the same time, she was keeping her mother alive.

'Good, good, turn the music off now. Where is Shabir?' asked Dominica, as she rose from the chair.

Hulou replied. 'He left and hasn't returned.'

No sooner had she got the words out of her mouth than Shabir bustled in from the corridor of saris.

He was dabbing his forehead with a stained handkerchief. 'Sorry, Ms Dominica. I had to pick up one of Yuri's guests. Her plane was delayed.'

As if a major nerve twitched in her neck, Dominica's head jerked. '*Her?* Did you say *her*?'

Shabir stopped wiping his sweaty forehead. 'Yes, I think she may be a new guard.'

Yalina would have looked away at this point under normal circumstances, but in her make-up and sari, she wasn't Yalina anymore. So, she stared at Dominica, enjoying the look of anger or jealousy on her face.

Shabir changed the subject. 'And is Yalina what you are looking for? I mean, is she—'

Dominica waved her hand impatiently. 'Yes, yes, she is fine. And this woman you collected from the airport. What exactly does she look like?'

'I believe she has short brown hair. Er, I wasn't looking at her face.'

Dominica let out a sharp laugh. 'You weren't looking at her face? Ha! You are not being honest with me, Shabir, because I see you, ogling all the girls. The younger, the better, and you have access to them for free. I know how you look at them, picking which one you will have every night. So, now, tell me, what did the new recruit look like!' She tapped her foot impatiently.

'I, er, don't touch the girls. I . . . I . . .'

'I don't care if you do, as long as you don't hurt them and leave bruises. The clients want them to look clean and pretty. Now, what did the woman look like?'

'She had short dark hair, blue eyes, and a dimple on her cheek.'

'A dimple, yes?'

He nodded. 'Yes.'

'Okay. So was Yuri there when you dropped off this new recruit?'

'Yes, he was.'

'I must go and meet the woman. Take me there, Shabir.'

Shabir was wiping his face again as he nodded.

'I will be back this evening when the clients arrive. Make sure, Hulou, that the girls are clean. You know what I mean.'

Hulou bit her bottom lip and nodded without taking her eyes away from Dominica.

'Don't look like you would kill me if you had a knife, Hulou. That look doesn't suit you.'

***

The journey from New Cross to Blackheath was gruelling. Dominica demanded Shabir drive faster all the while she was tutting, sighing, and grumbling under her breath.

As soon as Shabir drove into the gated property, he'd barely had the chance to brake, before Dominica threw open the car door, charged across the gravel drive, and pushed her way through the double oak doors into Yuri's London mansion. Jealousy was radiating from every pore in her body.

She had told Yuri that she wanted no woman around him unless they were part of the paid workers. She reasoned that women were hormonal and unpredictable. In truth, she didn't want another woman to take what she saw as hers. In his mid-forties, Yuri was ten years older than her. He was typically handsome, if you liked big men with long hair pulled tightly away from their face. She knew he was highly desirable because he had money and lots of it. But it was his mysterious ways that for her were a complete turn-on. And as far as she was concerned, all that seventeen stone of solid muscle belonged to her.

She assumed he had at least listened to her one demand regarding women. However, at the time, Yuri, as he always did, merely smiled and nodded. Few words ever left his mouth unless he was angry. Then, all hell would break loose. Waving the two guards out of her way, they quickly moved to the side, allowing her entry.

They didn't want to stop the hissing, spitting cat. Dominica had a reputation for throwing her toys out of the pram, especially when she'd been on the vodka. The two guards assumed that was her only attraction because with her spiteful features and skinny legs, she was neither attractive nor kind, yet no one dared to ask Yuri what he saw in her.

The clomping of her shoes against the marble floor echoed around the high ceiling of the entrance hall. She stormed through to the vast lounge, which was rarely used because Yuri wasn't one for entertaining guests – only a few businessmen and his advisor, whom she couldn't stand anyway.

She continued until she reached the room on the right – his plush office. Without so much as a knock, she barged in, only to find Yuri dressed in a casual blue cashmere jumper and jeans. With a rare smile on his face as he swung gently from side to side in his grand office chair, he couldn't have looked more comfortable and sexy if he tried.

Dominica glanced at the woman sitting opposite, who, oddly, for the autumnal weather, was wearing a white V-neck T-shirt, her cleavage briefly on show, and a pair of khaki shorts that showed off her sharply tanned legs. Her short dark hair enhanced her long neck, and from the side, Dominica could spot the dimple. *Cute.*

The woman's side profile had Dominica bubbling with envy. So much so, that as soon as the guest pivoted her head, Dominica felt like ripping her face off. She didn't know how to cool down the raging fury inside her that wanted to escape like lava from an erupting volcano.

'Kristi, this is Dominica,' said Yuri, shaking his head in annoyance at the interruption. He didn't move from his seat. He continued sitting as he usually did, his legs apart, leaning back into his chair, with his hands casually clasped together, resting on his lap.

The woman rose and turned her back on Yuri to offer to shake hands with Dominica.

But Dominica was too angry to reciprocate. 'What is going on, Yuri? You said you wouldn't employ a woman for security.'

She looked at the visitor.

The woman sucked air in through her teeth and placed her hands on her hips. Her ice-blue eyes were piercing as they tapered in anger. 'Who is this, Yuri!' Her Russian accent was hard yet crisp.

'This is Dominica. She is—'

'She is not part of my business with *you*, Yuri.'

'Dominica runs the private parties.'

Kristi huffed. 'But she isn't part of my business with you, so why is she here? I must insist that we talk alone.'

'I can go anywhere in this house that I choose,' spat Dominica, now fuming that the woman, in her opinion, had no right to speak to her in that way.

'First, you insult me by not shaking my hand, and then you insult me by assuming I am here to work as a guard. I am Kristi Pavlov, and my late father was Kristian Pavlov. I do not work for Yuri or you.'

Dominica noticed that Yuri looked uncomfortable. Perhaps it was the mention of Kristi Pavlov's father's name. 'Leave the room, Dominica. But first, you must apologise for your rudeness,' he demanded.

Dominica looked from one to the other. She didn't know whether to offer her sincere apologies or slam the door behind her on the way out.

Jealousy had its way. 'Who are you again, and what do you do?' She looked Kristi over.

The woman didn't look as if she had any standing in their type of business. In fact, she appeared as though she had just returned from a holiday. But Dominica was still eaten up by the woman's natural good looks. Her tanned face and blue eyes, without a smidgeon of make-up, were so attractive, it boiled her piss.

Kristi flicked her wrist dismissively. 'I will not deal with this woman, Yuri. I will go to my hotel and call you later. And, by the way, tell your driver to buy some deodorant. The car stinks.'

Dominica was gobsmacked. No one apart from her ever spoke to Yuri in that way.

'I am sorry, Kristi. Please allow me to drive you to your hotel. But why don't you stay here? There are many rooms.' He pointed to his right. 'That wing of the house has a separate entrance, and it is at your disposal.'

'Hmmm, and I will be left alone, yes?'

'Of course, Kristi.'

Dominica wanted to claw her eyes out. She knew Yuri only too well, and the way he was looking at the woman, she was convinced it wasn't to get inside her business brain. Most likely, it was to get inside her knickers.

Yuri pressed a button and immediately a guard opened the door. 'Please show Ms Pavlov to the east wing, and have her luggage collected.'

'My luggage is in the hall. I came here from the airport.'

Yuri grinned again. This time his eyes were smouldering.

'You don't mind if we search it, do you?' interrupted Dominica, now fuming.

Instantly Kristi lunged forward, grabbed Dominica by the hair, and with the other, she pulled a knife from her side pocket and held it to Dominica's throat. 'I would kill you back in Russia for ever speaking to me like that. Now, you have utterly insulted me.' She pushed Dominica away and turned to Yuri. 'I have changed my mind. I will stay at the hotel, thank you. I cannot be around silly, immature women. You understand?'

Yuri jumped up and glared at Dominica, his eyes wild and his lips tight. However, he deliberately relaxed his face when he looked back at Kristi. 'I will arrange a taxi for you, but don't ever touch Dominica like that again.' His last words reinforced his importance.

Kristi turned the knife around in her hand, knowing she had to impose her authority. 'I was told that you were a ruthless negotiator, a man of respect and not to be crossed. But I now see a man who is, as the English would say, ruled by his dick. My father was wrong about you. I have no time for business with a man who answers to his – his bit of fluff.'

They stared at each other before she sighed. 'It was nice to meet you, Yuri. I think I will take my business elsewhere. My father once told me that you could be good for our business, but he also had reservations about you.'

'I am sorry to hear that he passed away. I didn't know him very well. I carried out only a few transactions with him many years ago, and so I was surprised to hear he had a daughter.'

'My father protected me, and he kept our relationship private for my safety. We both know he had enemies, clearly, because, as you know, he was assassinated. But I am here to continue the business. I like England. The business is easy here, but I want to be working with the right people.'

Feeling the woman's power in her words alone, Dominica also felt the need to lower her gaze. She could tell that Yuri was angry with her. He didn't have to say anything: it was written across his face.

'I am sorry, Ms Pavlov,' said Dominica. It wasn't because she *was* sorry but because she didn't want to get a beating from Yuri for fucking things up.

Kristi studied Dominica's face for any sign of contrition. Believing that Dominica was trying to reduce the tension, she waved her hand dismissively. 'Go and take my luggage to this east wing.'

Dominica looked up, alarmed. How dare she? But one glance at Yuri, and she knew she had to do as she was told.

As soon as Dominica left the room, Kristi sat down. 'Right, shall we start again? What are you willing to pay for my Russian girls – the virgins?'

Yuri nodded, genially. 'Four thousand apiece and you will have ten per cent of all their earnings. I want them to arrive to me with the cocaine that your father promised me.'

Kristi nodded. She knew that Yuri was testing her. 'You mean heroin? My father never dealt with cocaine in this country.'

Yuri smiled. 'Sorry, I meant heroin.'

The gentle tap at the door made Kristi smile, knowing that she had browbeaten Dominica and had her just where she wanted her. Before the door opened, she looked at Yuri, her eyebrows now raised and with a smirk on her face. 'You must keep that guard dog on a tight leash. She is not good for your business. She is too emotional and has no sense. I will start with a small number, and we will see where our business leads.'

Another gentle tap compelled Yuri to shout, 'Wait!'

‘But, Kristi, we had agreed on a specified amount. Why have you changed your mind?’

‘You should be able to work that out for yourself, Yuri. Your girlfriend seems to me to be – oh, what is that word in English – somewhat volatile. It has made me rethink our relationship, which, you have to admit, has not got off to a good start. So, maybe, it is best we go about our business in this way until we can trust each other.’

Yuri bit his bottom lip and pressed the buzzer. The door opened, and in walked a guard.

Dominica was lurking outside the room, looking very sheepish.

‘Please take Ms Pavlov and show her to the east wing.’ He nodded as Kristi left the room, and the door closed behind her.

Almost immediately, the door opened again, and Dominica bowled in.

‘Well, that was rude. She held a fucking knife to my throat.’

Dominica observed Yuri studying her. She assumed that he wasn’t still angry with her because he was sitting with his head back and his hands in his lap.

He smiled and curled his finger. ‘Come here.’

Dominica saw the glint of mischief in his eyes and hurried over to straddle him, but he held up his hand and curled his finger for her to come even closer. She leaned into his face expecting a kiss, but he savagely grabbed her hair and pushed her face down to his groin. Her cheek brushed against his erect penis. And she knew then what she had to do. She also knew that the bulge inside his jeans wasn’t because she had turned him on. It was Kristi’s presence that had obviously aroused him.

Another stab of jealousy poked her in the chest. Yuri never got aroused simply by looking at her. She had to practically do a cartwheel naked before he would take her to his bed.

She lowered his jeans and held his penis, ready to place her lips around it, but, unexpectedly, he forced her head down, almost choking her. Shocked and humiliated, she had no choice but to allow his hands to force her head up and down repeatedly, making her gag and choke. Still, she didn't dare bite down to stop him.

As soon as he ejaculated in her mouth, he released his grip and slapped her hard across the cheek. She fell back and hit her head on the desk. But he didn't stop there. He smacked her aggressively again. This time, she got on all fours and tried to crawl away, but he was now up and on his feet, and with a swift kick, he caught her in the ribs and kicked her again until she screamed in agony.

'Stop! Please, Yuri, I am sorry!' She gasped and spluttered as she dragged herself towards the door.

Standing up, she felt as though she had been sawn in half. The pain shot up her spine and took her breath away. He had done a right number on her, and she knew that if she didn't leave now, he would do far worse. But as she turned the doorknob, he was there, his body stopping her from leaving. All her fears came home to roost. Every time he winked or smiled when he was carrying out his punishments on other women and girls, she had always felt smug that he was doing so on them and not on her.

Today, he stared at her with the same mocking look he gave the girls he owned. It was the same one as the day he bought her. She had been so young and eager to please him then because that way he wouldn't have her locked in a room for men to do as they pleased. As she had heard the other girls had been. She, however, was different. She had been a virgin at the time, and he had paid a reasonable price to have sex with her. The regularity of their sex gave her more freedom. She started by cooking for him and giving him massages until he fully trusted her, and she was allowed to work for him in a different way – by ensuring the girls were clean and ready for their punters.

Looking at him now, she knew she was back to square one. She was just a girl he owned.

CHAPTER THREE

'I should have kept you on a tight leash!' growled Yuri.

Dominica recoiled in fear when she saw his eyes narrow, and the curl of his lips was a sign he was disgusted. Her eyes were glued to him as he walked back to his desk. She hoped he would retake his seat, wave his hands, and dismiss her as he had in the past when he wanted time alone. He didn't, though; instead, he picked up the radio and called Casper, his number one guard and right-hand man.

'Bring me a dog collar and a lead.'

'Aw, no. Yuri, please, I am so sorry,' Dominica pleaded.

'Sorry? Sorry? I treated you well. Yes?'

Dominica nodded. 'Yes, you did. I, er . . . mean you do. And, and . . . and I promise I will be good. I'll do whatever you want.'

He nodded and smiled. 'Yes, until the next time that you are so content with our arrangement, you feel comfortable enough to embarrass me.'

'No, no, I swear, Yuri, I would . . . never.' She watched him open the top drawer of his desk and retrieve a pair of scissors. His lips twisted into a sneer.

‘What are you going to do, Yuri? Please, no,’ she begged, as sick images of the pain he could inflict on her crawled through her mind.

‘I paid for your hairstyles.’ He pointed to her head with the scissors. ‘Your clothes. In fact, everything. Yes?’

He stepped forward.

She nodded. ‘Yes, and I am grateful. You know how grateful I am,’ she begged, as her eyes locked on to the deadly-looking scissors.

Taking another step closer, he held up the implement, inspecting it as if it were a foreign object, and then he lunged forward, snatched a chunk of her hair, and cut it off.

Dominica automatically threw her hands to her face, but she felt relieved it was only her hair falling on the floor and not chunks of her flesh.

Suddenly, Yuri had turned into Edward in the movie *Edward Scissorhands*, furiously chopping at her hair until there was not an inch of a lock left.

When she thought he had finished, he began to cut her blouse, which he had already ripped. Each snip was so close to her skin that she was too terrified to move.

‘You will leave here as you came, with no property that belongs to you. You own *nothing* and I own you.’

By the time he had finished, she was standing there naked and shivering.

After two loud knocks, Casper walked in, followed by another guard, a younger man called Lenin.

Trembling, Dominica clocked Casper’s grin before he studied her with an unwavering predatory attention. She tried to cover herself with her hands, but Casper just sniggered. She didn’t want to look at him. She hated him because even though what she did was cruel at times, Casper was beyond brutal. He had a savage malignance sewn into his personality. At six feet seven and sporting a fifty-inch chest of solid muscle, he was also the most sour-faced man she knew. His huge square jaw and grey bristly hair made him appear older than his thirty-four years.

'Here, Yuri, the dog lead.'

Yuri nodded. 'Put it around her neck.'

'My pleasure.'

'Take her to the Kent holding cells and let it be a warning to all the girls. I will give you further instructions when I have decided what I want to do with her.'

Casper's grin grew as he eyed Dominica. 'Is she one of the girls now or—'

'Yes, Casper, she is. So do as you want with her, but don't kill her. Wait for instructions as to what to do with her once the girls have seen her.'

Before he left the room, he bellowed an inch away from her ear. 'You are a pet dog! You are not my equal. I bought you, I saved you, and this is how you repay me? You embarrassed me in front of Kristi Pavlov, and you damaged my reputation. But I will leave you now. I must have time to think about your punishment.'

Dominica felt sick with fear. If only she could turn the clock back; if only she had just kept her jealousy in check and her mouth shut. But it was too late. Her body began to tremble, and she couldn't control it; whether it was fear or shock, it didn't matter. She would probably be put to death unless Yuri calmed down and had second thoughts.

The door closed behind him, but not before he winked at Casper.

The realisation hit her. Yuri had given Casper the freedom to do as he wished with her. Her stomach churned. Her mouth turned bone dry. She was probably more afraid of Casper than Yuri. They had never liked each other. Up to a few minutes ago, she had always had the upper hand because Yuri tended to side with her over Casper if she threw a hissy fit. She was fully aware, though, that Casper, who had also been a school friend of Yuri's, had never agreed with her position in the business.

She didn't move or say a word as Casper tightened the dog collar around her throat. 'Kneel, doggy,' he mocked, as he patted his knees. 'Kneel.'

Dominica was still trying to cover her modesty.

'I said *kneel*, you dog!' His voice was deep, husky, and unforgiving.

With a hard thump at the back of her head, Dominica fell forward, but the tension on the lead yanked her back. She choked and gasped for breath as she clawed at the collar, trying to get her footing, before she hanged herself.

'You will kneel for me, or I will show you how I treat bad dogs.'

Dominica caught her breath and did as he said.

Lenin leaned against the wall smoking a cigarette and slyly eyeing her over. While he tilted his head from side to side, ogling and licking his lips, she guessed he was sizing her up.

'That's it,' said Casper. 'Now, walk around like a good doggy.'

On all fours, Dominica went into self-preservation mode and did as he demanded, while all the time taking her mind to a distant place.

***

As soon as Casper asked Lenin to leave the room, Dominica knew what would happen to her. She didn't fight it; she didn't even scream when he ripped her backside cheeks apart and rammed his manhood deep inside her. Evidently, he wasn't doing it for sexual pleasure. He was exerting his power over her; it was his way of revenge. Once he had finished raping her, he called Lenin to join him, and they spent an hour humiliating her. When she didn't react, Casper took to stronger physical punishments. He wanted to hear her scream; he loved that sound.

By the time they had finished with her, she could barely breathe, her eyes were mere slits, and her lips were too swollen even to beg the men to stop. Casper had slung her around like a rag doll, and then he'd kicked her muscles to mush so that she couldn't walk.

Out of breath, both Casper and Lenin left the room, with Lenin slamming the door behind them.

Dominica dragged herself into the corner, curled into a protective ball, and groaned in agony. She wished they'd had the decency to leave her unconscious and give her a few moments of respite from the pain.

After a few minutes of silence, she heard the crackling sound of the radios just outside the office door. Trembling from head to toe, she watched the door handle turn and the door open. Two different guards appeared. She couldn't quite see who they were as her eyes were so puffed up, but she knew the guards were from the Kent holding cells because they were dressed in black uniforms. She felt them grab her arms and try to lift her to her feet. Her legs gave way, and so she slumped.

'Please, let me talk to Yuri.' Her words were barely audible.

As she expected, they didn't say a word. She assumed they were acting under Yuri's or Casper's orders, but as they lugged her out of the office, she could see the blurred outline of Kristi. And although she was barely conscious, she still wanted to give Kristi a violent kick. She hated the woman.

'So, Dominica, you seem to have upset someone,' Kristi mocked.

The two guards held Dominica up in front of Kristi as she stepped forward.

'I understand that Yuri bought you.' She laughed. 'I am surprised that he even gave you a voice. Perhaps you should've learned when not to use it.' She waved her hand. 'I mean, he gave you a job, didn't he? But you abused the little power he gave you. I am not convinced that I should work with Yuri when he takes on a girl like you!' She held one finger up. 'A girl he probably paid good money for and who is stupid enough to let loose with her mouth.'

'I . . . w . . . was his girlfriend, until . . .' Her head slumped between her sagging shoulders.

Kristi tapped Dominica's cheeks. '*Was* is the operative word, Dominica. So now you are what, exactly?'

Dominica had lost all sense of any fight; she felt her inner strength leave her like a frightened ferret scurrying away.

'Take her to my rooms. I'm not done with her yet.'

'But Casper ordered us to take her to the Kent holding cells,' replied one of the guards.

'Yes, and you can, but first, I want to show her that she cannot ever talk to me in the way she did. You must understand,' she said, with a severe curt tone, while displaying a vicious-looking knife, 'or do I need to speak with Yuri about this concerning situation?'

'No, you don't need to speak to Yuri. We will take her to your rooms,' replied one of the guards.

Dominica tried to wriggle free, but she could barely move. Every inch of her body was in agony. Whimpering like an injured dog, there was no point in screaming. No one cared – no one. Her ears buzzed as her head throbbed, but the sound of Kristi's footsteps behind her only escalated her dread.

The guards dragged her past the main lounge area to the corridor leading to the east wing. From there she was taken into the second room on the right – the lounge.

Dominica already knew the layout, before she even entered the room. To the left of the lounge was the main bedroom, with a bedspread rich in animal prints and a plush mustard chaise longue. It had its own en suite bathroom and was accessible from the corridor. To the right of the lounge was a larger bedroom en suite, which was not accessible from the corridor.

But in Yuri's flash way, he had allowed Kristi access to all of it. *Who needs two bedrooms?* thought Dominica, momentarily drifting from her main concern.

'In here, Ms Pavlov?'

'Yes, in here is fine. You may go now.'

Dominica closed her eyes while the two guards dropped her onto a sofa. Once she heard the door close, she peered up, terrified of what she might see. She was surprised that Kristi wasn't brandishing the knife any longer.

Kristi leaned into her ear and whispered, 'Scream your head off, Dominica.'

She frowned. '*What?*' Stealthily, she looked for the knife that had been in Kristi's hand.

'I said, scream your head off, now. Or I'll give you something to scream about.'

Dominica hadn't grasped what was going on, but she certainly wasn't going to argue, so she took a painful deep breath and yelled as loudly as her broken ribs would allow.

Kristi nodded. 'And again.'

Dominica screamed again.

'Good. Now, those guards can go back and tell Yuri that I am torturing the fuck out of you.'

'W . . . What do you want from me?'

'I want information.' She held up her hand. 'And before you even think of running back to Yuri, remember this: you will never be his girlfriend. He has shown you that you are nothing to him but a puppet, a toy. He *owns* you.'

Dominica rested her head against the large arm of the sofa. The blood from her swollen lips stained the pale-green velvet arm. But her head hurt so much that she neither had the strength to move nor the will to argue.

Dominica blinked a few times and focused on Kristi. Observing the woman walking over to the drinks cabinet with confidence to have her back to her, she watched her pour a generous amount of brandy into a snifter glass. Naturally, Dominica assumed it was for Kristi. But with a serviette in one hand and the drink in the other, Kristi knelt beside her and helped her by gently angling the glass, so the amber-coloured liquid eased into her mouth.

Wary but grateful, Dominica drank the brandy, while she kept one eye on the woman.

'Here, take these,' demanded Kristi, showing Dominica two tablets.

Dominica stared and tried to figure out if Kristi was poisoning her.

'They are painkillers, that's all. Because killing you won't help me,' said Kristi, placing the tablets under Dominica's nose.

Dominica opened her mouth as wide as her swollen lips would allow her to, and Kristi popped them into her mouth before offering her more brandy to wash them down.

The long heavy curtains were closed, so the room was only lit by the side lamps and the chandeliers. However, Kristi jumped to her feet and opened one of the curtains when she heard tyres from a vehicle moving over the gravel drive.

Dominica blinked a few times because the light was so bright.

'Hmm, Yuri and two of his men have left the house. Good,' said Kristi. 'Now we can talk.'

Dominica stared at the knife that Kristi had just placed on the side table.

'Oh, for God's sake, I'll put it away in the bedroom.' She snatched the knife and literally threw it into the bedroom, in the direction of the bed, where it fell just under the animal print bedspread. 'There! See? Okay now?'

Dominica felt better, possibly because the fear of being carved up like a joint of scored pork had gone, and the brandy was undoubtedly helping to take the edge off the shock.

'Do you want to take a warm bath?'

Turning her head, Dominica didn't want to move an inch. 'No, I cannot move.'

Kristi hurried to the other bedroom next door and returned with clothes and a baseball cap. 'I cannot look at you naked and have a conversation with you. Get dressed.'

Taking the clothes from Kristi, her hands brushed over the softness of the T-shirt. Even the khaki shorts, similar to those that Kristi wore, were made of a soothing material. Every bone in her body hurt as she tried to put the T-shirt over her head. Eventually, Kristi stepped in and helped her.

'Thank you. Now, what is this information that you want from me?'

Kristi didn't answer right away. She poured herself a brandy first and then took a seat opposite Dominica. 'Before I have a discussion with you, I must warn you that I will deny everything if you even think of divulging our discussion. Trust me, Dominica, I have the power and the knowledge to convince Yuri that you begged me to help you escape.'

Dominica sensed the seriousness in the woman's tone. She was obviously no amateur but one dangerous bitch. She glanced to the corner of the room, knowing cameras were installed and everything would be recorded. She quickly looked back to see Kristi smiling.

'Yes, Dominica, I am fully aware of every camera in the east wing.'

Dominica nodded slowly, putting her hand over her mouth. 'That bookshelf is a false wall. It opens to the main lounge, so you are not entirely separate from the house. Yuri would never give you that much control.'

Kristi nodded. 'So those two points I already know. What else do you have to tell me?'

'Who are you, really?'

'I am Kristi Pavlov, and I want to know that if I work with Yuri, I can trust him, and you can help me to understand the man.'

Dominica sat up straighter and stared ahead at Kristi. 'Why should I help you? You ruined my relationship with Yuri, and he was everything to me. I still love him, you know.'

Kristi rose from her chair and stared out of the window. 'You love him, yes? A man who bought you and took you as a sex slave because that is really what you are. He has the right to sell you to anyone who will pay your debt. Because' – she paused and laughed – 'you still owe him a debt, don't you?'

'No, he has never said I owe—'

'Oh, be serious, Dominica. You all owe Yuri a debt. Just because he was allowing you into his home and helping him with the other girls' well-being doesn't mean you have paid off your debt.'

'So, I owe him some money, but he did love me. I know he did.'

'I am afraid you have no idea what it is to be truly loved because you are not a free woman. It is probably better for you to believe he does love you than to believe the opposite. But even so, can it ever stop the guilt you must feel for what you have done to those other girls? Perhaps, you feel you are better than them, watching how those girls feared you. You must have got a kick out of it.'

'What, like you are now doing to me, Kristi?'

'Ha, excellent, Dominica, but be careful, because the difference is *I* am a free woman. You see, you are disposable. I'm not.'

Dominica watched Kristi pace the room.

'No, you're wrong. Yuri doesn't see me as one of his girls, and he treats me very much like I'm a free woman.' She choked on some blood that trickled down the back of her nose and then she tried to clear her throat. However, her words sounded strained. 'Yuri and me, we work together. He needs me to manage the girls, and I know how the system works.'

Kristi stopped pacing the room and spun around to face Dominica. 'So why did he allow those two men to rape and beat you to an inch of your life? He plans to use you as a deterrent by making an example of you, and you know what that means, don't you?'

Dominica's eyes clouded over. 'No.'

'I think he will arrange a torturous death for you in front of the girls.' She paused and stared.

Dominica's eyes were wide, and the blood drained from her face.

'And yet, you tell me that Yuri loves you.'

Suddenly, like the collapse of a stack of dominoes, the realisation of what had happened in the space of a mere hour hit Dominica hard. 'You did this deliberately. You caused this argument. You made him want to beat me. I get it now, Kristi. You wanted me to view you as my rescuer and side with you. I understand now. You want to take over Yuri's business, don't you?'

Kristi smiled. 'You are very clever, Dominica, but I didn't think he would be prepared to kill you, so we both learned something today.'

'Stop it, Kristi. You are playing mind games with me.'

Shaking her head, Kristi gave Dominica a compassionate smile. 'No, I am not playing mind games. But I know it is common for the captive – in your case yourself – to think they are in love with the captor, who, in this case, is Yuri. It is called the Stockholm syndrome. Did you know that?'

'No, I didn't. But he does love me too. I made him angry, that's all. I should never have humiliated him, but you made it worse for me.'

Kristi nodded. 'Yes, I did, so that you would see what you are truly worth to him.' She smiled and tilted her head to the side. 'And, so now, after all the years you have given to him, with just one upset, there is a strong likelihood that he will sentence you to death.'

Despite hearing that, Dominica felt her body start to relax. The strong painkillers were kicking in. 'What if I refuse to help you?'

'Then I will let the guards take you away and do what they do.' Her vast satisfied smile lifted one of her cheeks, highlighting her dimple.

Dominica gazed in contemplation, desperately trying to recall a vision of the past. She eyed every contour, the shape of the woman's face, the slim delicate nose, and the round blue eyes.

'Oh, but you won't do that because you are not as evil as Kristi Pavlov. Or are you?'

'*What?*'

'You heard what I said. So stop playing games and tell me who you really are.'

Kristi frowned. 'You know who I am, Dominica, and you must have known who my father was.' She lifted her chin proudly.

Dominica nodded. 'I did know who Mr Pavlov was. Who didn't? I knew his family very well, and, Ms whoever you are, you may have Yuri fooled, but you haven't fooled me.'

It was the first time she had seen a flicker of concern on Kristi's face.

'You, Ms Fake, are not Kristi Pavlov because she didn't have a dimple, and I am sure that they do not appear as you grow older. She didn't have blue eyes either. I know that Kristi was kept away from her father for her own protection, but, you see, Russia can be a small place, and I remember seeing her when I was twelve years old. My mother worked for Mr Pavlov for a year before he fired her. If you were the real Kristi Pavlov, you would know why your father fired her. Do you remember what it was for?'

Kristi shook her head.

'I was in the corner of Mr Pavlov's enormous kitchen, waiting for my mother to finish her work to walk me home. Kristi crept into the room like a ghost, hovering around. My mother was cleaning the kitchen sides. She didn't hear or see Kristi and accidentally stepped back on to Kristi's toes. Like a drama queen, Kristi screamed the house down as if my mother had chopped her feet off. But Mr Pavlov was so incensed by his daughter screaming that he personally beat my mother with a stick. He broke her hands. Remember now?'

Kristi returned to her chair and sipped her drink, totally unconcerned. 'I don't care, nor do I remember.'

'But I care, and I *do* remember. I remember the sickening smile on her face and her eyes like black stones, lifeless and spooky. And I don't recall any cute fucking dimple.'

'You're mistaken, Dominica.'

Dominica shook her head, even though it still hurt. 'No, Ms Fake, I would never forget her face because right after that, my mother died. Mr Pavlov sent me to England to pay off a debt that my mother supposedly owed Mr Pavlov.'

Kristi shrugged her shoulders. 'I am not concerned with your stupid notions, and if you think that telling Yuri will give you a freedom pass, you are very much mistaken. I have enough photos of my father and me to make you look very silly.'

Dominica felt sudden waves of tiredness. 'It's over for me now, anyway, so do what you have to do.'

'It doesn't have to be over for you. I can stop the death sentence, but I need something from you.'

As Dominica's eyes flickered open, Kristi smiled. 'Ah, I thought that might get your attention.'

'I will help you because I don't believe you are Kristi Pavlov, and I don't want to die either. What do you want me to do?'

'Well, I have my own guards arriving this evening. They can get you out of here. I can say that I went too far and killed you, so my men took the liberty of getting rid of my mess.'

Dominica was now fully engaged; visions of escaping and living a free life shot through her mind. Eager to get started, she said, 'What do you want to know?'

'Where do you keep the new girls before you work them?'

Dominica's eyes, although puffy, widened slightly. 'You're the police, aren't you? I know what happens. If I were to tell you everything, I would get taken away and beaten and then dragged back, like the other girls who tried to escape.'

Kristi laughed. 'Police? How many Russian police are there in England, you fool?'

Dominica stared at the woman and realised she had sounded rather stupid. The woman was, without doubt, Russian, despite pretending to be someone she was not.

'Okay, so why do you want to know that?'

'You have courage, but you don't get to ask why. Answer the question, or I will hand you over to be disposed of. It's your choice.'

'Yuri has different places. One is . . .' She paused and looked around. 'It is inside a small hospital type of building. That is where he has the holding cells. They are going to knock the old hospital down soon.'

'Where is it?'

Dominica winced when she tried to shrug her shoulders. 'I don't know exactly.'

'Well, think harder.'

Tears welled up in Dominica's eyes. 'I really don't know where it is.'

'I need to know that he won't double-cross me, Dominica.'

'Ms Fake, I don't give a fuck, just as long as you get me out of here.'

'Okay, now, can you recall anything about the building? Any signs, any names?'

'I don't know. I think a building company owns it.' She stopped and frowned. 'I heard Yuri talking to someone about other derelict properties, but I don't remember his name. But Yuri keeps all of his accounts in his filing cabinet.'

Kristi laughed. 'He keeps accounts? What type of accounts?'

'They are for his properties, and imports.'

The door suddenly opened, and in stormed the two guards dressed in black. 'You have had long enough, and I see that she is still breathing. I must take her now.' The shorter guard frowned. 'Why is she dressed?'

Kristi jumped to her feet. 'I don't answer to you. How dare you question me! Stand outside my room, and if I get treated with hostility one more time, I will leave, and you will tell Yuri that our business relationship is over.'

The man nodded. 'I have instructions from Yuri to take her to the holding cells and—'

'I want her kept alive. I have a buyer for the feisty, fiery bitch. He loves torture, so you tell Yuri not to dispose of her and no more bruises or marks. My buyer is fussy.'

'But we have our orders.'

Kristi shrugged her shoulders. 'Take her if you must, but I will let it be known that I had a perfect buyer for her, a potentially profitable business venture.'

She watched as the two guards looked at each other. 'We will take her to the holding cells and not harm her. You can speak with Yuri.'

Kristi observed the two men help Dominica from the sofa.

As Dominica left the room, she realised that the guards were far more gentle with her than when they had dragged her to the room previously.

She didn't struggle. The drugs were helping her pain and allowing her to relax.

As Dominica looked back, Kristi could see the gentle hint of a smile – and it was a genuine smile as well.

CHAPTER FOUR

Hulou had called out for her mother a few times before she'd pulled back the curtain, and to her utter shock, she found her there with blood still pouring from her neck.

Yalina had never seen such grief as Hulou dropped to her knees and wailed while she threw the top half of her body around in a circling motion. Then her wailing turned to anger as she banged her fists on the floor. 'No, no, no!' she screamed, until she finally collapsed with the side of her face on the floor, her eyes lifeless.

As Yalina knelt beside her to comfort her, Hulou suddenly got up. 'Come, we must run. I will not allow my mother's death to be for nothing. Yalina, Bina, Sana, she died for all of us. She took her own life so that we could all escape. She would never have wanted to be the reason I was a prisoner. Come quickly,' she said, as she waved her hands for the others to follow.

But Yalina was rooted to the spot, too afraid they would kill her mother for her insolence if she tried to make a run for it. And besides that, where would they go? The police wouldn't help.

'No, you go, Hulou. Go, run,' she said.

Hulou didn't even put any shoes on her feet. She hoisted up her bright yellow sari and ran through the corridor of saris and vanished.

Yalina glanced at Bina. 'What do we do now?'

But it was Sana who answered. 'They do not pay us to speak or act. We must stand here and say nothing.'

Yalina's eyes widened. 'But will the guards blame us?'

'No, we are the invisible ones,' replied Bina.

Those words hit her like spears being flung into her chest. She knew now that Bina was right in what she'd said.

***

Assuming that Dominica would return to organise the evening party, Shabir turned his phone off and spent two hours devouring dishes that would have fed a family of four. After removing the serviette stuffed down the front of his shirt, he drank the last of the expensive wine and shoved the table away from him. As soon as he pushed himself out of the chair, he waved at the waiter. 'Put it on my tab.'

Without waiting for a response, he strolled through the restaurant's busy kitchen, out through the back door, and into the back alley. A cold gust of wind swirled around him and flicked dust into his eyes, causing him to curse and drop his car keys. Before he retrieved them, he blinked to clear his sight. He breathlessly climbed into his car with a glance up and down the alleyway. He had wanted to stay longer and finish another bottle of wine, but he knew that Dominica, with her big mouth, would start to question where he had been and act like the big boss. She loved to throw her weight around; she was the only woman working for Yuri who could. He smiled when he thought of how Dominica was seething with jealousy when he had mentioned that a woman had arrived to meet Yuri.

He was still smiling when he pulled into the back entrance to the sari storage warehouse, but his smile soon disappeared. Even in the darkness, he could make out two black jeeps and a limo. So Yuri was here.

Huffing and puffing, he struggled to lift his heavy weight out of the low car seat and almost threw himself out, regretting having eaten so much. He hurried along the corridor of saris and into the main room. This was where the party was to be held, assuming the guests would all be seated, and the only reason Yuri would be there was because they had a prestigious buyer. However, he almost skidded to a stop when he saw that the room was not filled with excited clients at all. No one was there. Although, all the lights were on, there was no music being played.

The first person he clocked was Yalina. She was standing on the stage with her head down. To the left of her were Bina and Sana. They were visibly shaking and clinging to each other. A Russian guard stood opposite with his arms folded.

Shabir turned to his left, where the curtain was always pulled across to hide the cleaning cupboard. He noticed two other guards with their radios switched on. As he made his way to find out what was going on, the guards stepped aside, and that was when he saw Hulou's mother slumped on a wooden chair.

At first, he assumed she had died of old age. That was until he saw the blood. Initially, he had thought the colour was from her top, but a moment later, he realised he had been mistaken. He glared down at the congealed blood. Then he noticed the blood down her arm and the knife on the floor. Her throat had been cut. *Had one of the guards killed her?* he wondered.

Unable to take his eyes away from her, he mumbled, 'What happened?'

Unexpectedly, Yuri appeared from the doorway that led to the front of the factory. His eyes were so dark and his face so immensely drawn that Shabir knew he himself was in some kind of trouble.

Yuri towered over him. 'You lazy fat bastard. While you were absent, Hulou's mother killed herself, and now Hulou has gone. If she is not found, and soon, you will pay, gravely.'

Shabir nodded before he darted off to use the bathroom. The fear had him leaving half his body weight down the toilet. Sweat dripped from every pore in his body, and he knew he had to find a way to get Hulou back, or they would dispose of him and have no qualms about it. Yuri had made him fully aware others in Pakistan would easily take his place. Bringing girls over from Pakistan was very straightforward but not so profitable as selling them on to the Chinese, which meant they didn't have to take the greater risk by bringing them to London.

After washing his face, he returned to hear the guards on their radios. He couldn't speak Russian, relying instead on their broken

English, but he could ascertain from their smiles and nods that they had a sighting of Hulou. She was heading down Lewisham High Street. His heart was racing so fast that his chest hurt, and he wondered if he was about to have a heart attack.

Then Yuri appeared again, pointing a finger at him. 'You are very, very lucky, Shabir. It seems they have found her.' He turned slowly to face the three young girls. 'The police are bringing her back for me, so remember this: if you try to do anything like Hulou, you will have to face the consequences, and you will see soon enough what they are.'

'Yes, so, Yalina, don't you think about running away as well. The police will only bring you back, but first, they will beat you,' added Shabir, to the annoyance of Yuri.

Yalina realised then that Yuri had very little time for the man.

'What will you do about her?' grilled Yuri, as he pointed a finger at the elderly woman.

Shabir showed the palms of his hands. 'Leave it with me. I will have it taken care of. You do not need to worry.' His words tumbled out in his efforts to make up for his absence.

Yuri gave a solitary confirmatory nod.

'Is Dominica here?' asked Shabir, peering over Yuri's shoulder.

'No, she no longer works for me. For the moment, I have someone else who will organise a new person to arrange the parties.'

Shabir felt uneasy. 'Who is that, may I ask?'

'Ask Ms Kristi Pavlov, when you meet her, as I am sure she will have someone in mind.'

'Ms Pavlov?'

'Yes, the woman you collected from the airport. We are to be business partners.'

'Business partners?'

'Are you a parrot? Enough with the questions. Take the girls back to the holding cells. There is no party tonight. And the new girl must stay intact. You understand me? Yes?'

'Of course, Yuri.'

Shabir felt a wave of festering anger. He hated being the underdog. Quickly, he clapped his hands. 'Don't just stand there, girls. Get changed. Hurry, hurry.'

Yuri was about to leave, followed by his two guards, when he stepped back and leaned in towards Shabir. 'And don't drive your car on to my property again. Your car looks like a taxi, and taxis do not come into my drive. You are stupid. Yes?'

Shabir could feel the wrath of the man merely by the man's breath on his cheek.

'It won't happen again.'

'You die if it does,' Yuri said, harshly, before laughing with his guards.

***

While the van drove over the bumps, Yalina continued to vomit. She couldn't get the vision out of her head of the dead woman and poor Hulou. As soon as they came to an abrupt stop, Yalina expected the guards to slide open the door and let her and the others out; but, instead, the door remained shut. She listened to the noises outside and the crackling sounds of radios. Then she heard another van stop and the unmistakable pleas from Hulou. Yalina covered her ears, unable to bear the blood-curdling screams and terrifying pleas for mercy. Unexpectedly, tears rolled down her cheeks, and she had to move her hands away from her ears to wipe her face. The screams were so horrific, she guessed Hulou's ultimate demise wouldn't be pleasant. There was silence, and a moment later, the side door opened, and a guard flicked his head for them to get out.

Yalina quickly gazed around before a guard shoved her in the back to move. She couldn't see Hulou, so she assumed she had been taken away. But what she did notice was a man dressed in a smart suit. His hair was like the moon on a dark evening. His thick waves shone like silver, and as he glanced her way, she caught the light of his eyes; one, oddly, was glistening brighter than the other. He stepped back into the shadows and continued his conversation with one of the guards.

Suddenly, she longed to go back to the room where she had been staying with her mother and feel her warm, comforting arms around her. But, she reasoned, it would be better for her mother to be in some beautiful house cleaning and polishing and enjoying a decent bed and food than residing in the rat-infested prison cell because clearly that was what it was.

As she reached Bina and Sana's room, the guard bellowed for them to halt. He opened their door, pushed them in, and locked it behind them. Then he looked at Yalina. She could see he was eyeing her over, and she hoped he would heed this Yuri man's words, that she was not to be molested in any way.

'Move on! Your room is at the end.'

As she walked on, she automatically glanced at the room, which was more like a bathroom, where she had seen the handcuffs. To her shock, there was a woman who looked as if someone had put her through a stone polishing machine. Her face was like a balloon, and her legs – what she could see of them – were black and blue. The woman's battered head was resting on her arms, which were held aloft by the cuffs.

An icy shiver ripped through her. This was like hell on Earth. Then she noticed the woman's eyes. They opened just enough to give her face a little character. Yalina gasped loudly; it was Dominica. Quickly, she slapped her hands over her mouth and looked ahead. *What had they done to her? And she was one of their own.*

***

Finally, as she approached the last room before the set of double swing doors, the guard demanded she stop. 'You're in here. And think yourself very lucky. I understand you must be kept well, so there is some good food and clean water.'

Not wanting to upset the giant man with his roaming eyes, Yalina nodded politely. 'Thank you.'

The guard pushed her inside the room and slammed the door shut behind her. Hearing the door lock, she instantly relaxed her tense shoulders. As she turned around, she noticed the door. It was made from thickened steel. A wired reinforced glass window had been fitted, allowing some light into the room. It was enough for her to see that she wouldn't be sleeping rough on the floor. To her relief, there was a metal framed hospital bed with a striped mattress and two blankets folded at the end.

Someone had placed a tray of food on a small wooden table and beside that was a bucket containing what she assumed was clean water because there was a bar of soap next to it.

Her stomach was rumbling, and she knew she had to eat to keep her strength up, but the aftertaste of vomit was putting her off. So she cupped her hands and scooped up the water, bringing it to her mouth to sip. Her eyes then scanned the tray, and she was pleasantly surprised. On it was a cheese sandwich that was wrapped in cellophane, an apple, and a packet of crisps. This wasn't her usual food back in Pakistan, but at least it wasn't half-eaten by maggots.

Starving, Yalina sat on the bed and unwrapped the cheese sandwich. As she was about to bite into it, she noticed the chest in the corner of the room. Curiosity outweighed the hunger, and so she got up and approached the chest. Having seen the brutal mess of Dominica and heard the terrifying screams from Hulou, Yalina's imagination was in a dark place. Was it a chest or someone's coffin?

She grabbed the leather strap and tugged it to lift the lid, taking a deep breath as she did so. In order to get a better view of the contents, she had to drag the heavy chest towards the door. The first thing she noticed was the emerald-green material, an exquisite sari edged in gold thread, and beside it was a jewellery box containing bangles and necklaces. Yalina held the gemstone necklace in her hand, and then, with her other hand, she stroked the beautiful sari. The top was a deep blue and encrusted with beads.

Her eyes grew wider. She recognised the dress. She had only ever seen it once before, when her father had almost slammed the chest shut on her hand. She recalled his words. 'No, Yalina, you must not touch it. Your hands are dirty. This belongs to your grandmother.'

She had been ten years old then, but she remembered the material very well, and as she brought the necklace to her face, she could actually smell her grandmother's scent. These were her things. Pulling the contents from the chest, she spotted a large box that she didn't recognise. Not only was it full of make-up, but there was also a picture of a woman with her face entirely made up, just as Hulou had done to her.

Inside the chest, there was also a note, and as Yalina opened the folded piece of paper, she recognised her father's handwriting.

Dear Yalina,

I hope you are being a good girl. You must do as you are told. And always remember you are doing this for your sisters. I will send for you and your mother as soon as we have paid the bank, which will not be too long if you are a good girl.

Father

Scanning the words a few times, she sat back, her shoulders slumped in complete and utter despair. With a lump in her throat, she mentally processed what was happening to her. It was so clear now. Shabir hadn't double-crossed them. It was her father who had sold her and possibly her mother as well. He had never loved her. Even in the note, there were no words of care, respect, or love. Her dreams of school and university were gone. This was to be her existence now. She would have to do as she was told for fear they were using her mother as collateral. She wasn't hungry anymore, but she was angry. Very angry.

CHAPTER FIVE

It was clear that something seriously dramatic had occurred. All barring one of Yuri's men had shot off in their cars as though an avalanche was on its way. The only guard remaining was Daria, who introduced himself to her. His appearance had Kristi wondering if Yuri had other reasons for employing the man. He was shorter and chubbier than the other guards, and his rounded shoulders accentuated his slovenly demeanour. Rather than holding his head high, he leaned against the wall rolling a cigarette as though he was manning the Dalton Highway in Alaska. He didn't strike her as being the sharpest knife in the drawer either, with his slow speech and nervous giggling. *However, looks and first impressions can always deceive*, she thought.

'Are you moving in here?' he asked, as he shifted from foot to foot.

Kristi tried to work out where the man was focusing since his eyes looked like they had swapped sockets. 'Temporarily, why?'

Daria shrugged his shoulders and randomly tried to blow a bubble with a piece of chewing gum. 'Yuri didn't mention that you would be moving in.'

'And would Yuri inform you of such matters?' she asked, as she watched him clumsily try to push a piece of card at the end of his roll-up. She realised then it was a joint.

Daria looked down. 'No, maybe not. So what are you doing this evening?'

Wanting to suss him out, Kristi didn't answer right away.

'We're on our own,' he said, trying to fill the silence.

Kristi was laughing inside. She could sense the man was feeling awkward. He was so unlike any Russian guard she'd ever met before.

‘I have my car arriving tonight, and my personal guards are not here yet, either, so would you please wait by the gate? The delivery man doesn’t have the code, and I don’t want my car to be returned.’

He nodded and licked the cigarette paper before finally sealing his joint.

She was about to walk away when she spun around. ‘Oh, Daria, is this place rat-infested?’

Daria frowned. ‘Rats?’

Kristi nodded. ‘Yes, rats or mice. Are there any rodents?’

‘Why?’

‘Because as I was unpacking my clothes, I am sure I heard one in my room.’

‘I don’t know. I haven’t heard them.’

‘But can you check for me? I hate rats.’

‘I don’t know how to check. Was there any rat shit?’

‘Daria, there are cameras in my rooms, which, by the way, you can tell Yuri I have covered over. I must have my privacy. Anyway, maybe previous footage shows the little bastards scurrying around. Because I will be honest with you, I am terrified of them.’ She put her finger over her lips and winked. ‘Our secret.’

Daria blushed slightly, offering a smile that was one tooth short of perfect.

‘Yes, Kristi, you can tell me anything. I won’t say a word.’

He looked down at his feet and then slowly looked up, tilting his head to the side. Their little secret had given him the hope that she was into him, and this was a come-on. ‘I should call in the rat people, anyway. I want you to be comfortable while you’re here. The camera footage is only live, not recorded. Yuri wanted it that way.’ He chuckled. ‘So I wouldn’t be able to rewind to see the little bastard as it scurried away.' He wiggled his fingers, imitating a rat running away.

Bingo! She had got the information she wanted about the cameras. She had needed to know if the cameras were only a live feed.

'Thanks, Daria.' She softened her otherwise sharp tone. 'This mansion is full of men, and mine haven't arrived yet. I could do with a friendly face around. Do you think Yuri would assign you to me for now?'

'Yes, if I ask him, he will. You're safe here, though, and all the guards will look out for you – especially me.' He winked. 'And Yuri did say that apart from us, no one in the UK knows you or knows that you're even here. I guess your father was a powerful man with many enemies, like Yuri has. So, you will have our full protection.'

Kristi was itching to get away, but she also had to gain Daria's trust and build some kind of bond.

'Well, I will feel much safer knowing that you, Daria, have my back. And thank you for looking out for my car. I appreciate it.'

As he walked towards the main doors, Kristi noticed that when he suddenly straightened his spine, his head became an inch higher. She was right to guess that he was the underdog and had been taken on for a more personal reason. Because he clearly wasn't the full ticket. However, he was carrying a gun, and for all his roaming eyes, he could potentially be dangerous. She had been brought up never to drop her guard, and she was well aware of making any assumptions about someone else. It had served her well in the past.

While Daria was outside the mansion, Kristi wasted no time hurrying to the bedroom, where she retrieved her work tablet, before making her way to Yuri's office.

As soon as she stepped inside, a cold feeling came over her. This was too easy. Suddenly, she felt painfully visible. Yet she was precisely where she needed to be. The filing cabinet she was most interested in was locked by a small key, not a technical coded lock. *Surely he wouldn't have been so stupid as to leave the key in the obvious place, would he?* She glanced around the room, working out the most plausible hiding places. The most likely one was the desk and the pencil pot was the best bet. She grabbed the pencil pot on the desk, but something made her pause and take stock. She was experiencing a sense of paranoia. Why had Yuri truly trusted her so explicitly? She sure as hell wouldn't trust him.

Needing to get into those files, she emptied the pot. Bingo! There it was on the desk. Wasting no time, she inserted the small key. The filing cabinet clicked open. Carefully, she slid the top drawer open, ensuring it didn't make a metal-on-metal high-pitched screech that would set her teeth on edge and also alert Daria to what she was doing. Although he probably wouldn't hear if he was outside awaiting for the arrival of her Mercedes.

Taking the first file over to the large wooden desk, she glanced through the initial few pages. Without reading every word, she merely surmised that it was the accounts for a random building company. No one had mentioned anything to her about building companies. She continued searching through the files, but they all seemed to contain building plans, architects' drawings, legal letters, and diagrams of renovations.

The second drawer was equally disappointing. The files appeared like any other business, with no details regarding the girls' personal information. And there was no information regarding their transport to the UK, and, more importantly, the places where they were kept.

She didn't have time to stand and stare to try to understand it all; instead, she used her tablet to take as many photos as possible. In the end, she wasn't even looking; she just turned over each page and snapped away.

Once she had finished, she opened the third drawer; inside, there were papers in a wallet folder. Now wishing she'd looked at those first, her heart was beating like a drum. If the guards returned and caught her, she could only assume her life would be cut short and probably in the grizzliest way possible. With perspiration peppering her brow, she removed the contents of the files. She noticed a letter heading: 'TR Corporation.' And then, when she saw the photo of The Click and a casino, her eyes widened, and she almost gasped aloud. She was longing to scrutinise the attached papers, but she simply didn't have time. All she could do was photograph them. But in her panic, she dropped the photo of The Click. It slid behind the cabinet before she had a chance to photograph it. *Damn!*

The last paper seemed to be some type of contract. Adjusting the tablet to get the whole document on the screen and in focus, she saw the name at the bottom. Her eyes widened, her breathing increased, and her sudden instinct was to run. She had to get away from the mansion. It was clear that no one had her back. However, taking that last photo of the signature had been a feat: her hands had shaken so much, but the result was a blurred photo.

She could feel her heart almost beating outside her chest when Daria called out.

'Kristi, your car is here.'

Relieved that it wasn't Yuri who was returning, she placed the paperwork back into the filing cabinet, snuck out of the office, and hurried to the large lounge, where she took a seat on one of the puffy sofas. As Daria called out again, she could hear his clodhopping footsteps approaching. She yawned the moment he saw her pretending to be relaxed and half-asleep. 'I was watching *The Bourne Supremacy*, an outstanding film.' She tapped her tablet.

Daria held up the keys. 'Nice car. I love Mercedes cars. Do you want to go for a ride? I can lock up here and come with you.'

Kristi wanted to laugh. This idiot of a guard had absolutely no idea. However, her mind was shot to pieces. She was struggling to keep a calm exterior, when, inside, she was frantically trying to piece together a very disturbing puzzle. She only hoped the concierge from her hotel who had delivered the car hadn't mentioned where she was staying.

‘No, you must stay here and guard the mansion. If Yuri comes back to find you gone, he will string you up by your balls on your return.’

‘Yuri won’t ever touch me. You see, I’m his brother.’

Well, that explained why Yuri employed him, she thought, before she wondered how the hell two brothers could look so different. One, she considered, would be judged by most people’s standards as a very good-looking man, while the other looked like something that had come out of a slow cooker.

‘I thought you two looked alike.’

Kristi smiled as she took the car keys that were dangled in front of her.

‘Thanks again, Daria. See you soon.’

Holding his hand out, Kristi frowned. ‘What?’

‘Your tablet. Give it to me.’

Kristi felt her mouth go dry. She had to calm her nerves. ‘It’s fine. I’ll take it with me. I won’t be long. I just need a few items from the supermarket. They are open this late in London, yes?’

‘Yes, but you cannot be too careful. Don’t walk about with your tablet. You might get robbed.’

‘I will be careful.’

She turned to walk away, praying that he would not stop her.

‘Drive carefully and on the left!’ he called out.

Kristi waved as she hurried to the car. The main gate was still open, and the moment she drove out and on to the road, she saw Yuri’s limo about to pull into the drive. With her pulse drumming in her neck and her hands covered in perspiration, she drove along the main road before exiting onto the A2 and heading for Greenwich. She had already booked into the Novotel London Greenwich for six weeks. She hadn’t considered that Yuri would offer part of his mansion to her as a guest.

So much was flooding through her mind that she had to slow down, reflect, and process the information with clarity. She checked her mirrors to make sure she wasn't being followed, and for the first time in her life, she showed every possible physical sign of fear. Never before had she felt so totally out of her depth.

Paranoia was creeping around like an invisible cloak and threatening to take over her mind. She opened the car window for a few seconds before she glanced in her rear-view mirror for the umpteenth time. So frantic that they would be upon her at any moment, she almost missed the turning on to Greenwich High Road, and that was when she realised she shouldn't be here doing what she was doing. She should be at home and preparing herself. She ran her hands over her stomach and slowed down before turning into the side road and on to the ramp that led down to the underground car park. She was made to wait at the barrier while the ANPR checked her car number plate and her booking. Seconds later, the barrier lifted and she was in. She had to go down another level to be able to park, and once she'd removed the keys, she leaned back and sighed. The car park was deathly quiet. As she got out of her car, she felt her legs feel like jelly; right away, she was angry with herself. *Get a grip.*

The lift took her to the lobby area, which was bright and welcoming. A young woman behind the desk smiled. Her face was heavily coated in make-up and her hair was practically glued flat to her head with a neat bun wrapped tightly on top, similar to the style worn by the air hostess on the Emirates Airline advert *We're on top of the world.*

'Good evening, Ms Pavlov,' she said, with an eager fake smile. 'Your key.' She slid the card from under the desk and handed it over to Kristi.

'Thank you.'

Kristi leaned closer to look at the girl's name tag and got a whiff of cigarettes and freshly sprayed cheap perfume. Rosalind. 'Oh, I need to post something. Do you have any padded envelopes, A4 size?'

The girl nodded. 'Yes, how many would you like?'

'Just the one, Rosalind. Thank you so much.'

Rosalind trotted to the room behind the desk. Her high-heeled shoes made a slap-slap sound on the marble floor. She returned seconds later. 'Is this okay?' She waved an envelope in the air.

'Yes, that's perfect. And what's your surname, Rosalind?'

The young woman in her early thirties blushed. 'Oh, er, sorry. Is there a problem?'

Kristi smiled. 'No, not at all. On the contrary, I wanted to email management of your helpfulness.'

'Oh really? Thank you so much. I need a good word, to be honest. I'm not in the manager's good books. Anyway, it's Rosalind Bacon.'

'I'll do it the second I go to my room. Oh, do you have a pen and a piece of paper?'

Rosalind was nothing short of an eager beaver, determined to get complimentary feedback. She had been in trouble for looking at her phone too many times. And she had been given a warning for sneaking off for a cigarette more times than her breaks allowed.

Kristi walked over to the seating area. She wrote a short note and then popped the tablet and the note into the Jiffy bag. After writing an address on the front, she hurried to the desk. 'Sorry, I was about to walk away with your pen.'

Rosalind smiled. 'You can keep it. I've got plenty.'

'I can't see how you would need favourable comments appraising your work, and I have never been to a hotel where the staff are so accommodating.'

Rosalind beamed. 'Will you put that in your email as well?'

Kristi nodded. 'And a lot more besides, Rosalind.'

'Shall I make sure that gets posted for you? I can pop it in with our normal post,' she said, glancing at the package.

'That would be wonderful, but how secure is it?'

Rosalind nodded. 'Oh, very secure. It goes in our postbox safe. Only the postman has the code to get in.'

'Perfect, thank you, Rosalind. You've been a joy.'

Once Kristi entered the lift, she tapped her foot impatiently listening to the monotonous background music until the door pinged and it finally opened. After glancing up and down the corridor, she ran to her room. With the door shut behind her, she felt enormous relief. She sat on the crisp white duvet covering the double bed and placed her hands over her face. There was only one person she knew she could trust with her life, and hopefully, the parcel would be on its way there.

Something didn't sit right. She knew Russians and how brutal and astute they could be, and yet Yuri wasn't, was he? It was as though he wasn't breaking the law even though he had mentioned he had been shipping over the girls. She tried to recall his actual words, but, of course, Dominica barging in had ruined that and now where was the poor girl? Was she rotting in some holding cell?

She had to find out where Dominica was, but she was fully aware that it was a tightly kept secret. Her only option was to pull herself together and return to Yuri's place. But what was so concerning was this: she was now on a completely different mission, with no help.

As far as her being here at the hotel was concerned, she could inform Yuri that she'd returned here for more of her luggage, which she'd had delivered two days earlier, because at the time, she hadn't realised that she would be staying with him.

Rummaging through her holdall, she retrieved another tablet containing photos depicting her in Russia as a child with her so-called father.

While the film *The Bourne Supremacy* was downloading, Kristi wandered into the bathroom and washed her face. The loud rapping at the door made her jump out of her skin. How the hell did they find her? Was it even him? She glanced at the tablet; it showed fifteen seconds before the film was completely downloaded.

Taking a deep breath, she called out, 'Who is it? I'm getting changed.'

Kristi glanced around the room. She was on the third floor and there was no escape. She didn't think she had sufficient time to grab a weapon from her overnight bag.

'It's only me, Rosalind, Ms Pavlov.'

Sighing with relief, Kristi opened the door and was met with a massive bunch of flowers that were shoved in her face. She had to step back to see who was holding them, and then her blood ran cold when she met the dark menacing eyes of Yuri's head of security, Casper, whom she'd been introduced to at the mansion, when she had first arrived.

He turned to Rosalind. 'Thank you so much, Rosalind. My wife was clearly not expecting me. And I couldn't allow the day to end without surprising her on our anniversary.'

Rosalind beamed like the cat that had got the cream. 'Anything for Ms Pavlov. Enjoy your evening.' She chuckled before hurrying away.

Kristi was too terrified to scream because pointing at her through the flowers was a handgun. And, also, she was too afraid that Casper would shoot the poor girl in the back of the head.

Both stared at each other for a few seconds and then she heard Daria's voice.

'Hello, Kristi,' he said, as he appeared in the doorway. 'I think it is best if you come with me for your own protection. I told you, London isn't a safe place,' he said.

'I was about to collect the other suitcases that I had sent here and return to Yuri's home, so why does Casper have a gun pointing at my face?'

Daria stepped forward into the room. 'It's okay. I will help you with those. It's not a problem.'

‘How did you know I was here, Daria?’

‘While you were photographing Yuri’s private records, I attached a tracker to your car.’

‘I wasn’t photographing anything. What makes you say that?’ asked Kristi, her mouth as dry as a bone.

‘I told you that the cameras were only live feed. That was true. However, the one in Yuri’s office isn’t only live, it records as well.’ He held out his hand. ‘Give me the tablet, Kristi.’

She pointed to the tablet on the bed. ‘Take it.’

As Daria stepped in front of Casper and attempted to retrieve the device, Kristi leaped onto the bed and fly-kicked Daria in the chest, knocking him back into Casper. With both men losing their footing, she had enough time to launch herself off the bed and give Casper a deliberate lethal elbow to the side of his neck. The angle and power should have brought the man to his knees, but he was a lot harder than she had given him credit for. But she was off, out of the room and racing down the corridor.

Casper, though, was soon on his feet. Dropping the flowers, he chased after her, his long legs and superfit body, giving him strength and speed over her.

He dived through the air and grabbed her legs, pulling her viciously to the ground, before he gripped her short hair and rammed her face into the floor. She was about to attempt a crocodile roll when Daria appeared with a syringe.

Her eyes widened. ‘Please, no! Daria, no!’

But he rolled his eyes, stuck the long needle into her neck, and before he’d even emptied the syringe, she had lost consciousness.

CHAPTER SIX

30th October 2012

As Michel jogged around Richmond Park, his earphones blasted Tchaikovsky's '1812 Overture'. It was familiarity of the music that brought back good memories from his much younger days in Russia, prior to his mother's death. It was also the time before his father and uncles cruelly mocked him for being so morally right all the time, when the country was running on immorality. In this dog-eat-dog world, it was the only way to survive. However, he couldn't live that way, and for his beliefs, he was beaten and then scarred so badly it only pushed him into silence. Of course, it hardened him and turned him against his own family and the country he was born in. Mentally, he wanted to rid himself of everything Russian, especially his accent.

Suddenly he stopped when he felt the vibrations of his phone buzzing in his sweatshirt pocket. He bent over, placed his hands on his knees, and took a deep breath before retrieving his mobile and glancing at the caller's name. Instantly, he felt his heart almost galloping outside his chest. Two words, *Brown Bear*, flashed. It was the code name for Charley's boss.

There had been no contact from his wife, Charley, for a week now, and although her operations manager Verity Mercer, otherwise known as Brown Bear, had reason to believe his wife was dead, Michel wasn't convinced. He had made it very clear to Verity that he would only be certain if they found her body; otherwise, he would assume she was being held captive.

He held his breath before opening the message, hoping that the news was good and that her team had located her – alive. He looked up to the grey sky. 'Holy Father, please do me this one thing: bring my wife back to me.'

His Russian accent was barely detectable now. In the last year, he had been studying English at a highly advanced level, even perfecting a London twang. It allowed his undercover personas, otherwise known as legends, to stretch into other realms. His primary roles were to infiltrate serious crimes committed by Russians.

He could go undercover as a Russian, having lived in the UK for most of his life; it enabled him to offer the suspects expansive knowledge of London and the underworld. His language classes had been invaluable, particularly because of the increase in Russian specific crimes. Not only were these cleverly organised but they now required input from the special intelligence unit and the employment of deep undercover police with his experience.

He opened the message – **Park Lane 1.30**

His brows snapped together. Park Lane would mean the London Aquarium, and 1.30 would be 3.45. He checked his watch and then sprinted to his parked car.

Part of his roles included being a quick thinker, but as the days passed with still no messages from Charley, his brain was less in gear; even jogging for hours couldn't clear his thoughts. He had instantly gone off the boil as far as his current job was concerned. And now his operations team had temporarily removed him from his post with some random cover story about a broken leg, which meant that when he returned, he would have to do so with a limp. As much as he could morph into a legend and take on a pseudonym, he found making the physical changes the hardest. Walking, talking, and even his mannerisms had to fit in with his new cover.

***

Once he had showered and changed into plain dark-blue jeans, a blue polo shirt, and a black bomber jacket, he was ready to meet Verity. His slim physique and simply styled short dark-brown hair left him indistinguishable from anyone else. And that was how he liked it. He could weave in and out of crowds, and no one would remember him. As he headed to the aquarium, he assumed their meeting would take place inside and by the shark tank. Moments later, he spotted her as he approached the entrance.

Dressed in black jeans and a pink sweatshirt and carrying a backpack, she, too, looked like any other tourist. Her fair shoulder-length hair was tied in a bun. Of course, she was attractive; when she was in a fitted dress, with her hair down and make-up on her face, she would easily stop traffic, and, sadly, she knew it too. But he didn't see her as anything other than Charley's boss. As he watched her flick her head towards the London Eye, he knew intuitively that whatever she wanted to talk to him about was of grave importance; he only prayed it wasn't to tell him they had found his wife's body.

He followed her lead but remained a few feet away until they were in the queue, and then, once she had purchased tickets, she waited until he caught her up. Handing him a prepaid ticket, she stood by his side as the pod slowed to let the people off, allowing them then to climb aboard. She showed the glass door operator two tickets and a police badge that instantly compelled him to step aside and hold his hand up to stop anyone else eagerly waiting to get on with them.

As the door closed behind them and the pod gently moved, Michel walked to the farthest point away from the door. He had his back to her. He didn't want to face her when she told him that Charley was dead and they had found her body, and he was sure that was precisely what Verity was about to say. Because if they had found her alive, she would have phoned, or someone would have called. They wouldn't have arranged this secret meeting.

The newness of his leather bomber jacket mixed with the sharp, tangy scent of his aftershave, filled the pod. She could see he had showered. His hair was still damp, and his face was freshly shaved. Seeing him like this led to a sudden surge of hope that he had made an effort with his appearance solely for her. 'You are a good undercover officer, Michel. I could do with you back on my team.'

Her voice was too seductive for his liking and compelled him to spin around. His eye twitched as his lips tightened. 'I am not here to play games. Tell me what you have to say to me, and then leave me alone.'

Maintaining a mask of indifference – despite wanting to rush over and kiss him passionately – she stepped forward, shaking her head. 'Don't flatter yourself, Michel. You know very well that ship sailed a long time ago.' She reined in her sharp tone. 'Sorry.'

Placing her backpack on the seat in the centre of the pod, she unzipped it and retrieved a slim black plastic file. 'I *am* sorry, Michel. Truly very sorry.'

When he met her eyes, he thought perhaps she was being genuine. He then looked away, his heart suddenly beginning to beat so hard and fast that he had to swallow a few times. Although the realisation that they had found his wife's body gave him finality, his heart then ached so much he had to sit down with his head in his hands.

Finally, he looked up at his wife's boss. He noticed how long Verity's fingers were when she gracefully removed a large A4-sized photo and offered it to him. He snatched it from her and took a deep breath before forcing himself to peer down. The image didn't hold back; it demonstrated the detailed macabre scene with gruesome clarity. It centred around a close-up of two charred bodies. Both were sitting upright in a burned-out car. One body was in the driver's seat and the other in the front passenger seat. They could have been mistaken for Halloween decorations – joke skeletons bought from a fancy-dress shop that would light up at any moment and shout 'Boo'.

Feeling his stomach contents rising, he knew he had to gulp in more air. His hands shook as he held the horrific photo. 'And you're sure it's her?' His voice cracked as he spoke, so he instantly coughed to clear his throat.

Verity sat down on the seat and slid closer. It was too close for his liking. 'That's her car.'

'DNA?'

Verity shook her head. 'The bodies were too badly burned. The report showed that an accelerant had been added to the fire, leaving the bodies indistinguishable.'

The lack of empathy was obvious from her words, never mind her tone.

'What? But the teeth? Surely, they can take a sample from the teeth? I have to know, and—'

He looked Verity up and down with contempt. 'Surely you have to be a hundred per cent sure, or is she just a commodity now? Clearly, she has done her job and so is she now dispensable?' He raised his voice. 'Is that it, Verity? Is that really it? Answer me!'

Verity shook her head before taking a deep breath. 'Michel, I am sorry, but there is no DNA.' She raised her hand to stop him from interrupting her. 'And the teeth of the two victims were removed. So forensics couldn't extract the pulp for analysis.'

Michel's eyes widened in horror. Visions of his wife being tortured and then burned to death sent shards of ice through his veins.

Verity looked away; she couldn't stand to see him so grief-stricken over another woman, especially Charley, the decorated officer everyone in the team, from top to bottom, found enchanting and yet smart. It was as if whatever Charley was saying should be taken as gospel. She only had to open her mouth, and silence would fill the room, awaiting her words.

If only things had turned out differently. Michel should have been with her, not Charley. But as soon as Charley became part of their unit, he was all over her like a rash. The fact that Charley spoke Russian fluently, as well as two other foreign languages, was probably the attraction because she sure as hell couldn't see why he would favour her. So Charley might have had a pretty but childlike face and been chunkier, not the size eight that she had been when he'd first met her. But whatever it was he had seen in her, there had definitely been a magnetic attraction between them. It seemed so unfair. But what was even worse, though, was that he had discarded her like an old toy before she could even get a second date.

But she wasn't about to give up on him just yet. She hoped she could be the one to help him through his grief process – the caring friend offering a shoulder to cry on and a warm bed at night. *Was now the right time to put her arm around his shoulders?* she wondered. Even though she wasn't good at handling grieving people, and she wasn't good with tears either, she was determined to find a way to be the go-to girl for him.

Desperate to escape and run, Michel jumped up from his seat to get the vision out of his mind. However, there was nowhere to go. *Perhaps that had been her plan all along*, he thought. Maybe she knew he wouldn't wait around and spend time in her company.

His fast and aggressive reaction knocked the file from her hand. It broke the moment it hit the floor. The paperwork inside splayed out like a fan. Michel scooped it all up, and, knowing he wouldn't have time to read everything before the glass doors opened, he began taking snapshots using his phone.

In a panic, Verity tried to rip the contents of the file from his hands, but he merely pushed her away. Not expecting the force of that push, she almost toppled backwards. Initially, she was astounded that he would have the temerity to put his hands on her, but her emotions were sidestepped as she tried to recall everything in that file. 'Give it back, Michel!'

Michel turned his back on her.

'No, I want to see the file for myself. She is my wife, and I have a right.'

'Look, Michel, you know you cannot just look through these papers. You are not part of this case. I only wanted to give you the news, and I guessed you'd want proof.'

She tried again by tugging his arm.

This time, he spun around. His eyes flashed and his nostrils flared. 'Get the fuck away from me, Verity.'

'Whoa, don't, Michel. This is not why I brought you here,' she replied, nervously.

She had been informed of how ruthless Michel could be, but it had never crossed her mind that he would ever talk to her in this way.

But she wouldn't be the one to back down. 'Give me the file. You understand the importance. Now, hand it over.'

'You won't tell me anything because I am Russian and so I can guess this target is probably Russian.'

'Oh, come on, Michel, it's nothing to do with you being Russian. Christ, you wouldn't be in the force as an undercover officer if you weren't trusted.'

She edged forward, but his suspicious glare made her hesitate.

'If you try to stop me again, I will break your fucking fingers.' His Russian accent was clear and quite alarming.

Seeing the sudden fear in her eyes as she backed away, he continued flicking through the file, taking photos of all the images and statements until he came to one that forced him to stop for a moment and stare. It depicted a squalid-looking bathroom. The tiles on the floor were stained nicotine yellow and cracked. Layers of paint, thick with dust and grime, coated the exposed pipes. And there in the centre of the photo was a set of handcuffs dangling, with only one cuff attached to the pipe. The walls were covered in oblong bevelled edge tiles and to the right of the pipes was a sink with one dull-coloured metal tap. Limescale had eroded the enamel, leaving a green outline where the tap water had run. He could almost hear the sound of a dripping tap and imagine the smell of stagnant pond water. The shocking point of the photo was the amount of blood. It was spattered up the wall and had pooled in the corner next to the pipes that held the handcuff.

'And this blood. What do you make of that?' he said, as he took another shot before shoving the photo under her nose.

Verity looked at the photo. She knew that one was in there, and she would have discussed it with him if he hadn't decided to photo everything. She couldn't blame him. He was like a machine. In fact, the deep undercover officers were all the same, and they had to be.

'No, Michel, we have no idea where this place is. An undercover officer working with Charley managed to take one photo and send it to me before they too disappeared. The photo was sent with a text saying that Charley had been held there before her murder. You can see from the amount of blood that she would never have survived. I am so sorry, Michel, but you know we're here to do a job, and we know the risks, but she was a good person, and she will be missed.'

Michel glared into the condescending eyes of Verity. 'You speak with so much finality.' He sighed. 'You show me a few photos, and you assume she's dead, and I have to accept it?'

Verity just looked at him, unsure what she should say.

'Who is this other undercover officer?'

Ignoring his question, she stepped forward to take the file. 'It's been a week. Face facts: you know the risks, and Charley knew them more than most. She had worked hard to gain their trust, and she simply must have messed up because right now we have nothing. My undercover guy informed me that the target had been tipped off and has now gone off the radar.'

'And this other undercover officer you had on this mission. Is he the other victim in the burned-out car?' He raised his eyebrows and glared, awaiting a reply.

'I shouldn't discuss it with you, Michel. You know I shouldn't. But as your friend and a friend of Charley's, I can tell you that we did everything in our power to find her.' She paused and gave an exaggerated sigh. 'I wish I had come to you with better news.' She held out her hand again to take back the file, her voice uncompromising. 'Delete the photos, Michel. It will only fuel your grief.'

'You didn't answer my question.'

'No, Michel, the other undercover officer went missing *after* we found the bodies. I believe our target had got to him also. We lost all contact, but to answer your question, no, he wasn't the other person in the car. All I can confirm is that the two people in the car were females.'

Michel slapped the file into her hand and glared at her starchy-coloured face.

'Don't shoot the messenger, Michel. They asked me to give you the news, considering we were once . . . friends.'

'*Friends?* Is that what you call it? Don't pretend we were once *anything*, Verity. You nearly cost me my marriage. Lucky for me, my wife is – or rather was – so good at reading people. And don't you dare pretend to me that you liked or even respected Charley because we both know you didn't.'

'That's absurd, Michel. I get that you are hurt and grieving, but please don't direct your anger towards me. Just because you harbour guilt over our—'

'Now it's my turn to say, don't flatter yourself. We dated just the once before I met Charley, and when we were on that stupid case in Scotland. You.' He poked a finger in her chest. 'You came to my room with clear intentions. You knew I had been drinking because I was missing my wife being stuck in that hotel. You and your constant flirting. And you think you were clever by calling out when my wife rang me on the hotel room phone. So, Verity, I don't feel guilty. I just feel sorry. Sorry for you.'

Her confident expression suddenly paled into hurt and shame before she faked a smile.

As he stared, he wondered if Verity was getting some kind of sick kick out of believing Charley was dead.

'Tell me, Verity, where was her last known position before her life was ended?'

'I know it's hard, but, Michel, you cannot get involved. This isn't your case. It was Charley's, and you cannot switch roles. You know that.'

'I'll ask again. Where was her last known position?'

Verity shook her head. 'We don't know. If we had her tablet, we'd have a better idea. You see, she went deep undercover, and she orchestrated the first meeting with our suspect. Look, you know she was on a huge case, the biggest our unit has ever been involved in. I am doing my best to find this target, for Charley's and my other officer's sakes. So just stay out of it, Michel. If you go into her last known position, and there are any dregs of the operation intact that my team can reactivate, and you go sticking your nose in, you will blow it for any future chance of nicking these suspects. I cannot tell you anything more.'

Suddenly, as the pod was about to open its doors, he nodded and gave his best defeated look.

'I understand. I'm sorry I was so rude.' He held out his arms to hug her.

As much as Verity knew him, she hadn't ever had the privilege of knowing him very well. Embracing him, he whispered to her, 'But I cannot stop until I find my wife, and I know she isn't dead. Goodbye, Verity, and thank you.'

Once the glass doors opened, he sprinted out of the pod, leaving her momentarily perplexed. Why had he run off? A cold, clammy feeling engulfed her. By the time she pushed herself away from the crowds, she could see him in the distance, weaving in and out of the bustling tourists.

Fear gripped her around the throat as she realised what he had done. Her phones! The unit had warned her to be careful. That was why she had chosen the London Eye to be safe. He would have nowhere to run. But she hadn't expected him to go through the file. Not that those notes and photos were a real problem, but the case details and messages on her phones could be. He was one of the most competent officers they had. He could get into her phones in a second, if he wanted to.

As she hurried away from the crowd, she dug deep into her backpack and found only her personal phone. Smoothing back her hair away from her sweaty face, she dialled Michel's number. It rang three times before he answered it. 'Michel, I promise you this, if you don't return those phones, you will be fired, lose your pension, and—'

'I resign!'

'We will arrest you!'

'You cannot arrest me. I have done nothing wrong!'

'My phones, Michel, my phones!'

'I do not know what you are talking about.'

CHAPTER SEVEN

31st October

Harper Kane pulled her jacket tighter around herself, and as she bent down to lay the bunch of red roses on Paddy's grave, she noticed how scrawny her hand looked. It had been a month since she'd had a proper meal inside her, even though her mother and aunt had insisted she at least tried to eat their home-cooked meals.

But it wasn't only Paddy's murder that made her feel sick all the time: it was those dark thoughts that plagued her mind. The wind blew, and she could feel her hair tickling her ears. Even that had grown way longer than she usually kept it. But her appearance didn't matter. Not now.

She hadn't gone to work at the club since the shooting. Lucky for her, Roxy, her good friend and a very competent barmaid, had taken over the role, giving her time, partly, to grieve and also to decide on her own future. She had cried enough, and now, although her eyes were dry, her heart was filled with rage. Her short-lived relationship with the tall Irishman had been beautiful, and only God would have known if it would have developed into a lifetime of marriage or fizzled away as the lust for each other left them. But that was the thing: she'd not had the chance to discover that for herself. He had been shot dead in cold blood, practically on her own doorstep. And she knew in her heart her ex, the father of her son, Teddy Ryder, was responsible.

Since Paddy's death, she had used every bit of her strength to keep up the pretence that she was unaware of Teddy having prior knowledge of Cody Deacon's involvement with the kidnapping and the torture of those innocent young women. It had been by chance that she'd seen the texts on Cody's phone from Teddy demanding money for a debt that Cody had run up in Teddy's casino. But what had disturbed her more than his demands was the fact that Teddy knew about a particular missing girl and was using that knowledge as leverage for payment. However, as frustrating as it was, she couldn't even tell Teddy why she hated him. She couldn't let on how she knew about his evil wrongdoings. Because then he would know what she had done herself, and he would hold that against her – she was sure of that.

Her anger was fuelled when she'd also only recently discovered that Teddy was responsible for Vadim's accident; it had left the poor man in such a bad way, he'd returned to Russia.

When she stared at Paddy's grave, she wondered if half of her was also grieving for Vadim. For a year with Vadim in an out of the country, she had convinced herself that they were merely friends with benefits. But was she really hiding her true feelings for him, to save herself from further heartache? She sighed to herself because those tears had been from nothing less than *heartache.*

She had understood from Paddy's brother that Teddy and two men had mowed Vadim down. They had cruelly left him a mess. But not only that, they had cajoled him into signing over the club and ultimately forcing him back to Russia. She assumed the reason Teddy had wanted Vadim out of the country was to get back with her.

But what had started as a few winks and hugs and trips down memory lane had now become an obsession of Teddy's, and, crucially, as far as she was concerned, it was one that most certainly had driven him to have Paddy murdered. She didn't have to prove all of this. She knew it. End of.

For the past month, sleep had been hard to come by. So she had lain awake devising a way to get her revenge on Teddy without killing him. It wasn't that she didn't want to: she did. More than anyone, she wanted to shoot Teddy – right between the eyes. However, she couldn't do it. How would her son feel knowing his mother had killed his father? Sensing Teddy was there in the car just outside the graveyard watching her, Harper sighed heavily before feeling her anger rise. He had parked where there were yellow lines on the road. No one else would have had the balls to park there for fear of getting a ticket from the boss-eyed moody ruthless traffic warden.

It was perfectly clear to her that Teddy was becoming even more of a flash fucker as each day passed. He swanned around like he owned this part of South-East London. In fact, he had turned into the type of cocksure man she despised.

Purchasing The Click had been shrewd to say the least. Not only was the club a regular cash cow, but when Teddy told her that the reason he'd bought it was because she was managing the place and so she and ultimately Eddie would be the beneficiaries, she could follow the logic in what he had done. But Teddy hadn't just done this for altruistic reasons. She knew he could have her right where he could see her.

But he couldn't have her under his nose now because she had told him she was taking time off. However, his seemingly constant watchfulness either by him or by one of his minions was beginning to irritate her like an annoying wasp that wouldn't bugger off.

She glanced to the side, and yeah, sure enough, there he was in his brand-new Jaguar. He waved and then got out of the car. Pretending she hadn't seen him, she walked in the opposite direction, towards Orpington High Street, where she had parked her car in the Walnuts Shopping Centre.

'Hey, Harps. Wait up, babe.'

Harper had to stop; but she needed to keep up the pretence. Turning around with a fake smile on her face, she said, 'Sorry, I didn't realise it was you.'

By the time he caught her up, he was out of breath. 'I kinda guessed you would be here. Listen, how about you and me have a weekend away from everything?' He held up his hands. 'No funny stuff. Just a break away as friends. You need to look after yourself, Harps. You're looking sickly, babe.' He attempted to embrace her, but she stepped back.

‘Teddy, I need time on my own. No disrespect, but I want me own space. I don’t need a holiday, a break, or even a night out. I just need to be alone.’

Teddy sighed. ‘I get it. Our Eddie wanted to pop in, but I told him to leave you be.’

Harper felt the veins in her neck drumming. She had to take a deep breath before she would let rip. ‘Teddy, you had no right. If Eddie wants to come over, then he can. I am always happy to see him.’

‘Why don’t you come to ours? We’ve got a big screen, a spare bedroom, well, three, and Eddie would love that, you know, being around his Mum and Dad.’

Harper breathed through her nose, afraid her mouth would open, and verbal abuse would tumble out.

‘I have to go, and please tell Eddie he can come to mine.’

‘Oh, uh, are you ok? Have I upset you, babe?’

She wanted to say ‘Upset me? Upset me? You have destroyed my fucking life!’ But, instead, she merely shook her head and turned to walk away.

But Teddy wasn’t going to give up so easily. He gripped her arm and spun her around. ‘Harps, what the fuck is the matter with you? You’re acting like you were in love with the man, coming to his grave every day. He was just a *doorman* at *my* club. Why are you so fucking grief-stricken?’

She ripped her arm away from his grasp. ‘Teddy, what happens in my life is none of your business. You don’t own me, so stop following me.’

‘I’m not following you.’

‘Oh no? So how did you know that I come here every day?’

‘That’s not important.’

‘Oh, leave off, Teddy. You *are* following me.’

'No, I'm not. But I have you followed because I am worried. I mean, whoever killed Paddy may come for you.'

She stared at his eyes. They stared back, unblinkingly. *He had balls*, she thought. Few men could have looked her in the eye pretending Paddy's death had nothing to do with them. But she knew. She knew he'd had Paddy shot. And the thing was, she couldn't say a damn word about it.

'Well, stop it! It's beginning to creep me out. And I'm not your girlfriend or your wife, so just back off, will ya.'

'You're the mother of my child, though.'

'Ha, yeah, the mother of your child when it fucking suits *you*. I wasn't for twelve years all the time I was in prison. You gave that role to me sister. And now I'm out, you agree I can see my son. But that's only limited to one sodding day in the week.' She turned to march away again, knowing that she was getting angrier and angrier by the minute.

But he still had hold of her arm. 'That's not fair, Harper.'

Turning to face him and removing his hand, she said, 'Teddy, life *ain't* fair, and, take it from me, *I* know. Now, if you don't mind, I have a very busy day.'

She reasoned that this little tiff wouldn't have him suspecting she knew more about his devious moves to get her back. She knew how his mind worked. He would assume she was just being moody. The new Teddy would never think it was his doing.

'All right, my treacle dumpling, I'll leave you in peace.'

When she glanced back, she saw him almost bouncing along the pavement towards his car. With his confident stance and wearing a thousand-pound suit, that vision of him suddenly jolted her into reality. She wasn't the type of woman to sulk around moodily and let herself go. She was a fighter, the tough one in the family, not a washed-out grieving woman.

As soon as she reached the high street, she walked into the hairdresser's, and an hour later, she walked out with her hair bleached short and trendy. The staff had also reshaped her brows and given her a manicure.

After calling into the supermarket and filling the trolley with plenty of fruit and vegetables and a couple of burgers, in the hope that Teddy would pass on her message to her son that he was welcome, she headed home.

CHAPTER EIGHT

Parking her car directly outside her flat, Harper hesitated. This was something that she had done ever since Paddy's death. And it happened because every time she walked from the kerb to her doorstep, she felt as though she was stepping over Paddy's grave. The vision of his lifeless body was ingrained in her mind and would be until the day she could exact revenge.

Holding the shopping bags in one hand and the front door key in the other, she realised she was feeling weak and needed to eat to get her strength back or she would be no good to man or beast. Finally, once she was through the door, she bowled along the hallway and into the kitchen.

Suddenly she dropped the bags, her eyes wide and her heart thumping. Sitting at her table was a menacing-looking man with a military buzz cut. At first, she didn't recognise him. Instinctively, she looked for her knife holder. To her dismay, it was empty. And then she saw why. When she glanced over at the man again, he was holding up the knives.

Then it dawned on her who he was. She'd only met him briefly when he was working undercover as one of the Russian traffickers and then again when her sister Charley had introduced him as her husband, while she was recovering in hospital.

'What the hell? You gave me a bloody fright. Where's me sister?' she asked, through fear that her brother-in-law, who, as far as she knew, could barely speak English, would relay some bad news. After all, Charley's job came with a serious health warning.

It shocked Harper when he answered in clear English, 'Harper, I am sorry for letting myself into your home, but I couldn't wait outside.' He flicked his head to the French doors behind him.

‘Blimey, have you been having speech lessons? So what’s going on? Where’s me sister?’ she asked again.

But the look on his face told her something was gravely wrong. Knowing he was about to make some revelation and the news wasn’t going to be good and wondering if she could handle more pain, she held her breath and waited.

‘I had to come here. I had no one else to go to. And your sister always said that you would welcome me, even help me, if ever I needed it.’

Harper nodded, hurrying him to get to the part where he told her that her sister had left him – *because surely, he wouldn’t say she was dead, would he?*

‘Charley is missing.’

A moment of relief allowed Harper to breathe. ‘Missing, then? Not dead?’ She had to confirm her own sanity.

He chewed his top lip and then stared her straight in the eyes. ‘The unit believes she’s dead.’

‘*What!*’

He shook his head. ‘Look, I don’t believe it.’

Harper felt the pulse in her neck throbbing, and her breathing intensified. She was trying to take it in, but she knew she was clinging on to hope.

‘Charley was involved in a deep undercover operation. A few days ago, her car was found in a field in Kent, burned out, with two bodies inside.’

Harper’s lips began to turn a deathly grey as she gasped and panted involuntarily.

Michel immediately rose from the table and came over and grabbed her arms. ‘Take a couple of deep breaths and look at me, please, Harper.’

Harper nodded but her face suddenly hardened in concentration.

After giving Harper a hug, they both sat at the kitchen table.

'I know her body isn't one of them. Please, you have to listen to me, because I cannot talk to anyone else.'

Feeling the lump in her throat, Harper swallowed hard. 'DNA will identify the b-bodies, though, surely?'

He nodded. 'Normally, that is the case. But when a flammable accelerant has been used, the only way to ascertain who the victims were is by their teeth. They can identify through dental records or source DNA.'

Harper nodded. 'So what did they find?'

'Nothing, Harper, because there were no teeth.'

'Jesus Christ, are you saying they burned the teeth too?'

Michel shook his head slowly. 'No, they were removed before the bodies were burned.'

'So, really, you don't know if one of those burned bodies *is* my sister.'

Michel glanced either side of him before he got up and checked that the French doors were closed.

She realised just then that he was bigger than she remembered. And that frame of his was full of rock-solid muscle underneath a blue shirt and jeans. His hair was far shorter than when she'd last seen him a year ago, but there was something else about him that she didn't recognise – was it fear? If this was the case, then they were both in the shit. Looking at him more circumspectly, the light seemed to have faded from his eyes and now they appeared like two lifeless dark pools of emptiness.

'What's really going on here, Michel?'

Sitting down at the table again, he said, 'I don't know yet, Harper, but your sister is very good at her job, and she would never blow her cover. She is the best there is, but I feel there is something else going on.'

Harper nodded. 'So what are you saying?'

'The only person she trusted is you, apart from her father and me. I mean her adopted father.'

'Okay, Michel, what's your point?'

'I need your help to find her.'

'But you're the bloody professional. Why do you need *my* help?'

'I have resigned from my job. I cannot work until I have found her. So that's what I'm going to do. But . . .' He smiled. 'You see, the day before she went missing, she embraced me tighter than usual and kissed me harder than she normally would. And another thing: she said, "You do know how much I love you, don't you?"' He blushed slightly. 'As soon as she left that morning, I felt odd, almost cold, as though she was about to do something extremely risky.'

'But your work and Charley's *is* risky, Michel.'

He nodded and steepled his fingers. 'Yes, I know. But that morning it was as if she was giving me a prior warning. She would never say those words. Before, she would say "love ya".'

'I have to be honest, Michel, I don't know my little sister that well. As you know, I went to prison when she was a young teenager. During that time, she was fostered out. The only time I got to see her was when she came to my rescue, and, of course, her visit in the hospital. Oh, yes, and a flying visit, just after Paddy was killed.'

'So are you really saying I have wasted my time coming here?' He jumped up.

'Stop, Michel. Wait a minute. You obviously don't know me and perhaps you have forgotten what I would do – what I have done – for my family. And I didn't say I wouldn't help. Far from it. Of course, I will help. I love my sister, and I couldn't contemplate the thought of something bad happening to her.' Her voice became firmer. 'Do you know why I served time?'

He walked over to the French doors again, this time stretching his neck. 'Yes, she trusted me with the truth. She wanted to be the best officer on the force and bring down as many of the *baddies,* as she called them, as she could. She was always pursuing the next big case. Charley had to pay you back by doing good because you paid the price for her, so, yes, I know all about what you did for Charley. That's why I'm here, Harper. No one would love her more than me, except you.' He returned to his seat and took a deep breath. 'And, look, I'm really sorry about Paddy. Please forgive my rudeness. I can imagine that you're still grieving, and you already have your own pain to contend with.'

'Right now, my sister is more important, Michel.'

Harper had a million and one questions, but she couldn't think where to begin. Then she recalled receiving a parcel in the post from her sister a few days ago. Charley's note read '*Keep this tablet safe. Don't let anyone know you have it. When the time comes, you will know what to do with it. I love you xxx.*'

Suddenly, an unexpected tear trickled down her cheek. She felt so guilty that she hadn't given the note or the parcel much thought until now. Acting like a mechanical robot, she had slid the parcel under the bed and completely forgotten about it.

Wiping her cheek, she said, 'What can I do? How can I help you, Michel?'

He handed her the phone. 'I will share with you everything I know. It's all in those pictures and notes and—'

'I can't see this on your screen. It's too small, so I'll have to print it out. I've got a printer in my bedroom.'

He frowned.

'Yeah, for late-night accounts when I can't be bothered to stay at the club.'

***

Michel sat on the edge of her bed, and Harper stood over the printer that was on a makeshift desk. Before the first copy left the printer, he said, 'The images are uh—'

'Michel, I'm no soft bird.' Her eyes glared as the first photo spat out from the printer. 'Fucking hell! No!'

Her hands shot to her mouth. The shocking image of the burned bodies, sucked all the air out of her lungs, causing her to stagger back.

Michel got up and steadied her. 'I know that's not her. I know it's not.'

Harper looked at his eyes, hoping for real reassurance. 'My God! But what if it is?'

'It's not!'

Once the printer had stopped, Harper gathered the papers and flicked her head for Michel to join her at the kitchen table. 'Are there any other surprises before we go through them?'

Michel wanted to smile because he was impressed with how Harper was taking control of the situation. *Maybe*, he thought, *it was her way with her family, and, after all, this was family business.*

'There is one photo that shows a lot of blood.'

'Is it hers?'

Michel nodded. 'Well, so Verity, her head of operations, thinks. But, then again, she is relying on a statement from an undercover officer who has since gone missing.'

Harper raised her well-defined brow and stared. 'I get the impression you're not convinced.'

Michel shrugged his shoulders, taking a deep breath. 'I am not convinced by anything anymore. We used to discuss our cases, not in great detail, but the odd little bit, but with this case, she kept everything close to her chest. She did say once that if she ever went missing, I was to come and find you and that she would try to find a way to get a message to you.' He stopped and laughed. 'It's so crazy. I have no one to turn to, and I hardly know you. But I guess you were close to her, and so was I.'

'Where is this photo with all the blood?' She tried to fan through them.

He took the pile of copies and found the image. 'Here, and I just wish I knew where this place is.'

Harper stared at the photo. 'There's a lot of blood.' She bit her lip, trying to stop her tears from escaping.

He nodded again. 'Verity said the amount would suggest that Charley wouldn't have survived. I am no expert on such things, but I just know in my heart that she's not dead.'

'Well, I have seen more claret piss out of a person who subsequently survived.' She was recalling the amount of blood that came out of Pasha's head the night she beat the living daylights out of her.

As Harper stared at the photo, trying to gain any clues, Michel pulled two phones from his pocket and stared at them. 'These I took from Verity Mercer, Charley's operations manager.'

'Why?'

'Because I don't trust her at all, and I hoped I would be able to access the phones from home using my computer. Only, when I got to my house, the intelligence unit had arrived first, and they'd ransacked the place. A note was left, telling me to hand back the phones that I had stolen.'

'Jesus, they ransacked your home for two poxy phones? A bit extreme, wouldn't ya say?'

'Either there is something damming on the phones, or they didn't want the phones at all. In which case, they were after something else. I have an idea of what it could be. I bet they want

Charley's tablets. She has two: one for work and one for personal use, but not even I know where they are. She took both of them with her a day or so before she went missing.'

He ripped at his hair. 'Oh God, I wish I knew her last known place.'

'And why won't this Verity bird tell you?'

He shook his head. 'The case is very high profile. That means the target is at the top of the food chain, and apparently that photo of the handcuffs is in an unknown area. The other undercover officer before he went missing said that Charley was held there. That's all I have. And believe it or not, if we go in deep undercover, the initial meeting is often very cloak-and-dagger. Verity, genuinely, may not know Charley's last position. Although I find it hard to believe. Something is not right about this case. Not right at all.'

'Hey, Michel.' It was her turn to be positive. 'We will find her. I'll make us a drink, and let's talk this through, starting with this business about my sister's work tablet.'

'I'll have a brandy, if you've got one.'

Harper smiled and left the table to find a bottle of Rémy Martin, which her mother had bought her ages ago, in the living room cabinet. Her distrustful mind was playing overtime. His slight Russian accent was enough to keep tugging her back to the trouble she had found herself in over the Russian traffickers, and now even a hint of a Russian accent was sending her into a dark place. *Yet if her Charley loved him, then he was completely trustworthy, wasn't he?*

After she returned with two glasses and the bottle of brandy, she placed them on the table and poured each of them a generous measure. 'What are your thoughts on why Charley left the house with her tablets? I mean, was she not supposed to?'

He gulped a mouthful of the strong liquor and swallowed the bitter taste. 'Yes, as I said, she used one for work, and they can usually track where it is, but she must have turned the tracker off, for some reason, and that's what makes me suspicious. Where is the tablet and why can't Verity and her team find it? Or is it that Charley doesn't want Verity to find it? That's why I am convinced there is something very scheming going on.' He took another gulp. 'There must be information on that tablet that will blow something out of the water. I have a feeling she has posted it somewhere – maybe to our holiday home in France. No one knows about it. But if I go there, they will follow me.' He smiled and nodded at her. 'Maybe you could go instead. We have like a PO box in the village. I will give you the details, money, and passcode. They won't follow you, Harper, because they have no reason to.'

'You trust me, don't you?'

'You're the only person apart from Charley who I *can* trust . . .' He paused. 'I know you have no reason to feel the same about me, but believe me, when I tell you, I love her so much, I will die for her. And . . .'

Harper noticed his face pale over and his tears begin to well up.

'I begged her not to do this case—'

'What is it, Michel?'

'She is pregnant, Harper. She's having our baby.'

CHAPTER NINE

It was eight o'clock in the evening by the time they concluded that it was impossible to get into Verity's phones. Michel guessed she had disabled her accounts; however, not before he clocked a few notifications. The first line of these had been visible without logging in, and there seemed to be a lot associated with gambling apps and, far more damning, a debt management application app.

Michel stared, and it was as if a dark cloud had passed across his face.

'What is it?' asked Harper.

'As undercover officers, we have an extensive background check carried out on us. It is needed to counter any serious concern. For example, if we are in debt or have any gambling issues or have an addictive personality. Because, as you must understand, we are dealing with criminals – rich criminals.'

'But those notifications are just random. They flash up on my phone sometimes.'

He stared at the phone, shaking his head. 'No, they *don't* flash up randomly at all. You would have to show some kind of interest, and the number of notifications would suggest that she has been dabbling, or, perhaps, the case itself is linked to some gambling. I have a feeling that Verity has more to do with this operation than being the head of the tactical team. Something stinks.'

'Really? So tell me about this Verity bird.'

Michel poured another brandy. 'She is, how the English would say, a right royal cunt.'

Harper hadn't heard Michel speak in that way before. 'So, were you once in love with her?'

Startled, Michel's eyes widened. 'No, no, I was never in love with her.' He grinned. 'She is too underhanded. When I did go on that date with her, I caught her going through my phone. She said she was sorry and that she had picked up mine by mistake, but even afterwards, I noticed her looking sideways at my text messages. You know what I am saying. And the way she speaks is all off to me. Her words are too cleverly scripted as if her existence is every bit thought out – even rehearsed.' He shuddered. 'Not like Charley. She's more fun-loving and spontaneous. I didn't ask Verity for another date. I found her, how you say, a pest. She kept texting and calling, and to add to that, she was so fake, she was putting on this false impression of herself. I think she forgot I am trained in identifying liars.'

'Fake? How could she be fake? She must hold a responsible position, mustn't she?'

'Harper, her father was a police commissioner. She didn't work hard to get to the top. It was laid out for her like a red carpet. And she's not that clever, not like Charley.'

Harper saw how his face lit up when he spoke of her sister.

'Charley is so intelligent and witty and kind.' He sipped his drink. 'She's not dead, and why Verity wants me to believe she is, I don't understand. She wouldn't tell me her last known position because she reckons she didn't know it herself.' He shook his head to indicate he didn't believe what she'd told him and looked into his empty glass. 'Maybe I am grieving too much to see what's really going on.'

Harper watched and listened; she concluded she could trust him. 'Do you believe Verity is after Charley's work tablet?'

He looked up through his long dark lashes. 'Yes, I do, but I bet it's in France, so will you go there for me? Hopefully, whatever is on that device will help me find my wife.'

'Wait there, Michel. I feel I need to give you something.'

With a suspicious eye, Michel watched her leave the room, only to return with a parcel, which looked to him like the shape and size of Charley's laptop, clearly unopened. It was wrapped in a Jiffy bag.

She placed it on the table and pointed. 'There it is, I do believe.'

Michel silently regarded her with brooding eyes. 'Why is it that after I have been here all this time,' he said, holding up the empty bottle of brandy, 'you did not tell me?'

'I wanted to be able to trust you first.'

He gave an agreeable nod. 'May I?'

'Yes, open it.'

A dog barking made Michel and Harper jump. 'Oh shit, I forgot to feed the neighbour's little dog. She will be barking all night. Excuse me for a minute,' she said, as she took the keys off the kitchen worktop and hurried along the hallway and out of the front door.

Michel stayed motionless, staring at Charley's tablet.

After a few minutes, Harper returned out of breath. 'Bloody little yappy mutt.' She smiled. 'He wouldn't bark to ward off intruders. He only yaps when he's hungry. I've left him in the garden for a bit.' She glanced at the tablet. 'Why haven't you looked?'

'Charley gave it to you, so you must be the one to turn it on.'

Harper looked at Michel and then back at the device. Although confused, she refrained from showing it. *He had told her earlier that he knew the passcode. Why hadn't he opened it? She knew she would have done had the roles been reversed.*

'Okay,' she said, as she took the seat next to him.

After she pressed the 'on' button, the device sprang into action. Right away, it requested a password.

Michel entered what he thought it would be but access was denied. 'This can't be her tablet.'

'Well, clearly it is because she sent it to me.' Harper sighed. 'But I haven't a clue what the password is.'

‘I think you do, Harper.’ His voice was cold and suddenly disturbing.

She stared at the screen with a deep frown, now feeling a little uneasy. ‘What makes you say that?’

‘Because you and Charley had a secret safe word.’

Harper’s heart began to beat fast; her skin tingled with fear. ‘Well, you said you knew it.’ She gave a false stilted laugh. ‘And I can’t remember a secret word from when we were kids.’

‘Charley was intelligent. She knew you would remember that secret word, so please don’t pretend you don’t know, Harper, or you will be insulting her intelligence.’

Harper stood up and stepped back. She wanted space between them, even if it was only to catch her breath. What was really going on here? She fathomed that he already knew that Charley had handed her the tablet for safekeeping. He had told her he knew his wife’s password and yet he had not used it to access the device. And the story about Verity? Well, as far as she could tell, it seemed to her a pile of shit.

‘Sit down,’ he ordered.

‘No, Michel. Please, I think you need to leave. You lied, and I hate liars.’

His face tightened as his eyes scanned her. ‘I have never lied. Now, sit down. We must find out what is on this device.’

‘No, Michel, leave. My son will be here soon. I don’t want you here.’

For a moment, Harper thought she saw the hurt in his eyes, but was that an act? She wanted to give him the benefit of the doubt, but she was getting mixed signals from him.

‘Just tell me the password, and I will go.’ He leaped from his seat. ‘Harper, this is not a game. Tell me!’ he bellowed.

The sound of banging at the front door stopped them both in their tracks. ‘That’s my son. You must leave.’

‘Does your son bang at the door so aggressively? That is not your son, Harper. That is Verity and her unit. Please don’t tell them I was here. Trust me, they are after something – either me, that tablet, or the phones. And, right now, I’m more inclined to believe it’s the tablet.’

Harper stared at Michel. For a moment, she was still unsure how this would pan out.

‘I have to go before they stop me from finding my wife. If you tell them, believe me, Harper, you will never see your sister again.’

Harper was amazed by how fast Michel could move. Taking the tablet with him, he flicked the switch off for the garden sensor lights and hurried through the French doors, over the stone wall, and into the neighbour’s back garden. His words were still ringing in her ears.

The banging at the door was now more brutal. ‘Hang on, please!’ she shouted, as she flicked the switch back on for the sensor lights to function again, before marching along her hallway to the front door.

As soon as she opened the door, a woman practically fell into the hallway. Instantly, she barged past Harper, followed by two huge men, who were built like brick shithouses.

‘Oi, who the fuck are you, storming into my house? What the hell is going on?’

With her hair tied in a tight bun and dressed in blue jeans and a shirred neck faux leather top, the woman ordered the two men to search the flat, totally ignoring Harper. She stormed through into the kitchen and pushed open the French doors. Right away, the sensor lights came on. It was clear from the surprised look on the woman’s face that she hadn’t expected that to happen. Pivoting her eyes, she scanned the small walled garden.

The two men suddenly joined her. ‘He ain’t here,’ one growled.

‘Search this place. You know what you’re looking for.’

Livid, Harper grabbed the woman's arm. 'I said, who the fuck are you?'

The woman stared at Harper's hand clutching her arm. 'Get your hands off me. And you should know who I am.'

'Should I?'

Harper let go of the woman, but, even so, she was bristling with rage; she could hear the two men ransacking her flat. It took her back to a time when the prison officers searched her prison cell. The screw who had taken a dislike to Harper the most during her imprisonment had not only turned her cell over, but she had screwed up photos, torn open the pillow, and deliberately smashed a mug that her sister Lexi had sent in to her.

The pulse in Harper's neck pumped so fiercely that she had to slow down her breathing before she knocked seven colours of shit out of the woman.

'What the fuck are they doing? What's going on?'

'Get back, Harper Kane, before I nick you for obstructing the police in their duties.'

'Where's your warrant?' asked Harper, now staring at the smug-faced bitch.

'You're on a life licence, so I'd watch your mouth, if I were you. Now, you are going to tell me where your brother-in-law, Michel, is.'

'And are you going to tell me who the fuck you are and what the fuck you are looking for?'

'You do surprise me, Harper —'

'Ms Kane to you, darling, considering I have no idea who the fuck you are.'

'After what the report said you'd been through, I assumed you wouldn't be so confident. PTSD, it said. But you don't look like a shell-shocked survivor to me. Now, where is Michel? I don't have time to mess about.'

Harper, with a smile on her face and her arms folded, leaned against the wall, staring straight at the woman.

'Michel has taken a crucial part of our evidence, and we need it back. And you standing there with that cocky look won't help matters.'

Harper watched as the woman shifted from foot to foot when she spoke.

'Your sister was on an undercover operation. She is missing, presumed dead. Did you know that?' Her tone suddenly softened, but the change was too sudden and false for Harper's liking.

'I won't ask you again. Who are you?'

'Verity Mercer, your sister's tactical operations manager. So now you know, stop fucking about. It's crucial that we find Michel.'

Harper could hear drawers being pulled out and doors opening and shutting. 'If your sidekicks don't put my home back to how it was, you'll get fuck all out of me.'

Harper made her way back along the hall and into the first bedroom. The state of the place made her heart sink. 'Oi, you bastard, you can fucking clean up this mess.'

One of the men, who was dragging her antique French wardrobe with the ornate Queen Anne style legs aggressively away from the wall, growled back, 'I'm just doing my job!'

When Harper heard one of the legs snap, fury filled her veins. 'Stop! Look what you're doing, you cunt.'

'I am doing my job. Now, back off. Get out of the room before you find yourself in handcuffs and down the nick.'

As Harper turned to leave them, she bumped into Verity.

Looking her up and down, Harper shook her head in disgust. 'So, you come into my flat, with no formal introduction, your bully boys proceed to destroy my home, and then you tell me that you need to find Michel because my sister is missing. And you don't think that telling me my sister is missing – considering the highly dangerous work she does – wouldn't be news that should have been delivered to me with care and understanding?' She flicked her chin up for a response. 'Who are you, really, *Ms* Mercer?'

'Oh, come on, Harper, you're a tough cookie. I've read your reports. So, coming here with a family liaison officer and a box of tissues would have been a waste of time. You will want answers, but until I get my hands . . . Until I find her husband, I can't give you any more answers other than he may know where she is, and I know the only place Michel would flee to is here. So, stop playing games. Your sister maybe out there somewhere – if she isn't already dead – and you can help us find her.'

'I don't get it. Why wouldn't her husband want her found? He works for your lot, so what's the crack?'

Verity pursed her lips and flared her nostrils.

'We have received evidence that he has gone rogue. He may have personal ties to our suspect.'

Harper's eyes widened, but then she grinned. 'Ya know what, Ms Mercer? I don't fucking believe you.'

Verity sighed. 'And why not, may I ask?'

'Because if you truly believed that her husband may be involved with your suspect, you would know full well that, of course, I would do anything to help you. But you push your way into my home like you're some kinda gangster. You have those two pricks ransacking my place. Michel is hardly gonna be fucking hiding in me knicker drawer, now, is he? And to top it all, you make all kinds of threats. That only tells me, Ms Mercer, that you're shitting yourself about something, and so there's more to this than my sister going missing.'

'Listen, Harper. I don't have time for formalities or niceties. We need to locate him and the property he has of ours that we thought he may have left here. He has nowhere else to go. And I looked into your case where your sister rescued you. Of course, at the time, there was no mention of the fact that you are sisters. I had to do some digging to find that out.'

'Why?'

'Because when any of our undercover officers go missing, we need to cover every eventuality—'

'Like what exactly, Verity Mercer? What the fuck are you implying?'

'You're perceptive. I'll give you that.'

'Get to the point.'

'We can't rule out that an officer who is deep undercover might be tempted by the lifestyle and so go rogue.'

When Harper stretched her neck, the skin tightened across her face. Taking a deep breath, she leaned into Verity's ear. 'If I was sure I wouldn't go straight back to prison, I'd bite your throat out for saying that my sister could contemplate going rogue. You, my darling, might be a detective, an operations head, or whatever the fuck you are, but, believe me, I ain't stupid. I can read you like a book. Twelve years in the nick gained me that qualification. So now you can stop playing games.'

She pulled away from Verity's ear and stared into her eyes that were alive with indignation. 'Now, tell your dogs to tidy my rooms and then we can sit down and talk.'

Verity was staggered by how Harper had managed to put the wind up her. Not many women had done that in the past, although maybe Charley had come close, with her sharp intellect and the ability to read people. And now, she realised, that having studied Harper's prison reports, she had read the woman all wrong. It had been a huge mistake to think that she would crumble under pressure.

Verity nodded and groaned inwardly before she walked past Harper and asked her men to tidy the rooms.

Surprised that the two men didn't moan and huff, Harper wondered if Verity did have a lot of clout. Possibly, but in their field, not in hers.

Once they returned to the kitchen, Harper nodded. 'Go on, then. Talk.'

Verity grinned. 'I think I do the asking here.'

'Tell me, Verity, when you say my sister is missing, how long has she been missing?'

'A week.'

'Where was she working?'

'I can't tell you that,' replied Verity, shaking her head. 'Look, this won't work. You must understand, I can't divulge information about the case.'

Harper barked a short laugh. 'But you can tell me that Michel has gone rogue and that he has property of yours and that you think my sister has gone rogue, but you can't tell me where she was working. Oh, why don't you just fuck off.'

Verity banged her fist on the kitchen table. 'Tell us where he is. I know he came here!'

Harper rocked back on her heels, her lips twisted into a sneer. 'It sounds to me like you're desperate. It seems to be more like a personal issue than a professional one, wouldn't you say, Ms Mercer?'

Verity was on the point of launching into a verbal assault when Harper lifted one finger. 'Don't waste your breath. Put your arsehole back in your arsehole and call your dogs off. I assume they're fucking house-trained, so get them out of my house, 'cos believe me, darling, I know nothing, except that you're a desperate cunt, and I for one, am a bit pissed off.'

'I'll drag you down to the station.'

'Good luck with that. My lawyer will have me straight out of there. I haven't seen my sister properly for twelve years. She was fostered and then adopted. I only saw her once when her unit rescued me, and again, briefly, on two other occasions, so I don't even know if I'd recognise her in the street. And another thing: I'd be the last place Charley or even Michel, for that matter, would come. So, don't you think you would end up looking a bit daft?' She tilted her head to the side and gave Verity an exaggerated smile.

Verity stormed towards the front door and called her plain-clothed officers to heel, but as soon as she pulled it open, she almost took a step back. There at the doorstep was a kid carrying a backpack.

'Oh, hello,' he said, politely, as he stepped aside to allow Verity and the two officers room to leave.

Harper watched as Verity ignored her son and hurried away down the path followed by the two officers. Not taking her eyes off Verity, Harper noticed that when the woman glanced back, her face was white as if the blood had drained out of her.

Slamming the door shut, Harper ushered Eddie into the kitchen. 'Eddie, babe, what are you doing here? It's' – she glanced at the clock – 'ten o'clock.'

Eddie dropped his backpack down on the floor beside the kitchen table.

'Staying for a few days, are ya?'

But Eddie wasn't smiling. He appeared down in the dumps. Even when Harper rubbed the top of his head, messing up his hair, he still didn't chuckle.

'Did ya dad drop you off, Eddie?'

'No, Mum, he didn't. And he doesn't actually know I'm here.' He looked up with his huge blue eyes, giving him a startled look.

'Had a row, did ya, babe?'

Harper was only half paying attention since Verity and Michel were still on her mind and feeding her thoughts with dark images and paranoia.

'If you must know, I had a huge row. Anyway, why were those two men and that woman here, Mum?'

‘Oh, something about local break-ins, that’s all.’

‘Well, perhaps we had better find somewhere else to live.’

CHAPTER TEN

Harper didn't know whether to feel angry, devastated, or emotionally drained. Having Eddie turning up should have been just the tonic she needed right now, but her mind was reeling, being pulled in all directions.

She was still staying away from the club. The decision to do so was partly an emotional one. Paddy's death had been a monumental shock. And because she was certain Teddy had a hand in it, she had vowed to herself never to work for Teddy. She could barely face him, let alone be in his company for too long. And if she did return to the club, he would have an excuse to hover around her like a praying mantis.

Another thing. If Michel was wrong in asserting Charley was still alive, it would floor her. But it was only an 'if'. So she was going to believe if her sister was out there somewhere she would fight tooth and nail to find her. Who could she trust to help her, though?

The third issue on her mind was her son, who, at fourteen, had the world on his shoulders. He wasn't the tough lad who would kick a Coke can around the streets, smoking a fag at the end of the road with his mates. He studied hard, was into his sports, and spoke with clarity and intelligence. Clearly, her son had issues, and so she needed to find out what they were.

Putting a smile on her face, Harper opened the fridge and pulled out a packet of burgers, waving them in front of him. 'How about a Mum special burger feast?'

Eddie was sitting at the kitchen table, with his head in his hands, looking thoroughly fed up. 'Yeah, Mum, that would be lovely, thank you.'

His polite words and manner made her feel like a stranger sometimes. She would rather he wandered in and helped himself from the fridge or the goodie cupboard and open up to her a bit more.

‘Cheese slice on that burger, babe?’

‘Thank you, Mum. Anything. I am starving.’

Harper flicked her eyes to the back garden as soon as the lights came on. However, on peering outside, she saw that it was only a fox nosing around.

She hoped that Michel would return soon. She didn’t think he was the bad guy, the bitch Verity had said he was.

‘Didn’t you eat earlier?’

Eddie shook his head, and as he looked up, she could see his eyes well up with huge tears, ready to fall down his already scarlet cheeks.

‘Hey, Son, whatever’s the matter?’

Harper dropped the cheese slice and held out her arms for him to fall into. He got up from the table and hugged her tightly, surprising her by how big he was under his sweatshirt. Her son was hurting, and if it was over a girl, then she would have to sit and down and tell him how it was all normal, and one day he would find the right one.

It sent her mind wandering to Vadim, and her heart began to beat fast. She hated admitting her feelings to herself, but she was missing him.

‘Talk to me, Eddie. You can tell me anything you like. Why are you so upset?’

He slowly unwrapped his arms and sat back down.

Sitting down beside him, Harper wiped his tears before she kissed his forehead. His voice had broken, and she could see he was growing into a man. ‘It’s fine, Eddie. You really *can* tell me anything.’

He nodded as he peered up through his eyelashes. ‘I can’t go back home – ever. Please let me live with you. I swear I will stay out of your way when you’re busy.’

His pleading words were so shocking that she needed to know what the hell had been going on, but she was also aware that she must tread carefully.

'Well, I guess you're at that age where you can make decisions for yourself, and I would love nothing more than to have you here every day.'

Those words brought more tears, and Eddie leaned into her and hugged her again before he began to sob.

'Jesus, Eddie Bear, what the fuck is wrong, babe? Has your father hurt you?'

With his hands over his face hiding his red eyes, he nodded.

Harper immediately jumped up from her chair. 'What the fuck did he do, Eddie, 'cos I swear to God, father or not, I will—'

'Please, Mum, please sit down. Don't do anything.'

Harper took a deep breath and sat down again. 'Okay, look, sorry, Son. But I can't have anyone hurt you. I know he's your dad, and you love him, but a father shouldn't hurt their child to the point they're sobbing their bloody hearts out.' She could have kicked herself. Why was she speaking to him as though he was ten years old? Her son may be crying but his words and tone carried a clear maturity.

'I *don't* love him, Mum. I haven't loved him for a long time.'

Those words hit Harper like a thunderbolt. She sat up straight.

'You what, babe? You don't love your father? Oh, come on, you've never mentioned it before. I know your dad adores you.'

Eddie got up from his seat and grabbed his backpack. 'Everyone thinks that, even you, but none of you get it, do you? My dad is a fucking *showman.*'

Harper was stunned. 'Wait, please, babe. I believe you. Listen to me. I'm just shocked, that's all. Sit and tell me what the hell's been going on.'

Slinging his backpack on the floor, Eddie retook his seat. 'Mum, sorry, I shouldn't swear, and it's not your fault.' He paused and rubbed his forehead with his forefingers. 'May I have that burger? I'm starving.'

Harper kissed his cheek and went back to the hob. 'I'll cook while you tell all.'

'Everyone sees Teddy—'

'Teddy, is it?' interrupted Harper, with a spatula in her hand.

'Mum, when I was younger, I had Erin look out for me. I didn't know a lot different. I mean, she was a little bit selfish at times, but she would give me a hug when I needed it. But when she broke up with Teddy, I still had Lena, our . . . well, my everything. She loved me. She even came to the football to watch me. She cooked all my favourite dinners and played on the PlayStation with me. But all that changed when, a month ago, he fired her.'

Harper turned around to see the tears angrily falling down his red cheeks. 'Why?'

Wiping his face with the cuff of his sleeve, Eddie said, 'Mum, Teddy isn't what everyone thinks he is. Lena and I were playing chess in my bedroom, and I wanted a drink, and she offered to get it for me. She used to make this delicious lemonade. I was waiting, and I thought she was taking a long time, so I got up and walked to the staircase. I heard what sounded like an argument going on, although it was hard to hear from where I was. But I knew it was Teddy growling at Lena. I hated it when he did that. Anyway, Lena came tearing up the stairs, and I hid in the bathroom, so she didn't know I was listening. She went to her room and began packing. I had never seen her so upset.' He stopped for a moment to wipe away more tears. 'I heard some cars pull up and so I looked out of the window on to the drive There were three cars with six men and an Asian woman standing there, Mum. Poor Lena looked devastated. I think she assumed this woman was going to replace her. How nasty is that, Mum? Initially, I think Teddy sacked Lena probably because she knew too much. After all, she was always in the house. And by taking on a non-English speaking housekeeper, he knew she wouldn't understand his conversations. He is so bloody anal about that kind of stuff.'

Staring at the sizzling burger, her knuckles white as she gripped the spatula, Harper listened intently until her son paused for breath. 'And how do you know those were Teddy's intentions?'

'Like I said, initially that's what I thought. I heard one of the men offering the Asian woman her services to Teddy, but, anyway, Teddy didn't take her on. Then I realised that Teddy wanted to get rid of Lena because he didn't like how close we were. I think he was jealous when I did everything with Lena, but, Mum, I had no one else. He said I couldn't go to you because you were always so busy, and, please, don't misunderstand me, but I know you have to work.'

Harper wanted to tell him it was a lie. She knew Teddy's game. He wanted to control her, and the only way he could was through her son. He'd already asked her countless times to move in with them. But even though she would then be able to see her son all the time, it would come at such an emotional cost. She hated every fibre of his being.

'Why are you still so upset that he fired Lena? Didn't you say that happened a month ago?'

She placed the burger in front of her son and offered him a can of cola. He nodded and took a huge mouthful of the burger, barely swallowing, before taking another bite.

'Woah, easy, tiger. You'll give yaself indigestion. There's plenty more. Slow down.'

It was the first time that she had seen him smile for what seemed like months.

Once Eddie had had enough to curb his hunger pangs, he took a deep breath. 'It's not so much that I miss Lena now, but I am lonely, Mum. Teddy is now the name I call him because he isn't a dad to me. Not a proper dad, anyway. I'm not allowed in his office. He slams the door in my face if he is on the phone. And I can't go to the lounge if he is having a business meeting, which he is doing most nights – that is, if he is even at home. It's been lonely, Mum. So lonely.' He stared off into space as if he was reliving a moment, and his face clouded over in pain. 'Mum, would you still love me, no matter who I was?'

Harper had no idea where this was leading, but it was clear that whatever was on his mind was breaking her son's heart.

'Babe, I would always love you. I love you selflessly. That is why I gave you to your father when I was in prison. I could have kept you with me for two years, but I couldn't do that to you. So, believe me, I would never love you any less if you chopped someone's head off.'

Sitting down next to him, she wiped his face and gripped his hand. 'Eddie Bear, tell me, what has happened? I can see you are so distressed.'

He took a deep breath. 'I thought Teddy and I were getting on okay. Lena had gone, and so I had to learn to cook, or it was a takeaway. I hadn't spoken to anyone for a whole week, not a single person. Then Teddy came home. He was a little bit drunk . . .'

Harper nodded for him to go on.

'We sat together. I'd cooked spag boll, and then I told him . . .' He took a deep breath. 'I told him, I thought I might be gay.' He sat back, staring into his mother's eyes, anxiously awaiting a response.

Cupping his face, she kissed him again. 'And what did he say?'

Eddie was shocked that his mother hadn't jumped up spitting feathers. '*What?* You're okay with it, Mum?'

Harper frowned. 'Of course, babe. You can't change what's in your heart. If you like lads rather than girls, then that's fine. All I would suggest is that you don't do anything about it yet.' She winked. 'You know what I mean. You're still so young. But I would say that, even if you liked girls too.'

Eddie screwed up his nose. 'I don't want sex, Mum. Ever, never, ever.'

The fierceness of his words worried Harper. 'Eddie, babe, what the fuck has Teddy *done* to you?'

That question had Eddie lowering his head in shame. 'He laughed in my face and told me I was a fucking Ryder, and Ryders are not gay. The next night, I was home in my room when I heard a car pull up. I didn't think anything of it until Teddy called me to come downstairs. Before I joined him in the lounge, he met me in the hallway. He said he had something for me that would show me I wasn't gay. I was about to walk upstairs away from him because I didn't like him when he spoke like that with his angry face on. But before I had a chance to do anything, he put his hands at the back of my neck and yanked me to him. He growled like a bear, into my ear, and whispered, "You fucking show me up, boy, and you'll wish you'd never been born."'

Harper flung her hands to her mouth. 'Oh my God, Eddie. How dare he put his hands on you. I'll kill the bastard.'

'I didn't think you hated Teddy that much.'

'Anyone who hurts my boy will pay. Now, tell me, what happened next?'

'He has two business associates who occasionally come to the house. Anyway, that night, they brought a girl along.'

'A girl?'

He nodded.

'And how old was this girl?'

Eddie shrugged. 'My age, I think, or maybe a little older.' He put his hand over his mouth as if he were about to describe a horror scene.

'It's okay, Eddie, you can tell me.'

'Will he get into trouble, Mum?'

'Do you even care right now?'

Eddie shook his head. 'Mum, I don't care if he rots in hell. What he did . . .' His lip quivered. 'What he did was disgusting. So disgusting, I . . . I hate him.'

'Okay, Eddie Bear. Tell me everything.'

He gulped his cola and leaned back on the chair, unable to look his mother in the eye. 'Like I said, two men came to the house with a young girl. One was a big fat Asian man with yellow teeth. He reminded me of Penguin out of *Batman*. And another man looked as though he may have been Eastern European. I heard a little bit of his accent. Anyway, the Asian man whispered in the girl's ear, but she was so scared that she couldn't even look up. Teddy then took me aside and told me that she would make me see that I am not gay and that I wouldn't catch any diseases because . . . because . . .' He gulped for air. 'She was a virgin. Oh, Mum. She looked just like a doll. Her face had so much make-up on, and she was dressed in this sari.'

'Okay, darling. Tell me. Did Teddy ask you to have sex with the girl?'

Eddie nodded. 'Before the two men left the house to wait outside, the fat Asian man whispered something in her ear, and she started dancing. But I could tell she didn't want to. And she had this fake permanent smile on her face. Anyway, once the men were in the drive, Teddy clapped his hands and nodded at the girl. He said to her, "You know what you must do." But just before he left the room, he winked at me and then he turned to her. He said, "Don't fail."'

'Did he know this girl?'

Eddie shrugged his shoulders. 'I think so. I'm not sure. But I knew what he meant, and I wasn't having any of it. And I assumed that if we didn't do something, Teddy would hurt her. I don't know why I thought that. It might have been the fear on her face when she looked at him. So I grabbed her hand. Oh, Mum, she was trembling. I took her to my room and locked the door.'

Harper wanted him to get to the point; she couldn't stand the suspense.

‘I sat her down on the bed, and I hugged her. I told her that I wouldn’t touch her but that I had to pretend I wanted to, for her sake, so I smudged that disgusting make-up on her face, and we ripped her sari. She was so frightened, Mum. So bloody terrified. I wanted to call the police, but she begged me not to. I knew Teddy would be listening, so I told her to scream a few times, which she did. She clearly didn’t find that hard. I pulled her to her feet and on to the bed and we jumped up and down, quietly giggling. Then when Teddy banged on my bedroom door, I saw that look of absolute terror. I wanted to hold her and run away with her, but I couldn’t, and I felt so helpless. She told me that if I called the police, the others would be hurt.’

Harper felt her chest tighten, and she had to take a deep breath. ‘And afterwards? Did they take the girl away?’

He nodded and ran his hands through his hair. ‘I still can’t get her face out of my mind. She looked back at me, like she was begging for my help, but that fat Asian guy grabbed her arm and pushed her into the back of the car.’

‘And what did she mean by “others”?’

He shrugged. ‘I don’t really know.’

‘And Teddy? What did he say?’

‘He didn’t say much, except for that stupid cocky look he has now and that wink. “See, boy, you ain’t gay”, he said.’

‘What a bastard, and what did you say?’

‘I just said, I guess not, but don’t ever try to choose my girls for me. You know fuck all about me. He didn’t take that too well and threw his drink at me, calling me a spoilt bastard.’

‘Does he know you’re here?’

‘Mum, apart from our holidays, we don’t see each other. He is in and out, building his empire, and I’m either at school or in my room.’

Astounded, Harper remained silent, trying to process it all.

'But the way he spoke about you, I assumed you were his be-all and end-all. I had no idea that your life was like that.'

'Mum, he has changed so much. I don't know him anymore. It seems to me that the more business he buys and the more money he has, the nastier he becomes. It's like being polite and kind is for the poor and needy.'

Now that Harper had a much clearer picture of her son's relationship with his father, she decided to make her own feelings known. 'I was never too busy for you, ever. He lied, and I think I know why he lied. He wanted me to move into his home. He is obsessed with me, Eddie. And the more I push him away, the more compulsive he becomes. So, you can move in here with me. You're old enough, and by Christ, you're tall enough to be regarded more as a man.' She tried to make light of what was a disturbing, serious conversation.

'Yeah, I've got bigger in the last few months. I am as tall as Teddy. Well, almost.' His eyes darkened. 'I should have stuck up for myself and smashed him in the face.'

'That's not like you, Eddie, and you can't hit your father. It would be best to walk away. Hold your head up high and be proud of who you are. You're a kind and gentle soul.'

'I don't take after him, then, because he is a bully – an arrogant nasty pig who I have hated for a while now. And I have had to bite my lip on so many occasions. I thought he would be the old Dad when we made our yearly trip to Egypt, but that was until I found out that it was a business trip to organise his shipment of metabolic steroids.'

'*What?* Was he dealing in drugs from Egypt while you were on holiday? Is that right?' Her anger was building up, just picturing the scenario.

He shook his head. 'No, it's legal to bring back steroids. Teddy organised a shipment of the stuff. But that doesn't mean to say he is one hundred per cent legitimate.'

The phone rang. Harper looked at the clock, and it was gone eleven. She glanced at the name flashing on the screen. 'It's your father.'

Eddie slumped his shoulders. 'Are you going to send me home?'

Harper smiled before she answered the phone.

'Harps, is Eddie with you?'

She wanted to scream at him, but, instead, she took a deep breath and kept her tone of voice neutral. 'Don't worry, Teddy. He is here, and I would have called, but I did ask you to let him know it was okay for him to come here, so I assumed you passed on the message.'

'Oh right, yeah, so what's he doing?'

'Oh, just watching a film and eating a burger. Anyway, he's fine. He's staying the night, and since he doesn't have school tomorrow, I thought we could go out for the day.'

'Oh, er, right, yeah, sure. So you're not coming into the club to work?'

'I'm not ready to come back to work.'

'Good. You take as much time off as you like. Do you two fancy coming to mine tomorrow? I can—'

'No, we're fine, Teddy. Speak soon.'

'Oh yeah. Uh, okay. I'll see you soon, then.'

Eddie's eyes were wide. 'I'm so glad you didn't tell him what we'd spoken about because he would go crazy.'

'I'd never betray your trust. I'm not in the mood to argue with him because I will be honest with you, Eddie Bear, the day I do that will be the day I rip the arrogance clean out of the man.'

Eddie looked sideways at his mother. 'You really do hate him, don't you?'

'Yes, I do, and I have my reasons.'

‘You think he was behind Paddy’s murder, don’t you!’

Shocked, Harper stared in disbelief. ‘*What?* Why would you say that?’

‘Because I think he was too. Mum, he is behind a lot of bad stuff. I don’t live in a house with him and not hear snippets of conversations. He is disgusting, and I’m not a grass, but he does need to be stopped. And I am not a baby. I can see what he is doing to you. I know he is obsessed, and that’s half his problem. He is fanatical and greedy, and he must have what he wants, including a son who is a chip off the old block and not someone who wants to be a marine biologist.’

‘The cunt!’ spat Harper, before she realised what she had just said. *I need to watch my language with Eddie around*, she thought.

‘He won’t let me live here. You do know that, Mum, don’t you?’

Harper grinned. ‘Ah, my son, I am a lot stronger than your father, and a lot braver. No one, and I mean no one, will get in the way of me and you. You might not know me that well yet, but one day, Eddie Bear, you will. Nobody hurts my family and gets away with it.’

CHAPTER ELEVEN

Harper lay in her bed staring up at the ceiling as her tears ran down to her ears. They were more through anger and frustration than grief. Because if she had let grief have its way, she would be sobbing uncontrollably into her pillow. The thought of her sister being one of those charred bodies was unthinkable. Another tear dampened her pillow. As she rolled over to hug herself to sleep, she heard a noise coming from the kitchen. At first, she assumed that Eddie had got up and was getting a drink. She listened and then heard the footsteps coming along the hallway.

Before she could get out of her bed, Michel was there in the doorway. 'Sorry for earlier. I didn't get—'

Harper put her finger over her lips, indicating that he should be quiet. The relief that he had returned made it evident that he wasn't the bad guy after all.

Sliding her arms into her dressing gown, she followed him back to the kitchen.

'Eddie is asleep in the spare room. I thought you had bleedin' scarpered.'

Michel sat on the chair and placed the tablet on the kitchen table. 'I was in your neighbour's house. You left the back door open, lucky for me. Cute dog, and nice coffee.'

'That Verity is a cocksure bitch. I could have swung for her. I know her game. She was attempting to use me to flush you out, saying that you had gone rogue. She even had the nerve to imply that Charley may have gone rogue. She was kind of insinuating that you were mixed up in all this. She even said I could help her find Charley, but she soon added' – Harper said, using air quotes – '"if my sister isn't dead". The woman is playing fucking mind games. But I know she was really after that tablet. Her two dogs turned my place upside down. Like I said to her, you ain't likely to be hiding in me knicker drawer.'

‘Turned rogue? That’s a bloody lie. And at least I know she is definitely after me now. I will endeavour to stay clear of her until I find my wife. Charley would never ever go against the law. And it proves that Verity must be desperate to get her hands on that tablet. I am still unsure, though, if she believes Charley is dead or not because what she said to me doesn’t correspond with what she is saying to you. Damn her!’

Harper flicked the switch on the kettle. ‘You really do believe my sister is alive, don’t you?’

He gave Harper a wry smile. ‘Of course. She is all I have. As I think I told you, my family back in Russia are all crooks. As you English would say, they have no time for me, because I am a police officer, and worse, I work for the British police.’

‘They would rather you be a villain?’

‘Yes. There are a lot of men back in Russia who have money. They are wealthy men but many of them have earned their money through illegal ways. Some of those are cruel, as you know for yourself. And some are the good guys, like Vadim.’

Pricking up her ears at that last remark, Harper poured two coffees and handed Michel one. ‘And did you ever know Vadim? I mean apart from the issues that went on in his club?’

‘I know *of* Vadim, but I do not know him personally. I have been told he is a good man, and a dangerous man too, if you are on the wrong side of him.’

Harper looked away, and a twinge of anger struck her as she thought back to what Paddy’s brother had told him on the phone. She had been standing right next to Paddy at the time of the conversation and had heard it all. Teddy Ryder would never have taken Vadim on alone. The bastard had had the poor man run over. They had really battered him.

She nodded to the tablet as she took her seat opposite Michel. ‘And I don’t suppose you managed to get into that thing, did you?’

Michel sighed, and then he ran his hand through his hair. 'No.'

'Why did you say you knew the password, Michel?'

'I didn't say that. When I said I have a passcode, I meant for the PO box in France.'

Harper blushed, feeling foolish.

'It's "turnip".'

Michel sat up straight. '*What?*'

'Turnip. Our secret code was turnip.'

Michel wasted no time in typing in the password. He looked at Harper and nodded. The tablet screen came to life and there on the screen was a folder – just the one folder and also a downloaded film. As soon as he opened the folder and scanned the documents, he frowned.

'What is it, Michel?'

He turned the tablet to face her. 'I don't know what all this is. It looks like business accounts. Why would she go to all this trouble to photograph these? They must be significant.'

Harper took the tablet and looked for herself. She swiped document after document until she saw a photo of some building plans. Getting up from her seat with the tablet, she walked around the table to sit next to him.

'Look, these are architects' drawings. Who was she employed to uncover, Michel?'

'Her covers have always been deep and risky because she was sourcing the human traffickers but at the top level. Why she has taken these particular photos, though, I just don't know.'

The next photo had Harper throwing her hands to her mouth. 'Jesus fucking wept. Look!' she said, excitedly. 'See. It says TR Corporation. I bet TR stands for Teddy Ryder. That's why she sent the tablet to me. It was sent as a warning. I am sure it was. I think I need to get back to the club to do some digging to see if

Teddy keeps any files in the office – anything with TR corporation stamped on them.'

Michel shook his head. 'No. Don't jump to conclusions. TR could be any company. Did you know Teddy Ryder had a building firm?'

Harper was shivering. It was probably from nervous anticipation. 'No, I didn't, but it seems like every day I am discovering more and more about how fucking dark and ruthless that man is.'

Michel swiped the screen across to the next document. He had to squint to see the detail. Then, slowly, he looked up and stared into Harper's eyes. 'How dark do you think Teddy Ryder is, Harper?'

She stared at the document. 'Oh my God. Look at this. It's The Click. And look. There's another document here. It refers to some other property, but there's no address. I can't read the other stuff. I don't speak Russian.'

Michel peered closer. 'These documents say that his business is jointly owned. And it mentions shares.' He glanced back at Harper. 'Who was Teddy in business with? Do you know?'

Harper shook her head. 'I thought I knew Teddy, but we were just kids at that time. We had a child together and that's probably as much as I know about him.' Her eyes looked down.

Michel sighed and swivelled his body to face her. 'Harper, you probably don't know much about our work.' He pointed to himself. 'I am trained to understand body language and I know when you are lying to me, so I will ask you again. What else do you know about Teddy? You have to be honest. I am trying to find my wife.'

Sensing his bubbling frustration, Harper could almost feel the rage coming off him.

'Look, Michel. Let me put you wise about what Teddy is capable of doing. He ran Vadim over and had two of his men beat him to an inch of his life. That's why Vadim sold up and fled

England. And another thing: I know that Teddy is completely obsessed with me. He even went to those lengths to get Vadim out of my life.'

Michel slowly shook his head. 'No, Harper, he didn't do it because he was obsessed with you. No one goes that far.'

'Look, don't get me wrong. I don't think that highly of myself, but he *is* obsessed. Even my sister Erin says so, and she lived with the man for years.'

'No, I don't believe that. He tried to kill Vadim because he wanted the club and he wanted Vadim out of the picture. But as to why, I am not sure. But rest assured, I will uncover those reasons. However, for now, I must read these documents and comprehend them. I don't understand why Charley didn't leave a message or even why she didn't film herself. She could have told us where she was.' He clenched his fist in annoyance. 'Why didn't she tell me? How can I find her with just these stupid building plans, documents, and fucking accounts?'

Harper sat back on her chair and stared at Michel.

'What is it? What are you thinking, Harper?'

With a sympathetic smile she replied, 'I think I know why. She didn't have time. She had to run, and so whatever is in those documents is vital information. What I wanna know is why she didn't post it to her boss, Verity, or to you, for that matter.'

'Me? Of course, she wouldn't post it to me. And as for Verity, I think the reason is obvious. She doesn't trust her. And if Verity is in some way involved, then Charley would want this information as far away from her hands as possible. And something else to think about: whoever is at the top of the food chain has enough power to influence a lot of people. Believe me, Harper, Teddy Ryder may be involved with those at the top, but I can guarantee you, he will be their puppet. I have no doubt they are Russians. The notes and accounts speak for themselves. They may even let Teddy believe he is at the top, but he won't be.'

With her eyes narrowing, Harper felt her anger rising. 'Well, I don't care how big they are. If they've hurt my sister, I will fucking kill 'em, and as for that Verity, I will make her talk. Believe you me, Michel, she will wish she was dead, if she sees me coming for her.'

Michel looked uneasy. 'No, you leave it to me. I understand this world. But you don't.'

Harper jumped up. 'No, Michel. You only understand one side of it. I have lived in a different world – in the prison and then at the hands of those evil Russian traffickers – so understand this: you may do things one way, but me, I tend to like kicking arse meself. People don't like to argue with a metal bat, especially when it's about to be swung at their teeth.'

Michel's face softened. 'Your sister was so right about you. She told me the stories of how you protected your sisters by using your fists and asking question afterwards.'

Unexpectedly, he rose to his feet, placed his arms around her, and pulled her tight. 'We will find her, Harper. And we will do it together.'

'It's *we*, now, is it?' she replied, slightly embarrassed.

'Well, you have made it clear that you are ready to smash down doors and beat anyone to death, so I guess maybe you have what it takes.'

Wiping her gritty eyes, Harper yawned. 'I need to sleep, and hopefully, by morning' – she glanced at the clock – 'I mean by late morning, I may have a clearer picture.'

Michel nodded. 'I have to go. I can't be seen here because Verity's team will be back. So I will disappear for a while.'

Harper nodded, and then her eyes widened. 'I'm going to move in with Teddy.'

'What? *Why?*'

'Because he has asked me loads of times, and if I'm in his house, I can find out what the hell is going on.'

'But you hate him.'

‘Yes, I do. I hate him with all my fucking being, but, Michel, I love my sister more.’

‘You would sleep with that man?’

‘I have done it before.’ She chuckled. ‘Hopefully, it won’t come to that.’

‘Do you mind if I take this tablet?’

‘No. You understand the content better than I do.’ She stared off into nothing. ‘I can’t understand how Verity would be involved in any of this. As she said, she is Charley’s operations manager. It doesn’t make sense. If you were involved and doing something dodgy, you wouldn’t send an undercover officer in to investigate, surely, would you?’

Michel’s face paled over. ‘Oh Christ, oh fucking Christ!’

‘What is it, Michel?’

He waved his hand for her not to interrupt his thoughts. ‘Months ago, Charley was on an assignment under Peter Bracken. He was an operations manager. She’d had a lot of training for this particular job and then Verity joined his team. There was a change in the tactical team and Verity became Charley’s ops manager and Peter was shifted to another team.’

‘Didn’t you find that odd?’

‘No, I didn’t. Not then. We can finish a case sooner or it can run over the expected timeframe so the teams can cross over. And our operations managers, or tactical managers, can have more than one job on the go. You have to understand that when we go undercover, we can be living a double life for months. So, a lot can change in that time. But I take your point. Something’s not right. That’s for sure.’

***

Harper was still shaking by the time Michel left. It was all too much to process, but the one thing she was sure of was that she wasn’t going to sit back and do nothing. But she couldn’t spend every waking hour worrying about Charley. She decided to return to her bed and get some sleep.

***

Harper finally awoke to the smell of coffee and feeling the side of her bed sinking. When she rolled over, she saw her son's smiling eyes and him holding a cup of steaming coffee.

Pushing herself up the bed, she sat up straight, before taking the cup. 'Aw, babe, that's nice. Thank you. Did you sleep well?'

'Yeah, Mum.' He smiled again. 'It's so different here. I feel safe, and, um . . . I feel wanted.'

'Ya know, your dad has asked me to move in with him and you. I think I should.'

The beaming smile completely vanished from Eddie's face. 'I don't understand. I thought you hated him. I thought you understood me. I thought—'

'Stop! Listen to me. I need you to be very mature about this, Eddie.'

'But you said—'

Harper nodded. 'I know what I said, but you have to hear me out.' She stroked his bare arm. 'Your father is, as I understand it, a very dangerous man. I mean seriously dangerous.'

Eddie nodded. 'I know that, Mum. He has a thing about being the big I am, and I know what he is capable of. Well, actually, more his bully-boy mates. I'm not blind or deaf.'

'Now listen, Eddie. When I was young, I used to row with my mum a lot, and I used to say I hated her but—'

'No, Mum. You don't get it, do you. You really *don't* understand. No one would!'

Shocked by her son's loud outburst, Harper was about to explain when Eddie turned and marched out of the room, but not before she saw the bruises on his bare back.

Quickly, she placed the cup of coffee on the bedside cabinet and climbed out of bed. 'Eddie!' she called out. 'Come here. I'm sorry, love, but you didn't let me explain what my plan is.'

By the time she reached him, he was back in the spare room and putting on his sweatshirt.

'I thought you were on my side, but I guess Dad was right about you and him. You two were meant to be together.'

'Right, Eddie! Stop right there and listen to me!'

The rasp of impatience in her voice, forced Eddie to stop shoving his belongings into his backpack. He turned to face her.

'Believe me, Eddie, there is no one out there who loves you more than I do.'

He lowered his head. 'I know that, Mum.'

'Do you, Son?'

He nodded.

'Good. Now, how about we talk like adults over a big fry-up. And let me explain about this idea of moving in with your father. And before you jump in again, first, I hate your dad, and second, I am trusting you with something that I won't trust anyone else with.'

Eddie's eyes widened. 'Okay. Sorry, I stormed out of the room like a spoilt brat.'

***

Harper had her back to Eddie as she turned the sausages over in the pan. 'So tell me, Eddie Bear, apart from your father practically ignoring you, and also, you know, the stuff he made you do with that poor girl, er, has he ever laid a hand on you?'

Her throat tightened as the silence continued. 'Eddie?' she said, almost afraid to turn around.

'No, not exactly.'

'How did you get those bruises on your back?'

‘There are a few lads at school who don’t like me, that’s all.’

Harper felt her blood boiling and her temper rising. ‘Are you being bullied, babe?’

‘It’s all right, Mum. Honestly, it is.’

Harper spun around. ‘No, it ain’t all right. Does your dad know about this? Has he seen the bruises on your back? Did he go up to the school?’

‘No. I asked him about that, but he said he didn’t believe in all that bollocks. So, instead, he sent me to have boxing lessons and told me to fight back and stop being a pussy.’

‘Oh, did he, indeed.’

‘Now, do you see why I don’t want to go back home?’

‘Nah. I will move into your house, and I will strip the man of everything he has, and by the time I’ve finished, he will be begging for forgiveness. I’ll make that bastard kiss your feet for what he’s done to you.’

Eddie had never seen his mother so irate. He knew then that the mere thought of his father hurting him had sent his mother into a complete nutcase.

‘Can’t I just stay here away from him?’

‘Eddie.’ She paused to catch her breath. ‘I love you with all my heart.’

He nodded. ‘There’s a but in there somewhere, isn’t there, Mum?’

Harper nervously bit her lip. ‘I am trusting you with something so sensitive.’ She paused and stared at her son, wondering if she could lay her plan onto his young shoulders.

‘Okay, Mum, go on.’

‘I believe your father is into something dark, so much so, that your average villain would shop him for what he is doing.’

Harper had expected a gasp, a look of disbelief – anything, in fact, other than an affirmative nod.

‘Did you understand what I said?’

‘Yeah, Teddy’s business stretches beyond the acceptance of any law-abiding citizen.’

‘And your thoughts?’ she asked.

‘Tell the police and have him locked up, Mum, because if he is into something, as you say that’s dark, he’ll go to prison. So let the prisoners deal with him. Mum, I know he is into some bad things because I heard Ben Marshall, one of Teddy’s employees, call him a wrong ’un. Teddy went mental, Mum. He had this other guy, a tall man, like a soldier, who was all dressed in black, hold Ben down while Teddy kicked and kicked Ben in the face. Ben was screaming “Stop!” but Teddy wouldn’t.’

‘I know Ben and his brother Josh.’

‘Yeah, they are always polite to me. I mean, Josh is a bit strange, but Ben is a good man, in a gangster kind of way.’

Harper shook her head. ‘You should never have been exposed to any of this.’

‘It’s the house Teddy bought, and the top is like a bloody lighthouse with windows everywhere. So I can see who comes, who goes, and who’s sunning it around the pool sipping cocktails and snorting cocaine.’

‘If I agree to move in with your father—’

‘Please, Mum, stop calling him that. He doesn’t deserve to be called “father” at all.’

‘Okay, if I move in with you and Teddy, I vow to look out for you. And that includes any dirty looks, bad words, or anything. I’ll break his fucking legs, and no Russian soldier will stop me.’

‘Russian?’

‘Didn’t you say Russian?’

Eddie shook his head. ‘No, I didn’t. He could be, but he didn’t speak, so do you think Teddy is mixed up with Russians, then?’

Harper nodded. 'Possibly, and if so, the chances are they are the worst kind of Russians.'

'Okay, move in with us, then, but you have to understand there are levels to his nastiness, so if you think he is out of line, don't say anything. I'll just storm off to my room as I always do. I don't want you jumping in and ruining everything.'

'Are you sure, love?'

'Mum, if you think you can stop him, then I am all for it. I can't live knowing that my father is a wrong 'un. I will never get that girl's terrified expression and her face like a doll out of my mind.'

'Okay, darling, but don't run away with the idea that I've moved in properly. I only need Teddy to think that I am edging my way in, but really, Son, I'm just playing detective.'

'I get it, Mum. No worries. You do what you need to do, and me, well, I'll tag along.'

CHAPTER TWELVE

While Eddie was taking a shower, Harper loaded the dishwasher and mentally planned her next moves. Aware that she would have to put on the act of the century, she knew there would be days when it would test her strength; she only hoped she could find what she needed quickly.

As she threw the last dirty spoon into the plastic rack, the doorbell rang, followed by three knocks – it was Teddy.

Taking a deep breath and forcing a smile, she opened the door. She noticed his less than confident stance right away – he was uneasy.

'You look better, Harps. Very pretty. Had ya hair done?' He almost tripped over his words as they fell out of his mouth.

Harper nodded. 'Come in, Teddy. You just missed a fry-up.'

Teddy wiped his feet as he entered. 'I thought I'd drop by and see if Eddie wanted a lift back home.' The fast pace of his speech was a telltale sign he was feeling uncomfortable.

'It was lovely having him over, ya know. I enjoy him being around.'

'Yeah, he is a good lad when he's not talking rubbish. You know what it's like, boys of his age. I bet he spun you a few yarns, eh?'

Harper wanted to smash his teeth out there and then, but she resisted venting her rage and instead said in her best nonchalant tone, 'He didn't say too much, only about school and footie, but it made me realise how much I miss him.'

She stopped just inside the kitchen and turned to face him. She knew she needed to come across as coy and a little awkward. Looking up with half a smile, she said, 'Teddy, about that offer . . .'

Teddy's face lit up, his cheeks reddened, and his eyes had their come-to-bed twinkle in them. 'You wanna move in? Is that what you are about to say?' He didn't wait for a reply. 'Yeah, it makes sense. I think he needs his mum and dad together under the same roof, and, well, you know how I feel about you. It's good for him to see a normal healthy relationship, ain't it?'

Harper smiled. She was more than pleased with her little bit of acting. Teddy couldn't wait to get her into bed. He was almost drooling at the mouth.

Teddy, for his part, was over the moon. Without a care in the world, he said, caustically, 'Yeah, I reckon our son needs a little bit of help in that department.'

Harper bit her lip. She assumed that now he was talking about their son possibly being gay.

'Well, anyway, we can see how it goes. I was thinking of going back to work tonight. I need to get my life back on track.'

Teddy glanced around the kitchen. '*Tonight?*'

She nodded.

'Why don't you get used to your new home first. No pointing in rushing back to work.' He was still gazing around when he said. 'You could sell this and get a good price and—'

'What makes you think I own this place?'

Instantly, she clocked Teddy recoil. 'Oh, er, I assumed you did, that's all.'

Harper knew then that he had been delving into her affairs because the only person who knew was her mother, Delores, and as things stood now, Delores didn't like Teddy, so she certainly wouldn't have told him anything.

'So, I'll see you at the club tonight, Teddy, will I?'

'What? Er, listen. Roxy's been managing fine, love.' He laughed nervously. 'I think she believes it's her job now. Maybe, I'll give her some notice. Because she's been a good girl while you've been away. And I don't want to suddenly rip the rug from under her. You know what I mean.'

Harper stared Teddy out, allowing him to spew out his bullshit. It was obvious he didn't want her back in the club now.

'Er . . . about moving into mine. Shall I organise a removal van or what?'

Harper bit her lip in disdain; but, inside, she was laughing at him and his schoolboy eagerness. 'No, Teddy, let's just see how it goes. I'll pack a suitcase, and, well, we'll give it a trial run for now.'

'Yeah, of course, and I promise you, Harps, you won't regret it. The house is the bollocks, babe. There's a huge kitchen with every gadget. We've got enormous TV screens and a spa bath, a swimming pool, everything.'

'I just want to be around me boy. I'm not fussed about spa baths and flat-screen TVs.'

'No, no, 'course not, but I'm just saying you'll be comfortable there, that's all.'

She could tell he had changed. Once upon a time, all that was important to him was his son, not the size of his TVs or swimming pool. Even his leather jacket was flash, and his gold watch was so large it made her wonder if the thing made tea. He was sending a clear message to everyone that he was wealthy. Noticing how white his teeth were, it was obvious he'd had veneers fitted. And his tan wasn't Spanish, more sunbed brown.

It made her question if his new look was something that had rubbed off on him from Erin. However, her sister had made a complete U-turn since her attack. She had ditched the sunbeds, the fake tan, and the hair extensions and was a toned-down version of her former self. Surprisingly, Erin had been like a rock to her; she would often call in to see her to check that she was okay – especially since Paddy's death.

'No need to take Eddie home. I'll drive him later.'

'Okay, no worries. You're looking good, Harps. A helluva lot better, girl.'

'Cheers, Teddy.'

She noticed how he was rubbing the back of his neck. He always did that when he was feeling uncomfortable.

'What's up?'

He looked around. 'Eddie's in the shower, yeah?'

'Yeah, why?'

'Listen, Harps, I know he's me son, and you know how much I love him.'

Forcing a nod, Harper thought, *finally we're getting to what was really on Teddy's mind.*

'Of course, so what's up?'

'Well, er, he can be a little bit of a drama queen. He is going through a phase of telling a few porkies, exaggerating shit . . . you know what I mean . . . so don't be surprised when you move in to find out how dramatic he can be.'

Harper was stewing, but she did her usual counting to ten to prevent herself from dismantling his perfect veneers.

'He ain't like us, Harps. I may have fucked up with getting him to go to the grammar school. You and me, we are streetwise, we know how to handle ourselves. You know what I'm saying, babe. But listen. Our Eddie, he is away with the fairies. He needs to toughen up a bit.'

She noticed his Adam's apple as he swallowed hard.

'Yeah, sure, but don't mistake drama for intelligence. I mean, if I had the chance, I know I'd have taken more notice at school. It would have been a lot easier than being educated in prison.' She smiled.

Teddy was caught off guard. He assumed that Harper would want their son to be a little cheeky tough cookie, like her and himself. However, he hadn't realised that she didn't actually like what she had become.

'Yeah, yeah, sure. All I'm saying is he can be easily led, and not only that, he does also tell a few stories.'

Harper couldn't help herself. 'What, like being bullied?'

'Yes, exactly, like that. He reckons there are a few lads—'

'A few?' interrupted Harper.

'See, again, I think he exaggerates.' He smirked. 'He reckoned four sixteen-year-olds jumped him.' He laughed. 'Well, he was talking a load of bollocks. If four sixteen-year-olds jumped him, he would be black and blue. Ain't that right?'

Biting her lip again, Harper held in her anger. Eddie hadn't told her that there were four older lads. 'So you believe our boy is lying about being bullied?'

'Yeah, Harps, as I said, he's a drama queen. Anyway, I sent him to the boxing club so that he could stand up for himself.'

'So, let me get this straight, Teddy. You think learning a few uppercuts will stop him from getting a kicking by four older lads? Is that what you're saying?'

Sensing that Harper wasn't buying it, Teddy sighed. 'No, Harps, not at all, but it's a start.'

'And what did the school say?'

'I haven't gone to them. I want Eddie to look out for himself, not running to the teacher grassing. You know how it was at school. We handled our own shit, right? You had loads of rucks. You know you did, Harps.'

Harper knew she had to shut her mouth, or this would end up with Teddy sporting two black eyes and a thick lip, or, worse, a carving knife right through his gut.

'Yeah, okay. You've made your point.' She needed to end the conversation. She was somewhat surprised that while he was at it, he hadn't mentioned this business about Eddie being gay. She guessed that would be on his mind. But she certainly wasn't going to be the one to raise it.

'So, you don't mind me staying for a bit?'

'I think you'll love it, and I'll bet my house on you wanting to move in for good.'

Cocky bastard.

***

Totally ignoring Teddy's idea of not going to work tonight, Harper stepped out of her car and approached the club. She paused and took a deep breath. The last time she had been there, Paddy was there to greet her. But this time, he wasn't. He was dead, murdered in cold blood. And there was no Vadim inside to give her a cheeky wink or a gentle kiss. Her mood was flat.

Before she had a chance to put on a fake smile, Roxy bounded up behind her.

'Harper!' she squealed, as she flung her arms around her. 'It's so good to see you.'

Taken aback, but secretly warmed by the embrace, Harper replied, 'I've missed you too, Rox.'

Roxy pulled away and winked. 'Yeah, right! Of course you did, Harper.' As she linked arms to walk the three feet to the door, she whispered, 'How long will we have a job?'

'What do you mean?'

Harper unlinked her arm and turned to face Roxy. 'What's been going on since I was away?'

Roxy looked around her. 'You don't know *anything*?'

Harper shrugged her shoulders. 'Clearly not. What do you know, Rox? Tell me.'

'Teddy had a surveyor in here. He said he was his pal, measuring up for improvements, but I know the prick because he used to work with me ol' man. He's in the building game. He was a right dodgy bastard, an' all.'

‘So how do you know that Teddy ain’t into renovating the place?’

‘Huh! *Seriously?* Harper, the club doesn’t need improving. You know it, and so do I. So what’s he really doing with the place?’

‘I’ll ask him outright.’

Roxy shook her head. ‘No, he’s right funny about anyone being nosey. He’s changed the lock to the office.’

‘Changed the lock? Well, he’d better have left me a key.’

‘No, his business advisor and or accountant – whatever hat he chooses to wear – has a key. He’s a right nasty piece of work, he is. Wanders behind the bar, helps himself to drinks, and talks to the girls like they’re shit.’

‘Oh, does he now? I will soon see about that. You know me, Roxy. I won’t have any of my girls spoken to like a piece of dirt. They’re here to do a job, not to be abused.’

Roxy smiled, took her pumps off, slid on her high-heeled shoes, pulled the band from her hair, and let her long wavy blonde locks tumble down her back. She shook her head, loosening the bunched-up sections, and followed Harper to the door.

‘It is *soo* good to have you back. I hate asking Teddy for anything. He always makes me feel like I’m a pest, the way he waves his hands and smiles, but he’s not smiling at me. Know what I mean?’

‘Well, I’m back, Roxy, so any questions, I’ll be answering them.’

‘Before you go in, Harper, don’t be alarmed by the changes.’

‘*What?* There are *more*?’

‘Yes, he’s already had the builders in. They’ve put up a stud wall and made like a private section for his so-called special guests.’

‘Special guests?’ repeated Harper, with a deep frown etched across her forehead.

‘Suits.’

The moment Harper stepped into the club’s back room, she knew something was different. The smell, for one, wasn’t the same. And the staff coffee station that she had set up herself was spotless. The teaspoons in the jar were shining like new, and the table and chairs were gleaming. Not that it was ever dirty, but now, it looked like new.

‘Roxy, has Teddy replaced our cleaners?’

‘I told ya, he’s made a few changes. He has two Asian women cleaning the place now. They don’t say a word but scrub the place until their hands practically bleed. Michelle and Maria got the chop.’

‘*What?* But they’ve worked here for years.’

Roxy gave Harper an empathetic nod. ‘Stan Nikki, this new business advisor, sent ’em packing and employed the two mute Asian women.’

The second she walked into the bar and flicked all the lights on, Harper heard the back door open.

Roxy sniggered. ‘That’s him, the short-arse wanker.’

Harper spun around. The man was dressed in a suit that was too big for him. His tie looked a mess, with a schoolboy’s lazy knot, and his hair had that look of a grown out short back and sides. She could smell his cheap aftershave and clocked his dirty fingernails before he even opened his mouth.

At first, he was startled to see two women in the otherwise empty club.

‘New staff?’

Harper stepped forward. ‘Not at all. I am the manager of The Click. And you are?’

Roxy loved how Harper could take control of a situation. Even the simple lift of her chin commanded attention.

'Oh, right, so *you're* Harper Kane?' He slung his briefcase on the bar. 'So, finally, you've decided to join us, then.' He grinned as though he had meant that comment as a joke.

If it was, it wasn't funny to Harper.

She held out her hand, and he assumed she was about to shake his; however, when he attempted to grab her hand, she pulled away and held them out again, palm up.

'Keys, please, for the office.' Her tone was cold, with a sense of finality.

He gave a quick sharp chuckle and nervously looked from Roxy back to Harper. 'You won't need them anymore.'

'Sorry, Mr, er, what's your name?'

'It's Stan. Stan Nikki.'

'So, Mr Nikki, I am the manager, and I have all the keys to the club, including the office. I will hand you the book and paperwork you need to do the accounts. I have done it long enough without an issue so far, so hand me the keys. I need to order in some stock.'

A conceited smirk slithered across his face. 'Actually, I noticed quite a few discrepancies in the books, Ms Kane, so it's probably a good idea to let the professionals do what they are good at, and you' – he looked Harper up and down – 'you do what *you* are good at. I assume it's managing the bar staff, isn't it?'

Roxy couldn't believe what she was witnessing. She put her hand over her mouth to hide the grin.

'Mr Nikki, let's get something very clear,' Harper said. She moved her index finger in a circular motion. 'See this club?'

His arrogant smirk suddenly disappeared. He hadn't expected Harper to keep his gaze with a confident glare.

‘I revamped this club, Mr Nikki. I designed every inch—’

‘With all due respect,’ he interrupted, ‘adding a few sparkles and a lick of paint doesn’t make you an accountant.’

‘No, Mr Nikki, you’re right, but it doesn’t make me a cunt, either, and as I was fucking saying, until you rudely interrupted me, I turned this club from seedy to slick. I created a club for the classier clientele, celebrities, footballers, and rich fucking businessmen who will pay two hundred quid for a cheap bottle of plonk. And so, before you open your mouth and try to belittle me again, you’d best have your facts straight. ’Cos, darling, how many clubs have you known to increase their turnover by fifty per cent in a year?’

Feeling his neck turn burgundy and his mouth slightly dry, Nikki wasn’t about to be spoken to like this. He felt his business position with Ryder and the other business associates afforded him the respect he deserved. Being able to do the accounts was only a small part of his role. So he was not going to be undermined by some arrogant tart.

‘The profit increase isn’t simply down to a revamp. You have to take into account many other factors, like—’

‘Ya know what, Mr Nikki, you’re boring me now. Hand over the keys so that I can open my office. I have stock to order and things to do, and if you are Teddy’s new accountant, then that’s great. I take it Teddy is no longer engaging the Lasson Accountancy Services?’

Nikki’s ferret eyes were now stormy with anger. He glared at Harper. ‘Accountant? I am a lot more than that. I’m a—’

‘A mug?’ Harper interjected, to Roxy’s amusement.

Ignoring her comment, he gave an over-the-top fake smile, showing his tiny teeth and prominent red gums. ‘Look, I think we have got off on the wrong foot. I am here to do a job, not to argue with you. I insist we discuss the boundaries before we move on as colleagues.’

Harper looked at Roxy. 'Is this prick for real! Boundaries? Fucking *boundaries*?' She glared back at Nikki. 'I ain't at bloody school. Now, if you're Teddy's accountant, then your job is to do the fucking accounts, not to pick over a few petty mistakes. You're lucky I don't hand over a black sack of receipts and the company bank account and let you do the filing. Now, for the umpteenth time, give me the keys.'

'I am afraid I can't do that, Harper.'

'It's Ms Kane to you.' She placed her hands on her hips, her head tilted to the side. She raised her eyebrow. 'And why not?'

'Because the office isn't solely for the purposes of the club. It is now my office. I oversee all of Mr Ryder's businesses. So are we clear?'

His last sentence had Harper raging. 'Are we clear? Are we fucking *clear*? I tell you what you need to be clear about. If you ever talk to me like that again, I will smash your soppy-looking face straight through that sparkly bar and shove the fucking accounts up your arse!'

His sudden hoot of laughter had Harper locking eyes with him, in a daring stance.

'You have no idea, Harper, do you?' He grinned, mocking her. 'You're so rude, but you will soon be reminded that I am the last person you will want to piss off.'

'Oh, I am not rude. You, though, little man, are merely insignificant to me.'

He gave another high-pitched laugh. 'Respect is good for you, Harper. It keeps your teeth in the right place. Now, why don't you fuck off behind the bar and leave me alone, or fuck off full stop. I can see that you, sweet cheeks, are gonna be a right nightmare for me.'

Harper stood aghast; she was almost flabbergasted. How could this pipsqueak of a man have the balls to talk to her like that? Surely Teddy would have told him who she was, considering she was also the manager. Unless there was something more significant to Teddy and Mr Nikki's relationship.

'What's the matter, Harper, did you think you could take charge in here? And over me?' He sighed. 'It's not how it works, darling, not here. And if you don't like it, go and work at your Aunt Desiree's club. I bet she needs staff.'

Even Roxy gasped at the aggressive nature of the man.

It was at the point that Harper felt the sudden effects of the revelation. Her head started to throb, and a pulsating pain began behind her eyes. 'Teddy is not your boss, is he?'

Smiling from ear to ear, Nikki grabbed his briefcase from the bar and walked purposely towards the office.

CHAPTER THIRTEEN

As soon as Nikki slammed the office door behind him, Harper fled to the back room, flopped down on a chair, covered her face, and sobbed. There seemed to be no let-up from the tears soaking her hands.

Never before having witnessed Harper so distressed and vulnerable, Roxy pulled over another chair and sat opposite with her arms around her friend.

'Bloody hell, Harper, this world is truly beating you down. Your face looks like it's melting in pain. What's going on?'

After swallowing a few times, Harper wiped her eyes with the tissue that Roxy waved under her nose.

'I can't . . . I can't tell you. I can't tell anyone. I'm fucking drowning in frustration, Rox. I don't know what the fuck to do.'

'A problem shared is a problem halved.'

Harper smiled. 'I know, Roxy, but I am in a world right now where I don't know who I can trust. I certainly can't even trust the poxy police.' Another hot tear rolled down her cheek. 'I have to stay strong, for my family's sake, Rox, and I don't know if I have the strength to do it. Inside, I'm dying. I'm fucking dying.'

'I know you're tough, Harper, and you have never let anything get to you, but even your smile is broken, girl. You can't fight the world. Christ, Harper, look what you have already been through. I couldn't have served a day in prison, let alone twelve years. And then there's those fucking Russians and what they did to you. I would have died there and then. And to top it all, Paddy gets murdered. I know how much you two liked each other, so nothing can be as bad as that now, surely not, can it?'

Harper looked around her before blowing her nose. 'Rox, everyone around me is either a friend or a foe. There's no in-between anymore and there can't be.'

'But *I'm* a friend, Harper,' Roxy said, as she rubbed Harper's arm.

'Are you, though, Roxy? As I said, I don't know who I can trust anymore. It's like I'm flipping a coin for heads or tails.'

'Jesus, I didn't know it was that bad, girl. I'll make us a coffee, eh?'

Harper shook her head. 'I'll have a brandy. Coffee just won't cut it. Join me, Roxy?'

Roxy hurried to the bar and grabbed two glasses and a full bottle of brandy from under the shelf.

'You'd better not let numbnuts Nikki see us.'

Harper smiled. 'He is the least of my worries. I'll glass the bastard if he gets mouthy again.'

Roxy poured a generous measure and slid it under Harper's nose. 'There you are. Get that down your neck.'

After a gulp and a shudder, Harper wiped her mouth. 'I'm moving in with Teddy, for Eddie's sake.'

Roxy frowned. 'Now, you might not want to tell me what's got you into such a state, but, at least, give me enough respect. Tell me the truth. Why are you *really* moving in with Teddy? 'Cos I know, girl, you don't love him.'

'Are you sure about that, Rox?'

Roxy poured another round of drinks. 'Girl, I've known you long enough now to know you, so what are you up to? 'Cos it ain't a cosy night in having sweet sex in front of an open fire or playing the happy housewife and cutting up cheese sandwiches for Eddie's packed lunch.'

'Maybe I've changed. Maybe—'

'Oh, come on. Seasons change, tides change, but as for you, Harper Kane – no, I ain't buying it.'

Harper couldn't tell Roxy about Charley going missing. She genuinely couldn't trust anyone, even though she was fond of

Roxy. However, Eddie, she decided wasn't such a risk. And, she reasoned, if confiding in Roxy about her son proved successful, having a really loyal and reliable friend in the club, who could keep her informed of what was going on when she wasn't there, might work to her advantage in the future. 'I don't think Teddy is treating Eddie right. I think he is bullying him. I mean, Eddie has some nasty bruises on his back—'

'Teddy?'

'No, not Teddy. It was some lads from school. So Teddy's idea of handling the incident was to send Eddie to the local boxing club.' She looked around her before whispering, 'But it wasn't so much that which has upset me. The other night, Eddie came to my flat in tears. Apparently, he'd let on to his dad that he might be gay, and Teddy gave him a hard time over it.' She flared her nostrils. 'I could kill Teddy.'

Roxy gulped back another mouthful. 'Eddie is old enough to decide if he wants to live with you now.'

Harper nodded. 'I know, and he will, but first, I have to get inside Teddy's gaff. I need to know what the fuck is going on.'

With a deep frown and a wrinkled nose, Roxy said, 'Like what?'

Harper stared at Roxy. Spilling the absolute truth of all of her worries momentarily crossed her mind, but, again, she decided not to tell Roxy quite everything. 'Paddy.'

Roxy's jaw dropped in disbelief. 'Fuck me. You think Teddy killed him, do ya?'

Harper waved her hand, indicating that Roxy should lower her voice.

'Oops, sorry.' Roxy looked behind her. 'No, seriously, you think Teddy may have shot Paddy, but why?'

'Jealousy.'

'Jealousy? That's a bit extreme, but nothing surprises me with Teddy. I know he is your ex and Eddie's father, but, Harper, he is not a decent fella, and believe you me, I have met some bad boys in my time.'

'D'you think Teddy is a wrong 'un, then?'

Roxy looked down. 'Sorry to say it, Harper, but yeah, he is slippery, mate. He's as slippery as a bucket of eels. I don't see him having it with the likes of the Brooks or the Clarks. They sometimes drink in here, but they rarely give him the time of day.'

'They could be sizing him up to take him down if he has become such a cocky bastard.'

Roxy shook her head. 'No, Harper, I've known those two firms for years. My father worked with the ol' man Henry Brook back in the day, so when I say I know him, I mean I know him quite well. Both men seem to me to be too polite when they cross Teddy's path. It's as though they are a bit wary of Teddy, but I know they ain't doing business with him. That's a fact. While Teddy has his own firm, believe you me, Harper, the Brooks and the Clarks are proper suits. However, there are some who ain't kosher. There are a few dodgy MPs – even some Ol' Bill – who I hear on the q.t. are as crooked as they come.' She squeezed Harper's arm. 'Call it intuition, but I think Teddy is a sly, sneaky fucker. He's probably quite happy to see some respectable faces in here to make everything else seem legit.'

'So, do you think he isn't the boss? It seems to me that ol' fish face Nikki alluded to the fact that he isn't. If that's the case, why else would Nikki have the nerve to talk to me in that way? Unless, perhaps, he isn't working for Teddy but someone above him.'

Roxy shrugged her shoulders. 'I dunno about that.'

'I'll ask Teddy outright.'

'No!' snapped Roxy. 'Don't do that. He will be guarded, trust me. Act like you suspect nothing and see if the truth surfaces. Meanwhile, girl, I will listen and take more notice of what's going on because I know there is something dodgy going on. I feel it in me bones.'

Harper chewed the nail on her little finger until Roxy pulled her hand away from her mouth. 'You must have manicured nails, remember. Don't bite them off.'

For a moment, Harper was back in a comfortable place with Vadim looking over at her, winking. Her mind went dark. So much had happened. So much, it was unreal.

'Oh, Harper,' said Roxy, as she watched her friend's face dissolve into grief. Her eyes were pulled down at the sides, her bottom lip quivered, and a torrent of more tears followed. 'Your nails. I forgot it was a Vadim thing. Are you even over him, Harper?'

Harper wiped her eyes. 'It was nothing, really. Just a bit of sex and fun.'

'Are you saying that because he went back to his sick wife and left you here on your own?'

Harper looked up, right into Roxy's eyes, her bottom lip quivering again.

'He didn't have a sick wife, Roxy.'

'*What!* You mean he used that as an excuse and just left you to fuck off back to Russia? Well, to be honest, Harper, I actually thought more of the man and . . .' She paused and frowned. 'That doesn't make sense. He loved you. I know you said it was just about sex, but not to him, it wasn't. He loved you to death. We could all see it.'

Harper wiped her face again and sighed. 'All right, Roxy, I'll tell you the truth, but what I'm about to tell you must never leave your lips again. Got it?'

Nodding wildly, as if her head might fall off at any minute, Roxy stared wide-eyed at her friend. She was struggling to believe they were even having this conversation. This was the first time that Harper had confided in her about anything. In a way, she felt honoured, and it was at that point she knew their friendship would know no bounds.

Roxy nodded fast. 'Go on, tell me what happened, Harper. I have a right to know. He was my boss, too, and I cared for Vadim, ya know.'

Harper raised her eyebrow.

'*What?* No, not like that. He gave me a job when no one else would, and he made sure I had enough money to cover me rent without selling meself.'

'Okay, I'll tell you. Vadim wasn't married. There *wasn't* a wife. Teddy forced him to sell the club to him. That's why he left.'

Roxy's eyes were out on stalks. 'You're fucking kidding me!'

'No, Teddy wanted the club, and by hook or by crook, the bastard was going to have it. And he fucking did.'

Unexpectedly, Roxy's eyes filmed over with tears. 'His accident was no accident was it, Harper? I bet Teddy was responsible for him being mowed down.'

'Yes, he was. So, now, can you see why I need to move in with Teddy? I need to find out who my son's father really is because I sure as hell don't know him anymore. And you can also understand why I think he had something to do with Paddy's murder.'

Roxy placed her hand over Harper's. 'Oh, Harper, be careful, mate. I mean, I never knew he did that to Vadim, and you do know how dangerous Vadim is. I was shocked when he returned to Russia, but it all makes sense now.' She frowned and shook her head. 'He loved this club, and he really loved you, Harper. And as much as you might think you and Vadim were like friends with benefits, I know you loved him just as much. I suppose I assumed you were denying your feelings. And all the weeks you were mourning Paddy, were you being true to yourself and crying over Vadim too?'

Harper's bottom lip quivered once more. 'Roxy, I miss Vadim. I miss him so much. Every day I think of him, his kind ways, and how he made me feel like a beautiful woman. I liked

Paddy a lot, and maybe a part of me knows it was on the rebound after Vadim. I wanted to replace the pain of Vadim leaving, with love and passion.'

'You've been through so much, and your heart needs to heal, so I will help you in any way I can. I promise. Call him, Harper.'

'I can't. He's probably living a new life back in Russia.'

'He would be back in a heartbeat if he knew you were suffering like this. I know he would. And I bet he's missing this club. Not as much as missing you, though.' She chuckled.

Harper looked up and saw the mischievous look on Roxy's face. 'Don't you call him.'

Roxy smiled. 'Me? As if I'd do such a thing.'

'No, I mean it, Rox.'

The sound of the back door opening, and the hustle and bustle of the girls' chit-chatting pulled both Harper and Roxy away from their deep conversation. Each girl, in turn, hugged and greeted Harper with kind words and broad smiles.

However, when Nikki appeared, the girls scooted off to the ladies' changing room. It was evident he had harassed them, which got Harper's back up right away. She hurriedly took her station behind the bar, and with her head held high, she glared at Nikki, silently goading him.

He ignored her confrontational look and lifted the flap. Standing three feet away, he arrogantly poured himself a drink – a double.

'That'll be five pounds fifty.' She held out her hand.

Nikki smirked. 'It's on the house to me.'

'Oh, is that right? Well, no wonder there was a discrepancy with the figures.'

'Are you saying that not accounting for a few freebies puts the figures out?'

Harper chuckled. 'No, I am saying drinking on the job probably does that.'

'You're a mouthy bitch, you. I suggest you keep that gob of yours shut, do your job, and don't piss me off.'

'Oh yeah, and what would a little midget of a man do about that?' She laughed again.

Looking back with a venomous glare, he hissed, 'I'll have you fucked up.'

'Oh, I see. You're too pathetic to do it yaself, then?'

'You will soon learn that you don't have the clout you thought you had when Vadim had this club. Things have changed, and you will soon be wise to the changes, if you keep fucking me off.'

There was something menacing about the way the man spoke; it was as if he had some muscle to back up his aggressive speech. And something felt odd. She thought for a moment that she recognised him. *But where from?* Most likely, she assumed, it was from here in the club, since he spoke like he knew Vadim. *That was it!* She had seen him once with Vadim in the office. She hadn't taken too much notice. With his large briefcase and wearing a suit, she had assumed he was from the brewery. However, it was the sneer on his face that she recalled. A sneer that said so much. Clearly, she had wrongly assumed he was a midget selling his wares. But she had looked twice that day because Vadim wore a look of anger on his face, before he had two of his best bouncers escort the man out of the club.

She decided not to say another word and instead ignored the man. As she was about to go to the ladies' changing room, to ensure they had everything they needed, the lights reflected off something on the floor. Harper peered down and retrieved a piece of jewellery. She held it up, trying to work out what it was. It had what appeared to be a sizeable decorative hoop with a gold chain and red stones embedded in it.

As Roxy poured the first drink, she leaned into Harper. ‘I see you have discovered another one. I found one last week. Well, it was something similar.’

‘What is it?’ asked Harper, turning it around in her hands, while admiring the intricate detail.

‘It’s Asian jewellery. It’s mad because I haven’t seen any Indian women in the club in full regalia, and I think I would notice a great bleedin’ ring like that dangling from a bird’s nose.’

‘And you say you found one last week?’

‘Similar. It was a bracelet or an anklet, but the chain was very much like that one. I found it by the stage area.’

‘How odd.’

CHAPTER FOURTEEN

By eleven o'clock, Harper was busy greeting the regular customers; their attention and the good wishes lifted her mood until she clocked Nikki lingering around and helping himself to another gin. She decided not to argue with him again; something about him disturbed her. Although she did laugh when one of the regulars, a popular Crystal Palace footballer, asked him for a round of drinks. When Nikki spun around to explain that he wasn't a barman, the footballer stepped back. 'Fucking 'ell, I didn't realise they were hiring ex-circus acts. Are you sure you can see over that bar? You need a pair of high-heeled shoes, mate.'

Harper knew the footballer had had a few drinks and was having fun with his mates, but Nikki didn't see it that way.

'Another comment like that, you flash prick, and you're barred!'

The footballer shrugged. 'Bar me, then, you miserable midget. I'll drink elsewhere and take me mates with me.' He turned to Harper. 'Sorry, love. I can take shit from you, but you see him?' He rudely pointed at Nikki. 'He has upset a few of my friends. I know you haven't been here for a while, but believe me, love, this ain't the first time he has pissed off your punters.'

Harper looked at Nikki, who was glassy-eyed and sneering at the young footballer.

'This ain't her club, so don't apologise to her. She's just eye candy for you bunch of suckers.'

His comment floored Harper. She couldn't understand how the man had so much front. Couldn't he see that talking in that way to the likes of a player from the first team squad at Crystal Palace Football Club would bring down the business?

'I'm so sorry, mate. Let me get you a drink on the house,' said Harper, who was quick to calm the situation.

The footballer shook his head, pulled out a card, and handed it to Harper. 'Sweetheart, I've enjoyed my time coming here. We all have, but that wanker kinda lowers the tone. Take my card, and if the owner gets shot of him, let me know, and we will be back.'

Harper and Roxy stood open-mouthed as the footballer and his entourage left. Suddenly, she realised the club was half-empty. It was then that she understood Nikki was not bothered about the club. She glanced back at the smug-faced bastard who was now perched on a chair ogling the pole dancers as if nothing had happened.

'Roxy, what the fuck just occurred here?'

'That's been happening for a couple of weeks now. That short-arse wanker is so rude. I tried to tell you. Remember?'

'Tried to tell you what?' came a voice from behind them.

Harper turned to see Teddy, who was all bright-white beaming smiles and stinking of Hugo Boss.

'That arsehole who says he's your accountant has to be the rudest man I have ever met. He has locked me out of the office.'

Teddy shifted from foot to foot, his cheeks glowing. 'I thought you weren't coming in.'

'No, Teddy, you assumed I wasn't.'

'Listen, my treacle dumpling, when you were off, I had to make a few changes. I had to get someone in to run the business. In fact, he looks after my other interests as well, so, anyway' – he said, his voice now more upbeat – 'it's less work for you to do, and I don't want you staying behind to cook the books.' He leaned in to kiss her on the cheek. 'You could be doing much better things with your time.'

Fourteen years ago, that kiss and that smile would have melted her heart, but not now. Now, she had to hold back from bottling the man.

‘Have you ever thought that maybe I like to do the accounts, the ordering, and actually *running* this club, as a manager is supposed to?’

Teddy laughed dismissively. ‘Come on, Harper, no one likes to do that. Anyway, I saw your suitcase in the hallway. Eddie’s over the flippin’ moon that you’re moving in, and,’ he winked, ‘I am too.’

‘Teddy, are you even *listening* to me?’

It was clear that Teddy was surveying the club. ‘What? Yeah, ’course I am. Now, don’t you go worrying about Stan Nikki. He is a funny old stick but he’s bloody good at his job.’ He turned to face her. ‘I know how feisty you can be, but don’t rub him up the wrong way. He is helping me make a shedload of money.’ He tapped her nose as though she was a child.

‘Good at his job? Yeah? Well, he’s halved your customers by pissing off the Crystal Palace crowd.’

Teddy was nodding as though he was listening, but, all the while, he was actually scanning the club. ‘Don’t worry, Harper. There’s enough money to be made, anyway.’

Teddy skirted around her and weaved his way towards the new sectioned off area, before she could probe his comment.

Harper kept her eye on him until he stopped in front of three men, who were all impeccably dressed in tailored suits. They appeared like civil servants; however, one man seemed slightly off. He was older, stockier, with thick wavy silver-grey hair and dark sunglasses perched on his nose. Teddy was talking to him, nodding and patting his arm. From nowhere, Nikki appeared. And, instantly, the man with the sunglasses pivoted and turned his attention to him by shaking Nikki’s hand.

Stepping away from the bar, Harper continued to stare, trying to absorb every little detail, because, right now, she had no idea what the hell was going on. *Were the three men villains or genuine businessmen?* she wondered. But when she tried to analyse it, she reasoned that no one would carry out business in a nightclub. Unless, that was, The Click was the business they were discussing.

Maybe Nikki was right; perhaps she should go and work for her aunt. She could do that easily since her aunt had offered her a management position at The Deacons, which had been the larger of her two clubs before she sold The Tone.

Since Cody's death, Desiree had given her two remaining sons, Byron and Dax, a share of the proceeds from The Tone to get them off her back. Byron took his share, put his house on the market, and went to Spain to retire. He couldn't stand the fact that Harper had not only annihilated him but that she was named as benefactor in his mother's last will and testament. So his father's legacy, The Deacons, would go to her. He knew he couldn't argue over the decision, yet he couldn't bear to even look at his mother now or face Harper again. It was no longer a secret that Desiree had left the club to Harper and her sisters.

Lexi was studying to be a solicitor, and Erin had set up a beauty business from a sum of money that Teddy had given her after their break-up. So the pair of them had no interest in working in the club. Charley had her work in the police force and was barely reachable under normal circumstances, and now, she was on the missing list.

Desiree's middle son Dax, however, had a different attitude; he was happy to work in The Deacons and share the profits with his mother, and he had even agreed to give up the weed growing business. Harper had yet to meet Dax. But after what his brothers and his uncle Oggie had put Desiree through – even though she'd heard that Dax wasn't so bad – she still wasn't in a hurry to make his acquaintance, family or not.

Teddy, the three suits, and the midget disappeared behind the false wall, the private VIP area.

Harper was left puzzled. She thought, perhaps with Nikki out of the way, she could have a nose around in the office. But, as soon as she approached the door, she was tapped on the shoulder by a huge man with short hair that looked like a trimmed toilet brush. He wagged his finger and shook his head, before standing in front of her, to block her entrance.

'Move, mate. I need access to this room, if you don't mind.'

The man wagged his finger again before looking over her shoulder and beckoning someone over.

'Excuse me!' Harper tried to move him aside.

'No.'

His accent startled Harper. She stepped back and frowned.

Almost immediately, another serious-looking man appeared. His black trousers, white shirt, and earpiece made Harper swallow hard. 'Who are you?'

'Not your concern. Go back to the bar and do your own job. This room is private,' said the tall muscular man with the grey bristly hair.

His stern features and harsh tone, clearly Russian, compelled Harper to walk away. Nothing made sense at all. *Who were these Russian men?* The original doormen, apart from Paddy, had been Londoners.

With her heart beating fast and her head spinning, Harper decided it was probably best that she leave for the night. Everything about the club was alien to her – except the girls. When she asked Roxy to take over and see to it that the girls received their wages, Roxy frowned.

'Harper, while you were away, ol' short arse, Nikki, took over all that stuff.' She glanced around her. 'You get off. I'll keep my eyes and ears open.' With that, she kissed Harper on the cheek.

'I'll let Teddy know I am going home.'

Roxy shook her head. 'Don't be surprised if you get told to fuck off. No one goes to that VIP section unless one of the girls is called over to supply drinks.'

Harper's heart was still beating at a rate of knots. 'Oh, really? Well, if he tells me to fuck off, he'll wish he hadn't.'

Roxy chuckled. 'I bet he will, an' all.' She had seen Harper bounce a few people out of the club and admired her greatly for it.

'Oh, and see that tall geezer? He's Russian, I think. He's the one with the grey spiky hair. Who is he?'

'I have no idea. I've seen him come in with the midget and go into the office, but he is just one of a few. I told you, Harper, the club has changed. I thought it would be like old times when you came back, but the management, like old fish face midget, is seriously bringing the atmosphere down, and Teddy doesn't care. He is always entertaining some suit or other. He's either oblivious to what's going on, or he has a total lack of interest in the club.'

Harper weaved her way through the loosely crowded room towards the VIP area. It was odd to have a false wall that went up as far as the ceiling to segregate the VIP guests from the rest.

One of her best dancers was on the pole and getting cheers and whistles from punters sitting close to the stage.

Uncharacteristically for her, Harper paused before entering the VIP area. Her palms were sweaty, and her neck felt hot. It wasn't like her to get anxious. She knew that only too well. But perhaps, she considered, it was the delayed shock from the Russian blocking her entrance to the office and his harsh accent taking her back to the torture she had sustained from the Russian traffickers.

Taking a deep breath, Harper walked around the wall.

Teddy jumped up as though he had sat on a wasps' nest. He tried to block Harper's view.

'What are you doing here?'

His words were fast and sharp.

'I came to let you know I was going home.' She attempted to look over his shoulder to see who he was keeping company with, but all she saw was the older man with the silver-grey hair. She clocked he had a large square jaw and a downward smile.

'Yeah, okay. Sorry, Harper. I'm in a meeting. Look, I'll see you at home later, yeah?'

Nervous fear marred his persona. Whoever the men were, he didn't want her to see them or talk to them.

'Okay. Look, sorry about tonight, Teddy. I don't feel well.'

He nodded fast. 'Call a cab and get off home, babe. You do look a bit peaky. Eddie will show you where the medicine cabinet is.'

Harper spun around and walked away. She was glad that Teddy was preoccupied; it would give her time to go through his office. She didn't hang about and drove like a nutter to Teddy's house.

She hadn't had a proper look in Teddy's place before. The only occasions she had visited his home were to take Eddie to football or to the cinema. Now, though, she could have a real tour, and she suspected Eddie would be only too pleased to show her around.

***

Roxy watched as Harper walked out of the club, with her head down, looking thoroughly defeated. She couldn't stand to see her mate like this. It was all wrong. Sliding her hand inside her bag, she pulled out her phone and glanced around to check no one was watching before she dialled the number saved under 'Boss'.

The phone rang a few times before a deep husky voice answered. 'Hello, Roxy. How are you?'

'I am okay, and how are you?'

'Yes, very good. Now, how is the club?'

'Do you mean how is Harper?'

'Well, yes, I do, really. How is Harper?'

She could sense his voice soften.

'She needs you, Vadim. Since Teddy and some fuckwit Stan Nikki took over and started to run the show, things haven't been the same. She has only just come back to work, and Nikki had her in tears, the fucking shit. So is there any chance of you coming to England to rescue her happiness?' She tried to lighten the conversation.

There was silence. 'Vadim, are you there?'

'Yes, I am, Roxy, but I'm not sure Harper needs me.'

'Are you both in denial? Jesus wept, the girl's in bits. Of course she needs you.'

'Roxy—'

Two angry punters called for service as Nikki rudely pointed to her. 'Serve them,' he growled.

'Sorry, Vadim, I have to go.'

'Wait—'

***

When Eddie opened the door, his face lit up. 'You're back early, Mum. I was hoping you would be.'

Harper kissed his forehead. She spotted the game controller in his hand and tutted. 'Eddie Bear, you won't become a marine biologist if you're playing cops and robbers.'

Eddie blushed. 'I have mates online who I play with.'

'Eddie, why don't you have mates over? I mean, you have this bloody great house and—'

She stopped when she saw her son's face drop. 'You do have mates, don't ya?'

'I did have, Mum. Well, one. He was my best friend, Calvin. It's a long story, but we fell out.'

'Tell me. I've got all night, as you can see.' She pointed to the suitcase that was still in the hall.

He walked on through the entrance hall into the kitchen that looked out over the expansive garden.

'Coffee, Mum?'

Harper smiled. 'You're a gentleman. Yes, please.'

As Eddie placed two cups under the dual coffee maker machine, Harper took her seat at the breakfast bar. 'So why did you fall out?'

'Are you sure you want to listen to my boring stories?'

It dawned on Harper that Teddy had never really listened to Eddie. He was obviously too busy making money. 'Sweetheart, I want to know every little detail.'

The coffee percolator hissed and buzzed and finally it spat out two hot drinks. As Eddie handed one to her, she raised her brow. 'Wow, this is very posh.'

Eddie nodded and took a sip. 'Calvin wasn't a best friend, as in friends since babies. Nothing like that. We were both in the same class, and he liked the same subjects as me, so we had lessons in common. I knew, though, Calvin was different, and I guessed he was more sensitive. He was a nerd like me, I suppose – nothing like his older twin brothers, Wesley and Duran. They're into their rugby and boxing because their dad was a boxer. I reckon he was also a bit of a gangster.' He looked up.

'Go on. I am still listening to you.'

Her son smiled, but Harper could see the sadness echoing in his tearful eyes. 'It's fine, babe. Tell me what happened. I am not like your dad.'

'Right at the end of the summer holidays, I was over at his house. His parents were out, his brothers were at some football game, and Calvin and I did something stupid. We smoked one of his father's cigars and made cocktails. I'd never had a proper drink before, and neither had Calvin. After three or four – I don't really know how many because we lost count – I was sick, but I didn't make it to the bathroom. It was all down me. So I stripped off. Calvin was also sick, and he didn't make it to the bathroom either. I had never felt so ill in all my life.'

It was clear to Harper that whatever had happened after that had mentally affected her son.

‘Go on, Eddie Bear, I want to hear the rest.’ In her mind, though, she was one step ahead of her son.

He took a deep faltering breath and stared into his coffee. ‘I don’t know exactly what happened after that. But I woke up with Wesley and Duran screaming at me. When I looked around, I was on their parents’ bed in my briefs and spooning Calvin, who was also only in his pants. It gave the wrong impression. We had done nothing, nothing at all. I don’t fancy Calvin, and, well . . .’ He sighed. ‘They didn’t see it that way.’

‘Didn’t Calvin put them right?’

He peered up, and a tear fell down his cheek. ‘No. He was too scared of his brothers. He didn’t say a word when they . . .’

‘When they what?’ urged Harper.

‘They beat me with a stick or something. It could have been a golf club, I don’t know. But I could hardly breathe, it hurt so much.’

Harper was holding in her rage by repeatedly swallowing. ‘Christ, Eddie, and did your father talk to their ol’ man?’

‘I didn’t tell him because their father came home and caught the twins beating me.’ He ran his hands through his hair and sighed heavily. His chin quivered. ‘I thought I was safe. I thought he would stop them, but they told him I was in bed naked with Calvin, and he just went mental. He grabbed Calvin by his hair and demanded to know what had happened. Well, Calvin said that I had got him drunk, and he didn’t know what I had been up to, while he was out of it.’

Harper was ready to erupt and go to the boys’ house and cause mayhem, but she breathed deeply. ‘Go on, Eddie, what the fuck did their father do?’

‘He grabbed me around my throat and made the boys rip my pants off . . .’ He stopped to wipe the tears away with the back of his hand.

Fearing the worse, Harper had to know the rest. Her heart was rampaging, and her throat was tight. 'What did he do, babe? What the fuck did he do to you?'

'He pushed me out onto the street and told me to fuck off. He told me never to come by their house again, and that I would amount to nothing but a dirty rent boy. So, I had to run home with nothing on, and with the twins chasing and laughing at me.'

'And the mother?'

Tears in his eyes welled up as he shook his head. 'I hoped she would stop them, but she didn't. She just gave me a dirty look.'

Finally, Harper had heard enough. She got down from the kitchen stool and pulled her son into her arms. 'I promise you now, Eddie, no fucker will ever hurt you again.'

Eddie hugged her back, sobbing.

'Now, listen to me,' she said, as she pulled away. 'You tell me everything, d'you hear? I mean, I wanna know everything. Did the boys do anything else to you?'

'Yeah, they did. They told everyone at school I was gay, and every time they saw me, they jumped me, along with their mates. Mum, I know Dad wants me to toughen up, but I can't fight four of 'em. I can't do it because I don't have any mates. I know I'm different. No one wants to sit with me. Even the girls look away.'

Harper stared at her son's sweet face; it was crumpled in pain. 'Eddie Bear, this is serious bullying, ya know. Tell me, how often do you get called gay?'

Eddie shrugged. 'When don't I, you mean. It's all the time. I must be gay, eh, Mum? Everyone else seems to think so.'

'But do *you* think you are, babe? Do you like boys or girls? And before you answer, as I said, it makes no difference to me. I love you whatever.'

He shrugged again. 'I don't know, Mum. I don't know even who I am anymore. I want to be left alone. I don't want to fight because, honestly, I’m afraid of what I might do if I lose my temper.’

For a moment, Harper could hear herself in her son’s words. However, she wouldn’t be afraid of what she might do this time.

CHAPTER FIFTEEN

Harper slept in one of the spare rooms, having been up until quite late playing a video game with Eddie, who was surprised how quickly she had mastered it. As she rubbed her gritty eyes, she rolled over to see the door slowly open, and there, holding a mug of coffee, stood Teddy. He looked flawless in his faded jeans and linen shirt. His blond hair appeared much lighter, and she wondered if, in the morning light, she was seeing the truer picture of the man. He'd possibly had highlights to go with his sunbed tan.

'Good morning, Harper. I bet you slept like a princess in that big bed, didn't ya?'

She smiled and sat up straight, relieved that she had slipped on her Rolling Stones T-shirt rather than slept naked.

'Teddy, can we get something straight.' She tried to keep her tone even, although, inside, she was seething. 'I know I said I would take you up on your offer of staying for a while. Ya know, to see how things pan out, for Eddie's sake, but I didn't leave me self-respect at the door, mate.'

Teddy bowled over to the bed, and ignoring the comments, he perched himself on the edge.

'Teddy, I'm not kidding.'

'Harper, me li'l stocking top, you have nothing I ain't seen before.'

With her jaw shot forward, she glared. 'Don't push it, Teddy. Seriously, I'll pack me bag and fuck off. So, either you give me space and privacy, or I'll go back to me flat.'

'Okay, okay, you can't blame me for trying. You know how I feel.'

Before she even responded, he placed the mug of coffee on the bedside table, stood up, and retrieved a small box from his jeans pocket.

Assuming that the present was an engagement ring, Harper stared at the small jewellery box, wondering where Teddy had got the idea that she would want to marry him. Her frown deepened before Teddy laughed.

'Don't look so terrified, babe. It's not a ring.'

Harper's shoulders relaxed as she accepted the box. When she flipped open the lid, she saw two diamonds twinkling.

'Your short hair suits you so much, Harper, but I think you would look even prettier with a diamond in each ear.'

'*Diamonds?*'

If he had given her this gift fourteen years ago, she would have cried and hugged him so tightly, but this was now, and everything she had once adored about the man was a distant memory. Teddy was not the sweet, kind, caring boy she had once loved; he was Teddy, the man she despised.

He nodded, beaming like the cat that swallowed the canary. 'Yep, they're beauts, ain't they.'

She held the box loosely in her hand. 'They're big.'

He nodded again, triumphantly, puffing out his chest. 'If you want them insured, they are worth six grand.'

And there it was, *the price tag*. She was getting the measure of the man with every move, word, and gesture.

Harper looked at the earrings and then back at Teddy. 'Six grand, eh? I could buy a new car for that.'

Teddy sat back on the bed again. 'No way, not six grand. Anyway, next week, me and you can go car shopping. You can take our boy to school in a fancy new Beemer or a Merc or . . .'

The loud popping sound as the jewellery box lid shut made Teddy jump.

'I bet you thought someone had shot you by the way you jumped, Teddy.'

He chuckled but stopped when he saw how her eyes appeared to darken.

'What's the matter?'

She shrugged her shoulders. 'You don't know me anymore, Teddy.'

'Of course, I do. Fucking 'ell, Harper, we were kids when we met, and we've loved each other ever since. We both know it.'

Slowly and firmly, she shook her head. 'No, you *don't* know me. Not now. We used to be very different. We had dreams once, Teddy. Our dreams. You know. You, me and our boy, our baby, a little three-bed semi in a semi-rural town, just enough to get us by, and a holiday once a year to Spain.'

'Yeah, and we can easily have that a million times over. Look what we can have together.' He gestured around the room with his hand. 'I can have a huge villa in Spain. You can sun yourself whenever you like. We can have our holidays in the Caribbean.' He laughed. 'Skiing in France, diving in Egypt, having the best clothes.' He paused before jumping up. 'Talking of which, how about when you drop Eddie off at school, me and you go up West, and I'll treat you to a new wardrobe?'

'And what's wrong with *my* clothes, Teddy?'

His smile bordered on a mocking grin. 'Nothing, except, well, you can see they're from the high street.'

Before she said another word, he went on, as if he liked the sound of his own voice. 'And you can have the best of everything. Cars, clothes, we can eat in the best restaurants, drink the best champagne. I swear, Harper, we can have it all, and I wanna wine and dine ya and show you that you are my queen. I can make up for everything in the past, show you how truly sorry I am for not visiting you in prison and for all that shit. We have one life, Harper Kane. Me and you, I promise, are gonna live our best life. Believe me, there is nothing I can't have. I mean, there's nothing *we* can't have.' He stopped, smiled, and leaned in for a kiss.

Harper turned away. And there it was, those words. 'There is nothing I can't have.' They would play in her head like an annoying kids' party song stuck on repeat.

Staring at him, she wondered if there were any more layers to him, or had he peeled every inch of mystery and now he'd exposed his true self, the arrogant, self-centred prick, with absolutely no moral compass whatsoever.

She grinned, but not because she agreed with him or was even entertaining his ideas but because she understood the true Teddy Ryder. And to think she believed he had changed for the better. But, clearly, he hadn't. Not one bit. He always wanted what he couldn't have. When they were kids, she loved him with all her heart, and she would spend most of her time with him. But even then, she remembered, the same flaws in his character were there – the clues to the man he would become. When she wanted to be alone, he would pester her for attention until she gave in. When she found out she was pregnant in prison, he wanted the baby. He almost brainwashed her to hand him over. It was all flooding back to her now. Everything that Teddy wanted, he got, one way or another, and so if she didn't give in to his needs, he would move on to the next challenge.

All the sexy winks, the come-to-bed eyes, and the sweet compliments meant nothing to her now. And the two enormous diamonds were merely a reminder that he could afford whatever he wanted, but the sad part was his money was dirty money. He was corrupt, and the more he had, the more he wanted. There was no way Teddy Ryder would ever pedal backwards.

Her phone buzzed, and right away, Teddy was craning his neck to see whose number it was.

Harper snatched her mobile from the bedside table. It was Roxy. She smiled but didn't read the message.

'Who was that?'

Harper raised her brow. 'Er, Teddy, I know you want us to be a couple, for Eddie's sake, but ya know what? I'm not used to being asked questions . . . Like who's texting me.'

Teddy chewed the inside of his mouth. 'No, I know, Harper. I only want to be a more significant part of your life, that's all. I'll leave you in peace to drink that coffee while I make us some breakfast. Scrambled eggs?'

Harper nodded. Without looking at him, she glared at her phone, and as soon as the door closed, she opened the text.

Harper, call me when you can x

Harper slid out from beneath the covers and crept over to the door. Slowly, she opened it and listened for any sound. There was silence. She looked over the vast banister on the landing to the entrance hall below, pleased that Teddy was out of sight.

Tiptoeing back to the bedroom, she closed the door behind her and called Roxy.

It rang twice.

'Hello, Harper. You got me message, then?'

'Yeah, I'm out of Teddy's earshot. Any news?'

'Well, they closed a little earlier than usual last night. There were only a few stragglers left. I think the club's gonna go right downhill with the fucking miserable midget in charge. So, as I was collecting my bag and bits, while the midget impatiently tried to escort me out of the club, I saw him fiddling with the code. He only went and changed the security code to get in or lock up. So before he turfed me out, I said I wanted to have a quick piss before I walked home.'

Harper was standing as far away from the door as possible so that even if Teddy was earwigging, he wouldn't be able to hear her. 'Go on, Roxy.'

'Well, I opened the ladies' window. It's unlocked, but it looks like it's closed. You know what I mean.'

'Yeah, well, then, I might have a nose around.'

'You're the manager. You can do what you like. Don't let the midget make you feel less than who you are.'

‘Thanks, Rox, you’re a good mate.’

‘Oh yeah, something else seemed a little odd, right? When I left, I saw a builder’s van pull up and park right outside the door to the interlinking flat next door. Nothing odd in that, but who pulls up outside a club in a builder’s van with men in high-vis jackets at two in the morning?’

‘Maybe Teddy wants to do up the little flat to sell it?’

‘Yeah, maybe, but what builders start work at two in the morning? Most of the ones I know barely have their hair brushed and teeth cleaned before eight in the morning, and if they are up earlier than that, either their one-night stand is kicking them out, or they’ve shit the bed.’

Harper laughed. ‘You have a point. I’ll have a butcher’s tonight. I take it, they haven’t changed the opening days while I’ve been away, have they?’

‘No, it’s still shut on a Monday. Listen, Harper, be careful. I don’t like or trust these men that work for Teddy, and I have a bad feeling about all of this.’

‘Don’t worry, Roxy, I’ll be fine. And listen . . . Thanks, mate. Really, thank you.’

‘Just be careful.’

When Roxy ended the call, Harper crept to the door and quickly opened it, to the horror of Teddy, who’d clearly had his nose pressed next to it. In fact, he almost fell in.

She stepped back and tilted her head to the side with a knowing smile.

‘Breakfast is ready.’

‘The text was from my Aunt Desiree. She wants to see me.’

Teddy blushed. ‘Oh yeah? What about?’

Harper crossed her arms and smiled again.

‘Sorry, again, none of my business. Anyway, breakfast awaits. Eddie is already stuffing his face.’

Slipping a pair of jogging bottoms on, Harper joined Eddie and Teddy in the kitchen. Teddy poured more coffee, and Eddie shoved the last bit of egg into his mouth before looking up at Harper and smiling.

He was dressed in his school uniform with the backpack already on his back. 'Dad, can you take me? I need to be in early today.'

Teddy gulped his coffee. 'Oh, what? I thought your mum might like to take you.'

'No, Mum's not even dressed. Dad, please, if you're not too busy.'

Harper heard the hint of sarcasm in her son's tone and then clocked Teddy's face, which had now turned to stone. *That remark had seriously narked him*, she thought. *Perhaps the truth hurts.*

'Okay.' He glanced at Harper, who was tucking into the eggs. She knew he had no choice but to drive Eddie.

'Will you be here when I get back?'

Harper shrugged. 'Well, I have to go and see my aunt. Then I want to pop in on Mum, and then I'll be here.'

'Great, I'll see you later then, yeah?'

'Yeah, of course.'

Not feeling hungry, Harper waited to hear the sound of Teddy's car leaving the drive, and then she threw the rest of the scrambled eggs into the bin. It was her chance to get into his office and go through his files to see what the hell she could dig up. She aimed to find out everything she could about the man she would bring to his knees.

She expected his office door to be locked, but it wasn't; in fact, it wasn't even closed. She stood at the entrance and scanned the room for obvious signs of any cameras, but there were none. None that she could see, anyway. And if Teddy asked her why she had been in his office, she could easily say she was looking for paper and pens to make her to-do list.

When she entered the grand room, which featured a large desk and a high-backed office chair, she almost laughed out loud. The place looked ridiculous. Behind the sleek desk and chair was wall-to-wall shelving units filled with books, from George Orwell novels to books on how to get rich quickly. She fingered the classics and grinned. She would lay a monkey on the fact that Teddy had never read one of these. However, she'd had enough time in prison to read widely, and she had – a lot.

A photo of himself on a boat holding up a giant fish was on the desk. But, strangely, there were no photos of Eddie.

Everything was set out neatly. Almost too precisely laid out. The brown leather desk pad with the inset blotting paper was fresh, with no doodles or scribbles. The computer wasn't even plugged in. This room was too immaculate. It was like a show office.

The one thing Harper clocked straight away was the lack of natural light. *How odd*, she thought. There were no windows in the room. Along the right-hand wall there were two filing cabinets. One was old and tattered with stickers on the drawers and a few dents. She recognised it: it was the one he used to have in his office at the scrapyard. She assumed he'd kept the battered piece for sentimental reasons. Knowing she didn't have long, she tugged on the filing cabinet drawer handle and was surprised by how easily it opened. When she peered in, she understood why – it was empty. The next one was the same. Now very puzzled, Harper searched his desk drawers. All she discovered were a few scraps of paper, some paperclips, a couple of pens, and a pencil sharpener. He had moved whatever had once been in those cabinets. And she had a pretty good idea where to.

***

By one o'clock, Harper had showered, put on a pair of jeans and a black jumper, and slid her arms into her black blazer with the gold buttons before driving to her Aunt Desiree's house. She already had a key, but, out of respect, she knocked at the door and waited.

When the door opened, Harper stepped back. She hadn't expected a man to be there. She knew who he was, though. Not that she had met Dax in person, but she'd seen photos of him, and Desiree had kept Harper up to date with what had been going on since Cody's death.

'I can guess who you are.'

His voice was gentle, not so harsh as Byron's or Cody's. He was slimmer, with his long hair tied back, and as Desiree had described him, he was wearing shorts, even on the coldest day in autumn.

'Come in, come in. Mum's in the bathroom.'

Harper walked past him and into the lounge, where a colossal bull mastiff greeted her.

'What the hell is *tha*t?' she asked, staring into the droopy eyes of the most enormous mutt she'd ever seen.

Dax skirted around her. Harper could tell she intrigued him by how he kept looking at her.

'That's Lido, and he doesn't bite. He just eats and shits.'

Harper smiled and patted the dog's head.

'Can I get you a drink?'

Harper wasn't sure if she was supposed to dislike the man or befriend him. It was a problematic situation. After all, she was livid that her aunt's sons had tried to take the club off her by attempting to have her sectioned, and yet if Dax was in her aunt's house, and her aunt was good with that, then who was she to cause a row.

'Er, no, I'm fine, thank you. So is Lido your dog?'

'Nah, he's Oggie's dog.'

Harper felt her throat tighten up at the mere mention of the man's name; she hated him now, having heard the truth about what he had done to her mother, more than she hated anyone, except Teddy.

'So why is he here? Where is Oggie?' She had a sudden uneasy feeling as if the massive lump of a man was about to walk into the room and start another fight.

'Didn't Mum tell you? He's in the hospital. A few days ago, a nurse called Mum and asked her if she would visit him.'

'And did she?' asked Harper, surprised.

'Yeah, he's dying. Some heart condition he has, so he wanted to make his peace.' He threw his hand up. 'Not that he ever could, really, but, anyway, she went, listened to his apologies and pleas, and got sucked into taking on Oggie's dog.'

With that, the dog began snorting and making a disgusting noise as he licked his balls.

Suddenly, Harper and Dax burst into laughter just as Desiree entered the room.

'I see you two have met.' She smiled. 'I'm pleased to see you, Harper. You look better than the last time. How are you feeling, love?'

Harper nodded. 'Good, yeah, a lot better, thank you. I am not here on a social visit, more of a business talk.' She shot a look at Dax.

He held up his hands. 'I'll take Lido for a walk.'

Dax was not at all how Harper had imagined him to be. He came across as gentle-natured, although she had heard he could handle himself. She respected the fact that he would give them their privacy and so she gave him a warm smile. 'Thanks, Dax.'

Desiree, smartly dressed as always in a green woollen dress with a black patent belt around her waist, sat in her armchair and nodded for Harper to take a seat. 'So this sounds interesting. I am all ears.'

'The Deacons is roughly the same size as The Click, yes?'

Desiree nodded. 'It is, but it's not picking up. I dunno if people haven't got the money these days, or they genuinely were coming in for the weed that Dax supplied. I am told it was good shit.'

'I know nuffin about weed, but, anyway, listen. Before I took over managing The Click, it was fairly mediocre. The club was dull, and the only reason the punters came in was for the girls. What if you revamped The Deacons? I mean, do a proper makeover, and turn it into the same kinda club as The Click.'

Desiree chuckled. 'You mean turn it into a bling palace?'

'And there's your new name.'

Desiree pushed herself out of her chair and wandered over to a small bar area. 'Fancy a stiff one?'

'Believe me, Dez, I doubled the takings the moment it attracted all the celebs, including the Premier League footballers. You know what The Click is all about. It sells classy sex, clean-looking pole dancers.'

Desiree poured two gin and tonics. 'And you reckon you could turn The Deacons into a bling palace, do you?'

Harper took the tall glass and smiled. 'I don't just think I can. I *know* I can. I designed The Click. Why not do the same to The Deacons?'

'Yeah, but in reality, Harper, The Click ain't all that far from The Deacons. So why would the celebs come to mine when they have The Click to visit?'

Harper pulled out a card from her jeans pocket. 'This will be the key to your success.'

Desiree took the business card from Harper and read it. She frowned. 'Isn't he that Crystal Palace football player?'

'Yep, and he has walked out of The Click and with no intention of returning, unless a certain person leaves, and that person is not me. He likes me, and I bet I could get him to bring his entourage to The Deacons and open it as well, if you do a reopening.'

As Desiree's eyes widened, Harper could see the excitement. It was like a flickering flame.

'And I have a few other ideas that will get you some new business, but good business.'

They clinked glasses.

'I've got a few grand in the bank. It should be enough, I reckon, to do an overhaul, and I will register the name. I never liked the name The Deacons.' She laughed. 'I kinda like Bling Palace.'

'Hmm, not so sure about the name, but if we're agreed, there's nothing to stop us from getting the wheels in motion.'

Desiree raised her very well-defined brow. 'Us?'

'Dez, in a few weeks, I would love to manage your club, if the offer still stands. And I would like to bring the girls with me. The pole dancers and the bar staff. You'll need more staff, with what I have in mind.'

Desiree clinked glasses again. 'Of course. I would want nothing more than having you around.'

CHAPTER SIXTEEN

The sound of the door opening didn't pull Yalina from her state of self-hypnosis. Sitting cross-legged on her bed, she swayed from side to side, with her arms wrapped around herself as a form of comfort.

'Yalina, what are you doing?' demanded Shabir, with his forehead heavily puckered.

Slowly, she opened her eyes and stared back, showing a complete lack of respect. He was her master, not her uncle. Not that she'd ever loved him as such, but she had loved her father – once upon a time – before he'd sold her to Shabir.

'How dare you look at me like that! And you should be getting ready! Get up, girl. Be ready for when I come for you.'

Yalina stared at him, her face not moving a muscle.

'Do as I tell you!' he bellowed, in frustration. 'You must look your best. You have . . .' He looked at his watch. 'You have fifteen minutes, and remember this, Yalina. Your mother is expecting good news from me.' He pointed a fat sausage-like finger at her. 'It's about you, and you don't want to disappoint her, do you? Now, chop-chop.' He clapped his hands.

Yalina noticed how exhausted and grimy he appeared.

He pulled a large soiled handkerchief from the pocket of his brown slacks and patted his sweaty forehead. 'You know what happens to disobedient girls, don't you?' he hissed, before he slammed the door behind him.

He was right; she did know what happened to disobedient girls, and all the meditation in the world would never remove those vivid pictures out of her head. Throwing her hands to her face again, she pushed her thumbs into her eyeballs, as if she would unsee what she had forced herself to see. However, the whole incident continually played over and over in her mind.

The horrific situation had taken place a few days after Hulou had tried to run for her life. The guards captured her, bundled her into another van, and drove her back to the underground unit. Yalina heard Hulou's haunting screams as she begged for mercy. The sudden silence convinced Yalina they had killed Hulou. If only they had.

The shocking discovery that the guards had ruthlessly kept Hulou barely alive came the same evening when eleven more girls arrived from Pakistan. Settled for the night, with her head on the stiff pillow and the blanket pulled up to her chin, she heard a commotion. There were sounds of girls, some crying, some whispering, and the unmistakable harsh voices of the guards hurrying the girls along the corridor. A few moments later, her door opened, and in the doorway stood a guard whose eyes wandered around with no direction. She'd seen him before and knew his name was Daria. He made her shudder, the way he looked at her. She was terrified of him because he carried a needle and syringe to drug any girl who became feisty, and she was so afraid of needles that he would only have to point it in her direction, and she would fall to her knees. He flicked his head for her to get up and leave the room. With the door open, she could hear the girls, and it was clear from their nervous chattering that they had no idea where they were going or even why. But she knew.

The moment she was off the bed and entering the corridor, Daria prodded her harshly in the back to walk on. She saw the crowd of young women who were barefoot and shuffling along the corridor. They were dressed in western clothes. From the jeans swinging around their ankles and tops too small or too big, they were obviously not their own. Like her, they had been stripped of their traditional clothes and forced to wear the fashion of the Europeans. She presumed it was for a safer passage.

Daria prodded her harder to catch up with the new girls, and as she did, she saw Bina and Sana among them. She bumped into one of the new girls when the guard stopped them from walking on. Instead, the guards escorted them through the see-through swing doors, similar to the ones she had seen near the exit, into a room on the right.

Once inside the barely lit room, Yalina discovered that it was large with a sign on the wall saying ‘No Patients Allowed’. It was then that the room itself confirmed her notion that the building was an old hospital or clinic, and they were probably standing in a teaching room, after she’d spotted the vast chalkboard on the far wall. She gazed around, trying to adjust to the lack of light, while clocking the other signs and posters, some faded and torn, showing medical adverts. A light came on, and all the girls were made to stand against the back wall.

Bina quickly sidled up to her. ‘Yalina, do you know what this means?’ Her voice quivered.

‘No, Bina, what is happening here?’

‘This is when they show us the consequences of disobeying them. Close your eyes if you can, Yalina.’

‘Close my eyes. Why?’

‘Because, Yalina, you cannot unsee anything once you’ve seen it.’

Yalina wanted to ask what Bina meant, but Daria marched over and screamed into Bina’s ear, ‘If you talk again, I will cut out your tongue!’

Bina’s eyes were wide like a bushbaby’s, and she suddenly looked down. ‘Sorry, sir,’ she quickly replied.

He walked backwards, facing all the girls until he was under a single pendant light that shone above what looked like a dentist’s chair. The downcast light turned his features into something that looked quite monstrous. ‘You must watch to appreciate that you will be found if you ever think of running away, and the worst will come to you. You must work off your debt. You understand? The police will bring you back after beating you first if you run away. I will show you what I mean, so that you do understand.’ He nodded to the guard standing by a door on the other side of the room.

Yalina stared, her heart beating so fast. She felt her pulse drumming in her temples.

Suddenly, two guards came in dragging a girl by her arms. Her head was slumped forward, and her long matted hair hung loosely; she was barely conscious. When she finally lifted her head, her eyes were so swollen that Yalina didn't recognise her at first. Then she recalled the yellow sari – it belonged to Hulou. Her beautiful yellow sari was heavily stained with blood and patches of brown. Her feet were swollen and black and blue. It was clear someone had stamped on them. *Maybe the police*, thought Yalina.

The two guards forced the girl down onto the chair and disturbingly tied her wrists to the metal arms.

Yalina heard a few gasps from the new girls, who were undoubtedly as terrified as she was.

Bina whispered again. 'Don't look, Yalina. Please, don't look.'

Daria pointed at the person tied to the chair. 'This girl was brought back to us by the British police. See what they did to her?'

He nodded to one of the guards, who pulled a pair of rusty ancient pliers from his black tool belt.

'Now, you will see what we do once the police have finished with you.'

Yalina wanted to close her eyes, but she couldn't, nor could she turn away. Something inside her was forcing her to watch. Intrigue? Disbelief? It could have been several reasons, but she didn't close them.

Hulou suddenly became fully conscious. Seeing the pliers in the guard's hand, her eyes became wide with terror. She began to thrash about, desperately trying to escape from the chair and the torture she knew was coming her way.

As the guard held her head back, the other one smashed the pliers into her mouth. Hulou screamed out in primal fear, not pain, but absolute dread when he gripped a tooth. Then, there was silent anticipation as she took a deep breath before the guard ripped the tooth from her mouth. Her head fell back as she stared in horror at the pliers being held up for all to see. The tooth was attached to a partial section of bone.

The girls couldn't remain quiet. They screamed and cried like any young women would until Daria yelled, 'Shut up!'

The room fell silent, with only a few sniffles.

Daria then directed the guards to take the girls back along the corridor to their rooms. As the girls left the room they could hear the blood-curdling sounds of Hulou's agonising screams, which were getting louder by the minute.

Yalina could hear her, again and again, begging for the guards to stop. She imagined that the bubbling and gurgling sounds were from the blood pouring into the back of her throat. She had slapped her hands over her ears, the moment she was pushed back into her room. And from then until now, she had fought to remove the vision and the sound.

It was the screams that haunted Yalina; she couldn't unhear them. And she couldn't unsee the man savagely detaching Hulou's tooth. She could only imagine that they had removed all of them.

***

The tooth extraction demonstration was to instil fear. She knew that, and it had worked. Within fifteen minutes, she was in her grandmother's precious sari, and her face was covered in heavy make-up.

Shabir unlocked her door and stepped inside. His shirt had substantial sweat stains around his armpits, and his face was puffy and red. 'Good, you are ready. Now, you must do as you are told.'

He stepped closer and studied her face.

She could feel his breath on her cheeks and smell the sour odour of stale whisky and garlic. She blinked and held her breath, as if his own would poison her.

'You must learn to put the make-up on better. You have the pictures.' He pointed to the magazines on the floor.

Yalina nodded; she didn't speak.

He patted his dripping brow. 'If you let me down, I won't be happy. Do you understand me?'

Yalina silently nodded again.

'Don't look at me as if you can see through me, girl!' He grabbed her arm and shook her. 'What is the matter with you? You must smile, and, Yalina, you have to dance like Hulou showed you. There is an exceptional guest who wants to meet you and . . .' He softened his voice and stroked her cheek. 'If he likes you, you may get to live in a palace. It is a huge place with everything you could desire – clothes, jewels, everything.'

Casting her eyes down, she had heard enough. She wasn't stupid. It was clear she was for sale or for rent. And it was also evident from what Shabir had said that she mustn't let him down. She had heard that he was on his last warning from the Russians, and she assumed they'd held him responsible for Hulou's escape. But although her eyes were cast down, her ears remained open.

'Right, come with me. We must go. And understand this, Yalina. I have gone out of my way for you. So if you disrespect me tonight, I will do more than remove your teeth. I will remove your insides.'

'Thank you, Uncle.'

'What did you say?'

Yalina looked up and smiled. 'I said, thank you, Uncle.'

'Hmm, yes.' He glared, uneasily. 'Good. And keep that smile. Don't look ugly.'

At that particular point, Yalina burst out laughing. The uncontrollable laugh even shocked her. But it was his words 'Don't look ugly' that flicked the giggle switch on.

'What are you laughing at, girl? Stop it, Yalina. You are acting like a fool.'

But she couldn't stop. She was hysterical. The more annoyed he got, the uglier he got. His jowls wobbled, his eyes sank beneath his fleshy eyelids, and sweat dripped down his forehead, along his nose, and speckled his light-grey shirt.

An unexpected slap across her cheek instantly stopped her laughing. She didn't clutch her face but stood motionless, like a statue, her face devoid of emotion.

'Now, move!' he demanded, as he pushed her in the nape of her neck. 'You dare laugh like that. You ungrateful girl.'

The journey was spent in the back of a van again, like before; it was dark, but she was aware of other girls present. She had seen them when the guard had slid the side door open for her to climb in, and the light from his torch had shone in.

As soon as she was seated and they were off, she rubbed her sore cheek. It hurt like hell and stung like a thousand bee stings. But her outburst could easily have resulted in something far worse.

The silence in the van was palpable. She could sense the fear oozing from every pore, the dread curling around in every girl's mind, and the nervous anticipation heard only from their shallow breaths.

CHAPTER SEVENTEEN

Sitting outside her flat in her car, Harper stared at the message – TR - **Where are you? I've been calling. Are you okay? Will you be home soon? xxxxxx Teddy**

She shook her head and wondered if she could keep up the façade. As much as she had a deep-seated hatred for Teddy, which she had mentally forced down in the depths of her psyche for now, to be able to take her revenge, she was also finding the man an irritant, on a more day-to-day level. The texts and the questioning reminded her of the old Teddy, but it had been so different then. She had liked his attention, had loved his jealous streak. She had been immature – very naïve – but at the time, she reasoned it was just his way of showing her he loved her. But as he said, he could have what he wanted.

She replied: **Teddy, stop texting and calling. I am busy.**

TR - **Busy? The club is shut tonight. Have I upset you? Have you changed your mind about moving in? Are you seeing someone else? I thought we could have a family dinner tonight, just the three of us.**

And that was it. He was obsessed with her – not as a person but as a possession. He couldn't stand the idea of her being interested in anyone other than him.

Teddy, I have family business to attend to. I'll see you later.

She looked at her watch; it was seven-thirty. She wasn't worried about upsetting Eddie. She'd half expected Teddy's reaction to her initial text, so when Eddie came out of school, she had FaceTimed him to tell him she would be late back. He'd winked at her as if he knew she was up to something. Lucky for him, he didn't look like Teddy when he winked. He came across as so much more sophisticated.

TR - **I was worried, that's all. I thought the diamond earrings had scared you off. I'll take it slower, I promise.**

He couldn't just say 'earrings'; he had to say 'diamond earrings'. She shook her head again at his words. *He will take it slower.* Again, he assumed that she would get back with him.

Just then, Vadim popped into her head and stirred the fire that burned in her gut and dragged out the feeling of hatred towards Teddy. But thinking about Vadim gave her an idea. Why hadn't she thought about it before? The flat next to the club. There was a way into the club via Vadim's former office. Would anyone know about the secret entrance? She doubted it. It was disguised as a bookcase. Taking a few deep breaths, she pondered over her options of getting into the club unseen. She had two.

***

Before climbing out of her car, she fumbled in her handbag for the door keys to her flat. With her back to the road, she heard a car slow down. It wasn't the type of road where a car would slow down unless they were going to park. As Harper spun around, the black car with the tinted windows shot off before she had a chance to see the driver. However, she thought she recognised the number plate and the vehicle. She recalled Verity getting into the same make of car and the plate ending in EPW. It could be a coincidence, but Harper didn't believe in those anymore.

As she pushed her door open, she was met with a scent, something sweet, with a sage undertone – aftershave. She might not have noticed a few weeks ago, but too many things now were assailing her senses, sending dangerous signals to her brain. Slowly, she crept towards the kitchen, listening for any movement. Seeing the French doors ajar, she held her breath and listened harder for any slight sounds. She hurried for the knives, which had always been her first thought. Dropping her bag onto the table, she snatched two of her sharpened kitchen knives and walked back along the hallway, pushing doors on the left-hand side open with her foot. But there was no one there. Apparently, whoever had been in her home had left.

The intruder hadn't turned the place upside down, but whoever they were, they had been through her drawers and cupboards. And they had even left a few photos on the bed.

Peering closer, Harper recognised them as the ones she had pinned to the wall in her prison cell. She hovered over them, wondering if this was a message for her, or had the intruder merely left them there by mistake? One photo was of her little sister Charley when they were all kids fishing in the River Cray on a hot summer's day. Charley was standing in the river in an old pair of wellies that leaked and wearing a pair of light-blue shorts that had been passed down from sister to sister. Her sun-kissed freckles peppered her pink cheeks as she proudly held up a bucket of minnows and sticklebacks. Unexpectedly, tears trickled down Harper's nose and dropped onto the duvet. 'Please, Charley, be alive. If you are, I will find you, I promise.' Another tear fell until she stood up straight, wiped her eyes, and sniffed.

The previous men who had ransacked her place were unnecessarily reckless, but whoever had rifled through her stuff this time was careful, even gentle. She wondered if Michel had returned. She hoped to God it was him. At least she would know he was alive. All she could do for now was to focus on Teddy's involvement in all of this. And without Michel or her knowing Charley's last whereabouts, they were fucked. She had to do whatever she could, but in the right way, before she would resort to pinning Verity down and strangling her until she told the truth. And that had to be a last resort. Because there would be no going back. Without question, a judge would lock her up for the rest of her life.

She checked every room until she was satisfied that nothing was missing and then returned to the kitchen, where she kept her spare set of keys to the flat next door to The Click.

Tipping her small kitchen pot upside down, she was puzzled – *where were the sodding keys?*

Racking her brains as to where they could be, she tried to remember the last time she had used them. *Was it a month ago?* And it was so odd because there wasn't anywhere else where she would keep them. Returning to her room, she pulled out her handbags from the bottom of her wardrobe and quickly emptied each one onto the bed. There was nothing but a few receipts, a lipstick, and some tissues.

Sitting on the bed, she sighed in annoyance. Her plan – the better option – was not going to work. It would have to be plan B.

After dialling her trusted friend Terry, the cab driver, on his personal phone, she waited. Unusually, it rang a few times before he answered it. But before he could even say 'hello', she heard a very familiar voice in the background shout, 'Tel, wanna another drink, babe?'

'Hello, Harpsichord, how are you doing, doll?'

'Oh, sorry, Tel, are you with me mum?'

'Er . . . well, ya see, it's kinda like, er . . .'

'Tel, I think it's great. You two finding friendship puts a smile on my face,' she replied, sensing the awkwardness in his voice.

'Yeah, that's it. We've found friendship. I meant to tell ya, but with you being, well, ya know, down in the dumps, like, I kinda thought—'

'Terry, it's not my business, but I want you to know I'm pleased, and to be honest, I ain't surprised.'

'Really? Oh, that's such a relief. So what can I do for ya, Harper? Need a ride?'

Harper heard her mother in the background. 'Tell Harper I said "hello". Is she all right?'

'Delores, I think she can hear ya.'

'Tel, let her know I am fine. D'ya think I could borrow you for a couple of hours, or do you have plans?'

'Delores, Harper wants to borrow me. Ya don't mind, girl, do ya?'

Harper heard her mother laugh. 'No, 'course I don't, as long as she brings you back in one piece.'

'Can you meet me at the club in an hour or . . .?'

'Yeah, give me a chance to get my shoes on.'

Harper giggled. 'Oh, I see, so you've got your shoes under Mum's table, 'ave ya?'

He coughed. 'Not quite, but I guess I'm working on it.'

There was no better man for her mother, and if their relationship became a serious one, Harper would be the first to congratulate them. Having her best mate and her mum under the same roof would be the icing on the cake for her.

***

Harper made her way to the club to meet Terry. And like a faithful dog, he was there, parked along the road. Harper pulled right in front of him, and that was when she noticed how happy he looked. In fact, she thought he appeared ten years younger.

Terry even sprang from his cab instead of having to push himself out. Smiling to herself, she noticed that he had lost weight. Clearly, from his smaller waist, he'd been training for the month she hadn't seen him.

'Tel, you look trim.'

He beamed. 'About time I tidied myself up.'

Harper placed her hands on her hips. 'Or is it for Mum?'

He blushed. *That was new*, thought Harper; she'd never seen him embarrassed before.

He clapped his hands. 'Right, so what's the crack?'

She hated to be the one who would turn his cheery voice into a sullen, cold state of concern.

'Tel, I know that you're in a good place with Mum and, well, I would never want to burst that bubble of happiness for either of you, but—'

Terry suddenly grabbed her hand. 'Fuck, what's happened? It must be something bad. I can see the pain written all over your face.'

Harper looked down, defeated. 'It's such a long story. I think I had better get inside the club and fish out the paperwork before I get into it with you, because, to be honest, Tel, I only have half a story. But listen. I think Teddy has moved his paperwork for all his business into the office in the club. There's a bloke called Stan Nikki, a short geezer, a bit like a pit bull terrier with an elastic band tied around his nuts. He's a right mouthy bastard. He reckons he's Teddy's accountant and some type of business advisor, but . . .' She shook her head. 'I dunno. I do know this, though. I need to get into that office while the midget guard dog and his minders aren't there. So will you be a lookout?'

'*Lookout?*'

'Yeah, you know.'

'Harper, I'll come in there with ya.'

She shook her head. 'This fucking Stan Nikki bloke has changed the security code. I can slide in through the window. Roxy has left it open for me, but once I'm in, I will have to go through the flat next door to get out, or all the alarms will go off. Because it's harder to climb back out of the window.'

'I thought you told me some time ago you could enter through the flat?'

'I can't find the keys. So it's gonna have to be the window.'

Terry tapped his stomach. 'I ain't lost that much weight to squeeze through windows.'

Smiling, she winked. 'It's a knack. Anyway, you've got me number. Call me if anyone shows up.'

Terry frowned. ''Ere, I've been dropping you off 'ere many a time, and I've never noticed so many classy-looking cars 'ere. They're all parked along the street.'

Harper shrugged her shoulders. 'I guess someone up the road might be having a party.'

'Monday night? You don't think there are people in the club, do ya?'

Harper shook her head. 'No, Tel, it's shut on a Monday. Anyway, call me if anyone goes near the place.'

'Are you sure you'll be okay?'

'Yeah, positive. As I said, the club's shut.'

Terry looked around him and nodded. 'Hurry up, though, and don't take risks, Harper.'

As Harper jogged towards the club, she said to herself, *if only you knew Terry. If only you knew.*

The alley to the back entrance of the club was well lit. The lamp that used to flicker had been repaired, but what she saw by the door made her pause. There was a cigarette butt still burning. She looked around but saw no one. *Maybe it had rolled from the street*, she thought.

The ladies' toilets were a few metres along from the back entrance. As Roxy had said, the window looked shut, but she knew she could open it. And she was also aware that it wasn't linked to the alarm. As she pushed the window open, she heard music. At first, she thought it was coming from outside, perhaps from a car window left open, allowing Asian music to blare out. However, by the time she had squeezed the top half of her body through the opening, she realised the music was actually coming from inside the building. Her initial assumption was that there was a private party taking place, but no one had mentioned anything to her about such an event. If this was the midget's doing, she would have something to say to him. She had taken an intense dislike to the man from the off because he was not only rude and aggressive but there was also something very underhanded about him. And that was probably it. He was organising private parties, and she guessed that Teddy didn't know a thing about it.

As she slid forwards and gripped the sink, her hands slipped, and she fell headfirst onto the tiled floor. More by luck than judgement, she managed to put out her hands to save herself, with her only injury revealed by a throbbing palm.

Harper had no time to dwell on it before the toilet door opened. And there, looking like something out of a Bollywood movie, she was confronted by a girl who flinched and instantly cast her eyes to the floor.

Harper, too, was caught unawares, and for a moment, she was at a loss what to do next. Almost immediately, the music became louder as the main door to the ladies' toilets opened.

'Yalina, what are you doing, girl? Come quickly!'

Completely caught off guard, Harper didn't have time to hide before she came face to face with a large blubbery-looking Asian man. His eyes were dark and spiteful, his waist was huge, and his beige trousers tapered down to rest an inch away from his chunky black trainers.

'Who are you, and what are you doing here?'

Harper folded her arms and tilted her head. 'What? Who the hell are you, more like? And what the fuck are you doing in my club with this young lady? And, more to the point, in the ladies' toilets?'

The fat Asian man said no more but grabbed the girl by her arm and pulled her out of the room.

Harper followed, ready to let rip, but she was immediately stopped in her tracks.

On the stage was a sea of colours. Young girls, barely sixteen, were writhing their bodies, albeit stiffly, as if someone had put them in a costume and pushed them on to the stage and told them to dance. They were dressed in long sequined skirts with slits up to their hips and what looked like satin bras that the girls could barely fill. Everything about the scene was wrong; worse, to her, it was even disturbing. How could this be a private party? Where were the women apart from the girls on the stage? And surrounding them, some on chairs, some on large cushions, were men, Asian men, of all shapes and sizes, and greedily leering – a couple even pawing at the girls. However, more worrying was the presence of the guards, who were built like brick shithouses and leaning against every wall in the club.

What the hell had she walked into?

As she was taking it all in, she didn't see the fat Asian man call over to Stan Nikki. Before she even had a chance to phone Terry, Nikki was there, straight in her face.

'What the fuck, bitch, are you doing here, and how did you get in?'

Two guards stood behind him by the time he had the words out of his mouth.

Harper knew then there was no way she could have a row, not with the pit bull and his Rottweiler lookalikes.

She held her hands up. 'Look, I was just passing. The front door was locked but I could hear some noise, so I climbed in through the window of the ladies' room to see if anyone was breaking in. Now, I see, you have a private party.'

Nikki looked her up and down. 'You fucking liar. You thought the place was shut, and you were going to do a bit of detective work in my office, weren't you?'

'No, I don't care about your office. Like you said, it's yours now, and me, I get to leave my job at the end of the night, and you can do all the paperwork. It's like a relief, really.'

He looked her up and down, huffed, and then grinned. 'Yeah, and my fucking coat does up the back. What are you looking for, Harper Kane?'

Harper shrugged her shoulders. 'As I said, I thought I heard noises, so I—'

'Bollocks.'

'Whatever, Stan. I will leave you to your party. Sorry to have bothered you.'

As she turned to leave, he roughly snatched her arm and swung her back around. 'Not so fast.'

She stared at his hand on her arm and then back at him. 'Get the fuck off me. You have no right to manhandle me. If Teddy knew—'

'Teddy? Your old boyfriend, *Mr Ryder*?'

Harper frowned. *What was he saying?*

He laughed, mocking her, and then he looked at the two henchmen. 'This one is so fucking naïve.' He chuckled and wiped his mouth with the back of his hand. 'She has it in her nut that I should be worried about what Teddy Ryder thinks.' He poked her hard in the middle of her forehead. 'Get it in that thick skull of yours that Teddy Ryder don't call the shots around here, love. And that makes you a fucking silly billy, who, quite frankly, riles me right up.'

'That's news to me, 'cos as far as I know, Teddy owns this place, so that makes him the boss.'

'Ah, dear, dear, dear me. You *are* in the dark.'

'Well, enlighten me, Stan.' The sarcasm in her voice was hot and sharp. 'So that I know who I'm supposed to suck up to.'

His thin humourless lips tightened. 'You think you're so clever, don't ya?'

Taunted by the idea that he was only cocky because he had two guards backing him, she badly wanted to punch him in the face. Deciding against it, she flared her nostrils and bit her lip, mentally counting to ten. However, anger had its way. 'Ya know what, Stan? I don't know what your problem is, but I am guessing it's stumpy man syndrome, because, for an accountant, you are one disrespectful prick, who thinks he's the Godfather's consigliere, but you're not. You're only a carnival clown who thinks he can count.'

She thought she was safe when she noticed the two guards snigger. However, all that did was wind Nikki up even more. He clicked his fingers.

'You're really starting to boil my piss.' He glanced up at the most prominent guard. 'Drag her out the back, away from here.

Give the sly whore a pasting, and then take her . . .' He paused and grinned like a happy psychopath. 'You know where to.'

Harper's heart suddenly sped up. She glanced at both huge men and knew she was confronted with impending danger. She had to run for it. But, instead of running to the back of the bar, she ran towards the lecherous Asian men, who were so engrossed in perving over the girls on the stage, they were oblivious to what was going on behind them.

But one guard was quicker than her. He grabbed her by her jumper and yanked her so fast and hard that she flew backwards and lost her footing, landing on her side. Her hip felt sore, but that was the least of her worries. If the strength of the guard's tug was anything to go by, she would suffer a heavy beating. The bigger guard now had her in a hold with her arm thrust painfully up her back. She didn't bother to struggle; it was pointless. She would save her strength and pray she could outrun them once she was in the alleyway.

However, as soon as they were in the back room, Nikki stopped them. He stood in front grinning with some sick satisfaction and bellowed, 'Take that, you bitch!' as he gave the first blow to her stomach.

She doubled over, but she wasn't winded. In fact, she realised he was no fighter. She'd suffered harder punches from women in prison.

'Not so mouthy now, are ya!' he yelled again.

He hadn't expected Harper to straighten up and smile before she lifted her leg and fly-kicked him right smack bang in the solar plexus. 'And you take that!'

He flew backwards, hit the fridge, and slid down onto his backside.

For a few seconds there was shocked silence, with the guards seemingly unsure what to do next.

But Nikki wasn't done. Coughing and spluttering, he managed to get to his feet, his face glowing red, matching his bloodshot eyes.

'Get her outside! Fucking rearrange her face and kick the cunt right out of her.'

'Seriously, Stan, what the fuck are you doing? This is madness. I only checked the club was okay. Come on, me and you might not see eye to eye, but what have I ever done to you? Why are you so hateful? You don't even know me.'

Now back on his feet, Nikki curled his lip. 'You think you still run this club? You ain't working for or even shagging Vadim, are you?' He grinned. ''Cos he's long gone, sugar tits, and along with the stubborn bastard went any influence you might have had. You see, I hate having to remind people where they stand in the pecking order. I am better at showing 'em.' He looked at the guard who now had her in his grip. 'Take her away.'

CHAPTER EIGHTEEN

Terry leaned against his car having a smoke. No one was coming or going to the club. He kept his eyes on the entrance to the flat next door. He knew an interlinking door joined the two premises, and he only hoped Harper would appear soon, either out of the club or out of the flat. But something felt very off about the situation. As far as he was aware, she was the manager, and she had her own set of keys to the place. So why all this cloak-and-dagger stuff? He knew almost everything about Harper, and so he sensed something disturbingly profound going on. And knowing her, it was almost certainly something dangerous.

Taking another drag, he noticed a black Range Rover drive past slowly, the tinted windows hiding the driver, but he wasn't too concerned, since the motor continued on. However, what then caught his eye was a motorbike. It stopped a few yards away. The rider sat on the seat with one foot on the kerb as though he was eyeing the club. Terry decided to get back into his cab and watch.

The rider, who was dressed in black jeans, a navy-blue Polo shirt, and a black biker's leather jacket, walked towards him. Slowly, he removed his crash helmet, looking about him as though he was casing the joint.

Terry stared intently, wondering where or if he had seen the man before. But, then again, he had been cabbing for years, so he could have given him a lift at some point. He assumed the rider was a deliveryman or he lived further along the street where there were some Victorian houses converted into flats.

But when the rider stopped and peered into Harper's car, Terry looked on with concern. And as soon as the rider tried the door handle, Terry leaped from his cab and marched over to him. 'Oi, what the fuck are you doing? That ain't your car.'

The rider stepped back and looked Terry up and down.

'Whose car do you think it is?'

'Well, clearly, mush, it ain't yours, is it!'

‘Who are you?’ asked the rider. ‘And why are you watching her car?’

Terry frowned. ‘*Her car?*’

‘Yes, Harper Kane’s.’

‘I know you from somewhere. Who are you?’ He lowered his tone. The feeling that he had seen him before felt linked to Harper.

The rider looked about him. He nodded, knowingly. ‘I’m her brother-in-law.’

As the cogs turned in Terry’s mind, things suddenly started to make sense. He had briefly met Michel when he’d exited Harper’s hospital room with her little sister, Charley. ‘I’m Terry, Harper’s mate. Well, I guess I’m more of a good friend of the family. I’m sort of dating Harper’s mum, Delores, now. Michel, isn’t it?’

Michel nodded. ‘What are you doing here?’ he asked, in a more mellow tone.

Terry pointed to the club. ‘She’s just gone into the club. I’m waiting for her to come out.’

Michel looked up. He knew the club like the back of his hand. It had been one location where he’d had to work undercover for several months before they’d apprehended Zavid’s trafficking gang. It had surprised him when Harper went back to work there, but he had to admire her for it.

‘And so you’re watching her back as well, are you?’

‘How d’ya know that?’

‘The club is shut on a Monday, and I can see you’re guarding her car. It’s merely an educated guess on my part, Terry.’

Terry grinned. ‘Yeah, well, maybe I should let her explain the cloak-and-dagger stuff ’cos I sure as hell don’t get it. And to be frank, I am not sure what’s going on. Anyway, more to the point, what are you doing here?’

Michel smiled briefly. 'I need to see her urgently.'

As Michel lit up a cigarette and offered Terry one, he caught a glimpse of light coming from the back entrance to the club. He straightened up. 'I wonder if she's coming out.'

Terry sparked up his cigarette and followed Michel's gaze. Sure enough, the back door was open, but all he could see was a thickset man all in black and also wearing a baseball cap.

'What the fuck is going on?' said Terry. 'The club's supposed to be shut. Shit! She didn't know anyone would be inside.'

As Terry was about to step around his cab to see for himself, Michel pulled him back.

'No, listen, you have no idea what you're walking into. We'll wait. Let's use our eyes and ears before we make any moves.'

Terry glanced at Michel's anxious face. 'You think Harper could be in trouble?'

Keeping his eyes firmly on the man dressed in black, Michel nodded. 'Yes, probably. And the guy over there looks like a bodyguard. If so, he could be armed. But why is he here?'

'No idea, Michel, but I guess this kind of work is right up your street, mate, ain't it?'

Michel didn't reply. Throwing his cigarette to the pavement and putting it out, he tugged Terry's from his mouth and stamped that out also. 'Sorry, but whilst he can't see us over here, he could see the cigarette smoke.'

Moments later, another guy appeared who looked even bigger than the first man. Holding Harper with her arm forced up her back, with his other hand, he held a clump of her short hair.

It surprised Terry that Harper wasn't hissing and spitting like a feral cat. 'Fucking hell's bells, Michel, they've got her. Look, they've bloody *got her*.'

The first man with the baseball cap began walking in their direction.

Michel pushed Terry down behind the cab. 'Shhh, don't move. Hold my crash helmet.'

Both men were talking to each other, and, in the still air, their voices carried. Although what they were saying sounded gibberish to Terry, Michel knew precisely what they were saying because they were speaking in his native tongue – Russian.

'He said he is going to fetch a car. The other guard told him to empty the boot.'

'Fuck me. *What?* They're taking her away? We've gotta stop 'em.'

'Shhhh, yes. Stay here. Do nothing.'

Terry knew he wasn't quick to think on his feet. So he decided to take orders from Michel, in case he himself potentially bungled it and only made matters worse. Crouching down behind his cab, he watched as Michel nimbly hurried after the Russian. It was dark enough for him not to be noticed because the only street lamps working in this part of the residential section of the street were further along.

Michel followed the Russian wearing the baseball cap at a safe distance and close to the garden walls, so he was less easy to spot. He watched as the man stopped by a brand new BMW 7 Series, a few feet away from the first in a line of street lamps.

When the man pressed the fob to open the car door, Michel launched his attack. He pulled a knife from the back of his trousers, and with one hand, he reached around the man's forehead, drawing him to his chest. The Russian struggled and tried to elbow Michel in the ribs but he was helpless. In one precise and fast movement, Michel ran a knife across the man's throat.

Everything was just a blur to Terry who had been watching intently. And what happened was so fast, that if he had even blinked, he would have missed it. He could see the stunned expression on the Russian's face as he clutched his throat with both hands. The gurgling sound seemed to echo but it soon stopped when he staggered backwards and fell over a low wall into a conifer bush.

Terry's eyes then went to Michel. He didn't look to see if the man was dead. Terry assumed Michel would have known that because he carried on with his mission. Having popped open the car boot, he removed cans of petrol, rope, and black sacks and placed them in the footwells of the back passenger seats. Terry thought he could easily be watching an action movie, but this was real.

Fury vibrated through Terry's body as he glanced back at the enormous Russian restraining Harper. When his eyes flicked from Michel to Harper, a strong sense of helplessness pricked him in the chest. It shouldn't be this way. He should have protected her instead of sitting in his cab smoking fags and being the lookout.

When he looked back at Michel, he clocked he was wearing the Russian's baseball cap. Like lightning, Michel hopped into the BMW, reversed along the road, and continued reversing into the side alley where the other Russian was holding Harper. Panic seized Terry's brain. He couldn't think straight and hoped Michel knew what he was doing. He saw the boot lid pop up as Michel came to a stop. So he would have appeared to the larger Russian that he was the smaller Russian who had driven the car, and before anyone could get a closer look, the boot would block the view. *Clever*, he thought.

After a couple of seconds, Terry saw the boot lid slam shut. He guessed Harper was inside the car, which baffled him. *Why hadn't she fought the Russian off?* He then noticed the Russian tap the car, signalling for it to move on. Holding his breath, Terry was willing Michel on to make a swift getaway, hopefully with Harper safe and sound in the boot of the car. However, what happened next took Terry completely by surprise. Michel unexpectedly put his foot down on the accelerator while the vehicle was still in reverse and mowed down the Russian. Hairs rose on the back of Terry's neck as he heard a crunch, some popping and thumping, like the sounds of Rice Krispies on loudspeaker. The BMW proved it was no lightweight vehicle. Terry assumed that it could take down a small elephant, never mind a grown man. The gruesome sounds were enough to turn Terry's stomach over, and he was no stranger to violence and bones breaking.

Michel shot forward and reversed again, over the flattened Russian. There was something very deliberate, planned, and professional in the second move.

It was only moments ago that Terry had looked into Michel's dark severe eyes. He could almost taste the bitterness somewhere inside him brewing. He had a way of intimidating someone without even saying a word; perhaps it was his poker face and lifeless eyes that had that effect. The violence mixed with the throat-clenching notion that the Russian had been ready to drive off with Harper made Terry feel physically ill. His legs wobbled and his heart skipped a few beats.

Michel drove out of the alley and paused. He stared straight at Terry and flicked his head, indicating that Terry should follow him.

Wasting no time, Terry jumped into action. He got back into his cab, took a deep breath, threw Michel's helmet onto the passenger seat, and tore off, following the BMW.

Michel didn't drive along the main road; he took a few lefts and rights until they were finally on the A21 heading for Sevenoaks. They took a sharp turning along Shire Lane and eventually came to a stop in a field accessed via a small country lane. It was pitch-black, so Terry left his lights on.

Throwing open his driver's door, he hurried to Michel, who had already opened the boot of the BMW. Once Harper managed to ease herself into a kneeling position in the boot, she was faced with Michel towering over her.

'Christ, you bastard, Michel, you're in on it. I fucking . . .' Before she finished, she then saw Terry and knew then they weren't her captors, and they had somehow rescued her. 'What the bloody hell are you doing?' she yelled at Michel, who offered his hand to help her out.

Livid, she tried to push his hand away and clamber out herself. Nonetheless, he gripped her tighter, helping her.

'Bloody Nora, doll. I thought . . . Well, I think if Michel hadn't turned up when he did, Gawd knows what would have happened to you.' He half expected a more relieved response from Harper.

Instead, she turned to Michel, and screamed, 'You fucking fool!'

As soon as her feet were on the ground, he let go of her arm. A deep crease puckered his brow.

'Fool? They were going to kill you! I'm no fool. If a Russian puts you in a boot, you're halfway to being dead, so—'

She angrily pushed him in the chest. Her face was a furious red as the tightness in her throat shortened her breath. 'They were taking me to somewhere. It could have been where they are keeping Charley!' She pushed him again, but emotion weakened her arms. 'But now, you've fucked it up! It could have been my only chance to—'

Michel grabbed her arms to stop her from pushing him again.

She turned her face from side to side, avoiding his sensible gaze.

'Saved her, Harper? Is that what you believed you would do? This isn't a game, and just because some Russian doorman puts you in the boot of a car doesn't mean you were off to the same place that Charley was last seen. You can't be sure that the Russians in the club are anything to do with Charley's case. Russian gangs are many. Russia is a huge place, so please don't go off believing that every Russian you meet has Charley held hostage. And you need to understand, this is my job. It isn't yours!'

'Looking out for my sisters has always been my fucking job, Michel!' she yelled, as she struggled to push him away from her.

Michel could see her tears forming, and he knew she was reluctant to let them go. He threw his arms around her to prevent her from falling to her knees. 'We will do this together.'

'Oh, Michel, I have to find her. I-I have to . . .' she stuttered, almost choking on the sob stuck in her throat. 'And you saw Teddy's name on those contracts.'

'Harper, Russians invest in buildings all the time. Half of London is owned by them. You don't know the extent of Teddy's businesses. He may well be getting into property development but that doesn't mean he has anything to do with Charley's disappearance.'

Terry frowned. 'What are you talking about, Harper? What's going on? I mean, there you are sneaking in through the club window like Catwoman and coming out with RoboCop shoving your arm up your back. And talk of Charley, you've always trusted me. So, will you please tell me what's going on?'

Harper sighed heavily and nodded for Michel to fill Terry in.

'We need to get out of here first. Harper, get into Terry's cab. I need to clean your prints and mine from the car.'

Terry nodded and guided Harper away, expecting Michel to pull out a cloth and wipe the steering wheel. However, Michel was acting very oddly. Firstly, he was rummaging inside the front passenger side. Then he stripped off, down to his boxer shorts, tossed his clothes inside the vehicle, and then his boots, before he dragged out a canister of petrol and doused the car. As far as Terry was concerned, this man was like no one he'd ever met. Michel's speed, agility, faultless deliberation, and quick thinking had him mesmerised.

As soon as Michel struck the match, the car was a bright lethal blaze licking the sky. Terry gazed like a child in amazement. He had burned out a couple of vehicles in his day, but no way was it at all as precise and successful as this operation. His recollection of the event was a bumbling, idiotic mess. He'd had to pour petrol over a car three times before it caught alight, and he and his mates had gone through an entire box of matches. And the result was a few measly flames that danced like fairies, until his best pal, Podgy, threw a petrol can in through the car window and almost blew himself up. How they ever survived their late teenage years was a wonder in itself.

Suddenly, Michel was in Terry's cab. 'Quick! Quick! Drive away now!'

As Terry slammed the vehicle into gear and shot off, he heard a loud boom; it was followed by the sky lighting up like a colossal orange mushroom, confirming that Michel had definitely removed any traces of fingerprints.

'So a duster didn't cut it, then?'

It was the first time Michel smiled. 'I like to be thorough.'

'Is it safe to say that my place is probably the best option for you two right now?'

Terry looked over at Harper who was staring out of the window; she hadn't even flinched when the car blew up. He gripped her hand to let her know he cared, and she squeezed it back, but she didn't turn to face him. He guessed she was crying, and he assumed it was because Charley was missing and Teddy was somehow involved. And somewhere in the centre of the issue were Russian soldiers or bodyguards or whatever they were. He realised they would be a scary reminder of what she'd been through.

CHAPTER NINETEEN

It was eleven-thirty by the time Terry reached his house in Farnborough Park, and all three occupants of the car were sitting in silence. He assumed Harper was still consumed by bizarre thoughts because, in reality, who gets nabbed by Russian bodyguards and thrown into the boot of a car, only to be rescued later, and then witness the car you were in being professionally blown up as though a bomb had hit it? He turned his car lights off before he drove into the drive. He didn't want any curtain-twitchers getting an eyeful.

Not that there was much chance of that. His drive was private. A person would literally have to walk up past his huge front lawns and peer down the side of his house to see his cab. On the other side of the drive, there were twelve-foot-high bushes.

Hurriedly, he got out of his vehicle and opened the door at the side of the house, nodding for Harper and Michel to join him. Of course, it would raise eyebrows to see a man dressed in boxers walking into his house, especially on a cold autumn evening.

Michel smiled as he passed Terry, who was still holding the door open for them.

Harper, with her shoulders slumped, followed behind. She took a seat in the kitchen while Michel awkwardly looked around him. Harper had been inside Terry's house a few times, but Michel hadn't.

Without words, he looked at Terry and then down at his partially naked body.

'Oh, shit, yeah, sorry, mate. I'll only be a jiffy. I think maybe a tracksuit will be the best fit.' Terry chuckled. 'My clothes will drown you.'

While Terry was out of earshot, finding something suitable for Michel to wear, Michel took a seat at the long white wooden table opposite Harper. 'Are you going to tell Terry everything?'

Harper chewed the inside of her lip, and her eyes were red when she peered up. 'You mean what we didn't tell him back there where you pretty well firebombed the BMW? Yeah, there's no point in hiding the truth, whatever the hell that is now. Because I am becoming more and more confused as the hours pass, and Terry, as an outsider, might put things into perspective better than I can.' She paused. 'Why were you at the club, anyway?'

'I came to find you. I went to your flat, and you weren't there, but I saw Verity. She didn't see me, but she's been following you. They can't find me, and I'm too, as your sister would say, "cute for them".'

Harper huffed and gave him a wink. 'She probably didn't mean cute in that way, Michel.'

Terry came back looking extremely pleased with himself. In his arms were a pile of clothes and a pair of trainers. 'I forgot I had these. I went shopping without my glasses. I ended up buying the wrong poxy size. They're new and will probably do you a turn. The trainers are a size eight. Any good?'

Michel's face beamed, which completely threw Terry. It was the first time he'd seen the man smile properly. It seemed to change his own perspective of Michel, seeing him more as a man than a machine.

'Thank you. I'm a size eight, and this is very kind of you.'

Terry waved his hand. 'No problem. Now, shall I get us all a brandy, or would you prefer a hot drink?'

'Brandy for me,' said Michel, holding his smile, while quickly slipping on the tracksuit and sliding his bare feet into the trainers.

Harper nodded, her eyes still heavy. 'A double for me, please, Tel.'

Terry didn't bother to go off to the lounge, where he had a small bar area. He pulled a bottle from the cupboard, grabbed three glasses, and poured generous measures.

‘So what’s going on?’

Harper gulped back her drink and shuddered as the liquid burned her throat. However, she reached across the table and helped herself to another shot. ‘It’s a long story and you know some of it, yet maybe I can sum everything up. Charley is missing. She was on the job, on the plot, they called it. Anyway, Michel, maybe you should explain what’s happened.’

Michel gave Harper a sympathetic smile. ‘Charley was acting undercover for a trafficking gang. Well, I assume so because that’s her speciality, if you will. Her operations manager trained her for the role. He was a good cop by the name of . . .’ He faltered. ‘It’s escaped me. I can’t think straight.’

Terry clocked his Adam’s apple bob up and down, and Harper instantly averted her eyes from the bottom of her glass to look at Michel.

‘His name *was*—’

‘Peter Bracken,’ interrupted Harper.

‘You remembered.’

‘Yeah, I remembered because when you mentioned him before, you looked like you were considering something, but you explained that it’s possible to swap tactical operation managers. Are you telling me he’s dead? If so, how?’

‘That was one of the things I wanted to mention to you apart from the fact that Verity has been following you. Peter Bracken was found dead in his home yesterday. At this stage, the word is he fell down his stairs and suffered a broken neck.’

‘But you think there’s more to that, don’t you?’ replied Harper.

He nodded. ‘I do.’ He leaned forward. ‘I called a trusted friend in the force, and he informed me that Verity has made it known that she has reason to believe that I have gone rogue, and there’s a warrant out for me now.’

‘Why would she do that if you are only trying to find your wife?’

Terry didn’t interrupt. He could see this was serious business.

‘Harper, there’s more to all of this.’

Suddenly Terry’s phone buzzed. It was Delores who was checking that he was okay. Erin had taught her mother how to text, and she was now ping happy. As he read the message, he looked at Harper. ‘Did you leave your phone in the club? Your mother has been trying to call you?’

She frowned and pulled her phone from her back pocket. ‘No. Oh, shit,’ she said, as she looked at the black screen. ‘My phone has run out of battery.’

Terry pointed to the USB socket with a cable attached next to the microwave. ‘You can charge it up over there. It’s a booster charger.’

Harper instantly thrust the cable into the phone. ‘I hope my Eddie hasn’t been trying to get hold of me. He’s a sensitive lad and will be worrying. I was supposed to go back to Teddy’s house tonight.’ She sighed and rolled her eyes. ‘What the hell am I gonna do now? I can’t go back there. What would Stan Nikki, his accountant, have told him? He couldn’t say to Teddy that he had two Russians throw me in the car and take me away.’ She stopped and looked from Terry to Michel. ‘And, by the way, how *did* you rescue me?’

Terry coughed. ‘I’ll tell her.’

Michel nodded.

‘Rambo, here, killed one of the guards who went to fetch the car, and then he used the man’s motor to reverse over the second guard once you were in the boot.’

With her eyes on stalks, Harper’s mouth fell open. ‘So you’ve actually killed *two* guards?’

Michel nodded. ‘They would have killed you, Harper, otherwise. Guys like those don’t take prisoners.’

‘Well, two down, and about another six to go.’

‘*Six?* What are you talking about?’

‘Inside the club, there were about twenty ol’ Asian perverts pawing over a handful of young girls dancing like they hadn’t a clue what they were doing. I couldn’t tell how old they were. Maybe sixteen. They had thick make-up caked on, so it was hard to gauge. But surrounding the performance were these guards, all in black. They reminded me of Zavid’s Russian soldiers who were involved in trafficking those kids.’

‘Don’t you think it would be wise to call the police?’ interjected Terry, with a scowl on his face.

‘And what will they do, eh? Stan would pass it off as a private party, and the club’s licence sadly allows for those,’ Harper replied.

‘But Russian guards? Underage girls?’

Harper shook her head. ‘They may not have been doing anything wrong – simply dancing, and there is no law against that. And besides, Stan seemed too cocky, and he wasn’t bothered, which makes me suspect the police wouldn’t touch them. He sure as hell ain’t as thick as compacted pig shit. He might look it, but he’s a clever tosser.’

‘But he’s pushing his luck having you taken away, and, well, what exactly were they going to do to you?’ asked Terry.

‘Stan demanded the guards rearrange my face, kick the cunt right out of me, and take me to, well, you know where to,’ replied Harper, using air quotes for the words used by Nikki.

‘But it makes no sense. Teddy owns the club, and you say this dickhead ordered the guards to batter you?’ queried Terry, leaning back on his chair and shaking his head.

‘Yeah, but he also said that Teddy wasn’t the man who called the shots, or words to that effect. He was even taunting me about it.’

Michel stood up and began pacing the floor. 'I'd hoped there were some details in that glove compartment of the BMW, but it's a hired car, probably under a fake name. I've got to make a plan.'

As soon as Harper's phone had enough battery life, it began churning out messages, one after the other. She stared at the endless missed calls from Teddy and the texts, asking where she was.

She showed them to Michel. 'He is persistent, this fucking arsehole.'

'You sound like you hate him,' said Terry.

'I do. I really do. He killed Paddy or had Paddy killed. He had Vadim mowed down and forced him back to Russia. And he's bullying my son. And if that ain't bad enough, some older lads from school are also bullying my boy.'

'Seriously?'

'I shit you not, Tel. My son is having a right hard time, and I'm not gonna stand by and let it carry on.'

'You've never let on to me that you thought he killed Paddy. I had no idea. Why would he do that?'

'Jealousy. Simple as that. He wants me to himself.'

'A bit extreme, wouldn't you say?' replied Terry, his face wearing a deep questioning look. 'So why move in with this jealous, I assume, unhinged killer?'

Harper glanced at Michel. 'Do you wanna explain while I make a call?'

Michel retook his seat and told Terry about the information on the tablet that implicated Teddy as potentially being involved in some way in human trafficking.

Harper wandered into the huge lounge away from the two men and dialled Teddy's number. It rang once, and she waited, listening to his breathing.

‘Harper, where are you?’

She could tell right away he was anxious.

‘I told you I had family business to attend to and that I would be late. My phone died, and when I charged it up, I had a million and one missed calls from you. What the fuck are you doing, Teddy? I’m not your wife or even your girlfriend, so why are you bombarding me?’

‘I was worried, that’s all. Where are you now?’ His voice wavered, a telltale sign that he was nervous.

‘With a friend of mine. Why?’

‘A friend? Are you okay? I mean . . . er, will you be long? Are you coming back to mine or . . . ?’

‘I dunno yet. I just have a few things to talk about, that’s all.’

‘Talk about? Like what? And who’s this friend? Is it a bloke?’

‘Just personal stuff. And no, Teddy, it’s not a fucking bloke, for Christ’s sake.’

He laughed nervously. ‘You know me. I just worry about you, that’s all.’

Michel leaned against the doorway, listening. She turned to him and smiled.

‘Oh, before I go, Teddy, who exactly is this Stan Nikki, the accountant?’

She was still staring at Michel when she said it and then she turned her phone on to loudspeaker.

‘Er, why do you want to know that? I mean, it’s an odd question. Who exactly are you with?’

‘I’m on my own right now, so who is he?’

‘He, er, he is the man who looks after my business and my accounts. He’s like an advisor, and believe you me, girl, he is gonna make me a rich man. I’ve already put me order in for a brand spanking new Aston Martin. And you, me little love muffin, will have pride of place beside me when we're whizzing through the country lanes in Devon.'

'Who else does he work for?' she snapped, ignoring his fantasy plan.

'*What?* What's that got to do with anything? Harper, has something happened? Tell me.'

'It doesn't matter, Teddy. Anyway, I've gotta shoot.'

'Wait, hang on.'

Harper sighed heavily as she ended the call.

'He has either learned to act or he is a clueless wanker.'

'I think this Stan wasn't lying when he gave you the impression that Teddy isn't the one calling the shots. That's not to say he isn't involved somewhere along the line, though.'

'Yeah, like owning The Click.'

Biting his bottom lip, Michel stared at the floor in deep thought. 'If they have so little regard for you and know the connection between you and Teddy Ryder, then it suggests a hierarchy is in place. And so we have to assume that Ryder isn't at the top of the food chain. And to be blunt, as you Brits say, if the Russians are involved, then it's big business, and I don't know if Ryder has that much clout.'

Harper listened intently. 'But he does have an awful lot of money.'

'Yeah, he probably does, and I bet every pound is dirty. Getting mixed up with any Russian gang is risky. If he has invested in them, believing they play fair, he will have a seriously rude awakening. It's in the blood of every Russian to make money. Their business structure is usually highly complex. When you think you have found the boss, there is always someone above him, and if he is corrupt, everyone else is. It is why your sister and I are trained to understand these matters and weed out the people at the top of the pyramid. However, we both know that when you cut the head off the hydra, a thousand will grow in its place. With Peter dead and Verity now enforcing a warrant for me, I am helpless, and I don't have access to anything. Also, they would have changed my passwords and passcodes by now.'

'Do you think the girls in the club were trafficked?'

He shrugged his shoulders. 'Who knows. But if the girls who were in the club are linked to Charley's disappearance, then I would guess so. That was her job. She specialised in human trafficking, and she was good at it. Bloody good, in fact.'

They both stared off, deep in their own thoughts, until Michel straightened up. 'Oh, yes, also, the last photo that Charley took on that tablet was of a contract. I couldn't make out the signatory because the photo was blurred. I can only assume that Charley was in a hurry at that point because she was too precise, too professional, so something disturbed her. I have a friend who is good with photos, but he's away on holiday. However, as soon as he comes back, he'll give me some idea of the name.'

'So it looks like it's you and me that Charley has now.'

Terry reappeared, having spoken to Delores. 'And me.'

'Thanks, Tel.' She peered up with an empathetic smile tugging at her lips. 'I need to collect my car. I can't be without my wheels, but I bet the place is swarming with police now.'

Michel laughed. 'The place won't be running alive with police. They were Russian guards, who, by the way, would be working for a Russian, not Teddy, and not, by the sounds of it, this Stan guy either. And so the Russians involved would clean up their own mess. They won't want the police looking into their business. That's the last thing they will want. But I will check it out, anyway, when I collect my motorbike.'

Michel drank the remainder of his brandy and peered at the bottom of the glass. 'I've had a thought. You are too hot to go back to the club and get into the office.'

Harper nodded. 'Yeah, go on. What do you have in mind?'

'You remember Katie French? Frenchy?'

Harper smiled. 'Yes, how could I forget her? She gave me a hard time when I started work at the club. And by Christ, she was good at her job. I had no idea she was working undercover.'

Terry walked over to the bar in the lounge and found another bottle of brandy. 'Top-up, anyone?'

Michel didn't answer; he held up his glass.

'Katie has been taking time off to look after her mother. She works mainly in the office on a more part-time basis, so she can still get access to the main computer for me. She could get into the club and do what she does best – act undercover as a member of staff. Surely, this Stan Nikki won't know every girl who works there. I believe she could be really useful to us and she *will* want to help. She is, after all, Charley's best friend. I will call her.'

Terry glanced up at the clock. 'It's gone midnight, mate.'

Michel laughed. 'Katie won't mind that. She is used to it. We all sleep an inch from our phones.'

Using a burner, he looked up to the ceiling and then dialled one of the many numbers he'd memorised.

Sure enough, Katie answered after two rings. She sounded as bright as a button. 'Hello.'

'Katie.'

'Fucking hell, Michel. What are you doing? Where are you?'

'Katie, what's happened?'

'Michel, half the force are out looking for you, and I hope they pissing find you. Peter was a good man. He trained me, you bastard. Why did you have to kill him? Isn't working for the Russians enough for you? I knew you would never be a fully-fledged Brit. Once a Russian soldier, always a fucking Russian soldier. Well, I hope you get hung, drawn, and quartered. If I find you, I'll kill you myself.'

'Whoa, hang on. That's all a lie!'

‘I trusted you, and I cannot believe that you and Charley, of all people—’

Harper had heard enough. She snatched the phone. ‘Katie, it’s me, Harper. What do you mean by “I cannot believe that you and Charley, of all people”?’

There was a pause. ‘Harper, your sister has gone rogue.’

‘Don’t be so fucking ridiculous. If you were her best mate, you’d know that my sister would never do such a thing.’

‘Harper, I’m truly sorry, but Verity showed me the evidence.’

‘What evidence?’

‘A total of two hundred and fifty grand was deposited in Charley and Michel’s joint account. One of the last messages from the other officer who was supposed to be working alongside Charley, before he went missing, stated that he believed Charley was feeding the Russians information for payment. We know how it works. But she must have underestimated the Russians because they like to leave a clean trail behind them, so they would have had her killed. And we guess they have killed the other officer because all communication ceased.’

Michel put his finger over his lips.

Harper understood, but she wasn’t letting it go. ‘What you’ve just reeled off sounds a bit wishy-washy to me. Do you have facts, dates, times, and names? I mean, anyone could put money into an account.’

‘What? A quarter of a million pounds? I have seen her bank statement, and Verity would never make an accusation like that unless she had proof. For crying out loud, our operations are so professional. Where we work isn’t a gangster club, ya know.’ She lowered her angry tone. ‘I’m sorry, Harper, and I’m sorry about Charley. I struggled to believe it. But it’s true.’

‘But you know her only too well. She just wouldn’t do that. I know she wouldn’t.’

'Living a legend as we call it, or going undercover, we have been known to get used to another life. The money becomes more exciting and appealing, not to mention the power it gives you. We live a fine line when doing our job, and I'm afraid both Charley and Michel have crossed it. And I know Michel, you can hear me, you rat.'

'Let me get something clear, Katie. You may have been her best pal, but I am her sister, and I am telling you she would never do that. She wouldn't because I served fucking twelve years for her. She'd never do that to me. Now you understand this: if you say that my sister has gone rogue one more time, I will show how fucking rogue I can be. Don't you dare fuel this ridiculous idea that Charley is a wrong 'un. 'Cos she ain't! No way. And do you think I would entertain her husband if I wasn't so sure he was right?'

'Harper, I need to think about this.'

'Well, do it quick 'cos I might need your help.'

'*Me?*'

'Yes, Katie. I don't believe my sister is dead. I need your help to find her.'

'Why should I help? I'm not convinced.'

Michel took the phone back. 'Because Charley sent Harper her work tablet, and it contains a lot of information about the Russians and others. Why would she send it out if she was corrupt, eh?'

'Harper, is that true?'

'Yes, it's true. I had to open it with a password that my sister and I had as kids.'

'What information was on the tablet?'

Harper gave a short laugh. 'You think I'm stupid? Well, anyway, at least we know where we stand. It seems the force is more fucking corrupt than the gangsters.'

'I'll help. What can I do?'

‘Really? Look, it’s after midnight now. Meet me later today,’ said Harper.

‘You say the place and time and I’ll be there. I owe it to you for what you did to save those girls.’

As she ended the call, she handed Michel the phone. ‘You’d better give me your number, in case I need it.’

He smiled, took her phone, and tapped in his number.

She returned his smile. ‘Cheers. Now tell me, did you know that money was in your account?’

‘No, I haven’t checked my account. I’ve been too preoccupied. And Charley always checked our joint account. Anyway, Verity would no doubt have had our account frozen by now.’

CHAPTER TWENTY

Yalina was still shaking as the guards pushed the girls into the back of the van. They hadn't even been given time to be seated until, one after the other, they were forced inside like tinned sardines. The squeals and cries were not for drama. They were real. No one dared cry out unless it was an automatic response to pain. They were all terrified of the Russians. And worse was Shabir, with his sly pinches, swift kicks, wandering hands, and harsh words breathing down their necks.

They had arrived at the club in two vans, but only one was taking them back.

The girls were all bunched up on the floor as the doors slammed shut. And it forced some to sit on the laps of others.

'Yalina, are you okay?' whispered Bina.

'Yes,' she replied.

'Sana, are you okay?'

'It doesn't matter anymore,' she replied to Bina. Her words were cold and robotic.

'Sana, what did that man do to you?'

'The same as the last man, and the man before him, and the one before him. They are cruel beasts, and I would rather die now than pay back the debt.'

Bina put her arm around Sana and pulled her close. 'Don't say that. One day, Sana, someone will come to rescue us. Keep that thought in your head.'

'I think someone did try to rescue us. The tall slim lady with the short blonde hair climbed in through the toilet window, but I saw the guards taking her away. She is probably dead now,' said Yalina.

'Yalina, please, don't ever talk to anyone. Never assume they will rescue us. And besides, they could easily have someone in disguise to test us. So don't say a word. You saw what happened to Hulou.'

Sana heaved and heaved and was suddenly vomiting as they turned a corner.

Another girl screamed. 'Oh no, you pig! I am covered with puke! As if being squashed in this horrid vehicle isn't bad enough.'

'I'm sorry, I'm sorry,' cried Sana.

'Sorry? I have the disgusting smell all over me now. Couldn't you have held it in until we stopped.'

'Shut up. When it's your turn, you will probably be sick too,' hissed Bina, protecting her friend Sana.

'My turn?' questioned the girl.

'Yes, er, what's your name?'

'It's Zuhr, and what do you mean by "my turn"?'

'Yes, what do you mean?' asked a second girl.

'How old are you, Zuhr?' asked Bina.

'I am eighteen, but my father said I am to say I am fifteen years old. That way, I will be favourable. They will pick me to dance in the shows.'

'What do you think those men are paying for? To watch us merely dance? No! We are dancing to show off our bodies while they decide who they will pay to have sex with.'

Zuhr gasped. 'No, that's not true. My father said I was to be a dancer, like in the movies. They are choosing who will be in a show.'

Yalina had heard enough. 'Ha! A Bollywood film?'

'Yes, yes, my father would never lie to me,' Zuhr indignantly replied.

‘Wake up. There is no Bollywood show, and why would you even think that, when you all saw how they tortured Hulou? That’s not Bollywood, is it?’

Zuhr began to cry. ‘No, you have to be wrong. What happened to that woman is something else. It wasn’t meant for me to watch. They made a mistake.’

‘Did you not hear the guards? We must do as we are told. We are prisoners, locked up, fed virtually dog food, and ordered to pay back a passage fee. And not by dressing up and dancing, but by sleeping with grown men. Those men at that place.’

‘No, no, they were old and fat and smelly and . . .’ snivelled Zuhr.

‘And wealthy. They were dressed in the finest clothes. They can pay for us. It will be our only way to freedom. We have no choice.’

Silence filled the van as the girls digested the finality of the conversation. The only sounds were the diesel engine and the clanging as the van drove over the bumps. But it was yet another message that they were, in essence, merely slaves.

Finally, the van came to a stop. The back doors opened, and the guards grabbed the girls by their arms, pulled them out, and literally threw them onto the ground like sacks of flour.

Zuhr, who had been quiet for the rest of the journey back, suddenly jumped up. As the guard grabbed her arm and tossed her, she landed feet first, hoisted her skirt, and ran like the clappers. Unaware of what was happening, a guard was about to drag the next girl out. But then another yelled something in Russian, and suddenly two guards pulled out their guns, pointing them at the girls while one guard took off after Zuhr.

Yalina willed Zuhr on to escape, to find help, not from the police, but from someone with an ounce of compassion.

However, any hope of escape was dashed. The guard caught Zuhr up and smashed her body to the ground.

As she scrambled desperately to get up, he bent down, snatched her ankles, and dragged her back towards the van. The sharp shingle cruelly ripped the bare skin of her arms and the sides of her pretty face. She screamed and begged for him to stop, but he wouldn't.

While the other guards looked on and laughed, Yalina gazed in horror.

Zuhr tried to twist and wriggle to stop her flesh from being burned down to the bone. Eventually, when the guard reached the other girls, he stopped and let Zuhr go, but she was covered in blood. Her cheeks were red raw and weeping, the tip of her nose was dripping with blood, and her arms were a wet sticky mess from having the skin abrasively scoured away.

Zuhr was shaking in pain. Yalina could see her teeth chattering and understood that the girl was going into shock. Her torn skin looked so sore that Yalina wondered if Zuhr would ever recover. But the girl had gumption; Yalina gave her that.

'Sho-ot me,' she stuttered, as she got to her feet. 'Please shoot me. I cannot do what you ask of me, and I will not do what you want. I won't give up my body to any man except to my future husband. I won't!'

Shabir appeared from nowhere; he must have been a passenger in the van. 'Shut up, Zuhr, and you will do as you are told.' He slapped the open wound on her face.

'But I can't.'

Shabir puffed up his chest to its full size, and Yalina assumed he was about to lose the plot.

However, he was distracted when Casper playfully nudged a younger soldier called Lenin. They spoke in Russian.

Yalina felt her blood run cold when she saw this younger guard confidently wink and join in. She had hoped he would have a smidgeon of compassion. But she was wrong: he was out to impress the older guards.

Suddenly, Lenin grabbed Zuhr by her shoulders. 'So I will show you how you do it. Come with me.'

'She is a virgin and valuable to the right customer. What are you doing?' implored Shabir.

Lenin pointed his gun at Zuhr. 'You don't ask me, Shabir.'

Instantly, Shabir shut up.

Yalina could see Zuhr's posture slump.

Zuhr's head bowed down to her chin as Lenin walked her to the van and demanded she climb inside. Without quibbling, she did as he told her. He closed the door behind them, to the mocking applause of Casper and another guard.

Before the guards rounded up the girls to escort them back inside the derelict hospital, a beam of light lit up the area, and Yalina could hear car doors slamming.

Heading towards the guards was a tall man with a ponytail. Yalina recognised him as Yuri. Accompanying him was Daria. The guards instantly stood erect, as if Yuri was an army colonel.

Yalina glanced at Shabir, who appeared ill at ease, especially when Yuri looked in his direction.

As Yuri walked towards Shabir, the sudden echoing sound of a gunshot stopped him in his tracks. It came from the van.

Yalina's heart was in her mouth. Poor Zuhr, she had believed that her father had sent her to England to perform in a Bollywood movie.

Yuri stormed towards the van and pulled open the back doors. He faced a naked girl, clearly ravaged by the unsavoury ordeal. Her face was covered in blood, her eyes were wide and terrified, but, more shockingly, she pointed a gun in his direction.

Yuri didn't move except for his eyes as he glanced down at the guard sprawled out on the floor of the van. One side of his head was missing, and as Yuri looked to his left, where he could hear a dripping sound, he saw fragments of the guard's brain and skull sliding down the inside of the van door.

Zuhr's hands were shaking uncontrollably. She waved the heavy gun, and her target could literally have been any of them, the state she was in.

Yuri instantly put his hands up. 'Put that down. If you shoot me, they will kill your entire family.'

His deep voice was demanding, and his words were like ice cutting through her.

Again, Yalina willed Zuhr on, this time to fire the gun at Yuri, but, instead, the poor girl, with her face drained of blood, had indeed had enough. She fell to her knees, dropped the gun, and covered her eyes, sobbing.

In a flash, Yuri retrieved the gun, and in one fluid and precise motion, he shot her in the head. The tremendous force of the bullet hurled her onto her back, and the sobbing instantly stopped.

A wave of gasps filled the dark sky. Once again, they had shown the girls the ruthless wrath of the Russians.

Yuri then marched towards Shabir, and with the gun still in his grasp, he belted Shabir around the face. 'These girls were to remain as virgins!'

Shabir wiped his hand across his swollen and bloody lip. 'But I asked that guard not to take her inside. I said she was a virgin and—'

Yuri stood with his hands on his hips, his head tilted from left to right. 'You're in charge of the girls! Are you telling me that you couldn't stop him from taking one of the girls for free?'

Shabir nodded violently as if his life depended on it.

This time the force of Yuri's backhander sent Shabir pivoting and him ending up on the ground, where he scrambled around to get to his feet. 'But he did,' protested Shabir. 'What could I do? I was not holding a gun. It was him. He held the gun to her head, and then he pointed it at mine.'

As he was talking, Yuri turned to Casper.

Casper shook his head, and in Russian, he told Yuri that what Shabir was saying was a load of bollocks.

Yuri stared at Shabir, who loosened his tie, swallowed hard, and brought a trembling hand to his sweaty forehead.

With a sinister grin, Yuri enjoyed seeing Shabir squirm. 'I see you would stab anyone in the back to save yourself.'

A frown flickered across Shabir's brow as he digested those words, and of course, Yuri was right. He would say anything to save himself.

'No, but-I-I will not be accused of something I didn't do. Look, Yuri, I was trying to protect your girls. Zuhr was worth good money, and she was fifteen and stunning. I had Mr Hussein offering ten thousand to take her for a weekend while he is in the country.' He nodded and gave a satisfied smile as though he had just moved the winning chess piece.

But among the young girls, one wanted revenge for him bringing her to this awful country. And so with a feeling of nothing to lose, Sana spoke up. 'No, she wasn't fifteen. She was eighteen, and Shabir pretended she was younger.'

Yuri shot a look at Sana. 'Who said you can speak?'

'I am sorry, Mr Yuri, but he is lying to you.'

'Shut up, you little whore!' said Shabir, as he lifted his hand to strike her.

Bina pulled Sana back, away from his line of fire. 'Mr Yuri, she is telling the truth. Zuhr was eighteen.'

'Be quiet, you stupid girls. You are not here to speak.'

Yalina glared at Shabir, and with all the hate she had for him, she knew she had to join in. 'No one could have asked for Zuhr because she didn't dance. She hid in the toilets all evening. No man saw her.'

Shabir's face reddened. He lunged at her but lost his balance.

'Stop!' bellowed Yuri.

Daria stood behind him, glaring at Shabir. He was licking his lips and grinning like a four-year-old who had just shoved the ginger cat down the toilet and gotten away with it.

Shabir instantly froze to the spot, his face sculpted in fear.

Yuri looked at Yalina. He studied her for a moment. 'You are not like the others, are you?'

His eyes returned to Shabir. 'Is she educated?'

'No, no! I would never select someone like that. No, not an educated girl.' His words fell out of his mouth fast and furious.

Yalina's dark eyes flashed, and her nostrils flared. 'Liar!' It was her chance to turn Yuri against Shabir; her way to at least see justice for this sinful life she would live now or die.

'How dare you!' he yelled, before Yuri gripped him tightly around his throat and squeezed.

'You greedy slimy man. You had orders – rules to be obeyed – and you have broken them too many times. Now I find that you have brought educated girls here.'

He let go of Shabir.

'No, no, she's not educated. She's just a village girl. She fetches water from the well and carries it for five miles. She—'

'Liar! I have never fetched water in my life. I go to school. I am studying to be a doctor.'

Yuri turned to face Yalina. He was surprised that she wasn't looking down like the other girls. Instead, she was holding her head high.

'School?'

Yalina nodded. 'Yes, to study medicine.'

Shabir glanced from Yuri to Yalina and back again, desperate to think of a way to stop the conversation.

'You want to make people better, cure people of their illnesses?' asked Yuri.

She shook her head. 'No, I want to make money, and, in my country, there is no such thing as a poor doctor.'

Yuri laughed. 'Hmm, yes, very clever and focused.' He turned to Shabir. 'And that is why I never have educated girls on my books. They do not do as they are told. They have ideas of their own – dangerous ideas.'

'I'm sorry. I must have misunderstood. Her father said she carried water, and I am as shocked as you are, Yuri. We can dispose of her, and she will cause no trouble.'

'It is not her who has caused the trouble, but you. And I am not sure what I should do about that.'

Shabir fell to his knees, clasping his hands together. 'Please, Yuri. I apologise for the misunderstanding. I will have more girls, and I have some already coming. They're beautiful girls. Hey, you can have them for free, no charge.'

Yuri tutted before shaking his head. 'Get up.'

'Thank you, Yuri. You won't be sorry.'

Yalina smiled sadly to herself as she tried hard not to fear the inevitable. She knew, given half a chance, Shabir would skin her alive, but she was proud that she had at least had the gumption to stand up for the girls in an attempt to take him down.

Through clenched teeth, she heard Shabir say, 'You will pay for this, Yalina. I will make sure your mother is put to death. And your father shamed.'

The thought of dying at his hands was one thing but the idea that he should use her mother as a threat forced her to spin around. 'And also, Mr Yuri, the girls are not all virgins,' she blurted out.

Yuri had his back to Yalina; he turned to face her. '*What* did you say?'

She flicked a wary look at Shabir. 'I said, not all the girls are virgins. I am not, and I was, but Shabir took that away from me.' She took a deep breath, waiting for a spiritual backlash for lying.

‘Stop it, girl. Why are you saying this? I never . . .’ His voice petered out when he saw Yuri’s eyes narrow.

Yuri shook his head. ‘I told you that you were never to help yourself, and Dominica told me you had a few freebies. But the virgins? My God, you feel you can devalue them?’ He inclined his head and glared.

‘No, I’d never do that. You know I’d never do that.’

‘He raped me too when I first arrived,’ said Bina.

‘And me,’ said another girl, who looked to be only thirteen.

‘And me also,’ said another girl.

Yuri glanced from one girl to another as they all nodded or shamefully looked down.

‘Daria, nail his cock to the post.’

With a grin and a chuckle, he replied, ‘My pleasure.’

Shabir’s attempt at an escape was dashed within seconds as two guards hurried to assist Daria. Forcing Shabir to the floor, they ripped his trousers and pants from his body.

Shabir let out an alarmed high-pitched scream. ‘No. Ahh, please, no!’

As they lifted him to his feet, Yalina couldn’t help but glare at him. She wanted to soak in the terror on his face, for the revulsion he had put the girls through, and probably countless other girls too.

Resigned to the fact that his fate would be imminent, Shabir’s face turned grey, and his eyes glazed over in a thousand-yard stare as if the shock had consumed him. He was dragged to a post.

Daria laughed as he skipped to his car, opened the boot, and returned to the post with a rope, hammer, and nails that he held between his teeth.

Shabir's legs buckled, and he retched through a series of dry-heaves. 'No, I beg you. I will pay you all my money, everything I own. Please, take it. Everything. Just don't do this.'

With a sickly eager grin, Daria carried on with his work. However, it took three of them to keep Shabir still as he desperately thrashed about to free himself. But after Daria punched him in the face a few times, the guards managed to wrap the rope around his chest and the post. Finally, once the guards held Shabir in place with his monkey nut-sized penis dangling between his legs, Daria removed a nail from his mouth.

Shabir looked down but could hardly see below his fat gut. 'No, no, please, no!' he screamed, as he felt Daria yank his penis, position the nail, and with a swing of the hammer, ram the nail through his manhood and into the post. The pain shot up his legs, into his groin, and vibrated along his spine. He assumed that was it, but no, Daria hammered another and another. Each time the pain got worse, until, finally, Daria slipped and hammered a nail right through Shabir's testicle. The shock and agony forced Shabir to lose consciousness.

Yalina watched. A small smile tugged at the corners of her mouth.

CHAPTER TWENTY-ONE

Much to Harper's surprise, she slept comfortably in one of Terry's spare bedrooms. Michel had also stayed over in one of the other spare rooms. The only reason she woke up was that she could smell bacon cooking. It was a warm homely smell that she had lacked growing up and never had in prison, but now, if she had guests over, the first thing she would offer them in the morning would be a full English or a bacon butty.

Pulling her jeans and black jumper back on, she shuffled into the bathroom. And then, staring into the mirror, she noticed her eyes were a tad bloodshot – the brandy last night. After splashing her face with water and combing her hair with her fingers, she rubbed her throbbing temples and made her way to the kitchen.

Michel was reading a newspaper while sipping a coffee. He looked as fresh as a daisy. No one would have known that he had drunk almost a bottle of Terry's brandy.

Harper, however, was hung-over.

''Ere ya go. Get ya laughing gear around that,' said Terry, handing her a mug of coffee.

She sat down and groaned. 'My head.'

Terry placed two tablets in front of her. 'They're only paracetamol.'

'Cheers, Tel.'

'A good fry-up will help that sore head of yours.'

'Lovely. Sounds good to me.'

Michel folded the paper and placed it beside him. 'Terry.'

Terry was sliding a fried egg onto a plate. 'Yeah, mate?'

'Would you mind if I stay a couple of nights? No one knows where you live, and at least before they arrest me, I'll have a chance to find my wife.'

‘No worries, mate. I have plenty of room as long as you treat it like your own. I ain’t one for waiting on people.’

‘I appreciate it very much.’

‘Oh, by the way, while you two were snoring your little heads off, I drove back past the club, and it was as dead as a doornail. No filth, no Russians, only a couple of work vans, and a geezer in a high-vis jacket.’

‘Great, I need my car,’ said Harper.

‘No!’ said Michel, in a firm tone. ‘They will find you in your car. Verity is following you, and you don’t believe that whoever these Russians are they will let it go, do you? You were instrumental in the murder of two of their men, and they won’t let you get away with that.’

‘No, I guess not, but I need to see my boy and . . .’

Terry placed the breakfast in front of her. ‘Forget the car.’

She realised then that she was acting stupidly and recklessly. ‘Okay.’

‘I’ll hire one for you this morning. You tuck into that before it gets cold, and I’ll make a few calls.’

Harper was so used to being in control that it surprised her when Terry took on that role.

She tucked into the fry-up and savoured every mouthful. ‘Tel, this is delicious.’

But Terry didn’t answer; he was elsewhere, too busy on the phone.

He returned five minutes later with a beaming smile. ‘All sorted. Finish your coffee, and we can pick up a hire care. It’s all ready for you. A silver Golf. Inconspicuous, it will do you a turn.’

‘Cheers, Tel. I am really grateful. You know that, don’t ya?’

Terry placed his hands on her shoulders and kissed the top of her head. ‘Anything for you, Harper. You deserve so much more.

How you helped save those kiddies, it's the least, I can do, sweetheart.'

She stopped drinking her coffee, and suddenly frowned. 'Tel, did you mention work vans? Were they outside the flat next to the club?'

'Yeah, why?'

'Roxy told me there were workmen going into the flat, but that was like in the early hours of the morning. I wonder what they're doing there?'

Terry shrugged his shoulders. 'Teddy's probably sold the flat, and the new buyers are doing it up.'

'But Roxy said they were there when she left the club at two in the morning.'

He shrugged again. 'I don't know – shift work maybe.'

As soon as Harper's phone buzzed, Terry pulled it from the charger and handed it to her.

'It's Katie. She said to meet at the club at seven this evening.'

Michel looked up at the clock on the wall. 'I wonder why the club? Maybe she isn't aware that Vadim sold it. But it's not a bad place to meet. It should be safe enough. It's hardly the ideal place for a set-up. There is only one road to the club and out again. And it would be too easy to see if Verity's team was surrounding the area.'

Harper placed her mug on the table, and her eyes narrowed. 'If that Verity bird turns up, I will serve time 'cos she needs a good bashing. I don't know why I don't just meet up with her and hold a gun to her head. She'll sodding tell me where my sister is then, won't she?'

Michel shook his head and sighed. 'You can't hold a gun to someone's head. She would have you back inside, and besides that, we don't know what her involvement in all of this is, just yet. All we do know for sure is she wanted me to believe Charley was dead and then she tells you that Charley is missing and *possibly* dead and also Charley had gone rogue.' He let out an exhausted breath. 'Or she is simply after the information on that tablet because it could bring down someone who is deemed to be highly significant – say the Russian mob's top boss. If that was the case, she would receive a commendation and that would impress her father.'

'And would she go to all these lengths – like ransacking my home and making out that you've gone rogue? I don't get it.'

'That's because she is ambitious, and, like I told you, her father was the police commissioner, and she sucks up to him as if he is some kind of god. It's sickening, but what do I know about family? Mine were all crooks who eventually turned on me.'

'And if her father has retired, why is she trying to impress him? Surely, there is the new commissioner she needs to suck up to.'

Terry laughed at her comment.

'Her father may have retired, but he is still important. He is highly regarded, and I understand he holds a major position in the Freemasons, and at the gentlemen's club where he drinks with the High Court judges, and he also plays golf with a few MPs.'

'Oh, I see. He's a pompous brown-nose prick.'

'I don't know what that means, but yes, probably.'

'It's all a bit extreme, and it seems, she is now accusing you of murder.'

He nodded. 'Yes, but that may be a ploy to have me dragged into the station.' He sighed again. 'Harper, it's easy to get carried away, and that's when sometimes you have to take a step back and digest the facts, instead of allowing your mind to go along the single thought track.'

She nodded, knowing what he meant.

***

Yalina hadn't slept much at all. Every thought shot through her head. Where was her mother? What would happen to her now she had spoken out? Would they kill her because she was intelligent, and what would happen to Shabir? Would they fix him up and allow him to carry on with his job, or, if not, were the girls going to be left locked away to starve to death?

The rap at her door made her bolt upright. She stared at the door, willing it not to be Shabir because she knew he would literally boil her head in a pot.

Instead, she saw Yuri and his wonky-eyed brother ducking their heads to step inside the room. Yuri was handsome; he was very tall and immaculately dressed. His navy-blue trousers fitted him perfectly, and his cashmere jumper was loose enough not to outline his muscular physique. She thought he looked gentle and kind, but she knew he wasn't.

Quickly, she jumped to her feet and stood to attention as if she were part of an army inspection.

'Yalina, is it?'

She peered up and then proudly lifted her chin. 'Yes.'

'Come with me,' he ordered, as he walked out of the room.

Daria followed him, and as soon as they were in the corridor, Yalina waited for a guard to escort her, but there wasn't one. She gingerly peered out of the doorway to see Yuri wave his hand to follow him.

Her legs felt like jelly as she walked a few steps behind him.

A car was waiting outside; it was a long black vehicle. She paused and looked to her left, where they had tied Shabir to the post and tortured him. But all that was there was the solitary post and a pool of blood on the ground. She wondered, at first, if he had bled out, but her science lessons told her he couldn't have; a nail wouldn't do that. When she saw the two lines and a trail of blood, she then assumed that they had murdered him and dragged his body away. This was merely a part of the horror she was living in – blood, pain, sex, and murder. And at that point, she realised they could kill her at any moment. As she stepped inside the car, she instantly felt the heat warm her cold bones. They had kept her in the room with no heating, and she had slept shivering and then waking up shattered from the constant shaking.

Yuri and Daria sat opposite her. The glass partition between the driver and the back was dark, so she couldn't see who was driving. Not that it mattered. She didn't know anyone in this country anyway.

'Do you want a drink?' Yuri asked.

The thought of something other than water made her mouth salivate. 'Yes, please.'

He lifted a flap that covered what appeared to be a centre leather table, and inside was an arrangement of drinks.

He gestured with his hand for her to help herself.

She glanced at his face, wondering if this was a test or a trap, but when she glanced back at the assortment, she decided she would take a can of cola. She'd only ever had cola once before at her cousin's wedding, and she hoped one day to be able to experience the taste again.

As she peeled the pull ring, the can exploded and its contents of sticky fizzy liquid flew over Yuri, drenching his cashmere jumper.

Yalina gasped in horror, her eyes wide with fright. 'I'm sorry, I'm sorry. I didn't know.'

He laughed, pulled a serviette from the side compartment, and dabbed the cola from his jumper. 'Accidents happen. Don't panic. Enjoy the drink. Next time, let me open the can.'

She stared in disbelief and was immediately suspicious. He was acting too nicely for someone who could order a killing or torture someone at the drop of a hat.

'Thank you, and I am sorry. I have never opened a fizzy drink before. Maybe there is a science behind it.' She smiled, hoping he wouldn't find her openness to speak as being impertinent.

He leaned forward. 'What is your ambition, Yalina? Money, knowledge, independence?'

She took a mouthful of the sugary drink and enjoyed the bubbles dancing on her tongue.

'All of those.'

'Would you like to make a lot of money?' His head tilted slightly to the side as if his eyes were boring into her soul, like Kaa, the snake, in Rudyard Kipling's *The Jungle Book*.

She smiled. 'Of course. I come from a family who are not poor, but my father lost his business and his house, and we became destitute.'

Suddenly, she recalled the accusation made by Shabir. 'Oh, but we were not so poor that I would carry water from the well. And I did go to school.' She remembered her father's words before Shabir took her and her mother away. She had been told never to bring shame on the family. And to do as she was told. She had no idea at the time that he had sold her.

'Never mind what Shabir said, okay. He is gone. Now the girls back there, do they all speak English?'

'Probably not. Some may do, though.'

'And you can speak in their language?'

'Urdu, yes.'

'You understand that you must pay your passage fee back to me?'

She nodded, wondering where this was leading.

'Good, Yalina. Now, what would you want for the girls?'

Yalina had no idea what he meant, but she decided to say what came from her heart. 'I would want the same for them as what I would want for myself. A decent place to call home, money, and never ever to have to sleep or dance for a man again, unless I am married to him.'

Yuri grinned. 'And if I could give you some of that, would you be happy to work with me?'

'I don't understand.'

‘It’s straightforward. You do as we say and manage the girls, and they will never have to sleep with a man.’

Daria chuckled. ‘Or a woman.’

Daria’s grin was short-lived. He was instantly silenced by a dig in the ribs from Yuri.

‘They will never have to sleep with or dance for a man again. They will be given good food and sanitation, a warm and comfortable bed, television, and free time, but I must add they have to work for me to pay off their debts.’

‘They won’t have to sleep with men?’

He shook his head and tapped her knee. ‘No! Never.’

Yalina frowned. ‘So what will they have to do? Will they be hurt in any way?’

‘No, they will not be hurt. I will explain what they will be doing nearer the time.’

‘And what if I say no?’ Her words came out before she had even contemplated them.

Yuri didn’t answer at first; instead, he studied her face before saying, ‘It’s very simple, Yalina. The girls will continue to dance and make money to pay off their debts by sleeping with clients, and my men will not feed them anything other than’ – he leaned back and laughed – ‘other than pig food. And your mother, sadly, will have to face the consequences of *your* actions.’

‘*My mother?*’ She felt her insides churning at the mere thought of her mother being hurt. She had seen enough to know that their punishments were brutal.

He nodded. ‘Yes, she is paying back *her* debt by working as a cleaner, but I can very easily stop her work and do with her as I wish. And the not knowing, Yalina, will forever play on your mind. Did I kill her? Did I chop off her hands? Did I remove all of her teeth?’ He looked down at his hands, turning them over. ‘Did I murder her with my bare hands? Or did I nail her to a post?’

His dark eyes peered up from beneath his lashes as a crooked grin graced his face.

'I can assure you, the guilt will darken your mind like a growing tumour and it will rip out your last droplet of happiness.'

He paused for effect and then said in a cheerful voice, 'So what do you say, Yalina? Is that a yes?'

She nodded, but reluctantly. 'I have no choice, and you know that.'

She had to have the last word. It was a trait her father had tried to slap out of her for years. She was seven by the time he'd managed to silence her. He had struck her so forcefully that she had fallen into her two-year-old little sister and made her nose bleed. From that day on, she stopped having the last say – until now. Maybe she wanted Yuri to slap her face because it overshadowed her guilt, knowing that she would be leading the girls into another form of slavery, which she was not privileged to know just yet.

'You do have a choice, but all choices have consequences. Some are good ones, some are bad. This life is cruel, and everyone in it is after something. You must learn that it's a dog-eat-dog world, and unless you want to be the dog being eaten, you must learn to be the dog having the feast.'

She nodded again because what he said was so true – well, it was in her world, at least.

'Great. Now that's settled, we will get along very well, Yalina. You will come to my house, and I have new clothes for you. After all, you must look like the boss. The girls must listen to you.'

His Russian accent appeared to have softened since she had first heard him in the corridor of saris when Hulou had escaped. She suddenly shuddered when she thought of the poor woman.

And again, she spoke, without thinking. 'Hulou. Will she be working with me?'

Daria laughed. 'No, she was barbecued.'

Yalina would have assumed that comment was meant to be a joke, but now, nothing the Russians did would surprise her.

'And Dominica?'

Silently, Daria licked his lips and offered her a knowing smile, leaving Yalina to guess the obvious.

To save her mother and herself, she realised that she would have to go along with whatever this new role was to be.

***

As the car stopped and the door opened, Yalina, for a moment, felt like a movie star. *Could she pretend she was someone she was not?* she wondered. In front of her was a huge house, and by the door stood a man dressed in black. No doubt he was another one of Yuri's guards. He hurried over and whispered something into Yuri's ear, and that was when she saw the usually chilled-out Yuri suddenly begin to flap.

He looked around and nodded for the guard to take her around to the back of the house.

She sensed there was someone inside of greater status than himself or at least of equal importance. She remembered her father's expression when her grandfather pulled into the drive. Her father would clap his hands and order everyone back inside the house to ensure the place was tidy. He would also shovel the youngest girls to the back of the house if they appeared unkept or scruffy. Then he would stand to attention before getting to his knees with his ritual of kissing his father's feet. All the feet kissing never made the slightest difference; her grandfather didn't offer to bail out his only son – her father – when he needed him to. She assumed her grandfather knew her father had sold her and that he simply didn't care. She wasn't so hurt because she had never really liked him much anyway. He either looked at her with sly eyes or he completely ignored her.

The guard guided her by pressing his hand into her shoulder. Finally, she was facing a small entrance door much lower and narrower than the main one. She guessed this was the servants' entrance from when the house was built in 1700, according to a plaque over the door.

Yalina was escorted through the long hallway with doors to the left and the right where there were small walkways leading to other rooms. The grand house was more like a hotel, with panelled walls, elaborate sconces, and fancy oversized paintings. In front of her, she could see a vast lavishly decorated lounge, which she'd only ever seen in films and on the TV, before they had to sell it.

The guard suddenly pushed open the door on the left, just before the large lounge area. He pointed for her to go inside. *Either he didn't speak English or he was mute*, she thought.

Once she was inside the room, he left, leaving the door ajar. She glanced around at the grandness and couldn't help but gently allow her fingers to dribble over the plush velvet chaise longue. It felt so luxurious that she wanted to lie down and feel the comfort of its fibres. Instead, she sat down with a straight back in exactly the way she had seen Queen Elizabeth do so and waited to be called.

She could hear arguing and a man's voice bellowing. He did not sound Russian at all. She imagined him to be in his sixties, maybe older, but his tone was full of authority, like that of an English headmaster. Then she heard Yuri's voice cut through the air. 'Andrew, you cannot come to me and make demands. I have the project completely under control, so stop interfering in the side of the business which has nothing to do with you. Now, any more talk of pulling out and I will remind you, my friend, that if this business is exposed to the police, I can leave this country like that.' He clicked his fingers. 'I have the transport, the money, and the means. You, however, will be left here and answerable to your own people. Remember, I have insurance that guarantees you will not be a silly man. So, stop making waves. Be patient, my friend – be patient. Soon, the new plan will be in operation, and we will be making more money than you could imagine.'

The conversation intrigued Yalina, and so, with her curiosity getting the better of her, she stood up and peered through the tiny gap in the doorway. She couldn't see anyone, so very gently, she pushed the door a little wider, until, suddenly, she saw the man Yuri was arguing with. Unexpectedly, as he turned his head, the light caught one of his eyes, and Yalina recognised him as the man with the silver hair whom she had seen when Hulou had gone missing.

As soon as he spotted her spying, he bellowed, 'Who is that girl? Why is she here in this house? Now, she has seen me!'

Yalina gasped and pulled away from the door. With her heartbeat racing, she felt sick. She assumed Yuri would kill her for this. Sitting on the chaise longue, she covered her eyes and waited for the backlash. But there was no sudden rush to have her dragged out. In fact, the yelling appeared to have calmed down.

After a few minutes, Yuri appeared in the room and demanded that she stand up. Gingerly, she removed her hands from her face and rose to her feet. This time she kept her eyes to the ground.

'Right, I will show you to your room. I have had some clothes sent from the shop. I think you will look better with your hair cut short. It will give you a more modern style so you will not stand out so much, and there will be fewer questions.'

'That man, was he mad at me?'

Yuri placed his hands on his hips and stared at her. 'You are not significant. It doesn't matter. You are one of my girls, nothing more. He understands that now.'

Those words resonated with her. She was indeed insignificant, a term that she understood and could relate to, especially when she was a child. Her father had always said he wanted boys, not girls. She wasn't an essential member of their family. Never had been, in fact.

'Who is he?' she asked, feeling more at ease.

Yuri frowned. 'Let me remind you that it is not your place to ask questions. I will let this matter go on this occasion, but you listen to me. I don't owe you any answers.'

Yalina nodded and lowered her gaze again.

CHAPTER TWENTY-TWO

It was just coming up to three o'clock when Harper collected the hire car. Earlier, at lunchtime, she'd called Eddie to say she would be picking him up from school because she needed to talk to him.

Harper drove over to St Olave's Grammar School where she waited for her sister Erin and her mother. After the long discussion informing them that Eddie had been bullied not only by older lads but by their parents, they agreed that this situation needed a firm hand and should not be left to Eddie's headmaster – who had a reputation in the community for being something of a snowflake – to sort out. Terry, seeing himself as a family member, agreed to help.

Forty-five minutes later, the Kane family were outside Eddie's school. Erin and her mother were sitting in Harper's Golf. While they waited, Teddy called, probably some twenty times, and continued with his barrage of text messages begging for her to answer him. Finally, as Harper stared at the screen for the umpteenth time, she decided, reluctantly, to return his calls and messages knowing that she wouldn't get a minute's peace, otherwise.

After a few rings, he answered. 'Harper, I've been—'

'Yeah, a fucking pain in the arse! You keep on texting and calling. I swear, right now, you're like static on a radio station. What the hell is the matter?'

'Oh, I was worried. You said you'd be back later.'

'Teddy, how many times do I have to tell you, I am not your wife? I am beginning to think the idea of moving in was a mistake. You're doing my nut in.'

'I'm sorry. Look, I worry that's all. You're Eddie Bear's mum and—'

She stopped him dead with a cutting remark. 'I am Eddie's mum when it fucking suits *you*. I wasn't when you were shagging me sister, was I?'

'Harper, what's got you so upset? Look, I'll back off. All I ask is that you let me know where you are.'

'*Why?* I mean seriously, Teddy, why should I? What's the big issue with you having to know my every sodding move?'

There was a pause, and she could sense he was thinking. She could even visualise him biting his lip.

'Okay, I'll be honest, babe. My business is a little kinda risky.' He half laughed. 'You know how it is. You play with fire, and you can get burnt. Well, I've built a business by, let's just say, shaking hands with a few nasty people.'

'What are you saying, Teddy?'

'Anyone with my kinda money is a target, yeah?'

'No, Teddy, not everyone is a target just 'cos they have money, unless, of course, your money is dirty money, and it has attracted a few undesirables, and you are in over your head.'

He laughed again. 'Christ no, babe, nothing like that. Yeah, maybe I've done a bit o' business with a few, let's say, villains, but I'm not in over my head. Anyway, I wanna know that you're safe, okay? And the club is a bit of a target, if, of course, anyone wanted to cause me grief. I'd rather you not go there anymore. I'll pay your wages, though. That's not an issue.'

'Oh, fuck off, Teddy, I like my job and the club. I don't, however, like Stan.'

'Where are ya now?' he asked, ignoring her statement.

His voice had changed, she realised, and now he seemed even more concerned.

'You're breaking up, Ted. I'll call ya later.'

She ended the call and stared at the lads coming out of the school.

He called back, but she didn't answer. She didn't want to argue with him, and, in any case, she couldn't stand hearing his voice anymore.

Delores spoke first. Not one to be reticent, or shy away from offering an opinion, she didn't hold back. 'Christ, my girl, Teddy is bleedin' well obsessed with you. I never realised he was that bad. I know he has changed. I mean, money can change a man, but—'

'No, Muvver,' said Erin. 'Money doesn't always change people, but it can definitely unmask them for who they really are. There is a lot more to Teddy, believe you me.'

'She's right, Mum,' said Harper. 'He ain't the same person. He walks around like his shit don't stink. Anyway, let's not talk about him. I have more pressing issues to deal with.'

Staring at the iconic steeple of St Olave's, Harper couldn't have felt more proud that her son went to a grammar school.

She had been watching the boys tumbling out of the school gates, some with their backpacks, as neat and tidy as they had been when they left for school. And there were those others with their ties loose and their shoelaces untied and their hair sticking up in all directions.

Right on cue, the heavens opened, and the rain gushed down. The boys didn't stand a chance. They pelted for the bus stop, their faces red and glossy.

Her eyes scanned the crowds for her son. And finally, with his shoulders slumped, she saw him. He was wearing a rugby top instead of his shirt and blazer, and he looked totally downtrodden. She watched him with his head down as a few boys skipped past and laughed at him. One even poked him in the arm.

Harper felt her anger rising; her stomach acid was whipping up a molten storm. She wanted to leap from her car, slap the kid around the face, and breathe fire over him and his friends like a mother dragon. But she knew she couldn't. She had to sit and wait for him.

It wasn't long before he spotted her waving at him and heading towards her car. He didn't wave back; he just smiled.

'Aw, love him. He is a handsome boy. He's just like you, Harper,' said Delores.

'Thanks, Mum.'

'Watch out for these older boys, Harper,' warned Delores.

'The little fuckers. If only he'd told me, I would have—'

'Shut up, Erin. Don't kid yaself, girl. You wouldn't have done much.' Harper softened her voice. 'Back then, I mean.'

'I do love him, ya know, in my own way,' she said, tapping Harper on the shoulder. 'And I thought you had forgiven me for going with Teddy.'

'I have, Erin. I was just winding him up, that's all. And I know you love Eddie. Now then, if you can remember what these twins look like, point the bastards out, will ya?'

'Are you sure we shouldn't let him fight his own battles? It will toughen him up.'

Harper was about to launch into a slanging match when Delores sarcastically interjected, 'And you fought all your own battles, didn't ya, Erin?'

'Look, I was just thinking aloud, that's all.'

'In fact, Erin,' Delores continued, 'if it wasn't for Harper, you would have probably been bashed up every day at school. So think yourself lucky that when you ever told anyone you were Harper's sister, they would run a mile, but our Eddie Bear hasn't got a big brother or big sisters, so—'

'Okay, you've made your point, Muvver, and yeah, you're right. Anyway, it's been a while, and I only met them once when I dropped Eddie off to see their bruvver, his so-called best mate.' She tapped Harper's shoulder again. 'There, look over there, by the wall. That's Duran and Wesley. Fuck me, their ginger minge muvver must have stuck 'em in a growbag. Look at the size of

’em, and you mean to tell me those brick shithouses have been bashing Eddie?’

‘Yep, and their father, like I said, humiliated my kid, so do you still wanna help, or what?’ Harper growled.

‘Kidnapping is a serious crime.’

‘So is fucking murder, and anyway, it’s hardly kidnapping, but, Erin, if you want out, I understand.’

‘No way, we’re a family. We stick together, and if Teddy is too much of a wanker to step in, then we’d better do it ourselves.’

Harper stared at the two lads and tutted. ‘What the hell are they doing? Why aren’t they walking home like the other kids?’

‘What are we gonna do, Harps, if they don’t walk towards my car?’

‘Let me think.’

Her phone buzzed, and she read the text from Terry.

The lad’s father has just gone indoors through the back door. The wife’s just gone out in her car.

‘Right, Erin, follow me and Eddie Bear when he shifts his bloody legs and gets in the motor. I bet the mother is coming to pick the bullying bastards up ’cos it’s raining.’

Erin and her mother clambered out of Harper’s car and returned to Erin’s white 4x4. As they hurried to avoid the rain, Harper grinned to herself. Erin had made an effort to become the more natural version of herself; but every so often, she would wear something that would remind Harper of how Erin used to be, and today it was the fur-trimmed pink boots.

Harper also noticed how well her mother appeared. She had undoubtedly slimmed down, and there was a glow to her cheeks instead of the dull mustard tinge that had graced her face for years. The drinking was now down to the odd glass of wine instead of a bottle of vodka. And she’d packed in the cigarettes. Maybe, she and Terry were genuinely good for each other. The sparkle in her mother’s eyes would suggest so.

Finally, Eddie opened the front passenger door and threw his backpack onto the rear seat. 'Mum, I'm so glad you picked me up. That bag is hefty.'

His hair was soaked to his scalp. 'Are you cold, babe?'

'Yes, Mum, it's freezing out there,' he said, while shivering.

Harper turned the blower to full blast. 'Why are you wearing your rugby shirt?'

He chewed his lip, which she often did. 'I got mud all over my blazer.'

'The truth, Eddie, please, babe. Did those twins push you in the mud?'

He nodded. 'Yep, there is a deep muddy puddle at the back. They thought it was funny. Anyway,' he said excitedly, whilst also changing the subject, 'I got a B in chemistry for my test today.'

'You got a B? That's fantastic, Eddie. Well done. Eddie, did they push you in the mud before you started your lessons?'

He nodded. 'Yeah, 'course. Why?'

''Cos you would probably have got an A if you weren't soaked and covered in wet mud. It's still in your ears, babe. You know I can't have older kids, or any kids, for that matter, bullying my boy.'

He shrugged his shoulders. 'Mum, you've often said shit happens and it's certainly true in my case. Look, you can't fight my battles. I'll be okay when I go to uni because there's no way they will end up where I'm going, so it'll all be fine in the end.'

'So that's okay, is it, Son? 'Cos in my book, it ain't, babe, and I'm gonna do something about it, once and for all. Their father is a right cunt!'

Eddie put his hand over his mouth and laughed at her colourful language.

'He can't bully you.'

‘What are you going to do, Mum? Call the police?’

Harper nearly choked. ‘Call the police? Are you mad? No, Son, I’m gonna smash the fucking granny out of him.’

Eddie laughed again, thinking she was joking. That was until they pulled up behind Terry’s cab, outside the twins’ house.

‘No, seriously, Mum, what are you really gonna do? I mean, he is a big man, and the twins can fight, Mum. They beat me up. I know what they can do and—’

She pulled up the handbrake and turned to face her son. ‘Eddie.’ She paused when she looked into his innocent eyes. She knew that as much as he had probably witnessed skulduggery around his father’s dodgy dealings and had probably heard some unsavoury things, he was possibly about to see something that may disturb him. So she decided it would be best for him to remain in the car.

‘Eddie Bear, I’ve had to fight for my life on a few occasions,’ she said, as she paused and sighed. ‘Sooner or later, I might end up back in prison because there are some things I may have to do. But listen: don’t try to stop me. If I have to go back to prison, I’ll know that my boy, my precious boy, won’t be bullied and can finish the school years with a smile and not for ever be looking over his shoulder awaiting the next kick or punch.’

Eddie tilted his head to the side. ‘Mum, please, I can handle it. I have until now. You don’t need to do anything.’

‘Oh, but I do. It’s what I was born to do.’

He grabbed her arms. ‘No, Mum, you were born to be my mum, and I need you on the outside.’

Harper kissed his forehead. ‘Listen, I might get locked up not for what I’m about to do today but for what I might have to do in the future.’

‘What can be so important that you would risk your freedom, Mum?’

‘Your Aunt Charley’s life, that’s what.’ She put her finger over her lips. ‘But that’s between us, yeah?’

‘Okay, between us, but, please, whatever you do, I can’t lose you again, Mum.’

‘You won’t, my Son. Never again.’

CHAPTER TWENTY-THREE

Eddie's eyes were drawn to the white 4x4 being driven slowly past them.

The vehicle drew up on the other side of Terry's cab.

'That's Erin and Nanny.'

Eddie then saw Terry's vehicle.

'What are Erin, Nan, and Terry doing here?'

'As I said, Eddie, I can't have my son bullied.'

Suddenly Eddie ducked down. 'That's them, Mum. That's Simone, their mum, driving the car.'

Harper watched the woman manoeuvre her Polo into the driveway next to a Jaguar. Harper smiled to herself. *So he has the top-of-the-range flash Jag, and she has the silver Polo for doing the shopping and getting her nails done. But it clearly wasn't for a trip to the hair salon.* Harper could see the woman's bushy ball of orange frizz on her head like a Willy Wonka Oompa Loompa bouffant. Unusual for a woman in her late forties.

Their house was a four-bedroom detached property with neighbours a good hundred feet away and separating them was a seven-foot-high brick wall. She wondered if the neighbours had built their boundary wall, which was different in design, to maintain privacy from Simone and her sons. She watched as two boys got out of the car and wandered through the side gate, ignoring their mother. Watching the woman struggling to climb out of her motor was painful. Being so big, she had to push herself out of the vehicle. Then she had to steady herself before she reached in and grabbed the two backpacks the boys had left on the rear seats.

'Eddie, do they lock the back door?'

‘Not while they’re in the house. I don’t remember them worrying about locking doors. Brent, their dad, thinks he is so hard that no one would break in while he is in the house.’

‘Good. Now, Eddie Bear, you stay in the car. Oh, where is the youngest boy, your old mate?’

‘He’s at football practice.’

‘And you don’t go? I thought you like footie?’

Eddie’s solemn stare said it all. *So the bullying had extended to the sports grounds too.* Harper’s blood was boiling, and she wanted to rip Brent’s head off. She wanted to beat the life out of the twins as well, but she had to keep reminding herself that they were sixteen not twenty-one.

‘Stay here, babe,’ she said, as she got out of the car.

She nodded sharply to Erin, Delores, and Terry to join her.

They crossed the road together. Terry was in front with a baseball bat in his hand, Erin had her handheld cosh, Delores had a brick in her handbag and a knife in the waistband of her trousers, and the only thing Harper carried was rage – but buckets of it.

With every step she took, she felt the anger rising to the top ready to explode. She visualised her son being stripped naked and chased through the streets; he must have been terrified.

Storming towards the house, Harper suddenly couldn’t contain herself. She snatched the baseball bat from Terry. ‘Sorry, Tel, I need this.’

Terry didn’t attempt to stop her. He knew she would lose it with the lad’s father, anyway, so bat or no bat, the outcome would no doubt be the same – complete and utter carnage.

Erin and Delores ran behind her, along the drive, through the side door, which led straight into the open-plan kitchen-cum-dining room. It was a fair size, wide enough to accommodate a twenty-foot concertina glass door that opened out onto the large walled garden.

The marble top centre island had stools on the other side, five in total, and the dining table behind that. From the kitchen, you could also view the lounge area. An enormous TV dominated the room. Two beanbags were strategically placed opposite, with a couple of game controllers wired to the games console on the floor and the three-piece suite behind.

Simone had her arse sticking out of the fridge and hadn't noticed Harper burst into the room. She assumed the racket was from one of her noisy kids.

The twins, however, saw Harper right away and they were stunned.

When Duran saw the baseball bat in Harper's hand, he screamed. 'Dad! Dad!' His eyes then darted to the three other people who almost fell in behind the woman with the bat.

Hearing the scream, Simone suddenly spun around and jumped, dropping the tray of steaks.

'What the hell are you doing here? Who are you?' She looked Harper up and down. 'A baseball bat? I think you've got the wrong house, lady,' she said, as she reached down, picked up the tray, and slapped it onto the marble worktop.

Erin, meanwhile, had skirted around the centre island and grabbed one of the boys before he legged it upstairs. 'Not so fast, ya little rat-faced bastard.'

Wesley, the cockier of the two, attempted to throw a punch, but Erin managed to whack his fist out of the way using her cosh. 'Do that again, and I'll shove this right up your fucking jacksy, you little scrotum.'

The boys stepped back and stared at Erin, who was now waving the cosh in front of them. 'Move, and I'll smash the pair of ya.'

Simone shifted her eyes from Harper to Erin. 'Oi, leave my boys alone. What the hell is going on?' she shouted, as she tried to pass Harper to get to her sons. 'Get out of my house before my husband comes downstairs and creates merry hell.'

But Terry blocked her move.

'And who are you?' She glared at Terry, as he instantly stopped her from getting to her sons.

'Me, I'm just acting as a ref, I guess.'

'Ref? Oh, I see, so you're the joker, are you? And you?' She looked at Delores.

'Me, I'm here to even the odds,' said Delores, as she took up her stance beside Harper.

Simone was twice Delores's size in height and weight, with a head the size of a bowling ball and arms like oven-ready legs of lamb.

Simone looked down at the middle-aged woman, and for a split second, she wanted to laugh. 'Give me a break, ol' girl. I ain't into granny bashing. Now, who is the fucking organ grinder, 'cos I ain't wasting my breath on the circus monkeys?' She spat the words out with her hands firmly on her hips.

'You talk the talk, I gotta say,' said Harper, with the bat still firmly in her hand. 'So, do your little brats take after you or your ol' man?'

Simone stared for a moment and then her confidence took a back seat. The woman's eyes held a darkness as though fighting was in her DNA, and she looked as if she didn't give a shit because what she was doing here was old hat to her. She had seen that look before when she'd been on remand in custody for a week, back in her youth, for fighting.

'What's got you so pissed off to come storming into my house with the last of the summer wine?' She pointed a fat sausage-shaped finger at Delores.

'You cheeky mare, I ain't bleedin' old!' hollered Delores.

'Come on, tell me, what's this all about?' Simone asked, glancing back at Terry.

'Your vile sons and your disgusting husband have bullied my boy,' said Harper, through clenched teeth. 'He stripped him and beat him and sent him running home naked while your little bastards beat him with a stick or a golf club.'

Simone leaned back and folded her arms. 'Ah, now I've got the picture. You're the little gay boy's mother. Come to fight his battles for him, have you?'

Harper's blistering pulse forced her head to rock with the beat slowly, like a demented nutcase. She grinned and nodded. 'So you knew about your husband hitting my boy, did ya?'

Simone put her hands up. 'Now, you fucking reel ya neck in, woman. My Brent never hit your kid. My sons did 'cos your gay boy tried to turn my youngest into a homosexual, the dirty little bastard.'

'So have I got it right? You were there?'

'Oh, that's right, I was there, and he's lucky I didn't get my hands on him, or I'd have beaten him up myself. You ought to be ashamed of yourself. You're not bringing that kid up right. He got my son drunk and then tried to sleep with him. Where did he learn that from, eh?' she replied, smiling, as she looked Harper up and down. Pleased with her comeback, Simone was oblivious to the fact that Harper was sensing the red mist.

Harper couldn't understand how a mother could allow a young boy to be physically and emotionally traumatised like that. Poor little Eddie couldn't even run into the woman's arms for help.

It pushed Harper over the edge. She dropped the bat, and in a reckless movement, she launched herself at the woman, grabbing a huge chunk of her frizzy hair and slamming Simone's head onto the worktop. The sound was sickening, similar to a bird hitting a car windscreen.

Simone was stunned. Nevertheless, she tried to go for Harper's throat. However, she was too big and much too slow for her opponent.

Harper darted out of her reach and, this time, she grabbed the woman's hair with both her hands. Viciously pulling her head down, she ruthlessly kneed her in the face. 'You nasty cunt!' she yelled, as she kneed Simone for the second time.

A fine mist of blood shot out of Simone's nose. But Simone didn't give up and desperately tried to get a grip of Harper to steady herself and at least stop the blows.

But Harper was in a frenzy.

'Terrorise my son, will ya!' she barked. Letting go of Simone's hair, she punched her in the face. Simone's head rotated as though she was about to collapse.

Harper stopped to assess the mess she'd made of Simone's face. The woman was still standing, but completely dazed. But she wasn't on her knees. After two fast and hard bone-breaking blows to the ribs, she ended with the third, a ferocious uppercut under the woman's sternum, ensuring that Simone would not be able to catch her breath properly for at least six weeks.

Harper stood up straight with her throbbing hands by her side and watched as Simone slid down the white shiny kitchen units like a sack of shit, leaving specks of blood everywhere. Her eyes were swelling up so much she could barely see.

'Now, that's better. You won't be hurting my boy again, will ya?'

With that, Harper gave Simone an added bonus. To ensure the woman's ribs were well and truly broken, she savagely pulled her leg back and kicked her hard under her arm.

Amazingly, Simone wasn't unconscious but she was gasping for breath. 'Please . . . please . . . I . . . I . . . can't . . . breathe. I can hardly see,' she stuttered, desperate to catch her breath and to pull herself up from the floor.

'You can't see 'cos your face now looks like a decomposing arse, and you can't breathe because I probably broke your ribs.'

Harper bent down and retrieved the bat. 'And d'ya know why? 'Cos, my little boy ran home terrified of your two cunting bullies. He was out of breath. He couldn't *breathe* because he was running for his life and for his dignity. And what boils my piss is that he would have looked to you with begging eyes to help him. My boy would have trusted you, but, no, you all turned on him like a pack of wolves. You're a disgusting fat piece of dog shit who should be locked up for child abuse.'

Harper took a few deep breaths and glanced at the two boys, who were now wide-eyed and too fearful of moving because Erin was wearing her Dobermann face, angrily baring her veneers.

Harper spat at the woman, still struggling to get to her feet. 'Mum, make sure she don't get back up.'

Delores patted her bag. 'She won't.'

Walking towards the boys, Harper listened for any sounds upstairs. 'Where's your father?' she hissed in Duran's face.

Duran stepped away from the mad woman. 'Upstairs, and when he sees what you've done, lady, he'll start a war.'

Harper laughed. 'Start a war? Is that right? I bet the prick can't even start a fucking lawnmower.'

'He will sort you out,' snarled Duran, as he attempted to swing a punch. But he only managed to catch the side of Harper's face before she grabbed his wrist.

'I can't beat you up because you're only sixteen, and I'm an adult, but you shouldn't have done that, silly boy.'

'No! You shouldn't have!' bellowed a voice from behind Harper.

Before she could turn around, Eddie was there bare-chested, gripping the sleeves of his rugby shirt, which he now used as a rope to flip over Duran's head. In an instant, using the sleeves as leverage, he yanked Duran down with such unpredictable force, he fell forward. Eddie lifted his knee and smashed the boy in the face.

Duran cupped his broken nose and wobbled about over the floor, with blood dripping between his fingers.

Then, Wesley attempted to throw a punch, but Erin pushed him back. 'Oh no, 'cos, I don't care what age *you* are. I'll be happy to fucking add to the disfigurement of your ugly face, an' all.'

Wesley was hopping from one foot to the other, his fists up in a fighting stance. 'Come on then, gay boy, me and you, yeah?'

Harper glared at Wesley. 'Yeah, let's make it a fair fight, like you and your brother did when you beat Eddie.' She handed her son the bat. 'Now, it's fair.'

Wesley dropped his stance and backed into the corner of the room. 'No, leave off. He's got a bat!'

Eddie nodded, and as Wesley covered his face, Eddie swung the bat hard and fast. He had always been the top batsman in rounders, a slogger, the gym teacher called him. The force of the blow as it hit Wesley's shoulder was bone-crushing. He let out a scream so high-pitched, it could burst an eardrum.

Suddenly, they heard a door being opened upstairs. 'Simone, what's going on down there? Lads, stop the screaming, and, Simone, where have the towels gone? Can't a man have a bloody shower in peace with a warm towel to dry off with! You're a useless cow!'

Wesley was about to scream up to his father when Eddie whacked him again with the bat.

Duran wiped his watery eyes, and in a temper, he rushed at Eddie and punched him in the back of the head. But before Harper could intervene, Eddie spun around, and with a face like a devil on steroids, he swung the bat so hard at the back of Duran's legs that he instantly fell to his knees. And another blow to the shoulder ensured Duran wasn't getting up unaided.

The bang, bang, bang sounds of heavy footsteps, as Brent finally came hurtling down the stairs, had Terry standing behind the door ready for action to add to the element of surprise.

Harper placed her arm around her son, kissed his head, and relieved him of the bat. 'Go and wait in the car.'

Brent burst into the room naked and still dripping wet. 'Where the fucking—'

He stopped shouting and glanced around at the carnage. First, he eyed Wesley in the corner of the room; he was as white as a ghost and hugging himself. Then his eyes went to Duran who was on the floor, his nose pouring with blood. Finally, his brain registered that there were strangers in his house equipped for a fight.

'What the fuck?'

Harper stood square-shouldered in front of the man.

'So you're the cunt who fucked with my son, are ya?'

Eddie stared, his heart beating so fast. After all, he was scared for his mother because he knew what Brent was capable of. He only hoped that Terry would help if Brent tried to hurt her.

Brent wasn't the least bit bothered that he was buck naked. An evil grin parted his lips, and he shot a quick look at Eddie. 'Your son tried to fuck my boy. You're lucky I ain't had him locked up. Now, get the fuck out of my house, you long cocky streak of piss.'

An uncomfortable silence crept over them as Harper stared unflinchingly.

He moved two steps forward. 'Didn't you hear me? Your son tried to turn my son into a homosexual. Now get out of my house before you get hurt.'

'Nah, that ain't the truth, though, is it? And those lads of yours – Dumb and Dumber – have brutalised my son. They are nothing but cowardly bullies, a bit like their—'

Harper looked down at his groin area. 'Oh dear, their maggot-for-a-dick father. Now, I could have you nicked for being a paedo.'

Brent's eyes widened, and then he laughed sarcastically. 'That's right, bitch, I'm a fucking paedo. I love little boys, so what are you gonna do about it?'

'I thought as much, you dirty stinking scumbag!'

‘What? You what? You stupid bitch, of course I’m no poxy paedo. Now get out of my house.’

Harper held the bat in one hand and tapped it methodically in the other. ‘You had me son stripped naked. You like seeing boys naked, do ya?’ She shook her head. ‘And you instructed your sons to beat him with the weapon you gave them. You like watching naked boys being beaten, do you? Get off on it, do you?’ She paused for effect, watching the realisation whirling around in the man’s brain. His face said it all.

Then Brent clocked Eddie with the phone in his hand. ‘Why, you fucking little bastard!’

He lunged forward to snatch the phone, but it wasn’t Harper who smashed him in the face but Delores.

She hadn’t been told the complete story about her grandson, and so hearing Harper repeat it all back to the boys’ father, it sent her over the top. She flew around the kitchen island and swung her handbag.

Brent would have laughed in her face, but the force behind the clout instantly brought him to his knees.

‘Take that, you fucking nasty, evil bastard!’ she screamed, as she swung the handbag again, catching him around the head. ‘If you or your boys ever, and I mean ever, look at my grandson the wrong way, I’ll not just brick ya, I’ll fucking bury ya.’

Terry couldn’t help but laugh. As a grown man there to protect as he saw them his family, he was left there feeling like a gooseberry. These women were wild, but he loved every one of them. Putting his arm around Delores, who was now puffing and panting with rage, he steered her away from the mess she had made of the man. ‘Come on, my duchess, let’s move out of the way.’

‘Jesus, Tel, I would have killed him. I mean it.’

‘Yep, doll, I know you would. That’s why I had to stop you.’

Brent managed to get himself into a sitting position, but his ears were ringing so much that he didn't risk getting to his feet. He held his head. 'What do you want from us?'

Harper smiled. 'Your boys will go back to school and put right all they did wrong!' She poked him with the bat. 'And if I hear that you or they or your missus have called the police or have upset my boy, then I will make sure that every social media platform will see the video my son has just made that clearly shows you admitting you're a paedo. I mean, who admits such a thing?' She looked at the two boys in turn, who seemed to be defeated. 'Got it, lads?' She raised her bat.

Duran nodded. 'I'm sorry, Eddie.'

Wesley looked away.

'Do you fully understand the consequences?'

Biting his lip, Wesley sheepishly nodded.

'Great, so we are all clear now. That was easy. So any comebacks and that video is one little tap away from being shown to the whole fucking world and its mother.'

CHAPTER TWENTY-FOUR

Harper drove Eddie to her mother's house; he was the most excited she'd ever seen him. It was as if someone had waved a magic wand and lifted her son from the doldrums to euphoria. His cheeks glowed and his eyes were alive and dancing as he said, 'And did you see me, Mum? I stood up for myself, and I wasn't going to let him hit you. No one beats my mum and gets away with it. I would have rearranged his face for him.'

Inside, Harper was smiling because her son was well spoken, yet there he was talking about fighting like a streetwise Jack the Lad.

'Anyway, Eddie Bear, they won't touch you again, and if they come anywhere near you, then, you remind them of the video you have.'

Eddie suddenly looked down. 'Actually, Mum, there is no video, and when they find out—'

'Find out what? How would they ever know? But what they will be worried sick about is what their father said.' She laughed. 'Imagine if that went viral. They would be mortified, and it would open up a whole can of worms. No, Son, there is nothing to fear now. Even if they snatch your phone to check for themselves, you tell them that you sent it to me and deleted it off your phone because it made you feel sick knowing that you were once friends with a lad whose father is a paedo.'

His excitement simmered down. 'Did you get hurt, Mum?' he asked, in a sober fashion.

'Me? Good God, no way!'

'You are so much harder than Teddy.'

'Teddy? I see you're still annoyed with him by not calling him Dad.'

'Mum, I can't get that girl, Yalina, out of my head.'

Harper suddenly had a flashback. She felt her skin tingling and the blood pumping in her temples. A man called out for a girl in the ladies' toilets in The Click. She was a young girl, around fourteen or possibly a little older, and her name was Yalina. She had remembered it because she thought how pretty her name was.

'Yalina? Was she from India?'

'No, actually Pakistan, why?'

Harper swallowed hard. Her mouth felt dry. 'Fuck! I think I met her.'

'Mum, what is it? What's going on?'

'I think something so unbearable is happening that right now, my son, I can't speak the words because if they are true, then your father is into something that—'

Eddie was staring at his mother's face. Her eyes were wide and her face seemed to pale over.

'Something that what, Mum? Tell me!'

Suddenly Harper blinked, took a deep breath, and glanced at her son. 'Sometimes, Eddie, I think of you as my little boy of three years old. You were dressed in an Aran knitted jumper, a pair of beige trousers, and a little baseball cap, and you were waving at me with a beaming smile as you left the visitors' room at the prison. You had no idea that you wouldn't see me again for a long time. And now you're a teenager, and it's hard for me to think of you as almost an adult, but you're so bright and intuitive that I think I should treat you more like a man. After all, I think you are far more sensible and manly than your father.'

Eddie nodded. He thought so as well. 'So tell me, Mum. What's going on?'

'That girl was in the club when the club was supposed to be shut. She was there with other young girls, and to me, it seemed like they were kids that were, were . . .' She took a deep breath, struggling to say the word and have to live through the concept all over again.

‘Mum, *what*?’

‘I think they were there involuntarily, possibly trafficked. You mentioned a while ago she was worried about the others, didn’t you?’

Eddie stared ahead. The enormity of what his mother had just said stung him.

‘I’m sorry. It’s a lot to take in, and I might be wrong.’

He shook his head. ‘No, Mum, that girl was terrified of the police, and it was so obvious that she was at the house against her will. And, yeah, I did mention that.’

‘I have an idea. We can help her and them.’

‘Oh, Mum, yes, we must. She was so nice. I felt helpless when she had to go, and that’s why I hate Teddy.’

‘Well, far be it from me to turn you against your father, but if those girls have been trafficked, I think it has something to do with him because the club belongs to him. Surely, he must have known what was going on? And having that same girl brought to the house for – shit, I can’t even think about that. The bastard.’

‘He is into bad stuff. I know that because he never talks to his so-called colleagues or businessmen in front of me or takes a phone call when I’m around. He waves his hands for me to leave or scoots into another room. Mum, does this have something to do with Aunty Charley going missing?’

Harper choked as she replied, ‘Maybe it does, babe, so I need your help.’

Eddie was sparked up again. ‘Yeah, Mum, anything. I’m no coward. You’ve seen me now. I can stand up for myself.’

‘Eddie, this isn’t about fighting, babe. It’s about knowledge. It’s a real long shot, but I need you to find out some information for me, which involves Yalina.’

Eddie nodded. ‘Go on.’

‘Your father brought her to you—’

‘No, this big Asian man did.’

‘Fair enough. What I mean is, did your father organise it?’

‘Yeah, he did.’

‘Can you ask for her again?’

Feeling part of something bigger than himself, he replied excitedly, ‘Yes, of course, I can. I’ll say I still have thoughts about men, and I want Yalina to convince me I am wrong to have those thoughts.’

It turned Harper’s stomach to think that Teddy, his own father, of all people, had made Eddie feel that way.

‘Are you sure you wanna do this, Eddie? Only it’s a huge deal, and a good mother would keep her child as far away from trouble as possible.’

Eddie laughed. ‘*Really*, Mum? And how do you propose to do that? I live with my – I live with Teddy Ryder, who is so dodgy the police would need a lifetime to take a statement from him, and my mother is one badass bitch who would easily give Black Widow from *Avengers* a run for her money.’

Harper had to laugh at how he’d just put on a London gangster accent.

‘What I need you to do . . . Oh God, forgive me for this.’ She took a deep breath. ‘Take Yalina to your bedroom, out of Teddy’s earshot, and record the conversation for me. Don’t call me because you know what it’s like with bad reception, and I have to get the facts straight. And also I don’t want Teddy to hear.’

‘Yes, and what do you want me to ask?’

‘Firstly, who is she working for? Does she know the name Teddy Ryder, and, if so, in what context? Why was she in the club dancing? And, most importantly, ask her if she knows of Charley.’ She paused in thought. ‘Charley would, of course, go under a different name . . . I have a photo of her. I’ll text it to you so you can show it to her. Oh, and I will send you another photo. It’s of a room. It’s not a nice photo. Actually, it’s pretty gruesome. It shows handcuffs attached to a pipe. See if she recognises the place.'

He nodded.

'Also, get names and descriptions and find out where she's staying.'

Harper stopped the car outside her mother's house. Terry and Erin had arrived before her, although she had taken a detour to give herself private time with Eddie.

As they approached the back door, she turned to face her son. 'Eddie, I know what I am asking of you is a lot, and I wouldn't if I didn't think it was for the greater good. You do understand, don't ya?'

'I'm not two anymore, and as you know, I am smart. Please let me help.'

'Okay, babe, I'm gonna talk to your nan and your Aunt Erin. I think I need to be open about what's going on. I won't tell Lexi because she is cramming for her law exams, and so, until we know anything concrete, we'll keep her out of it.'

'Don't they know?'

Harper shook her head. 'I hoped I would have heard some good news about Charley so that I didn't have to worry them all, but time's getting on, and so, sadly, it may be that I will have to give them the devastating news. And you know your nan. She will scream blue murders for keeping her out of the loop.'

Suddenly Eddie burst out laughing. It was a real raucous laugh that went from a low to a high pitch, evidence of his voice breaking. 'I wouldn't want to cross Nan with her handbag. She is . . . she is . . .' He couldn't talk for laughing.

It lifted the serious mood and it had Harper joining in. 'He wasn't expecting that. I bet Nanny thought she was at a birthday party, and he was the piñata.'

Her sense of humour had Eddie doubled over. Tears filled his eyes as he laughed his head off.

***

But that brief moment of levity left Harper as soon as she arrived at the back door of her mother's house. Her mind had switched to how her family would react to her news about Charley.

Delores stood up from the kitchen table when Harper and Eddie walked in. 'Are you okay, Harper?' she asked, genuinely concerned.

Harper smiled emphatically. 'Mum, let's go into the living room, shall we? I need to tell you something.'

Terry smiled compassionately at Harper. He could tell something was kicking off. It was written across her face. And he was in agreement with the idea that the family should all be involved in the situation. He understood that it would take a lot for Harper to loosen those heavy bricks on her shoulders. She was the type of woman who wanted to protect her loved ones from harm and also to shield them from emotional pain. Up to now, she had. But he had told her many times that a problem shared is a problem halved.

'This sounds ominous, Harper. You're not sick, are you?'

'No, Mum, I'm not sick. I'm just exhausted, that's all. It's our Charley. She is missing.'

Delores flung her hands to her mouth. 'You're joking. Please say you're joking.' She understood the seriousness of the situation concerning Charley's work.

Erin appeared in the doorway. 'What's going on?'

Harper insisted everyone sit down and not interrupt as she told them everything from Michel turning up at her door, to the information on the electronic tablet, and to the business with the club.

'And you believe Charley is alive?'

Harper bit her bottom lip to stop it quivering. She merely nodded.

'Right then, what do you want us to do?'

Erin was frowning. 'I'm not clever, and I'm not hard like you, Harper, but it's time I womaned up, and, well, had *your* back now.'

The kindness of her sister had Harper cupping her face to hide the tears.

Eddie put his arm around her. 'Mum, you're not alone.' He looked at Erin. 'And how can you say you're not hard? You had Dumb and Dumber shitting themselves.'

'Language, Eddie Bear,' said Delores.

'Language? I'm only talking like me family do.'

Harper wiped her eyes. 'I like you all posh.' She ruffled his hair. 'Right, you need to go home for now and carry out the plan, yeah?'

'I'll drive you home, little man,' said Terry, as he kissed Delores. 'I'll be back in a jiffy.'

'Mum, I'll text you to let you know what's going on.'

'And, Eddie, delete the text afterwards. This is serious.'

She suddenly felt her skin alive with goosebumps. 'Wait, no, stop, stop, I can't have you doing this, babe. It's all wrong. What the fuck am I thinking? See, I am exhausted and desperate.'

She rubbed her temples with her fingers.

'Mum, if it means that I may help save girls from the most despicable crime, then I'm in.'

'Harper, he's not a baby. Let him,' said Delores, firmly, squeezing her daughter's shoulder. 'He is a Kane.' She looked at her grandson. 'Definitely not a fucking Ryder.'

Nodding, Harper flung her arms around him. 'You, my sweetheart, may help us find our Charley.'

'I will do whatever it takes, and I'm not afraid because as much as I don't like Teddy, I don't think he would hurt me badly if he were to know what I was up to.'

Harper would like to believe the same, but she didn't know Teddy anymore.

'Right, I'm pinging over the photos. And remember, delete them when you're done, yeah?'

'Yes, Mum. Trust me, I can do this.'

***

Harper was two minutes away from the club when she parked the car out of sight and walked the rest of the way. She saw Michel sitting on his motorbike with his crash helmet still on his head. She didn't wave or acknowledge him because she didn't have to. He'd said that if Katie had arranged the meeting as a set-up, he would flash his light. There was no flash – so she assumed she was safe.

Standing by the back door to the club under the lamp was a woman she barely recognised until she got closer.

Katie had a wavy blonde bob with a side parting. Her face looked a little different because she wore a unique style of make-up – thick top lashes and eyeliner along the top lid. Hugging herself in an oversized coat, Katie smiled.

'It's okay, Harper. I am here alone. I see Michel across the way. He could have been less conspicuous.'

Harper smiled and hugged Katie. 'I think he wanted you to see him.'

'Ah, that'll be it. I know Michel is one of the best, and he never makes mistakes.'

'So, you believe him?'

Katie nodded. 'Let's talk.' She sighed. 'When you said that you trusted him, then I knew something very shady was going on with this case that Charley was working on.'

Harper looked around, still nervous about being spotted by not only Verity but by Stan. 'Can we go somewhere else.'

'Yeah, sure. My car is over there.'

Harper raised a questioning brow.

'You're safe, you know. I'm not going to go anywhere except a coffee shop or a burger bar.'

Feeling she had little choice, she followed Katie to her MINI Clubman and clambered inside. She noticed a briefcase on the back seat but she didn't say anything. Her suspicious mind conjured up thoughts that maybe Katie would tape their conversation from inside the car, so she was mindful of what she would say.

***

The small late-night café in a side street off Catford's main road took Katie only a few minutes to drive to, and she knew all the shortcuts. The warm air as they entered the greasy café hit them, and instantly Katie removed her cumbersome coat and swung it over the back of the chair. 'Tea and a fried egg sarnie? They do the best in town.'

The cooking smells had Harper salivating; she hadn't realised she was so hungry until Katie mentioned food.

'Yeah, go on, then, but I prefer coffee with my sandwich.'

After placing her order with a thick curly-haired rotund Greek man, Katie returned with the two mugs. 'Spiros will bring the sarnies over in a minute.' She attached her bag to the back of the chair, took her seat, and hurriedly sipped her tea. 'I needed that.' She relaxed her shoulders. 'Look, Harper, I love your sister like she's my own flesh and blood, and after our conversation, I knew I had to give you the benefit of the doubt. You see, Charley is so good at her job. She once said it was her sole purpose in life. And I knew the truth behind why she does her job before you told me, because, like I said, she and I were close. I know in my heart that she wouldn't turn against the system for money. I guess I was programmed to believe the boss.' She huffed. 'Well, I suppose you do. I mean, someone like Verity, the woman who has had mountains of success and who is evidently good at what she does to reach the top, is hardly going to fabricate shit. Well, at least, that's what she would want everyone to believe.'

Harper placed her mug on the table. ‘So you don’t believe Verity, then?’

Katie shook her head. ‘If Verity is claiming Charley and Michel have turned, as in villains “gone rogue,” because of the colossal amount of money deposited into their joint account, then whoever is behind it must have had that kind of money as surplus, to go that far to implicate two top undercover officers. So, whatever is actually going on, there is a significant amount of money at stake. And Verity loves the finer things in life, put it that way. She came from money. Her father’s well off. And she is driving around in a new 4x4, and they aren’t cheap. I also know she’s been looking at buying a new house. I saw her laptop open at some estate agency that only sells the manor type houses. So she could be the traitor. But who knows.’

‘The scheming bitch! I served time with the most devious of women, and you kinda get to understand their way of thinking, so tell me what else you know and let’s see if we’re on the same page.’

‘Right, well, Charley is the best because she can morph into the hardest of legends. We call the characters legends.’

Harper nodded, already fully aware.

‘She worked on major crimes involving the Russian mobs, or the Russian mafia as we call them, but gangs that are very separate to each other, so that she isn’t recognised, because hiding her true identity is paramount. She is highly valued in the force, and so the one thing that made me think something was not quite right’ – she paused to take a deep breath – ‘was when she went missing and then when I heard she’d been killed. Quite a few officers were suddenly shifted to other cases. The two bodies in the photo—’

‘You saw that photo?’

‘Yes, we all did. It was on the case board, along with other photos, and they filed the case away the next day. They didn’t have enough evidence to support the budget they would need to take down this gang once Charley was assumed dead. They were after the top guy, and what Verity told us was that her undercover officer, who, by the way, is now missing, had witnessed the Russians kill Charley and drag her body away. He told the team that Charley had tipped the Russians off, and they took her out, maybe as a warning to the British police before they fled. They left nothing behind – no trail of the girls, human trafficking, or anything of that nature. These Russians are so rich that they can exit in a flash and return under a different guise.'

Harper frowned; she was still unconvinced. 'But if Charley had tipped them off, I would have thought they would have protected her, not killed her?'

'These are Russians we are talking about. They would never have trusted her, even if she claimed to be on their side. The payment may have been part payment and the rest to be paid at a later date, and if they got what they needed, they would dispose of her and not pay the rest.'

'Surely Charley would have known that?'

'Russians can be convincing.'

'How did the other undercover officer inform Verity of what was going on and even manage to pass on the photos?'

'By text.'

'And that's all they have. I mean, anyone could have stolen his phone – one of the Russians even – and sent photos and messages to put the police off the scent.'

'It's possible.'

'Why is Verity after that tablet?'

'Look, after our phone conversation, I began to think about the evidence on the case and I remember Verity acting shifty. I recalled her being very selective with the facts that she put on the board and evasive when the team asked her questions. She was also vague about Charley and the disappearance of the other officer. And, like I said, the facts from the other undercover officer were simply from text messages. I don't know why she wants the tablet, but I can only guess it has incriminating evidence that could expose Verity's involvement.' She held up her hands. 'If, of course, she is implicated.' She sighed heavily.

'So tell me what was on the tablet?'

Harper waved her finger. 'I'm not sure I should say. I don't know how to trust you. I'm sorry if I'm wrong.'

Katie smiled when the messy fried egg sandwiches arrived. 'Cheers, Spiros.'

'My pleasure, Katie. No Charley tonight?'

'No, she's on her holidays.'

'Shout if you want more tea or coffee.'

'You come here with Charley?' asked Harper, sipping her coffee.

'Yeah, if we've had a few too many drinks, we come here in the early hours. Look, I need you to trust me if I am to help you.'

She turned around, lifted her bag from the back of her chair, and pulled out her phone. 'I want to show you something. No one knows about her because of the work we do, yeah, and I am trusting you with this so that you will trust me.'

She showed Harper a photo of a little girl in her arms. 'She is two now, my little Jasmine. There are only three people who know about her – her father, Charley, and now you, except, of course, the babysitter.'

'Ahh, she is adorable.'

'Eat your food and think about it,' said Katie, nodding towards the sandwich.

Smiling back, Harper made up her mind to trust Katie. 'Okay, Katie, how can you help me?'

'Well, first off, do not email or copy the information on the tablet to an external drive. It could end up in the wrong hands and pose a risk to your family's safety.'

Harper frowned. 'How?'

‘If Verity is after the tablet, because it contains sensitive information, then the same could be said about Charley’s original target – probably a Russian gangster. So, if that data should leak, and the recipients knows the source, then someone may come for you and or your family. Charley would have been undercover on a mission with some ruthless people. They will stop at nothing to retrieve any information she managed to collate.’

Harper could feel the fear grabbing her around the throat. ‘So what do I do with the tablet?’

‘You can give it to me. I’ll take it to the Police Commissioner, and it will be locked away in the evidence department.’

‘And Verity?’

Katie waved her hands. ‘I won’t mention it to her, only the Commissioner. It will be out of her hands, and you, my friend, will be safe.’ She bit into her sandwich and munched away as the gooey egg dripped down her chin.

‘So, you are seriously considering the notion that Verity may well be a wrong ’un. Is that right?’

Katie looked about her. ‘Yeah, I am.’

‘Okay, let’s meet tomorrow and I’ll bring the tablet. Let’s hope you can make sense of it.’

Katie smiled and patted Harper’s hand. ‘Believe me, I will do whatever it takes to find your sister. Although you must prepare for the worst.’

CHAPTER TWENTY-FIVE

Eddie sat on a high stool at the kitchen bench while his father paced the floor, his phone in his hand. The pungent smell of his aftershave dominated the room.

'And where is your mum?'

Eddie shrugged his shoulders. 'She mentioned something about a spa. I don't know, Dad, but I, er, I need to talk to you about, well, about being gay.'

Teddy stopped staring at his phone and peered over at his son. 'Sorry, what did you bloody say?'

With that tone, Eddie would typically have walked off to his room. But the fight at the twins' house had really boosted his confidence and self-esteem. He knew now that he could stick up for himself, especially when push came to shove.

'I said, I want to talk to you about my sexual preference.'

'Your *sexual preference*? For fuck's sake, Eddie, you're a *Ryder*. Now, I don't wanna hear any more about it. In fact, I think, mate, you'd look better with your hair cropped instead of those girly fucking curls.'

'So that's it, is it? You just want me to man up, as you put it last time.'

Teddy ran his hand through his own curls. 'No, Eddie, but you're way too fucking young to come out with statements like that. Gay, my arse. You don't know yaself yet. Anyway, I thought . . .' He paused and tried to choose his words carefully. 'That girl who came . . . Didn't you? You know.' He nodded and grinned.

'Did I shag her, you mean? Shit, Dad, that's what she was paid for, wasn't it?'

Teddy suddenly looked into his son's eyes, and for the first time, he saw a man, not a child. It was the intensity of the look.

'Did I do the wrong thing?' he said, in an understanding tone, a far cry from the last time they'd had the conversation.

'Maybe not, Dad. I just wish I was more sure, that's all.'

'And the girl didn't change your mind?'

Eddie grinned and winked, which also caught Teddy by surprise. 'You liked her, then, I take it.'

Eddie nodded. 'I wouldn't mind seeing her again.'

'Oh, Son, I dunno about that, mate. You're a kid, and I was probably overreacting. Let's forget it ever happened.'

'No, Dad, I can't forget it happened, and I don't want to. What I want is to see her again.'

'Eddie, she's not your girlfriend, mate. She's . . . well, it's her job.'

'I know, but I felt comfortable with her. She can teach me how to be with a woman. Oh, come on, Dad. I've already, well, you know . . . with her, but I'm still not a hundred per cent sure if I like girls over lads.'

Eddie could see his father cringing as soon as he mentioned 'lads'.

'All right, I'll make a call, but this cannot be a habit. It ain't right. You're fourteen, not sixteen.'

'All my mates have lost their virginity.'

'Well, it's changed since my day.'

To reinforce the importance, he said, 'Dad, that's why I thought I could talk to you about being gay. We are supposed to tell our parents.'

'Right, I'll make a call, but please, Eddie, no more talk of being gay. It's a fad, that's all.'

***

Yalina was still unsure of Yuri's proposal. If only she knew what this work entailed. Yuri had purposefully left her alone with her thoughts and in a room that was the grandest she'd ever seen, apart from those in the James Bond movies.

Yuri would have known that she came from a family whose fortunes had nosedived, resulting in the family having to downsize to a much more modest home – and a rented one at that. He was doing a good job of selling this new job to her, knowing that she had virtually no options available.

The bed was a case in point. It looked to be a queen-size, so bigger than a double bed. On the bed was a beautiful satin leopard print bedspread and sumptuous velvet cushions. The carpet was a rich deep burgundy and so soft on her bare feet that when she wiggled her toes she was able to enjoy the soothing sensation.

The clothes on the velvet chaise longue were very British and expensive. Yalina felt the soft cream jumper between her fingers and wanted to slide it over her bare arms. When she noticed the price tag, £150, her eyes nearly popped out of her head. That amount of money would pay the rent on their house for a month or three. She then picked up the tweed jacket and held it against herself while standing in front of the long ornate mirror. The clothes and the suggestion from Yuri for her to have hair styled would indeed give her a completely fresh look. And one that perhaps she would appreciate. She certainly enjoyed the feel of the clothes. They were warm, and they would be perfect in this cold English weather. Her conscience tugged at her as though her mother was wagging a warning finger. Was she saving herself but condemning the other girls?

After folding the clothes, she was on the point of placing them neatly beside the others, when she spotted something shiny sticking out from under the bed. She glanced at the main door before bending down and retrieving the shiny object. The moment she realised it was a knife, a large vicious-looking weapon, she dropped it like a hot brick. Shooting another wary look at the door, she decided that there was nowhere where she could hide the knife except back under the bed. She used her foot to slide it under, and then she breathed deeply, before having an all-out panic attack.

She needed the toilet but was reluctant to ask. However, there were two other doors inside the bedroom, so she hoped one of them was the bathroom. Gingerly, she gripped one of the handles and slowly opened the door. It was dark inside, but a light automatically came on as she pushed the door wider.

The brightness of the white tiles, the roll top bath, and the marble flooring made Yalina blink. It was stunning and so modern. She could imagine herself as Vivian Ward in the movie *Pretty Woman* – which she had seen at a friend's house when she was very young – where she was in the tub with bubbles flowing over the top. Closing the door behind her, she quietly used the toilet and then had to figure out the flush system. She eventually found out that the system flushed automatically after use.

When she came out of the room, Yuri and Daria were there. She noticed right away, Yuri's demeanour was different. He was nervously rubbing the back of his neck while Daria spoke in Russian.

Daria also appeared agitated. In particular, his hand gestures were forceful. She could sense that he was trying to convince Yuri of something. And when Yuri looked her way, she guessed that Daria was talking about her.

'Yalina, I made you a promise. You and the girls will never have to have sex with a man again.'

She nodded, but she could feel her heart sinking. Had Yuri changed his mind?

'I am not a man to go back on his word.'

Daria sniggered and was promptly shoved out of the room.

'I am sorry. As I was saying, I am a man of my word.' He steepled his fingers and flicked his front tooth with his thumb. 'But I will ask you to do one thing for me before you begin your new job.' He glanced around the room. 'That is, if you still want the new job.'

She stared silently.

'There is a boy. You went to his house. Yes?'

She blushed. 'Yes.'

'He has asked for you again. I said I would ask you, but, as I promised, I will not force you. I can, however, ask one of the other girls, maybe the little one, whose name is, wait a moment.' He opened the door and shouted to his brother. 'Daria, that small girl. What is her name?'

'Sana.'

'Yes, Sana, the pretty one, who our clients like very much.'

With her stomach churning, she recalled Sana being sick at what that last man had done to her.

'No, you promised me the girls won't ever have to do that again.'

Yuri inclined his head and darkened his eyes. 'Your tone is too sharp, Yalina. That is not good.'

'No, I'm sorry. What I meant to say is, I'll go. He wasn't so bad. Not as bad as Shabir.'

'Ah, I see. You like this boy, then?'

Yalina fervently shook her head. 'No, but I know Sana is not well right now. She needs time.'

'Okay, I will have Daria take you there.' He stared at her for a moment. 'Yalina, what do you know about this boy?'

She shrugged her shoulders. 'Nothing at all. He just wanted to have sex, that's all.'

'Did he talk to you?'

She shook her head. 'Only to ask me to take my clothes off and . . .' She looked down.

Yuri laughed. 'Don't worry. I don't want to know the details.' He clapped his hands. 'Right, wear the sari that you have on because I am sure he would like that. Be good. His father is to be kept happy. When you return, you must go back to the girls.'

Yalina's face dropped in disappointment. She'd hoped she would be returning to this plush room, but she didn't say a word.

'I want you to be clear that you have made the right decision to work with me and manage the girls because there will be no going back. You will never be offered a better position, not in this country, anyway. And if you choose to go against me, the consequences of doing so, which we have already discussed, will be harsh.'

'I understand.'

'Good. Then, that old room will be a reminder for you.'

He turned and left, leaving her alone. She sat pondering over meeting the boy again. He was kind, and he had not touched her at all. So why did he want to see her again? A sudden sense of excitement shot through her. Maybe he would help her escape, or perhaps he or his father could buy her.

While in contemplation, she stared at the second door, and her mind quickly became inquisitive; it was another trait her father had smacked out of her. She had asked too many questions, as far as he was concerned. He slapped her hands if she peered into a pot to see what was cooking, and he pinched her nose too hard if she looked over his shoulder when he read the newspaper. But the door was calling her. She jumped up from the edge of the bed and tried the handle. It was locked. Instinctively, she put her ear to the door and listened. She thought she could hear someone calling out. 'Hello, is anyone there?' she whispered, but the only sound she heard was a faint howling. Maybe, she surmised, it might be a groan or it could be the wind blowing through a crack in a window.

Daria wasn't long in coming to her room. Without knocking, he opened the door and stood there with a cigarette dangling from the corner of his mouth and grinning at her.

Yalina didn't like the look on his face and his stare. It was almost as if he was undressing her.

‘Come, now!’ he ordered.

She followed him and wondered how he could be related to Yuri. He was so different. His eyes, for a start, were round and too big for his face, and his stature was shorter and coated in a layer of fat, unlike Yuri’s lean and sleek physique.

She imagined their mother telling Yuri to let his younger brother Daria join in with the games, to include him all the time, and to look out for him at school. And now, as an adult, he was the tagalong who could get away with a lot because he was that brother who always had. She knew the set-up because her little sister was the same. However, her little sister was also her father’s favourite.

Daria opened the car door, and even though she was climbing in, he had to give her a shove just to show her he was in control. The windows were blacked out inside to prevent her from seeing out, but she managed to take in her surroundings before stepping into the car. The house was on a road that surrounded a huge green.

While Daria drove to the boy’s house, Yalina shut her eyes and listened to the songs being played on the radio. Apparently, he had chosen Capital FM and they were playing ‘Gangnam Style’ by Psy. It was a song she was familiar with back in Pakistan.

After every song, the radio presenter gave the time, so Yalina was able to work out that by the time they reached the boy’s house, it had taken around thirty minutes.

Daria opened the car door for her and poked her in the back. He hissed in her ear. ‘You fuck him good. Any complaints, and I will have to show you how it’s done.’

She replied with a simple ‘okay’, which somehow riled him up.

‘Don’t you fucking answer me like that. You are nothing, and Yuri is stupid to offer you a position of authority over the girls.’ He tutted. ‘Very stupid. Now, go and fuck him. I’ll be waiting outside.’

He didn't need to ring the doorbell. The door opened. Daria guessed Teddy Ryder had CCTV installed. A man in his position would be stupid not to. He grinned to himself. The man was a fool and too full of himself to understand what was going on right under his nose.

He nodded at Teddy. 'Here she is, but this is the last time she comes here.'

Teddy folded his arms. 'Oh, is that right, mate?'

Daria had to hold down his temper. He clenched his fists and his teeth.

'I think my boy likes her, so my money is as good as anyone's, or is it not now?'

Daria sighed and walked away. 'I'll wait in the car for her.'

Teddy flicked his head for her to come inside. He couldn't look her in the eye.

Yalina noticed it. *Maybe he was ashamed*, she thought.

Eddie came down the stairs and gave his father a look.

Teddy held up his hands. 'All right, I'll be in my office.' He sniggered. 'So you can make as much noise as you like.'

Eddie tutted at his father's disgusting insinuation.

Snatching the newspaper from the console table in the hallway, Teddy then pulled his son close to him, now annoyed that his son hadn't seen the funny side of his comment.

'Remember, Eddie, this ain't a bloody date, all right? You've no need to be cooking or entertaining.'

'Okay, Dad. Go, will you.'

Teddy laughed as he slammed the office door shut behind him.

***

'Hello again. Would you like something to eat and drink?' he said, with a welcoming smile.

Yalina shrugged her shoulders. 'I don't mind. Whatever you want to do.'

'Shall we grab a drink before we go to my room?'

For a moment, Yalina wondered if he now wanted to have sex. He seemed far less nervous and less uncomfortable than when she was here last time.

'I'm going to have a Coke.'

Having already experienced the taste and enjoyed it very much, she nodded, 'Yes, please. I'd like one too.'

Was she selling her virginity for a can of Coke?

He led her to the kitchen, opened the large American style fridge-freezer, and pulled out two cans of Coke. 'Would you like ice?'

She shook her head and relieved him of the can. She dragged the ring and waited, hoping the liquid wouldn't spray all over this beautiful gleaming kitchen.

'Come up to my room, Yalina, and listen.' He leaned into her. 'I just want to talk, nothing else.'

He could see her shoulders visibly relax, and her face brightened. 'Thank you.'

'No, don't thank me. You shouldn't be made to do this, anyway.'

'They told me I have another job now, but they are yet to disclose to me the details.'

It surprised her at how much tidier his bedroom was. She wondered if he'd been expecting her.

'I, well, my family need your help, and we also want to help you escape, but we must know what we are dealing with.' He pointed to his bed. 'You can take a seat.'

She sat down and sipped her Coke. The bubbles went up her nose and made her eyes water. She suddenly let out a loud burp and instantly put her hand to her mouth.

Eddie laughed and followed her with a loud burp of his own.

She blushed. 'I am sorry.'

He smiled. 'Coke always gets to me.'

'How can I help you, Eddie?'

Without wasting time, he opened the photos on his phone. The first one was of his aunt. 'Have you ever seen her?'

She took the phone and studied it.

He enlarged the picture so she could see Charley's face more clearly, but he felt gutted when she shook her head. 'No, I haven't. I'm sorry.'

'Yalina, I need to ask you a few questions, but I have to record our conversation.' He noticed her flinch. 'Don't worry. It's only to help us to find my aunt.'

'*Your aunt?*'

'It's a long story, but she is missing, and her disappearance may be connected to the people you work for.'

'How?'

'Please can I explain afterwards? Only we don't have long.'

She nodded and took another swig of her drink.

He turned the phone recorder on and gently stroked her bare arm. 'Don't worry, it's fine. Now, this photo is, well, let me show you.' He handed her back the phone, and her eyes widened.

'I know, Yalina, it's nasty.'

Studying the photo, she nodded. 'I have seen this. Those handcuffs, they are on the wall in the room along the same corridor where my room is.' Her eyes filled with tears.

'Tell me, what is it?'

'The last time I saw that room, Dominica who worked for them was hanging by those cuffs.' Her words were slow and distant. 'I think she was dead or almost dead. Her skin was grey, her mouth was swollen, and she was covered in dried blood. They probably removed her teeth.' She shuddered as tears trickled down her cheek.

Eddie wiped them away. 'I'm so sorry, Yalina.'

As he digested her words, his whole body became alive with goosebumps. He found it hard to understand that medieval torture like that really went on in this day and age.

'Do you know who you work for?'

'His name is Yuri. He is a Russian man. That man outside your house is his brother, Daria.'

'Do you know the name Teddy Ryder?'

She shook her head. 'No.'

'Do you know where this Yuri lives?'

'The car windows are too dark to see out of, but before I left his house to come here, I noticed that his place is like a mansion. It's huge. It's on a road, and in front is a big green area. It's about thirty minutes from here.'

'And you live there?'

'No, they lock the girls and me in the basement of an old hospital, asylum, or medical building. It's derelict, and I think they are rebuilding it because there are workmen's signs, wire fences, piles of sand, and a digger, or something like it.'

'But you don't know where this place is?'

She shook her head. 'Oh no, there are guards who transport us in these vans that are dark inside. They will never let us know where we are.'

'What does this Yuri make you and the other girls do?'

'When I first arrived, I was taken to a place where they made or sold saris. There were rows of them, and there was a room with a stage, and we were made to dance.'

'Is there anything else you remember about that place?'

‘Yes, we went back to learn this dance, and Hulou, a woman there, escaped and’ – she took a deep breath and wiped her brow – ‘they said the police had beaten her, before they, I mean the Russians, brought her back. Then’ – she paused and took another deep breath – ‘they made us watch as they pulled one of her teeth out.’

Eddie clocked how she was shaking and placed his arm around her shoulders. ‘Christ, Yalina, they made you watch? This is the most horrific thing I’ve ever heard in my life. You must have been terrified.’

‘Yuri has said that I have a new job and that the girls will be working under me, but I don’t know what it involves, but he assured me that we will not be sleeping with men.’

‘When these Russians take you in the van, is it just to this sari shop?’

‘No, they also took us to a bigger place with a bar and a big stage. There were a lot of guards, and then suddenly, while the girls were dancing, the music stopped, and we were pushed into one van when we had previously filled two. It was terrible. We were all on top of each other, and the driver sped off, flying over the bumps.’

‘How long did it take you to get back to this derelict place where they keep you?’

‘I don’t know exactly. But I would guess around thirty minutes.’

‘Yalina, please, can you think of anything that would give us a clue where they are keeping you?’

With tears in her eyes, she shook her head. ‘I don’t know. I wish I knew more, Eddie, I do, really.’

He stopped for a moment to hug her. ‘You are doing so well, considering it must be challenging for you.’

Yalina looked at him and smiled.

‘And you say Yuri is the top boss?’

'Er, no, not the head man, but he supposedly is my boss.'

'So who is above this Yuri, then?'

'I am not sure of his name, but he came to Yuri's mansion. He had hair like the moon and an eye that shone like a star.'

'Did he look Asian, Russian? Is there anything else about him that you can recall?'

'He looked very much British. He wore a smart suit. I think he was about sixty-five, maybe even a little older. He is a big man, bigger than your father. I saw him once outside the hospital building and then at Yuri's house.'

'And how do you know he is the boss?'

'He was like a headmaster, very loud, and he wasn't afraid of Yuri at all. I just assumed he was in charge.' Her pupils dilated into a thousand-yard stare, and suddenly, she excitedly said, 'Andrew! His name was Andrew! Yes, that's it, and Yuri spoke about having insurance in case this Andrew was to be a silly man, or something like that.'

'Anything else you remember, anything at all?'

She stared again, trying to recall anything in her desperate bid to help in any way she could.

Suddenly, Teddy bellowed up the stairs, 'Eddie!'

'Shit, time's up. Let me smudge your make-up.'

'I'll do it. It's fine.' She smiled as she also rubbed her hair to make it messy.

'I'm going to call my mum. I was going to call her before you arrived, but I thought you would be coming tomorrow.'

'I believe that Yuri and his men like the element of surprise. He and the girls, including myself, are heavily guarded. And we are never prewarned that we will be taken anywhere.'

'Were you brought to England against your will?'

Yalina went over the facts, calmy and honestly. ‘No, my father needs money so I came with my mother of my own free will, I suppose.’

‘So, you weren’t stolen off the streets?’

‘No, but I have a debt that I need to work off and then I will be free.’

‘And the other girls? Were they taken off the streets and brought here against their will?’

‘I don’t know for sure, but there are around twenty girls, and Yuri will be putting us to work to pay off our debts, but in what capacity, I don’t know. He promised me it wasn’t to have sex with men.’

‘Eddie, you need to come down now!’

‘Is there anything at all that you remember about the mansion?’

‘Oh yes, he showed me a room that would be mine once their new operation was underway. There was a door in that room that was locked. I thought I heard whining, like someone was in there, but then again, I shouldn’t be so surprised. He keeps twenty or more girls locked up in the basement of that abandoned hospital or clinic or whatever it is.’

‘Eddie, answer me, will ya!’

‘Coming, Dad.’ He gently hugged Yalina. ‘Thank you. I hope we can rescue you soon. If I had known when you were coming I could have arranged for my mum to follow you and find out where they are keeping you.’

‘It will be too late now, anyway. They are moving us soon.’

‘Eddie, hurry up, mate, will ya. The geezer outside is pacing the drive, the wanker!’

‘We’re coming!’

CHAPTER TWENTY-SIX

Daria opened the car door as soon as Yalina appeared. He didn't look at her; he looked at Teddy Ryder and smirked.

As soon as Yalina was seated in the back seat, Daria said, 'I hope you did what you were paid to do.'

His sneers and the smell of stale whisky on his breath unnerved her. She nodded fast. But she sat nervously on her hands.

'If the father calls to say you were not good in the bedroom, then I will show you, as I said.'

She didn't look at him, too afraid of making eye contact.

He leaned in further and gripped the back of her neck, pulling her towards him. 'Don't ignore me.'

'I'm sorry. Yes, I think he was happy.'

He let go of her and laughed before he lit a cigarette and walked around to the driver's door. As soon as he got in, he lowered all the windows to let out the smoke.

She shivered as the cold midnight air crept into her bones. She wished she was wearing that soft cream jumper and tweed jacket instead of her thin sari. As he tore away, skidding on the gravel drive, she saw Eddie looking down from his bedroom window and then giving her a gentle wave. Yalina closed her eyes to stop the tears. He was the only person in England who had been kind to her, and she hoped he would find a way to rescue her.

She wondered if Daria had forgotten she was in the back because he was still driving with the windows open. It might be okay for him. He was wearing his thick flannel coat, but she was hugging her bare arms to keep herself warm. As they reached the end of the road and stopped to give way to traffic, she stared at the large and beautifully kept houses.

A car pulled into the street. That was when she heard Daria growl under his breath. The driver of the car was the man with the silver hair. He glanced her way, giving her a piercing glare, and she could see his face reddening with anger.

Daria stopped his car, acknowledging Andrew with a roll of the eyes. 'Why are you here?'

Ignoring Daria's question, he growled through gritted teeth, 'What is she doing in your car, man? Are you an imbecile? She can see around her.'

Daria glanced back and realised that all the windows were down. 'It's fine. She doesn't know where we are,' he replied, in his sternest native accent.

'Get rid of her. This is the second time she has seen me. Now, I won't tell you again. Get rid!'

Daria wagged his finger. 'You have no right to tell us how to run the business. Do not make demands!'

'Us? There is no *us*, Daria. It is your brother who I deal with, not you. Now, do as I say, or this business will fall to its knees. I cannot afford to have any slip-ups.'

'Why are you going to Ryder's house?' Daria asked, as he blew smoke into the cold air.

Andrew curled his lip. 'Harper Kane is still hiding. Your men lost her. Unfortunately, she knows too much, so I want to find out if Ryder knows where she is.'

'And you go alone?'

'Yes, alone. My methods of extracting information are more diplomatic than yours.'

'But, Andrew, she isn't his wife or girlfriend. She is his ex. So why would he know?'

Shaking his head and sighing, Andrew replied, 'It is lucky that one of you has brains, and it certainly isn't you, you fool. Apparently, she isn't just an ex-tart. They share a son together. And he kept her on at the club when he took it over.'

‘Well, I know she does not live with him.’ Daria barked a short laugh. ‘And, yes, she was working in the club. And if she meant anything to him, with his money’ – he rubbed his fingers together – ‘she would not be serving drinks to men who come to watch the pole dancers. Yes? She would be at the hairdresser’s, in London, shopping maybe, and doing what rich women do. Yes?’

‘Whatever their relationship is, we need to find her before—’

‘Before what?’ interrupted Daria, now smirking. ‘Before she goes to the police and says she killed two Russian bouncers outside her club that was hosting a private party! A club she works in but one where she didn’t know about the private functions? See how it sounds? I tell you, it sounds stupid. She has gone, and probably, seeing it all from a different angle, she is running for her life. How long would she get in prison, in this country? Ten, maybe twenty years, for a double murder?’

Andrew hadn’t thought of that. His focus had been on finding her. ‘What are you doing with that girl in the car?’ He frowned and looked ahead. ‘Does Ryder like young girls?’

Daria laughed again. ‘No, but his son does. His father can afford the real thing for his son. He doesn’t need to buy dirty magazines.’

But Andrew’s eyes were wide. ‘*What!* You took one of the girls to Ryder’s house for his son? Are you both so stupid?’

‘Now stop, Andrew. You don’t tell me what to do.’

‘Someone needs to. That girl could tell his son anything.’ He peered closer at Yalina, who, he could see, was holding her head down, and, apparently, too afraid to make eye contact.

‘Relax, Andrew, why would Ryder’s son even ask questions? She was only there to fuck.’

‘Because, Daria, Ryder’s son is Harper Kane’s mother.’

Daria shrugged his shoulders. ‘So what? You are paranoid and maybe not good for business. I will tell my brother of your concerns, but I think he will have concerns of his own about you.

You make everyone nervous. You are always looking for a problem with the plans.'

Andrew puffed out his chest. 'I will look for faults to make sure we aren't bloody caught, you imprudent man. And having one of the girls – particularly that one – could be the bomb that blows the whole thing out of the water. So, tell me, Daria, how did Ryder know about the girls?'

Daria shrugged his shoulders. 'He asked Stan to arrange for this girl to go to his home.' He pointed over his shoulder to the back seat. 'His son was pleased. He must have enjoyed getting his little willie wet.' He curled his little finger and wiggled, insinuating that the boy had a small penis. 'He asked for her to come back.'

'Oh, Jesus fucking Christ!' screeched Andrew, as he bashed his hands on the steering wheel. 'And in your pea-sized brain, didn't you think that was odd? I mean, look at her. She is hardly . . . well, hardly experienced. I bet the only cock she has ever seen before was on a bull roaming the dusty streets in Pakistan. How could she have given him such a good time that he wanted her back?'

Daria spun around and looked the girl over. 'Stop worrying. I will take her to the lock-up, and then I will find out if she said anything to the boy.'

In a split second, Andrew's face turned from raging red to milky-white. 'If she's told that boy anything, you realise it will be over for all of us, don't you?'

'Stop worrying, Andrew. She knows nothing!'

'You cannot be sure about that. Get rid of her. She knows too much now. Look at her, man. The girl is pretending she isn't listening. Bury her deep, Daria. Very fucking deep. If Ryder starts to question me, then it will come back on you for being so stupid. Why would you use one of the girls? You're all nuts. No, actually, you're not nuts. You're simply greedy.'

'The correct term, Andrew, is Russian.'

'Just dispose of her tonight.'

With a nod by way of confirmation, Daria pulled away.

***

Eddie watched as the car left the drive before he picked up his phone. Instantly, he texted his mother, sending her the recorded message.

***

Harper was surprised to see her son's message so quickly. She, like him, had assumed that if Teddy had agreed to arrange for a prostitute, or, in this case Yalina, to come to the house, it would have been tomorrow night at the earliest. She was sitting facing Michel and Terry at Terry's kitchen table when she put the phone down and pressed 'play'.

When Yalina spoke about the abandoned hospital and those handcuffs, Harper's skin was alive with goosebumps. Her throat closed up. She looked across at Michel. His eyes were trance-like, his lips slightly parted, and his posture was upright and rigid.

'What is it, Michel? What is it?' she asked gently, as she placed her hand on his.

'Can you go back to the beginning, please?'

She played the recording again while Terry jumped up and opened the man drawer in the kitchen, where he retrieved a notepad and pen and slapped them onto the table.

Once they heard the part in the recording about Yalina's journey to Teddy's being about thirty minutes, the three of them looked at each other with excitement. This was the first piece in the jigsaw puzzle they had been gifted. And it was a crucial one as well.

'I need a map,' said Terry.

When Terry left the room, Michel almost let out a deep breath. 'I need to think.' He rose from his chair, ran his hands through his hair, and paced the floor.

'Please, Michel, tell me?'

'There is only one man I know with silver hair and a shiny eye. Actually, it's a glass eye, and his name is Andrew.'

'Is he dangerous? How powerful is this man? Would he hurt my sister?'

He rubbed his face. 'Oh God, this is a mess, but now it is all beginning to make sense.'

Harper, in her frustration, barked, 'Will you tell me who this bloke is because I will hold a gun to his head and make him tell me where Charley is?'

'He is the former Metropolitan Police Commissioner, Sir Andrew Mercer.'

'Mercer, Mercer? Where do I know that name from?' Suddenly, the penny dropped. 'Oh Christ, alive, he is that fucking bitch Verity's father!'

Michel slowly nodded. 'Yes, and he has to be the most respected man in the world of the gentlemen's clubs that I know of.'

'Katie told me that Verity's father is rich. Do you know if he came from money? Because if he didn't, then he has to be the biggest crook of all.'

When Terry hurried into the room, he didn't initially notice the startled looks on their faces. He was too determined to find the abandoned hospital. But once he had set out the map on the table, he looked at Harper and then at Michel. 'Okay, what's going on, you two?'

'Andrew, the silver-haired man with the shiny eye, is the fucking ex-Metropolitan police Commissioner, no less,' said Harper, her eyes bright and alert.

Terry straightened up. 'Oh, come on. Are you sure? There could be similarities, but a man of that level of standing connected to a Russian mob who imports young girls? Nah, I can't see it myself. I mean, think about it. To be a police commissioner, you would have the words “law-abiding” ingrained on the brain like wearing an anchor tattoo permanently reminding you that you served in the Navy.’

Michel shook his head. ‘How many men do you know – actually, how many people, period, do you know who have a glass eye?’

Terry shrugged his shoulders. ‘Er, I dunno, really.’

‘How many men with the name Andrew do you know?’

‘Er, three.’

‘How many men with the name Andrew have silver hair?’

‘One. Well, he has nine hairs in a nit, but they are grey.’

‘Can you see what I am saying? The probability that Andrew, with one eye and silver hair, *is* the former police commissioner is pretty high.’

Terry nodded. ‘But fuck me, that’s the kinda geezer you’d trust with ya life,’ he said, stunned.

‘And he happens to be Verity Mercer’s father, and—’ said Michel.

Harper interrupted. ‘The same bitch who turned my flat upside down looking for that poxy tablet. The same bitch who is my sister’s operations manager. The same bitch who is now following me. Christ, the evil fucking cow deliberately sent Charley to the death chamber!’

‘See, that makes no sense either. Why send an undercover copper into a crime that her father is part of?’

‘But she didn’t, did she? Verity only took over the case from Peter Bracken, who is dead, and I am in the frame for his murder,’ replied Michel.

‘Right, well, we need to find Charley ASAP,’ said Terry, as he smoothed the map out. He worked out the distance a motor vehicle would travel for thirty minutes non-stop based on information from Google, and then, using a piece of string, he placed one point on Teddy Ryder's home and let the other end produce a circle. He repeated this to produce a circle with its centre at The Click. When he had finished, they could see the likely maximum distance a vehicle could have travelled through three hundred and sixty degrees.

Michel thought it would have been easier to use a computer to achieve the same result. But he hadn't counted on Terry's knowledge of the streets in this part of Kent.

After smoothing out the old map again, Michel stared at the area. It was too big to guess where the hospital would be, and he sighed. 'What we're looking for could be anywhere.'

Michel asked to use Terry's laptop. 'I may know a way to find this place.' Of course, he knew how to do that; it was part of his job.

In seconds, he had the screen up, and after tapping the keys, he spun the laptop around to show an old cottage hospital. It was built in 1800 and left to go to rack and ruin. It had never been a landmark building because it had been privately owned and used as a convalescent home and then as an asylum before it was sold to a property developer back in 1996. There was no other information.

'Look, can we go there now? I mean, what if my sister's there and Yalina just hasn't seen her?'

Michel shook his head. 'We cannot go storming into the building. We're not the SAS, and I'll have to go on a reconnaissance mission first.'

Terry raised his brows. 'Really? See, even that sounds like what the SAS do, to me.'

Michel nodded. 'You forget I was a soldier before I worked for the British force. If Russians guard that place, understand this: they will shoot to kill. They will be guarding a profitable business, so marching in will get us shot.'

'Why don't we call the police? We can say we heard screaming coming from the building.'

Michel shook his head. 'Look, I don't trust the police. There is something very fishy going on and clearly the ex-commissioner is involved. Not forgetting he is Verity's father. That place will be flagged up as a no-go area, with an "Under Surveillance" notice in place. No officer would go there because it could potentially jeopardise their operation. They would never want any backlash for interfering with a big operation like that. If Verity knows that there is a criminal activity linked to her father in connection with that abandoned building, she will do whatever it takes to protect him, won't she? So, I can guarantee, that on the system, it is coded as "Under Surveillance".'

Harper could feel her anger rising. Her head was hot and her mouth dry. 'I can't simply sit here doing nothing. I swear to God, I will smash that Verity all around the place.'

'Calm down, Harper,' said Michel, getting up from his seat and doing some posture exercises. He was getting a pain in his back from sitting hunched up over the laptop. 'Or you will be next to useless. Look, call Katie. We have to keep her up to date, and she will know what to do at her end.'

Terry walked around the table and squeezed Harper's shoulder. 'Listen, doll, Michel knows what's best. This is his thing. I'll pour you a warm brandy, and you allow him to think for you for a change, okay?' he said, before kissing the top of her head.

'Okay, I'll call her.' After the phone rang a few times, Katie answered. Her speech was sluggish. 'Hello, Harper.'

'Katie, are you okay?'

'Yeah, just tired. I've been trawling through everything I could get out of the mainframe about Charley's operation, but it's futile, and there's nothing of any significance.'

'Katie, we know who is behind it all, and we were right. It is Verity, but, more importantly, also her father, Andrew Mercer. They are holding the girls in an abandoned building. It's five miles from Faversham on the way to Whitstable in Kent.'

'What! How? I mean really?'

'Yeah, we have good reason to believe so.'

'You're amazing, Harper. And you're quite sure?'

'Yeah. One of the girls who they are holding against her will gave us all the details.'

'And where is she now?'

'The Russians have her.'

'Bloody hell. Right, let me contact our chief. You stay put, and I'll get it sorted at my end. And let's hope to God we find your sister alive. If she is, Harper, I promise you I am going to do my best to get her back for you. Where are you now?'

'Me, er, I'm at a mate's.'

'Who is that?'

'Why?'

'I just want to make sure you are safe, that's all. It seems to me that there is no one we can trust,' she replied, but her words sounded a little sluggish.

'Are you okay, Katie?'

'Yeah, just so tired from going through all the paperwork trying to find anything to help me find Charley, but a strong cup of coffee will do the trick. Now, I need to call the chief and have him execute a raid. Where is this hospital?'

As soon as Harper ended the call, she glanced at Michel and sighed. 'The poor cow's shattered.'

Michel laughed. 'She's been on the wine.'

'What? Katie? But she seems so together.'

'Yeah, but this job can get to us all. She says she's been off, but I would guess she has been undercover, and it is very taxing. Why do you think I can drink a bottle of brandy and have no hangover? It's because I am used to it,' replied Michel, as he retook his seat.

Terry took three cups from the cupboard, poured out percolated coffee, and added a tot of brandy. ‘’Ere ya go.’

Michel gratefully accepted his, cupping his hands around the warm mug.

Harper smiled and stared at the coffee.

‘So, what do we do now?’

‘Well, I am going to check out this abandoned hospital to see if there is any activity. I’m going to find my wife.’

‘Are we not going to wait for the police to raid it?’

Michel shook his head. ‘They won’t go there right away. They have to make a plan and get a SWAT team together. But once they discover it is under surveillance there will be hoops to jump through first. Like I said, they cannot balls up an undercover operation. So they will have to have every form signed and sealed, before they go trooping in.’

Harper snatched up her phone from the table and slid it into her pocket. ‘Come on, then. What are we waiting for? Let’s go.’

‘Woah, no, you cannot come, Harper. This is too dangerous.’

Terry sighed. ‘Michel, you do know that she won’t listen, don’t ya? She’s as stubborn as an old goat.’

Michel tutted. ‘Well, you must do as I say, or you could get me killed as well as yourself.’

‘Okay, okay, let’s go.’

‘Wait!’ said Terry. ‘We might need a few items that could assist us.’

Michel tutted again and rolled his eyes. He wondered what on earth Terry could come up with.

However, when Terry returned, he held up two shotguns. He grinned. ‘Are these any good?’

‘Tel? What the fuck, mate.’

'I told you that me and me pals were a little bit naughty in our younger days.'

He threw one of the guns to Michel, who turned it over in his hands and smiled. 'Nice tool.'

Harper held out her hand, but Terry shook his head. 'No, Harper, you won't need one.'

Annoyed that she didn't get a gun, she said, 'All right, then, I'll take this motherfucker.' She pulled out the biggest knife that was attached to the wall magnet.

'Go on, Harpsichord, get in the cab.'

CHAPTER TWENTY-SEVEN

The car windows were up and the privacy glass was preventing Yalina from seeing anything outside.

But that wasn't her immediate concern right now. Her mind was on this man called Andrew. He was the man with the voice of authority. In fact, she didn't know who scared her more, Daria or the silver-haired man with the strange shiny eye.

She only hoped that Daria would leave her be, but, in her heart, she guessed she was about to face a torturous inquisition.

Daria slid open the blacked-out glass partition that separated the front from the back. 'Hey, what did the boy ask you to do?'

Yalina hoped she could convince him, but, in reality, she didn't know anything about married life. Her parents hadn't even promised her to anyone. 'He made me take my clothes off.'

'And then what?'

'He took off his.'

'What, all of them?'

Yalina sensed his surprise. 'No, just his trousers and shorts.'

'Then what did he do?'

'He touched me.'

'Did he? Where?'

Yalina's cheeks were burning up. *How do I answer that*, she wondered, *when I know absolutely nothing about sex?* 'Between my legs.'

He stopped asking questions, but he didn't close the glass partition.

She could see through the windscreen. It was dark, but she could see in the distance the entrance to the hospital. It was lit up by a couple of large industrial lamps that construction sites use when working late. Her mouth was dry, and her palms were sweaty, even though she was cold.

Her heart felt as though it was beginning to beat outside her chest. The vision of Hulou and those evil men tying her down before they extracted her tooth, along with the blood-curdling screams, played out again in her mind.

Daria edged slowly up to the closed gates and flashed his lights. A guard approached and smiled, allowing him entry.

He drove right up to the entrance of the hospital. But once he got out, he lit another cigarette before casually sauntering around and opening the rear passenger door 'Come, Yalina, I need to talk to you.'

Yalina could barely walk; her legs felt like jelly, and she also felt faint, but Daria's sharp tone as he urged her to hurry brought her to her senses. She could guess what lay ahead of her; she only hoped she could stick to her guns under torturous conditions. As it was, her stomach was churning with every step.

'Move!' Pushing her through the double swing doors and along the corridor, passing each room where the others were being held, he then went past her room, and, more shockingly, through the next set of double swing doors. 'Now stop!'

Yalina was struggling to breathe. She recognised the door that led into the room where Hulou had been tortured.

Using his foot, Daria pushed the door open. 'Go inside,' he demanded, as he flicked on a switch that brought back memories of that fateful occasion. The chair was as it was, and there was a considerable amount of dried blood still there on the floor. *Surely having teeth removed wouldn't cause that much blood loss, would it?* she thought. *But then, what did she know?*

She leaned against the wall because suddenly she felt very light-headed. The blood drained from her face, and she felt a prickling sensation. And then, as if a bird was inside her flapping its wings, or was that her heart, she felt sure she was having an attack. Moments later, she was gasping for air, on all fours.

Daria's words sounded distant, like an echo. Eventually, his words became more distinct as she came around. But as she looked up at him, she didn't like what she saw. Not only was his face almost contorted like that of a rabid dog about to attack its victim, but he was leaning over her, holding those same pliers that were used on Hulou.

'Get the fuck up! You have a choice: you tell me what you told the boy, or I take your teeth out, one by one.'

Her tongue stuck to the roof of her mouth, and a warm sensation covered her upper thighs. She had wet herself.

'If you are afraid now, think about how you will feel pain like never before after I remove your teeth. You can stop that by telling me what he wanted you for!'

'He-he-he wanted to have sex with me.'

Irritated, Daria spat, 'Yes, but what actually happened?'

'I have just said. Sex.'

'No, no, what *questions* did he ask you?'

'He didn't.'

'*What?* Are you lying to me? I'll make you tell the truth!' He banged the pliers against the wall, making her jump.

She shook her head and hoped he would believe her.

'What did you talk about?' Spittle flew from his lips as he waved the pliers in her face.

'Nothing, I promise, nothing! Nothing at all. He just wanted to do things to me. And that's what he did.'

Daria crouched down at face level and gripped her jaw, squeezing it tight. 'Tell me the fucking truth.'

Her eyes widened, begging him to let go of her. When he then forced the pliers into her mouth, the fear compelled her to scream so loudly that even Daria was struck dumb.

But just as he was about to grip her tooth, the door opened, and Yuri appeared, flanked by two guards.

Yuri looked flustered, and, although he was speaking in Russian and she couldn't understand him, she could see he was angry. He was shouting and waving his hands about before he stormed off. *Would Daria now leave her alone?* she wondered.

'Get up. You must come with me,' Daria demanded.

Relief flooded her veins when he leaned down and reached out his hand to help her up. As soon as she took it, he dragged her back along the corridor, joining the chaos at its peak. Girls were being pulled out of the rooms on either side of the corridor and pushed towards the entrance before being forcefully loaded into the vans.

All she could hear was 'Hurry, hurry! Move! Quick!'

Guards were running in all directions, pulling down the workmen's signs, rounding up the girls, and shouting at each other in their own language.

At that moment, the main lights that illuminated the entrance were turned off. They were now in total darkness.

This was her chance to run. Every time she had been led in or out of the van, she had deliberately scanned her surroundings and memorised the layout in the hope that one day she could escape this hellhole. To the right of the double doors that led down to the cold damp basement was the main entrance. The imposing double doors themselves had been boarded up but on either side were huge pillars. Behind them appeared to be recesses, but it had always been too dark to see what lay in the shadows. She could imagine at one time that it would have looked quite grand. Except now it was a derelict building with medical signs being the only clue that it was a former hospital. And the grounds would have been impressive. She could visualise a wash of coloured roses and flowers, judging by the vast expanse of bushes with millions of rose hips, rambling brambles, and weeds.

Daria now had his attention on the two lamps. His voice took on a new level of stress as he bellowed and waved his arm.

Yalina sensed they were panicking over something pretty serious. What with the lamps having just been turned off and all the girls now out of the building and into the vans, something was definitely going down. The guards were literally throwing the girls on top of each other. To her relief, she saw that no one was actually checking the girls from a list. That being the case, she knew she wouldn't be missed – at least not yet, anyway. So she would use this opportunity to hide and prepare to escape.

She took three steps back, and the moment she could make out Daria hurrying to the driver's side of the van, obviously to turn the headlights on, she spotted her chance. She fled behind the pillar and backed herself into one of the recesses. She leaned against what she thought was a wall until she felt the rough grain of the wood. Instantly, she spun around and realised that it was a door. A dilapidated one, too, judging by the splits in the planks of wood. She felt for a handle, but her heart sank when she couldn't find one. Gripping the edge with her nails, she tugged, hoping it would open, and it did. Without considering what lay behind that door, she entered and closed it behind her.

She breathed as quietly as possible, even though she was petrified that a guard would find her. But in keeping quiet, she could hear someone behind her breathing and then softly enunciated words. 'Don't speak.' The words were followed by a hand over her mouth, but they weren't harsh words like those of the guards.

The voice of a man said gently, 'I am not here to hurt you. Stay quiet.'

She knew she had to trust whoever was in the dark room with her. She nodded, and he let go of her mouth.

'Where are they taking the girls?' he whispered.

'I don't know, I promise.'

'Okay, stay here and stay quiet.'

'I will, I promise.' Yalina felt relieved, believing there was hope in the form of a man with a soft but firm voice. He disappeared to the back of the room. Yalina assumed there was another door that would lead to the main building, but she did as he asked and waited.

***

Suddenly the door was ripped open. Before she could even run, Daria's hand snatched her by the hair and dragged her outside, hissing into her ear, 'You cannot escape me, Yalina.'

Still with his hands gripping her hair, he hauled her towards his car. In the distance, she could see the vans climbing the steep hill. Were they to be murdered, and was she? Terrified of the consequences, she desperately tried to remove his hands, but he viciously tugged her hair harder, almost breaking her neck as he bent her backwards, until he reached his vehicle.

With a hard blow around her face, she buckled to her knees. He then bundled her into the boot. All her hopes were dashed.

'You dare to try to escape from me. I will show you what happens,' he hissed, before he slammed the lid down.

***

Harper sat in the front of Terry's cab and stared at the field, specifically the cordoned off, lonely, and even haunted-looking building. She had shuddered when she'd watched Michel go off to see the lie of the land.

She could only make out part of the front of the building where it had been lit up, but now it was in darkness. So, she guessed Michel had turned off their generator.

'Oh, Tel, I hope he's all right in there.'

'He's a clever bloke. He knows what he's doing, and we've gotta do our bit as well and follow any vehicle that comes out of there. We need to find out where this top dog lives.'

Before he started the engine, two black vans and a car with their headlights off shot out of the lane and took Terry by total surprise.

'Shit, here we go. This is our job. Hold on to your hats. We're off.'

Harper was ready for action, and as they tore off, slipping and sliding on the lanes of wet mud, Harper screeched, 'Can't you go any faster? Look, they're bleedin' miles in front.'

Terry put his foot down, but unexpectedly, the car behind the two vans slowed up and stopped in the middle of the road.

'Bollocks, they know we're following them.'

'So! Tel, just swerve around them.'

'No, Harper, I'm not. The man in that car will fucking shoot us, and believe me, my girl, they will be an excellent shot. I'm backing off.'

'But, Tel, my sister! Please, we need to do *something*!'

'Harper, no! I am not driving you into the line of fire. Now, I'm sorry, babe, but it ain't happening.'

Harper sighed; she knew he was doing the right thing, but she was so desperate to find her sister. It was now eating her up inside.

The car drove away as soon as the vans were out of sight.

She pulled her phone from her pocket to see if Michel had messaged her, only to find an unopened text message from Hatty, Paddy's sister. She frowned; it was so late. Why would Hatty be texting her at this time?

Hi Harper, I hope you are well. I thought you would like to know that the police have arrested a man for the murder of Paddy. I had my suspicions, but they confirmed it when they found the gun in his wardrobe. I wished to God my sister had never got involved in the family, and then at least my Paddy would still be alive. You take care – love Hatty.

''Ere, doll, you're shaking. What's up? Is Michel—'

'It's not from Michel. It's a text from Paddy's sister. They have arrested a man for his murder. He is the man Paddy nearly killed and was put away for.'

'That's good, isn't it? You can have closure now.'

'No, Tel, you don't understand. I thought Teddy had murdered or paid someone to kill Paddy.'

'Why would he?'

'Because he wants me all to himself, and if anyone gets in the way, he would have them killed.'

'Hold up, babe. Being obsessed with you is one thing, but having a man killed is another, and, clearly, it isn't Teddy Ryder who the police have arrested, is it?'

'Yeah, but he had Vadim beaten and run over because he wanted Vadim to sell him the club so that Vadim was out of the picture.'

Terry found it absurd and wondered if Harper was actually more affected by Paddy's death than she was letting on or even knew herself. 'Who told you about Vadim?'

'I spoke to Vadim myself. He said that Teddy wanted the club because he wanted me back.'

'If I remember rightly, when Vadim had his accident, well, what I thought was an accident, he had suffered from a serious concussion. Even you said he was not himself. Are you sure he got it right? Because listen to yourself, Harper. Buying a club is a big thing and most people tend to do it for business reasons not through matters of the heart.'

Harper mused over the idea that between herself and Vadim, the story may have been misunderstood. She sure as hell felt guilty that she assumed Teddy had murdered Paddy. She straightened up and looked away from the phone screen. 'He still had Vadim run over, though.'

'Oh yeah, don't get me wrong, Harpsichord. The man is still a right royal cunt.'

'Tel, where are you going now?' she asked, as he reversed past the lane leading to the hospital and parked up just after a bend.

‘We might as well wait for Michel, now we can’t follow the car and those vans. And. if anyone comes, we’ll see their headlights, but they won’t see my car. Let’s get out. We’ll walk over to that tree and we can hide in those bushes. No one will see us. ’

As they hurried to the bushes with an overshadowing oak tree, Harper clocked a set of headlights. ‘Look, Tel, a car.’

‘Yeah, babe, it is a road.’

‘No. Look, I think the car is heading down the lane.’

‘Stay down, then,’ Terry whispered.

The car shot past the bushes and down the narrow lane to the hospital. Harper noticed only one person in the vehicle. The driver was a woman.

‘Did you get a butcher’s as to who was in that car?’

‘A bird. Come on, Tel. I’m going down there.’

‘Whoa, hold your horses. What are you gonna do when you get there?’

‘I’m gonna find out who the fuck she is.’

‘But there might be guards down there.’

‘And there might not be. You wait here, then, Tel, but give us your gun.’

‘No way. You might shoot yourself in the foot. Oh, fuck it, come on then, Calamity Jane, let’s do this.’

The field sloped down to the hospital, and so they were able to pick up speed.

‘Slow up, doll, before I lose my footing.’

But Harper wasn’t listening. She had a good idea who the woman was, and if she was right, then she’d smash the life out of her.

As soon as she reached the gates, she stopped and turned to look around. The place was dead quiet, with only a dripping sound. But even in total darkness, she spotted the car.

Harper bent down and picked up a rock from the broken bricks and concrete pile. Slowly, she walked towards the vehicle. She stopped when she saw the double swing doors.

A woman with a torch appeared, and she shone it in Harper's face.

Harper lifted her arm to cover her eyes. 'I fucking knew it was you.'

***

'Back away, Harper Kane, or I will have you arrested and banged up again.'

'Oh yeah, really, Katie fucking French? You conniving two-faced bitch. And I almost trusted you. But there was something niggling in the back of my mind. You mentioned the hospital when I didn't think I had. I doubted myself for a moment, but on the way here, you popped into my mind, along with an uneasy feeling. When you sat opposite me eating that egg sandwich, you really didn't seem to take the situation seriously. Except for the fact that I shouldn't copy the tablet or email it, but I should hand it to you instead.'

Katie grinned. 'Your sister said you were very bright. And you are fearless, I have to give you that, but I can't have you sticking your nose into business that doesn't involve you.'

'Well, that didn't work, did it?'

'You think you're the fucking superhero of the hour. But you and the rest of them had no idea, did you? When you cut off the head of the hydra, a thousand will grow in its place.'

'Yeah, I've heard that expression before.'

'I know you have because it's what happens in my business.'

‘But how could you do this? To kids? Katie, they are fucking kids. I don’t get it. Why ruin your life by going rogue?’ asked Harper, genuinely interested.

Terry held back. All the while Harper was talking, he watched and listened.

‘Going rogue! Ha, are you serious? I haven’t gone rogue. I haven’t changed at all.’

‘But you work for the police.’ She stepped closer, gripping the rock.

‘Do I? Or do I work for another corporation just as corrupt?’

Katie’s cocky stance and sour words compelled Harper to grit her teeth and get ready to break every bone in the sly bitch’s body, but she knew she had to hold back for a minute or two.

‘I dunno, you fucking tell me. Because, right now, darling, I have no idea who the fuck you are. All I wanna know is what happened to me sister.’

‘See, now that’s the thing. Charley was the best. Not me, not anyone in the team, but *she* was, and Peter was the top ops manager. In the blink of an eye, a team was set up, but clever Peter decided to keep it under wraps, you see. But he wasn’t that smart, and neither was Charley.’ She laughed and pulled her coat tighter around herself. ‘She got a little bit lapse. I don’t know what made her go off the boil. But—’

‘She is pregnant,’ interrupted Harper, trying to gauge Katie’s reaction.

‘What?’ Clearly, she was surprised.

‘Yeah, she is having a baby, and so if you or your lot have killed her then you’ve also killed me unborn niece or nephew.’ She could feel the red mist descending again, merely thinking about her baby sister dying, especially while she was pregnant.

‘If you’ve killed me sister, I wanna know how she died. So tell me.’

The way Katie shrugged her shoulders sent Harper off her head. She launched the rock with everything she had, hoping to smash the woman in the face, but it only hit her shoulder and bounced off.

Rage ran through every fibre of her being as Harper ran at Katie. She was only used to street fighting, so when she was struck with a long baton at the back of her legs, she buckled and fell to the floor. The baton came crashing down on Harper's back. Still, in her unbridled fury, Harper felt no pain and jumped to her feet, snatching the baton and ripping it out of the woman's hands.

'You fucking evil . . .' She rammed Katie back towards the building. 'You snaky . . .' She rammed her again. 'Nasty, fucking bitch.'

Harper had Katie pressed against the wall with the baton firmly against her windpipe.

'You will die, Katie French, or whatever the fuck your name is, unless you tell me where my sister is or her body is.'

Desperately trying to push the baton away, Katie gurgled, choking, her face red and her neck filled with popping veins. 'I-I don't know. I-I-swear.'

Finally, Harper pulled the baton away and watched as Katie slumped to the ground, gasping for breath and swearing simultaneously.

But with a last-ditch attempt, Katie grabbed Harper by her ankles and tried to pull her to the ground.

Although Harper lost her balance, she still managed to swing the baton and clump Katie around the face, completely stunning her.

Terry ran to her aid, but, as usual, he could see that Harper had everything in hand.

'Tel, can you see if Michel is okay?'

Terry nodded and hurried inside the building using the torch on his phone.

'Ha! He will dead in about' – she looked at her watch – 'five minutes.'

Instantly, Harper smashed Katie again around the head and watched as blood spurted from her temple like a geyser.

Katie put her hand to her head to feel the damage.

Harper looked on, confused by Katie. Her blank expression, her sudden hoot of creepy laughter, and those dark shadows behind the eyes signalled something. Harper thought she knew what it was. She had seen it before when she had served time. It was methamphetamines – the woman was on drugs.

Wiping the blood away from her eyes, Katie looked at her watch again and grinned. 'Four minutes.'

An unexpected deep throb hit Harper in the chest. So they had already set the place up for demolition, and Katie had the detonator. She stooped down and pulled open Katie's heavy coat, but there was nothing.

'You fool, I am not a suicide bomber. The building is set to blow. It only needed to be activated, and that's my job, which, Harper fucking Kane, you can't stop now.' She chuckled. 'Because I have already pressed the button. The dimwits forgot to do it before they scarpered.'

Harper glanced at the blood still seeping from Katie's head and was astonished that the woman was still conscious. 'You cunt!' she roared, before she kicked her hard in the chest. And then, as Katie fell to the side, Harper ruthlessly kicked her again.

With her adrenaline pumped to the max, Harper tore into the building screaming, 'Terry! Get out! Get out! This place is gonna fucking blow up. Tel! Tel! Can you hear me?'

The only reply was the wind howling through the corridor.

'Terry!'

With still no answer, all she could do was turn around and run for her life. Grief strangled her as she tore past Katie who was struggling to get to her feet. Realising that only Katie would hold the answers to where her sister was if she was still alive, she ran back. Grabbing Katie by her coat and using every ounce of strength to pull her to her feet, Harper dragged her to the motor.

After Harper ripped the car door open, she helped Katie into the back seat of the car, before climbing into the driver's seat. 'Jesus, Katie, the key. Give me the fucking key.'

Katie was struggling to sit upright, but she managed to say, 'Press the accelerator.'

Completely perplexed with the newfangled system, Harper simply did as Katie instructed. She slammed the car into reverse and then rammed it into first gear before shooting out of the gates and up the lane. When she reached the top, she stopped the car and looked back at the building, praying she could see Terry and Michel somewhere away from the building – somewhere safe – but it was so dark, she couldn't see anything.

Exhausted, she got out of the car and slumped onto the damp grass, with her head in her hands, praying the men were far enough from the building before it exploded. If only she hadn't gone down there, she wouldn't have risked Terry's life or ruined any chance of happiness for her mother.

A sudden boom lit up the sky. Every bone in her body vibrated from the impact and her ears were ringing as though someone had stabbed each eardrum with a toothpick. The explosion was no Mickey Mouse affair; it was enormous. The building fell to its knees. Above the fifty-foot flames was a black cloud of dustlike particles, which spread like a million orange lights. The sight was stunning, yet, at the same time, horrific. She clasped her hands together as tears streamed down her face. 'Please let them be alive.'

CHAPTER TWENTY-EIGHT

With her ears still ringing, Harper didn't hear Katie behind her until she felt the rumble of a car starting up. The moment she jumped to her feet and spun around, she saw Katie with her face covered in blood.

With a fiendish smirk on her face, Katie gunned the engine of the MINI Clubman.

Fuming, Harper, bellowed, 'You fucking bitch! I could have left you there!'

Katie reversed past Harper and then stopped a few metres away before thrusting the gear into first, slamming her foot down on the accelerator, and aiming the car directly at Harper.

In a moment of panic, Harper eyed the tree in the distance and ran for her life. The woman was deranged, and Harper knew that Katie wouldn't stop until she killed her. The cold air ripped at her lungs as she legged it across the field. But she didn't look back, even though she could hear the car on her heels. *If only she could make it to the tree.* The first time she had run to the bushy outcrop, it had been pitch-black. This time, the headlights behind her lit up the way, and there in front, just before the tree, was a gully. Harper leaped across and hoped that Katie hadn't spotted what was happening.

Too intent on mowing down Harper, Katie didn't see the gully until the car actually nosedived. As the car screeched and banged and was knocked off course, Harper ran to the tree and stood beside it.

After a few wheelspins, Katie couldn't manage to drive her way out of the muddy gully. The engine coughed, spluttered, and hissed as steam forced its way through the grill. Katie's potential murder weapon was now a useless pile of metal.

But Harper was not only in a state of shock, terrified that her best mate Terry and her brother-in-law could be dead, but livid that she'd saved Katie from becoming bite-sized pieces of barbecued meat, considering she had risked her own life to save her. She stormed towards the car and glared at Katie, who, she had to admit, did look done in. But that wouldn't stop her because anger seemed to affect her in a way that she couldn't control, and counting to ten right this minute wasn't going to cut it. She almost ripped the handle off the door, leaned in, grabbed Katie by her collar, and dragged her out of the car before she gripped her throat with one hand and punched her clean in the mouth with her tightly clenched fist.

Katie couldn't put up a fight. She could barely stand, having used her last bit of energy to drive the car.

As she fell to her knees, Harper gave her one last kick and watched as the woman flopped flat onto her back.

'No more, Harper. Please, no more,' she begged.

'No more? No fucking more!' Harper screamed, through clenched teeth. 'Where's me sister?'

In a flash, Harper was on top of Katie and straddling her. At the same time, she gripped the woman's face and glared into her soul. 'Don't think I won't kill you. Because you know, Katie, that I have no qualms about murdering anyone who hurts my family. I killed for Charley once, and, believe me, I'll do it again. Now, you will tell me where my sister is, or I will take you away and remove your body parts bit by bit, starting with your eyelids.'

Without the cocky shrug, she replied, 'Look, I swear to you, I don't know. I was told she was dead.'

'I don't believe you.'

'I loved her too, you know.'

Those words were like a shard of ice being rammed through Harper's heart. 'How dare you. You don't fucking know what love is. Me killing you is love – love for my sister who you betrayed.'

Just as Harper was about to pull her fist back again, she heard sirens, and in the distance, she saw flashing blue lights, and then through the buzzing sounds in her ears caused by the explosion, she heard Terry's voice.

'Harper! Harper!'

A surge of relief knowing that he was alive compelled Harper to retract her fist and climb off Katie. She waved frantically. 'Over here.'

As soon as he approached, she flung her arms around him. 'Oh, fucking hell, Tel, I thought you hadn't made it. I was at my wits' end.'

He hugged her back and kissed her head. 'I couldn't leave you to sort this mess out alone, could I?'

'And Michel?'

'He's by my cab, breaking his bloody heart. He's got it in his head that Charley was in that building and he wasn't able to save her. I only found him because he was banging on what I can only describe as a prison cell door. That cunt there' – he pointed to Katie, who was flat out on the ground – 'locked Michel in one of the rooms. I managed to let him out. And we ran through the back door and behind a hill. That Michel knows what he's doing, all right. I would still have carried on running if he hadn't rugby tackled me to get down on the ground. And just in fucking time, an' all, before the explosion. My ears are still a bit fuzzy, but we're alive. Come on, let's get out of here. I guess we'd better bring that bitch with us.'

In no time at all, Terry had thrown Katie over his shoulders and staggered halfway up the hill before they were met by Michel, who lifted Katie as though she was a sandbag. With no care or finesse, he threw her into the back of the cab.

***

By the time they reached Farnborough Park, the sun was up, and everything seemed to be a dream to Harper. Terry appeared a little subdued as he drove. He gave an occasional glance at Katie who was sitting next to Michel in the back. Harper had done a proper number on the woman, and he wasn't surprised. Harper was never going to give Katie an easy time now, knowing that she was involved with this despicable Russian cartel.

As Harper went over what had happened, a sudden panicky thought ran through her mind. Her son. She grabbed her phone from her jacket pocket and dialled Eddie's number. It rang and rang, and with every ring, her heart was beating faster and faster. Visions of the Russians taking her son were filling her mind with dread. When Eddie answered, she put the call on speakerphone.

'Mum? Sorry, Mum, I was in the shower.'

'Listen, Eddie, get out of the house, yeah. Go to Nanny's.'

'Do I tell Teddy?'

'No, babe, just go. Don't ponce about. Fucking run. Don't call a cab. Just get out of there.'

'Mum, are you okay?'

'Yes, my little Bear, but I think the Russians will try to flush me out and use you. They are brutal, so run, baby, run. And when you get to Nan's, tell her to take you to Mr Baker's. He lives opposite. You wait for me there.'

'Okay, Mum, I'm on my way.'

'Good lad.'

'Mum, I've been thinking about what Yalina said. If they are not selling the girls for sex what is this other work they will be doing that warrants holding girls against their will?'

'Eddie, don't think, just run.'

'Okay, okay, I'm going now, Mum.'

***

Once inside Terry's house, Michel used cable ties to bind Katie's wrists and ankles and to secure her to the chair.

'Blimey, isn't that a bit OTT? She ain't going to get away,' said Harper.

‘Not really. She is trained to escape, but I am trained to keep a person hostage. She won’t get away. You can sleep with both eyes shut.’

‘I am so tired, but I must see my son.’

Michel shook his head. ‘You cannot go near him. Terry is going to visit your mum. He knows what to do, but you must sleep.’

‘He had a point, though. What are they going to do with the girls?’

‘Look, Harper, again, we cannot take what this teenager says as fact. It’s hearsay and from an unscrupulous Russian as well.’

Harper flopped into an armchair. ‘You’re probably right. I am tired, but I need a coffee, and then a bath to wash this’ – she looked at her hands and then at Katie’s bloodstained face – ‘blood off me.’

Michel left the room to make Harper a coffee. He used the excuse to compose himself. He didn’t like to let on to Harper that having seen the layout of the basement and the number of rooms, it would be reasonable to assume that Charley could have been in any one of them. He realised they could have locked Charley down there and no one would have known. But that was precisely what the Russians might have done. They used old buildings to hide their illegal activities from prying eyes. And what better place than a demolition site – a former hospital no less – with guards.

So his hopes of finding her alive were gone. The blast would have killed her. And so he would have to live with the guilt that he hadn’t had enough time to search the entire building. He pictured her there tied up, praying for someone to rescue her, praying for the baby’s life. Because she was like that: she always put others before herself. A tear escaped, and he allowed it to follow the contours of his nose. He stirred the cup and jumped when he felt an arm around his waist.

‘She might not have been in that building, Michel. Please don’t give up now.’

He quickly wiped the tear away. 'How did you know I was thinking about that?'

'Because it crossed my mind, too,' said Harper. 'But if they took the risk of removing those girls, then maybe they also removed Charley.'

'Yes, possibly. I have to know where they would take them. Once I have rested, I am going to track down Andrew.'

'And do what? Who would believe that he, of all men, is part of a Russian mob carrying out the most heinous crimes?'

'I have a way of extracting information.' He grinned. 'I am a Russian, remember.' He handed her the coffee. 'I have nothing to lose because you are right. The police would never believe me, a former Russian soldier, and you, a former inmate, over the former Police Commissioner. They would look pretty incompetent if he was found guilty. They protect their own.'

'But surely not to this extent?' replied Harper, although she knew how corrupt some authorities could be. She'd had enough experience in prison to know that.

'Harper, he is a powerful man.'

'He needs to be filmed in action and shown to the new Police Commissioner.'

Michel's eyes suddenly lit up. 'They would confiscate the film, but they would have trouble if we're to go on—'

'Social media!'

'No, not social media. I was going to say if we go to various police stations and the Met because not everyone will want to cover that up. I can leak it to the press, and, yes, it could go onto social media, but you leave that to me.' He glanced at Katie. 'And that piece of shit will help me do it.'

Harper nodded and sipped her coffee. She suddenly screwed her nose up. 'It's quite sweet, Michel. Never mind, I'm gonna drink this, have a bath, and get an hour's kip. Are you sure about her?' She pointed to Katie.

Michel nodded. 'Yes.'

Harper stared at her coffee and suddenly felt her shoulders relax. 'Ah, well, I'd best have a shower then because I will drown in the bath once the sleeping tablets kick in.' She tutted and rolled her eyes.

'You need to rest, Harper. A machine can't run without charge or fuel.'

'I know.'

She yawned and left the room. In any other circumstances, she would have gone mad at Michel for what essentially amounted to drugging her. However, she knew that whatever Michel did would have been for the right reasons.

Before she stripped off to step into the shower, her phone vibrated. It was a text from her mother – **He's here x**. Harper smiled. Her mother was getting with the programme, by keeping her text messages short and generic.

As the fine shower spray massaged her aching shoulders and stiff neck, she could feel her mind drifting into a dreamlike state. The shower wasn't helping her to stay awake. She managed to wash the dirt and blood from her hands and face and watched the water turn pink as it swirled down the plughole. She hoped she had also scrubbed enough of the muck from the rest of her body before she dried herself with one of Terry's brilliant-white towels. Once she had planted both feet on the bamboo bath mat, she could sense herself losing balance. She snatched a towel from the heated towel rail, wrapped it around herself, and swayed as she dragged her feet, which felt like lead weights, to one of the spare rooms.

'What the fuck have you given me, Michel?' she whispered to herself, before she crashed onto the bed and fell into a deep sleep.

CHAPTER TWENTY-NINE

Michel had slept for only three hours before he woke up. He got up from the armchair and walked over to Katie, who was still tied to the kitchen chair. She was awake. With his hands on his hips, he stared at her until she couldn't look away from him any longer.

'I told Harper, I don't know where Charley is. They told me she was dead. That's all I know, Michel.'

'You know I will torture you, don't you, Katie?'

'They will kill me anyway.'

He lowered his voice to a soft pitch. 'But, Katie, I don't understand. You were good. You brought down Zavid and his mob and saved those girls from being sex slaves to the fucking Arabs. You worked with my wife and me, and now you are going against everything you stand for. All I can assume is that they are paying you a lot of money.'

'Or have you ever considered it is for something greater than money and power?'

Michel tilted his head to the side. 'What is the reason you turned your back on the force – and your integrity and moral values?' He raised his voice. 'Tell me, Katie!'

Her eyes darkened, and then her lip curled. 'Love, Michel. For love.'

'Who?'

She looked away. 'I can't say. You can torture me all you like. I'll suffer worse if I tell you.'

'Oh no, you won't, Katie, because I know worse. I am Russian, and I know the horrific things they do to get answers.' He smiled, turned away, opened Terry's man drawer, and fingered through the contents. 'Oh look, Terry has some tile nippers. They are like the very ones that you were asked to cut off Harper's finger with.' He held them up. 'Remember?'

Katie's eyes widened, and he could see her face pale over.

'Hmm, you were hesitant then. Everyone thought it was because you didn't want to hurt her. But I saw your face the second that Russian snatched the tile nippers off you and removed her finger. You were about to faint. It's odd that. I would have thought you would be used to blood by now.'

She stared at the tile nippers and nervously licked her lips. 'What are you going to do?'

He could tell she wasn't listening to him. Her fear level had reached its peak; all she was focusing on was the tile nippers. He watched her breathing increase and wondered if she was about to scream.

'You may have been afraid to use them yourself because you don't like the sight of blood, and you won't like pain either. You have an enormous fear, and when this tool cuts through your bone, you will experience the most excruciating pain ever. The men I have tortured scream for their mothers when I do this.' He snatched her hand and placed the tile nippers over her little finger.

'No! Please, I'll talk. Please, not that.' Her eyes were like golf balls as she glared at the tool in his hand. A layer of sweat coated her brow, and her hands were still trembling, even though she was secured to the chair.

'Right, let's start with the obvious question. Where is my wife? Is she definitely dead?'

She shook her head. 'I don't know. There were two burned bodies with their teeth removed. I can assume she was one of them. But I don't know for sure. Please, Michel, put that thing down.'

Ignoring her, he went on. 'Who are you working for?'

She glared back, her eyes empty.

'Who!' he demanded, as he lifted the tool to her cheek. 'This cut would never heal. Your skin will peel open like a hot scored peach.'

Sweat appeared on Katie's brow and she strained every sinew to lean as far away as possible from Michel and his deadly implement.

'Who is Yuri?'

'Yuri?'

'Yes, and don't deny you fucking know him. I've listened to a detailed tape recording from one of the girls he has kept captive.'

'I don't really know him. I swear, I don't. I only know him as Yuri the Russian.'

'You think I'm stupid? Katie, give me some respect. Now, who is he?'

He slid the sharp edge of the tile nippers across her cheek, enough to graze it and allow it to sting.

She squealed in pain, which startled Michel. He stared in astonishment. He'd hardly touched her, and yet her face was probably very sensitive because of all the cuts and bruises sustained at the hands of Harper.

'Stop playing games, Katie. That didn't hurt you so much. Now, who is Yuri? I need to know where to find him, or you will be screaming next time for real.'

'I don't know where he lives. I don't know much about him. Only that he promised to pay me well.'

'You said you did it for love?'

'I lied. No one goes that far for love. Of course it was for money.'

Michel stood back with his arms folded. He was still gripping the tile nippers while he stared. He thought he knew the woman, but now she looked different. Her expression was cold.

'And I thought only a Russian would stoop that low.'

'She is a Russian,' came a voice from behind him.

Katie's eyes were on stalks. 'You don't know what you're talking about, Harper.'

'Oh! No? Give me those cutters, Michel. I wanna see if she pisses blood like a fucking Russian an' all.'

Michel handed her the tile nippers.

Grinning, Harper turned the tool over in her hand. 'Oh, I know how much this fucking hurts. A Russian removed my finger. D'ya remember, Katie, or whatever the fuck your name is?' she said, as she grabbed Katie's little finger.

With her body now shrinking into the seat and her eyes wide with terror, she cried out, 'No, please, Harper. Please don't!'

'Okay, Katie, is my sister alive? This is your last chance to tell us the truth.'

Katie began sweating buckets, and as the droplets of sweat dripped into her eyes, she blinked furiously to stop the stinging. 'Oh no, please, I'll talk. Okay, I'll talk.'

'Is she alive?'

'Okay, okay. I *will* tell you the truth. Just don't cut my finger off. As far as I know, up until yesterday, she was alive, but I swear I have no idea where she is.'

'You told me a few minutes ago, she was one of those charred bodies in the burned-out car. Now you've changed your story. That makes no sense to me. Who has her captive and if they know she is an undercover cop then why have they kept her alive?' asked Michel.

'I assume Yuri has kept her alive because she has information on him and his business partners. They saw a recording of her photographing confidential documents in his office,' said Katie.

'And by business partners, do you also include Andrew Mercer?' asked Harper, in a calm serious tone.

Katie shook her head. 'I don't know who the business partners are, but he isn't one of them.'

'Fucking liar. It's Andrew Mercer!' yelled Harper, making the already nervous Katie nearly jump out of her skin. 'You know it's him. I told you he was involved. That's why you tipped off this Yuri geezer and were at the hospital blowing the place up because you are in cahoots with them all, including Andrew Mercer.'

'No, no, you've got it wrong, Harper.'

Yalina would have had nothing to gain by making up a lie such as that, thought Harper, *but there was only one way to know the truth.*

'Liar. Now, Katie, the truth, or else.'

Katie stared, and her body trembled as she braced herself, hoping that she could handle the pain, because Harper wasn't going to believe her. 'It's not Andrew Mercer.'

Harper stared her straight in the face while holding the tile nippers over her little finger of her right hand. 'This is for Charley.' With both hands, she clamped down hard and fast until the two metal nippers connected.

As Katie began convulsing in the chair, the ties around her wrist cut through her flesh. Then came the pain. Her mouth opened, her eyes rolled back, and she began to let out an almighty scream.

Michel snatched a tea towel and shoved it into her mouth.

Right away, Katie opened her eyes and thrashed about, shaking her head until she finally stopped and tried to gasp for breath.

As Michel removed the tea towel, Katie, who was now dripping in perspiration, gingerly looked at the bloody stump where her little finger used to be. A sudden whoosh of vomit protruded from her mouth, narrowly missing Harper.

Totally unfazed by the mess, Harper chuckled. ‘Right, that little piggy went to market, so let’s see if this little piggy will stay at home. Now, Andrew Mercer, the ex-police commissioner, is he the main man – the boss – the one who calls the shots – or what?’

With her eyes now glued to the tile nippers hovering over her middle finger, Katie swallowed hard. The throbbing in her hand was travelling up to her armpit, making her feel so sick and faint, she couldn’t stand it.

‘Please no more, Harper. No more. Michel, please stop this.’

Michel paced the floor tapping his forefinger on his chin when he stopped and spun around. ‘Stop this? Me? Really? Look at Harper. Do you think I could stop her? No, I would answer her questions, if I were you.’

‘Let’s try a different question, then. Let’s go back to Yuri. Who the fuck is he?’

With tears suddenly streaming down her cheeks, and sweat dripping off her, Katie slowed down her breathing to be able to speak through the pain.

‘I came to England as a child with my mother. You don’t understand. I had to leave everything behind.’

‘So, you are Russian, like I fucking said. I knew I wasn’t going mad, when I heard you swear in Russian when I held that baton against your windpipe.’

Katie offered Harper her saddest expression. Even with her bruised face, she gave her best puppy-dog eyes look. It was one that Harper detested on anyone, let alone Katie.

‘My mother took me from Russia to escape my father, but she couldn’t take my two brothers.’

‘So Yuri is your *brother*?’

Katie nodded. But she paused, trying to catch her breath.

‘Leave her for a minute, Harper. I want her talking with clarity.’

Harper didn't argue; she waited until Katie looked capable of speaking.

'Carry on.'

'I thought it would be good to have my brothers in my life. I invited them over. I hadn't seen them for years, and I barely recognised them. They were in rags when I left, but when I saw them again, they were wearing designer clothes. And Yuri was so kind and sweet too. It feels good to have family around you, and you know that yourself. He was proud of me for everything I had achieved on my own. I'm so sorry. I wished, I just wished I hadn't got involved. I am so afraid he might hurt my daughter if I don't do as he says.' More tears ran down her cheeks. 'Please give me some water.' She tried to lick her swollen lips. 'I'm so sorry. I really don't know what else to tell you.'

But to Harper, her words sounded too soft and soppy.

'Oh, fuck off, Katie, or whatever your name is. I don't buy the sob story that you're spinning us. The fact is you used your position to traffic innocent girls. You're a cunt!'

With her irritation peaked, Harper clamped the tile nippers firmly over the middle finger.

'No, please no!' wailed Katie.

'Yeah, it fucking hurt, doesn't it, losing a finger? Now, you will talk. Tell me about Andrew Mercer.'

'Please stop. I will talk, I swear, but no more. I can't handle it.'

Harper guessed she was telling the truth. Then, suddenly, she heard a heavy dripping sound. When she looked down, she realised Katie was wetting herself.

Michel pulled Harper away and whispered. 'Leave her to rest for a few minutes. She needs to get her strength back to speak. I'll give her a drink of water and a brandy.'

Harper assumed he had done this before, so she allowed him to take the lead. Putting the tile nippers on the table, she walked away and used the downstairs cloakroom to wash the blood off her hands and face. As she peered into the mirror, she stared for a moment at her reflection. She had become a torturous robot, all for the love of her family. All she wanted was to be a mum and to enjoy life with her son. As she splashed water onto her face again, she focused on what she needed to do next. She couldn't live a happy life if she didn't do her best to find Charley, alive or dead.

When she returned to the kitchen, she was surprised to see Katie looking more with it. She had stopped sweating, and her eyes were more alert.

'My name isn't Katie. It's Katria.' She glanced back at her hands and the stump still dripping with blood.

'You set us up. Was that Andrew Mercer's idea?' asked Michel.

'Yuri made me do that.'

'You knew our bank details to put the money into our accounts because you were in and out of our house so much. When you ran out of cash, you borrowed my bank card. We fucking trusted you with our lives. You fitted me up for Peter's murder, didn't you?' He slapped his hands against his thighs. 'You could have taken my boots, my hair, anything from my house, to fabricate evidence, and we stupidly trusted you so much.'

Harper felt sick. Katria had carried out the biggest betrayal, and the thought whirled around in her head like a constant torment. 'The baby in the photo?'

That was the spark that snapped Katria out of her sorry-for-herself expression. 'What about her?'

'You said in the café that she is yours. Who is the father?'

With her eyes round and worried, Katria remained silent. Yet her feet, although bound, began tapping.

Suddenly, Harper began to see the pieces fitting together. 'You were protecting the police commissioner. You even lost one of your fucking fingers for him. It's him. You were fucking ol' Mercer, the one-eyed wanker. That kid is his as well, ain't she? And Verity made it all look like a fucking top undercover cop who had gone rogue.'

Katria stayed silent.

'Of course! It fucking makes total sense now. Why else would a middle-aged man in his position go along with such a terrible crime if it wasn't for love and money?'

'Look, you don't understand. I came from nothing. I had nothing! And Andrew was—'

'A fucking meal ticket, you bitch. And he was a fucking sucker, an' all, by the sound of it. But you had choices and a chance in life, Katria. You had a good mate in me sister, and you had more than most. Unlike those kids, you weren't trafficked and sold for sex, you greedy cunt!' Picking up the tile nippers, she squeezed them tightly over Katria's middle finger once more and glared into her eyes. 'Start by telling me the truth or you will lose all your fingers one by one.'

'Wait! Do you think I'd go for an older man who was so feeble that he barked like a dog if I told him to? Andrew didn't get rich by working for the police force.' She sighed in defeat. 'No commissioner is that well off.'

'So he was bent before you met him, was he?'

Looking up at Harper with a half-cocked grin, Katria replied, 'Of course he was. Why do you think I was with him? Come on, Harper. You hardly get rich by being a law-abiding member of society. We both know that.'

Harper scrutinised the woman's face and concluded that Katria was being the most honest she'd been. Now ready to ask the next question, Harper felt her heart skip a few beats, and, in some respects, she didn't want to know the answer. She placed the tile nippers on the table.

'What does Teddy Ryder have to do with all of this?'

At first, Katria seemed puzzled. 'Who? The property developer?'

'The nightclub owner. The father of my boy, Teddy fucking Ryder.'

Katria shrugged her shoulders, as much as the restraints would allow. 'I don't know. All I do know is that his name is also on the deeds of the properties we use and he is paid handsomely for it.'

'Did he own the hospital that you blew up?'

'Yes. He was knocking it down anyway to build flats, but Yuri and his associates paid him a large sum, enough to build on the land, once the hospital was flattened.' She took a few more deep breaths and whimpered every time she glanced at her hand.

'Does he know what your business is all about?'

'I-I-don't know if Yuri or Daria would trust him with that sort of information.'

'And where do Yuri and Daria live?'

The blood drained from Katria's face. 'Oh God. I swear to you on my baby's life, I promise, I don't know his address. He lives somewhere in Blackheath. I know that much but I don't know where. I have never been to his house. He only ever came over to mine.' She stared at the tile nippers on the table and Harper's hand hovering over them. 'Please, Harper, I swear, I don't know where it is.'

Harper turned to Michel. 'I'm gonna knock on every door around Blackheath.' She turned back to Katria. 'What cars do your brothers drive?'

'Daria drives a Lexus. Yuri doesn't drive. He has a driver, so he is usually in a limo.'

'Ah, so Yuri is a flash prick, an' all, then, is he?'

'Yeah, I guess he is.' The manner in which her words came out so slowly gave Harper the impression that Katria had come to the realisation that she had been used by her own brothers.

'Penny dropped, has it, Katria? Yuri was all out for himself, was he? I mean, who sends their sister to bomb a building? I'd send one of the experienced guards, but he sends you. What exactly did you tell your brother before he sent you to blow up the building?'

With her head down, she replied, 'I only had time to inform him that one of the girls had been telling all, and he must move all of the girls from the hospital, in case it is raided. He then called me back and told me to detonate the building.'

'And the tablet? Did you tell him about that?'

'No, I was hoping to get it off you myself.'

'Christ, I bet you haven't informed them that I'm Charley's sister, have you?'

Katria appeared startled.

'You fucking haven't, have ya?'

'No, if you must know.'

'Oh, I get it now. You wanted to be the one to hand me and the tablet to your brother on a fucking plate. So that you can show them your worth. Well, that didn't work out quite right for ya, did it.'

'Think whatever you like, it doesn't matter now, anyway.'

'It seems to me that no matter what kind of plan you had in mind, your brother couldn't give a flying fuck about you.'

Harper could see Katria was looking defeated. 'So d'ya wanna make my search quicker for me, Katria? Where does he live?'

'Harper, seriously, as I said, I don't know his exact address. I've never been there.'

Harper exaggerated her surprise. 'And didn't that ring any bells for you? Your long-lost bro, this Yuri guy, hasn't even invited you over for afternoon tea and a little catch-up?'

Katria shook her head and bit her lip. The tears were forming.

‘Fuck me, how used and manipulated do you feel right now?’ Harper laughed. ‘At first, your brothers probably played the family card. We all stick together, all for one and one for all. That was to get you to screw the one-time police commissioner. Not any ol’ copper but the former top police bod. Not only that but Yuri knew that being in the force, you would have access to fucking everything. He played you good an’ proper, didn’t he? But, see, you ain’t right tight with your brothers, are you? All along, they have been keeping you at arm’s length.’ She laughed again, mocking Katria. ‘Looks to me like they really don’t trust you, and you mean nothing to them. Like when you cut off the head of the hydra, a thousand will grow in its place. Those were your words. Remember?’ She clicked her fingers. ‘Just like that.’

Katria couldn’t stop the fat tears falling down her cheeks. The reality was all too clear now. She had desperately wanted to have a family. After her mother died, she would have done anything to be close with Yuri and Daria. Harper was spot on when she said that her plan was to hand her and the tablet on a plate to her brother, and now she wondered why she had even bothered.

‘And your boyfriend, the ex-commissioner. Doesn’t he know where Yuri lives either?’

Katria’s eyes were instantly lined with surprise. She looked up, her mouth open. She didn’t have to speak; her face said it all. She had been a general dogsbody not only to her brother but also to Andrew, the man she had fallen in love with.

‘Yeah, I thought as much. You really are bloody stupid and—’

Michel finished her sentence. ‘And, Katria, when you said you did it for love and money, you were telling the truth. You still had built into you that Russian mantra to use people to get what you want. And I bet you were initially using Mercer, but then you fell in love with him. By then, the tables had well and truly been turned. He was using you to get what he wanted, wasn’t he?’

Katria’s face was white as she silently absorbed the truth.

'So enlighten me, Katria. Who is the boss? Yuri or Mercer?'

As if a light had just come on, Katria's face flushed pink and her eyes once again became bright, and she couldn't unmask her satisfied expression.

It was then that Michel realised she had one over on them. Who *was* the beast in charge?

The back door opened, which caught them all by surprise.

Katria peered up. Seeing Terry, she hoped she was saved.

But to her horror, he shook his head and said, 'I go out for a couple of hours and come back to a right ol' mess. It's like leaving two teenagers home alone.'

CHAPTER THIRTY

Having kept Yalina locked in the boot of his car for over ten hours, Daria finally let her out. The only warmth she could find in that cold dark boot was a standard picnic blanket. She had lain there shivering relentlessly for what seemed like forever. The only respite was being able to have a catnap: then she was at peace.

The bright afternoon sun made her cover her eyes. As she climbed out of the car, her legs gave way. They were tingling with pins and needles. Glancing around, it was clear that they were outside the mansion, but he had driven somewhere else since putting her in the boot of his car, where he had cruelly left her.

She looked up at Daria, but his face was alive with rage and frustration. His eyes darted in all directions as he dragged her by her hair through the mansion.

'Yuri, Yuri!' he bellowed, checking to see if his brother was in the house. He guessed he wasn't because the limo wasn't in the drive. He suspected that his brother and Casper would still be orchestrating the move to the new premises since receiving the tip-off from Katria that the hospital would soon be raided. He only hoped she managed to set off the detonator before anyone discovered the place. The best way to get rid of all the evidence had been to blow the building to smithereens. But he was uneasy about one thing: the lights had shut down as if someone was already there.

'Yuri!' he called again. But a few trunks and a box overflowing with paperwork on the floor in the entrance hall caught his eye. *Yuri must have forgotten them between all the toing and froing.*

A threat to their operation had set the wheels in motion. As a result, they needed to vacate this mansion and move to their other house, a South-West London pad. It wasn't as grand as this one, but it would do for now. With no answer from his brother, he stopped huffing and puffing, let go of her hair, and turned to face Yalina.

'So it's just you and me, Yalina.'

A cruel smirk slithered across his face as his good eye twitched, and he licked his red lips.

Seeing Daria up close and personal, his leering eyes and the smell of garlic on his breath, made Yalina's skin crawl. But something told her he wasn't going to torture her. He wanted something else.

Staring at her for a moment before grabbing her hair again, he steered her past the main lounge area, along the corridor leading to the east wing, and towards the bedroom where Yuri had previously taken her.

Yuri's offer for her to manage the girls briefly came to mind, but she reckoned that the chances of that ever happening now were very slim. But she was still concerned for the girls, though. *Where had they been taken?*

She knew the last thing Daria would do would be to tell her where the girls were. She could see his mind was definitely on something else. *Was he going to rape her?* The thought nearly made her sick, and she knew she needed to put all her efforts into escaping from this place.

'I said I would show you how to please a man. Now, I will show you how it's done.'

'But, Daria, please. Yuri promised I would never sleep with a man again.'

'Ha, and you think he would agree now, after you tried to escape? No, no, no. Every minute you please me, be grateful, because you are still alive.'

He shoved her into the room with the leopard print bedspread, where the clothes she was hoping to wear were still on the chaise longue.

She didn't even have time to draw breath before his brute force knocked her onto the bed. And before she could even think about fighting him off, he had one hand on her chest and the other up her sari to get at her underwear.

She hadn't realised until now that preserving her virginity would mean so much to her that she would fight tooth and nail to keep it. Dread gnarled her insides, compelling her to shake uncontrollably. Wriggling and writhing to stop his grubby hands from reaching her intimate parts, she knew then that her efforts were futile. The pressure on her chest was too much.

His contorted face and eager eyes, like that of a panting dog, made Yalina feel nauseous.

'Please wait. I'm going to be sick.'

Daria stopped for a moment and stood up. When he began to undo his trousers, Yalina realised that he wasn't going to let up. He didn't care that she could throw up at any moment; he was too intent on raping her.

Her eyes bulged when she saw his protruding penis. The sight raised her fear, and like a cornered wildcat, she hissed and spat and tried to claw at his face as he lunged forward. Her nail caught his eyes, and he instantly pulled back and clutched his face. But he was angry. She could see he would kill her before he would ever let her go.

She rolled to her side to escape his fist and fell off the bed onto the floor. Frantic with fear, she suddenly remembered the knife. She slipped her hand under the bed and almost cut herself on the blade. It was there, within her reach.

Now her heart was really pumping. She had been given a chance in life. *Could she get the knife in her hand before Daria reached her?*

Daria climbed off the bed and crawled along the floor to her side, where he grabbed her ankles and yanked her to him.

Her long hand searched for the handle of the knife. *Eureka!* She had it in her grasp before he pulled her away.

Taking a deep breath, she screamed; simultaneously, she plunged the knife into his side.

When he sat up in horror at seeing the knife and the blood, she couldn't stop. She was now blinded by fury, and as she pulled out the jagged blade, she rammed it into his stomach.

His eyes widened in terror. He looked at the knife now deep in his gut. Then he stared at the girl. A girl had done this to him! *How could this have happened?*

He knew he was in trouble. He could feel his senses shutting down. But even in those last few seconds, the urge to stay alive was still uppermost in his mind. As his eyes pleaded with Yalina to save him, he was met with a cruel grin of contempt.

Yalina withdrew the knife, but she hadn't finished. Far from it. In a frenzy, she plunged the knife into him again and again, all over his chest, until she was breathless.

She watched him fall onto his side, now completely soaked in blood. The shock forced her to get to her feet and as far away from him as possible. She staggered back and hit the wall. All she could do was stare as the man gurgled his last breath.

Stiff with fright, she remained still, watching his blood drip from the knife, which was still locked inside her grip.

When Daria's phone rang, she almost jumped out of her skin.

She half expected him to answer it as if what she had done wasn't real. And the sound of the phone should have brought her to her senses. But it didn't. It continued to ring.

Slowly, she looked down at herself and took a short intake of breath. Her ripped sari was covered in blood. As were her arms and her legs.

She glanced at the bathroom door and paused as though she was about to run through a piranha-infested river. Reaching the door, she opened it, where, once again, she was met by the brightness of the room as the automatic light reflected off the brilliant-white tiles.

She locked the door behind her and pushed a few knobs on the bath. To her surprise, a shower above the bath came on. She stripped off and got in. However, she kept the knife firmly in her hand and allowed the gentle spray of water to massage her head. There was no shortage of soap and shampoo bottles displayed in the wall niches adjacent to the bath. After lathering her hair and body, desperate to get the thought of sex and the metallic taste of blood off her, she wrapped herself in a towel and warily crept out of the bathroom.

She peered over at the neatly folded clothes on the chaise longue across the other side of the bedroom and didn't hesitate to put them on. Her mind was awash with panic and how to escape, knowing that the police would grab her, beat her, and bring her back for Yuri to finish her off.

She hugged herself in her cashmere jumper and beige-coloured jeans. She'd never worn jeans before, but these were comfortable and warm. The trainers felt like gloves on her feet; they were a far cry from her flat hard-based sandals back home.

A sudden groan alerted her. She looked around the room. The sound was the same unearthly noise she thought she'd heard the last time she was here.

Hurrying back to the bathroom, she picked up the knife, which she'd left on the edge of the bath, and gripped it tightly before trying to open the door where the sound was coming from. The door was still locked. Hearing the groans becoming even louder, she realised the sound was like someone who had their mouth taped up.

She darted around the room looking for a key. Eventually, her eyes were diverted to Daria's pockets. She used her index finger and thumb to pull out his keys. As she grabbed them, a few other objects came out, including a gun, a filled syringe, and his phone. It took her almost a minute before she found the right key. Something told her that this moment would be one that she wouldn't forget. Taking a deep breath, she cautiously opened the door.

She was looking into a lounge but there was nothing in here that would have made that noise. Keeping very still, she listened and that was when she heard the sound again. It was coming from behind another door straight in front of her. As she crept towards it, she detected an unearthly smell. It was so strong, it made her pinch her nose. Having recognised the smell from her experience with a dead calf, she continued to approach the door with caution. This one wasn't locked.

What she saw was nothing short of disturbing. To the left was a woman tied to a metal hospital bed in a room that was otherwise furnished in sheer luxury. But more shocking was the scene to the right. A man who was clearly dead was left to rot on another hospital bed. A syringe was still hanging from the back of his hand. From the purple colour of his skin, it looked as though he had been dead for some time.

Yalina instantly glanced back at the woman and noticed she had a cannula in her arm. Her mouth was taped up, but her eyes were wide and alert, although the huge bruises around them suggested she had been beaten. Seeing the dried blood around the woman's ears and in her hair and the nasty weeping sores around her wrists, Yalina surmised that this poor woman had not just been beaten but probably tortured. Briefly examining the cable ties, Yalina wondered where to start. She noticed a few sharp-looking instruments on the bedside cabinet, which included a pair of scissors.

'It's fine. I'm not your enemy. I'll cut the ties,' whispered Yalina, before she glanced back over her shoulder.

After she had used the scissors to cut through the first plastic restraints very carefully, the captive took control. Yalina was shocked to see how fast and strong the woman was considering her arms and hands were covered in bruises. Even when she ripped the tape from her mouth, she didn't flinch.

'Thank you . . .' she said, as she pulled the cannula out and carefully clambered down from the metal bed.

'My name is Yalina,' she said, as she looked at the woman's bare legs covered in scabs over the cuts.

'Yalina, who's in the mansion?'

Yalina was still mesmerised by the woman's ability to suddenly switch into action. 'No one. I have just. I've just . . .' Her face turned pale. 'Er, I've just killed a man called Daria.'

Giving Yalina a brief hug, she smiled at her. 'It's okay, love. That was a smart move. He would probably have killed you, given half the chance. I know how evil that bastard can be.' She sighed. 'It's lucky for me, though, he had orders not to kill me. His brother, Yuri—'

'Yes, I know Yuri. Did he hurt you?' asked Yalina, looking at the marks all over the woman's chest and neck and the blood stains on her vest. 'Silly question.'

'I'm okay. Don't worry about me. I'm alive. I will heal, unlike my colleague,' she said, as she glanced at the dead man on the other hospital bed.

Yalina was shocked that the woman was so in control. If it had been her having sustained all of those injuries, she wouldn't have been able to stand up.

'Now, I need your help. Could you fetch me the coffee?' She pointed towards the lounge.

Yalina stared at the machine and noticed the box of coffee powder. Surely, she didn't mean that? But there was nothing else. After darting back into the lounge and grabbing the box, she handed it to the woman who opened her mouth and poured in a mountain of the dry coffee powder.

Instinctively, Yalina grabbed one of the bottles of water from the bedside cabinet, removed the lid, and handed it to her.

The woman greedily gulped it down. 'Right, that should shove my backside into gear.'

'You are Charley, Eddie's aunty, aren't you?' said Yalina.

'Yes, How did you know who I am? Oh Christ, is he okay?' Her voice suddenly became serious.

‘He’s fine. Your sister is looking for you. Eddie showed me a picture, and I can now see how much you look like your nephew. You both have the same coloured eyes.’

‘Thank God. Now, we must get out of here before they return. And are you sure there is no one here? No guards anywhere?’

‘No, they were all at the hospital removing the girls, and I think they are about to leave this mansion. There are still a few trunks and a box in the entrance hall.’

‘Shit, so they will be back. Do you know where they have taken the girls?’

Yalina shook her head. ‘No. What are you going to do?’ she asked, totally in awe of the woman.

‘I am going to find the girls. If Yuri is shipping them out of the country, we need to track them down, or they could be lost forever.’

Yalina frowned. ‘I don’t think that’s what is happening. Yuri has a job for them and it’s not to do with sex.’

A wave of puzzlement spread across Charley’s face, until her eyes suddenly lit up as if a light had come on. ‘Shit, the architects’ drawings. It all makes sense now. Listen, we need to go and find the girls. I think I have an idea where they are.’

‘What? On our own? Will you not call the police?’

With a deep sigh, Charley wiped her dry eyes. ‘I don’t know who I can trust, Yalina, except my own family. And I cannot get them involved. Listen, please can you be a lookout? I need to find some things.’

‘Can I help?’

‘No, sweetheart. I need my phone and . . .’ She stared at Yalina’s huge brown eyes. ‘No, just shout if you see anyone coming or any cars arriving.’

Sensing the authority in the woman’s voice, Yalina hid behind the tall window in the entrance hall while Charley, like a whippet, ran around the mansion.

The coast was still clear when Charley returned. She had Daria's phone, car keys, and a knife in one hand and a gun in the other.

'Right, we need to get out of here first, sweetheart, before they return.'

The second Charley opened the car door, Yalina hopped into the front seat. 'Charley, may I call you Charley?'

Charley nodded.

'Who was that dead man in the room with you?'

'He was my co-worker, my undercover partner, a rookie. It's a shame because he was a nice guy. Those bastards killed him because he was no use to them.'

'Why did they keep you alive?'

'I was useful to them. That's all you need to know.'

'Thank you, Charley. You've spoken to me like I'm human again and not a slave.'

Before Charley pulled away, she hugged Yalina. 'Good because you will never be one again.'

The phone rang before Charley managed to leave the drive. Yuri's name flashed on the screen.

'Bastard,' she growled. Before she answered the call, she put Yuri on speakerphone.

'Daria, come to the club. We have a meeting. And make sure you have loaded the trunks and that box from the hallway. I won't have time to pick them up. And make arrangements to get rid of the woman. I have decided I don't want her. And dispose of that stinking corpse. Daria, can you hear me? Daria!'

She ended the call and started the car.

'Did you understand him?' asked Yalina, totally in the dark.

'Yes, Yalina, I speak Russian. Now, while I drive, you take this phone and dial the number I reel off.'

Yalina did as Charley said. She dialled the number, but it just kept ringing. Without prompting, Yalina rang it again. But this time, it went to voicemail where the greeting was generic.

'Shall I call again?'

'No, sweetie. I need to get my head clear, before I . . .' She glanced to her left as if she had seen her for the first time. 'How old are you, Yalina?'

'I am fifteen. All the girls are about my age.'

CHAPTER THIRTY-ONE

Delores was in fidget mode: she just couldn't keep still. With one eye on what she should be doing and another on Mr Baker's house, she kept dashing from one room to another, her nerves now shot to pieces.

Morris Baker lived opposite, and he had a great deal of love and respect for Delores's eldest daughter, Harper. He'd always looked out for her and continued to do so, even after his own daughter, Harper's best friend, died. Now he had a new job: he was looking out for Eddie.

Delores was pacing the kitchen floor, her eyes glancing at the vodka bottle, which had always been her go-to drink when anything rattled her nerves. Although she had ditched the booze to prove to all her daughters that she could be a better person and be the mum they deserved, she wondered whether that was asking too much of her. Perhaps it was a little too late, but, nevertheless, she vowed to spend the rest of her life trying.

'Muvver, please, will you sit down? You're making me dizzy. Put the kettle on. I'll have a cup o' tea.'

'I dunno, Erin. How did Harper get mixed up in so much bleedin' drama?'

'Aw, come on, Mum, Harper has the biggest heart. I hate to admit it, but she is the one sister who, if there is a God, will be welcomed into Heaven with open arms.'

'You've changed your tune, Erin. You hated her for years.'

Erin tried to pull her black skirt nearer to her knees as she stared at her mottled fake tanned legs. 'Jealousy, that's all that was. Anyway, it's not about her and me. It's about her and how the fuck we can help her to find Charley, if me poor sister is still alive.'

Delores filled up the kettle and bit her lip. 'It should've been me fighting for Charley. She's my daughter.'

'It's all right, Mum. Look, we know what happened, and we don't judge you for it. Charley was brought up by another family, that's all.'

Erin got up from her chair and walked over to her mother and placed a hand on her shoulder. 'You love her, Mum, and always have. I reckon you were hurt because she chose a different family. It doesn't mean she didn't love you, but the circumstances were different back then.'

Delores nodded and wiped an unexpected tear away from her cheek. 'I was a pisshead, and . . .'

Out of character, Erin hugged her mother. 'And you had good reason. It was a tough time. Your boyfriend was murdered, Harper went to jail, and Charley was fostered and adopted. But look, our lives are very different now. We've *all* changed, Mum. Even me.' She looked down at her low-cut jumper. 'Well, at least a big part of me has.'

Delores shook her head. 'No, Harper hasn't. She's still the one fighting for us, and it will kill her one day. And that's what scares the shit out of me. I just couldn't bear it if she went before me.'

'Aw, stop being daft. Anyway, I need the loo. Any biscuits with that tea, Mum?' Erin asked, before she skipped off out of the kitchen and ran up the stairs.

As soon as Delores reached for the bourbons, she heard Erin's footsteps. They sounded like an elephant hurtling back down the stairs. 'Muvver! There's a bloody great 4x4 monster of a jeep or something parked up outside. I dunno, but four men have got out. I swear, Muvver, they ain't from around here. They're all in black suits, but they don't look like they're going to a funeral. They look bloody menacing.'

'Never mind that, do they look like Russians?'

'Well, they don't look Chinese, that's for sure. They could be Russians. They're big. I know that much.'

Delores dropped the biscuit tin, ripped open the drawer, and grabbed the first kitchen knife she could lay her hands on.

‘Muvver, what are you gonna do with *that*?’

‘I ain’t. *You* are. ’Ere, take it. I’ve got something else.’

She got to her knees, opened the door to the cupboard under the sink, stretched her arm in, and rummaged about until she pulled out a dirty-looking plastic bag.

‘Muvver!’ gasped Erin, as her mother got to her feet, opened the bag, and revealed a gun.

‘Don’t be so dramatic, Erin. It’s only a fucking shooter.’

‘*Only?* Shit, don’t you go shooting anyone. You’ll get nicked. Fuck me, Muvver. Where did you get it from?’

‘Never you mind, but finders keepers, and all that. Now, what did these geezers look like?’

‘Bodyguards.’

‘It’s those Russians that Terry was banging on about. Fuck me, they’re ’ere for Harper. I might as well tell you. They believe she killed two of their guards.’

‘Well, she ain’t ’ere.’

‘I know that, you divvy, but they don’t,’ said Delores, shaking her head in disbelief.

‘So what are ya gonna do? Simply shoot ’em if they knock at the door?’

Delores looked at the gun. ‘Well, no, probably not. But if they force their way in, then I might.’

The moment she said those words, they could see a black figure through the frosted glass of the back door.

Delores looked at Erin, who was now gripping the knife with white knuckles. ‘Jesus,’ she whispered. ‘They’re sodding here. Where’s me big sister when I need her?’

Delores flicked the gun. ‘Get out of the way.’

'Muvver, it could be the police.'

Delores shook her head. 'No, it ain't them. They normally announce themselves.'

The loud knock at the door made both women jump.

Delores put her finger to her lips and stared wide-eyed at Erin.

'Delores, are you at home?' came the deep, unmistakable voice of Vadim.

Swallowing hard, Delores opened the back door. Totally gobsmacked, she couldn't speak for a moment. Firstly, she hadn't expected ever to see him again, and secondly, he looked so different. His hair was cropped close to his head, a wide red scar graced the side of his head, and he was more prominent – much fitter. And even his eyes were alert compared to the last time she'd visited him in hospital after the attack on him.

Erin gave him the once-over. His striking blue eyes captured her attention; she liked a blue-eyed man, but this was someone she would never make a play for. She'd already done that with Teddy, and she wished with everything she had that she had never betrayed her sister in that way.

'Where is Harper?' His English was clear, but that hint of a Russian accent gave him a strong, stern tone.

Delores didn't know what to think. Terry had filled her in on the situation with the Russians and the need to keep Harper's whereabouts a secret paramount.

Erin was still in shock seeing Vadim in person standing there over six feet tall in her mother's kitchen.

'She's not here, Vadim.'

'She is not at her flat either. Do you know where she is?'

Slowly, Delores shook her head. 'No, sorry, love, I don't.'

He stepped forward and held out his hand.

At first, Delores frowned. That was until she looked down and realised that she was still holding the gun. 'Oh my daze. I'm sorry. Whatever was I thinking? We both thought, well, I dunno. Er, I'll put this away.'

Vadim stood silently, square-shouldered, with his hands now outstretched, still expecting something from Delores.

'Sorry, Vadim, what is it that you want, love?'

He grinned and raised his brow. 'My gun back, please, Delores.'

'Oh, this? I thought it was Harper's. I mean, she left it somewhere once, and I thought I should take it for safekeeping.' She sighed. 'Anyway, how do you know it's yours?'

He took the gun from her and pointed to the V that had been moulded to the butt. 'See this V? It stands for Vadim.'

'Okay, fair enough. So what brings you here?'

Vadim smiled, showing his perfect white teeth. 'I have, as you English say, a few loose ends to tie up and some unfinished business to take care of. Where is Harper? And why were you holding a gun, Delores? Expecting trouble, were you?'

Delores suddenly blushed. She was either staring at an enemy or lying to a friend. 'Well, er, an ex-boyfriend. You know how it is. You can't be too careful.'

Vadim then turned to face Erin. 'And you must be Erin. We didn't get to meet before. I suppose you have trouble with your ex-boyfriend too? Yes?' he said, sarcastically, before he took the knife from her.

Erin blushed as she stared at the man, right in his eyes. He was gorgeous all right.

But Vadim wasn't interested. He looked at Delores. 'Listen to me, Delores. I do not have to know where Harper is. I just have to know if she is safe.'

'Yes, she is safe.'

'Good. Please tell her to stay away from the club tonight.'

'Vadim, what's going on?' asked Erin, nervously.

He looked from Erin back to Delores. 'I can assume from you holding a gun and you a knife that you have a good idea what is going on.'

Delores leaned heavily against the kitchen unit. 'Please, Vadim, tell me that you are not here to hurt my Harper.'

'*Hurt her?*' His face dropped. 'Hurt her, you say? Are you mad, Delores? I would *never* hurt her.'

Vadim placed the knife on the worktop, and without being invited, he took a seat and unbuttoned his sheepskin coat, which made Erin look twice at his muscles popping out from behind a tight white T-shirt. She could see why Harper had had a sexual relationship with the man, and now she had seen him for the first time, if Harper hadn't been in the frame, she knew she would have tried. Her relationship with the doctor had fizzled out. They'd remained friends, but he wasn't the right fella for her. He was too nice and sweet. What she really hankered after was a rough and rugged kind of man, with maybe a beard and a few tattoos. Perhaps an available version of Vadim.

'You look better than the last time I saw you,' said Delores, still feeling a little awkward.

'Thank you. Yes, I went back to my country, and a good friend of mine, a doctor, saw that there was something very wrong and took me to his friend, one of Russia's best surgeons. He had found some small clots on my brain, so he operated and gave me medication. Another surgeon put a plate in my leg, and it has healed much better. I had to work hard in the gym, but I am well.'

'Yes, love, I can see that. Coffee, Vadim?'

He rubbed his hands. 'Yes, please. It is cold today, but I should be used to the cold.'

Delores smiled. 'Yeah, I bet. You lot always wear those fur hats like the busbies the Queen's Guard wear.'

Vadim chuckled. He liked Delores because she never minced her words.

'Can you tell me what this unfinished business is? Does it have anything to do with Teddy Ryder?'

Vadim smiled. 'Not exactly.' He held his hand up. 'And, no, I won't do anything terrible to him. I understand he is Eddie's father, and I wouldn't hurt him because he is also Harper's son.'

'You really loved her, didn't ya?' said Erin, mesmerised by the man's expressive eyes and deep husky voice.

'*Did?* No, Erin, I *do* love her. I crawled away back to my country like an injured dog, to die. I was so sick I thought I was going to do so, but the neurosurgeon fixed me up, and I am now back to put some things right.' He smiled again, winked, and then tapped the side of his nose.

'Oh,' said Erin. 'It's all right. I swear, I won't breathe a word, Vadim.'

Delores handed him a coffee and watched him knock it back as if his mouth was lined with asbestos.

'Thank you, Delores.' He stood up. 'I must go. Please make sure Harper stays away. I don't want her hurt.'

Delores nodded, but she knew the moment he was gone, she would be on the phone. However, as soon as the door shut behind him, it was Erin who dialled Harper's number herself.

When Harper answered the call, Delores snatched the phone from Erin. 'Harper, love, listen, you'll never guess who has just been here.'

'Mum,' replied Harper, 'I haven't got time for games. What's going on?'

'Only your Vadim's back, babe!'

'You *what*? You're kidding me. What's he doing back in England? I thought he was staying in Russia.'

‘No, girl, believe me, he is not the same man who left for Russia. The man with the limp and slurred speech. No. Vadim’s been operated on, and you have to see him to believe what you see. He is like the fucking Hulk – totally massive and on the ball.’

‘Mum, what’s he doing back ’ere?’

Delores could hear the excitement not so much in her daughter’s voice but in her rapid breathing. ‘He is back *apparently* to sort out “some unfinished business to take care of”, were his actual words.’

‘Is it anything to do with Teddy, by any chance?’

‘Well, I dunno the ins and outs, but he said he wouldn’t kill Teddy because of Eddie. Anyway, he said to make sure you stay away from the club tonight. He wants you safe.’

‘*Really?* What the hell’s going on, then, Mum?’

‘He didn’t stay long enough for me to find out. He was with three other men, although they didn’t come into the house. Erin reckons they looked like bodyguards. Listen, Vadim still loves you, Harper. That’s a fact, babe.’

Harper gave an exaggerated tut. ‘No way. It’s a figure of speech with him.’

‘Harper, are you okay, love?’

‘Yeah, Mum. Just keep an eye over at Mr Baker’s, will ya?’

‘Okay, love, just stay safe. Oh, is Tel all right?’ she asked, trying to sound nonchalant.

‘Yeah, Mum, he is just fine.’

***

Time was getting on, and Michel was pacing the floor, trying every which way to contact Verity, but the main office had told him she was on annual leave and her mobile phones, personal and work, were both switched off. After further interrogation, Katria had said Verity was on holiday for a week in the Philippines. A gift from her father for her birthday.

The six o'clock evening news showed footage of the explosion from a neighbouring village taken on a mobile phone. Terry was dozing in the chair but was wide awake when the news flashed up. He shook his head. 'How the fuck we weren't all toast, I'll never know. Someone was looking out for us that day, that's for sure. I don't understand why they would blow up the building, though.'

Michel stopped pacing and stared at the television screen. 'Because of the evidence inside those walls. And the police would trace it back to them.'

'What kind of evidence would warrant an explosion like that?' asked Harper, as she stood in the doorway.

'Anyone locked up in those rooms would have left so much evidence that they had been there. Think about DNA. And often, we have found lock-ups where prisoners and trafficked victims have used their blood to leave messages or carvings in concrete using an old nail or anything they can find.'

'Shit, that's bloody sickening.'

'But there is something odd about that explosion.'

'What?'

'The colours. The way the building blew up. It was like a firework effect. It seemed odd, that's all.'

'Not really. It was an old hospital building, and they could have had gas bottles lying around.'

Michel nodded silently, but Harper could see there was something else on his mind, and yet, like him, she had more pressing issues to think about, such as the unbelievable news that her Vadim was back in the country.

'Tel, would you mind if I use your washer and dryer for my clothes? I look disgusting.'

'Actually, Harpsichord, there's a box in Misty's room. I say Misty's room. She lives near Denmark Hill to be close to work, now. Anyway, she said to take those clothes to the charity shop because she's put on weight. I hope it's because she's content now. Love her. Come on, I'll show you,' he said, as he walked out of the lounge and up the stairs to the last room along the landing. He pushed the door open, and the cool air hit her. She realised that he had turned the radiator off, so she guessed that Misty's room was now permanently empty.

'Do you still see her, Tel?'

He smiled and nodded. 'Yeah, I pop over and have dinner with her once a week to make sure she's doing okay. She looks well. I guess time is a healer, and she has a couple of close friends who know her past, and they take good care of her as well, and the pharmacy department is a busy place, so, yeah, she's okay. Anyway, the clothes are mainly jeans and jumpers but knock yourself out.' He pointed to the enormous box in the corner of the room.

Harper kissed Terry's cheek. 'You, Tel, are my guardian angel. Do you know that?'

He blushed. 'No, but maybe I'm the nagging voice that sits on your shoulder,' he replied, before he left the room.

As she peeled open the box, she saw a neatly folded pile. They still had their fabric softener fresh smell. It was evident that the two girls Terry had fostered had been looked after well. She removed a plain black jumper, felt the silkiness of cashmere, instantly removed her smoke-ridden smelly top, and slipped on the jumper. It fitted perfectly. She pulled the other tops from the box and laid them on the bed before she lifted the jeans and found a pair of Levi's with the label still attached. They were her size. Having never owned a pair of 501s before, she felt her childhood memory return when she put them on. All the girls and lads had worn them, but she hadn't – ever; her mother had never had the money back then. At one time, she had felt cheated regarding the past. However, knowing the truth now had washed every ounce of anger away.

Quietly, she snuck down the stairs and past the lounge into the kitchen where Katria was still sleeping. Her head was slumped forward, and she was snoring her head off. Harper grinned. She wondered if Michel had forced her to take one of his heavy-duty sleeping pills. He'd clearly had the decency to clean her facial wounds and bandage her hand to stop the bleeding.

Sliding her feet into her shoes and gently removing her car keys, she quietly crept out through the back door and hurried along the path. She couldn't tell Terry or Michel where she was going because they would have stopped her. But she had to find out what had happened to her sister. She couldn't just sit there, and Michel, it seemed, was getting nowhere fast. She was getting frustrated, and now Vadim's reappearance added another worry to the mix.

CHAPTER THIRTY-TWO

Michel had gone over and over the information he had forced out of Katria. He dialled Verity's number again. He knew it was a national ringtone, the second it rang. So she was in the UK, not abroad. When she answered it was a simple 'Hello.'

'Verity, I need to talk. Are you in the car? Where are you going?' he asked, firmly.

'Look, Michel, don't be my enemy. Please join me. I need you on board right now.'

'Please, Verity, stop it.'

'No, I mean I need you. Meet me?'

'Sure,' he replied, as he looked down at his gun. One way or another, he would find his wife. Even if it meant putting a bullet through Verity's head.

A missed call popped up on his phone. Then came another. It was the same number but he didn't recognise it. In any case, he didn't have time for stupid sales calls.

***

Harper's mind was all over the place. Her main objective was to find her sister, and yet now, hearing that Vadim had some unfinished business to deal with, which wasn't necessarily linked to Teddy, she was struggling to work out what to do first.

She decided to speak to him and find out what the hell was really going on. Slowly, she cruised past the club, turned the car around, and drove back again, parking away from the residential area and near the overhanging trees, so she wouldn't be spotted.

The club was due to open in thirty minutes, and it was quiet. She noticed Annalise, one of the dancers, with a rucksack on her back and a thick woollen hat on her head, bowling along the road. Harper smiled to herself because when she wasn't wearing the

Doc Martens, ripped jeans, and the oversized coat, she was one of the best figure-perfect dancers that money could buy. But it was just a job to her, and outside of work, she was like any regular person. She saw Annalise skip along the side of the club only to return a few moments later with a small brown envelope. It was a wage packet, one of the old-fashioned wage packets. They hadn't used those in quite a while. She looked down at her packet of cigarettes and ran her fingers over the lighter. She was anxious and needed a fag to calm her nerves.

Her mind raced, wondering why Vadim had really returned; a part of her hoped it was for her. However, she felt he had been cold and distant with her during the last phone conversation she'd had with him. She took it that he had given in too easily. He shouldn't have gone back to Russia. He should have stayed and fought for her. If, of course, there really was more to their relationship than just friends with benefits. She shook her head and angrily snatched the packet before lighting up and taking a deep drag. When she looked up, she saw Roxy hurrying towards the club, and, like Annalise, Roxy came back into view with something in her hand.

Roxy was her close friend, but she couldn't get out and greet her, not tonight. It was evident that something heavy was going down because as the girls arrived, someone from the side door sent them packing, but Harper couldn't see who it was because her car was too far away from the side entrance.

Suddenly, her phone rang, making her jump. She fumbled to retrieve it from her jacket pocket. It was Teddy.

She had to answer it, or he would keep ringing. 'Yes, Teddy. What now?'

'Harper, is Eddie with you?'

'Teddy, it's nearly seven o'clock, and you don't know where your son is? Seriously, what kinda father are you?'

'Oh, don't, Harper, he is not a baby. So is he with you?'

'He is at his mate's for the night.'

'Oh, right, er, and what about you?' he asked.

Harper could hear the background noise and guessed he was driving.

'I'm at the gym.'

'The gym?' He laughed. 'Really?'

'Yep, and where are you, Teddy?'

She suddenly spotted his car as it pulled into the drive at the front of the club. It was a flash new Aston Martin. She swallowed the disgust, thinking about him making money from the Russians' crimes.

'Me, oh, I'm gonna call into the club. I've got a business meeting that shouldn't take long. Um, shall I pick you up from the gym? We could then go and have dinner.'

'Nah, you're all right, Teddy. I might come into work meself tonight.'

'*What?* No, it will be quiet this evening. You don't need to do that. Look, I tell you what, why don't me and you sit down together over a bottle of champagne, and I'll tell you all about my new ventures that I have invested in, which you, my little treacle dumpling, can be a huge part of, if you like.'

'Bloody hell, Teddy, where do you get all this money from?'

'Babe, my businesses are doing well, and there is plenty more where that came from.'

'Oh, is there really?'

'Yeah, I have gone into the property development business, and I tell you, Harper, I am having it right off. I can easily retire soon.'

Harper could feel her throat tightening up and her blood surging through her veins. The sheer arrogance of the man. He must know that the Russians wouldn't be paying him for nothing. He must have a scooby that they were committing some serious crimes. Was he so fucking greedy he would turn a blind eye? But, of course, she knew the answer to that already. He had used what he knew about Cody, known as Taboo, to blackmail him into paying the debts he owed him. It seemed the man had no shame or scruples for that matter. She shuddered and stared at the vehicle. It was a head-turner, all right, with its British racing green paintwork. What happened to you, Teddy Ryder? Clearly, money had gone to his head.

Her phone beeped, letting her know another caller was on the line. She glanced at the screen. It was Michel. 'Teddy, I have to go.'

She ended the call before Teddy even had a chance to say 'goodbye'.

'Hello, Michel. Sorry, I snuck out . . .'

'It's okay. Listen, Terry called your mother to find out where you are. She said that knowing the person you are, then you're most likely at the club. Harper, I need you to stay away.'

'What? Why? What do you know?'

'Harper, just do as you are told. I have been given some vital information. You need to keep away.'

Harper looked up to see Teddy get out of his car and straighten his suit jacket. He tugged on his shirt sleeves and tightened his tie before running his fingers through his hair.

'Harper, do you hear me?'

'What? Yes, Michel. Who did you speak with? What's going on?'

'Harper, just stay away, please. It is now out of our hands. Trust me on that.'

Harper ended the call and continued to stare at Teddy. Who could she ever really trust except herself right now? Who was sending Roxy and the dancers away? Was it Vadim? Had he called Teddy to go to the club to take his revenge on him?

Like a bolt of lightning penetrating her brain, she panicked. The fucking Russian mob! 'Shit! Shit! Shit!' she said quietly, as she fought to release the seat belt before almost falling out of the car.

'Wait!' she called out to Teddy. So many things flooded her brain. The mob. They would have used him. Paid him to be the bleeding blind fool. But as he would have too much on them, she could only guess they would kill him – the father of her son. And as much as she couldn't stand him now, she couldn't see him shot down, not as Paddy had been.

A vision flashed through her head when Teddy smiled at her before walking out of the visiting room that day with their three-year-old son, knowing it would be the last time she would see him until he was twelve years old. She blinked away the pain and the hatred. But she felt obliged to save Teddy, even though he probably didn't deserve her gallantry.

'Teddy, wait!' The chilly night breeze rattled the heavy-duty bins, drowning out all noise. Moments later, he was out of sight. He hadn't heard her calling him.

With her hands shaking, she called Teddy's number, but he'd turned his phone off. She dialled Roxy's number to find out who had opened the side door. But Roxy didn't answer either. 'Damn!' She dialled again, but there was no response.

She sighed. All she could do now was to try to sneak in and find a way to warn Teddy. Because she knew he was too full of himself to consider that the Russian mob would finish him off.

The cold air made her face tingle, and she wondered if it would snow. Her mind shot back to the girls having to live in that old hospital building in this weather. Slowly, as she approached the club, she looked about her. The lamp by the bins, which often flickered, was off. The sounds of footsteps and chattering forced her to spin around to see who was coming. It was a group of about twelve dressed to the nines and ready to party. They walked past her and stood by the entrance. Harper then realised she didn't look like the manager or even a punter. The door opened a fraction, and she noticed the light from inside shine on the excited potential guests. However, a deep voice, with a Russian tone, told the group that the club wasn't open tonight. By the time the man with the deep voice waved them on, another group appeared. Then a cab drew up with more people ready to party. Finally, instead of leaving the door ajar telling people the club was closed, the man stepped out and stood with his arms crossed and with a face like thunder. He growled at every guest that the place was shut for the evening.

Keeping out of his view, Harper could hear in his voice that he was pissed off. The man's demeanour didn't improve when he had to inform the next lot of punters and the next, until, eventually, he stepped back inside. Moments later, he returned with a sign, some barrier poles, and rope. He waved approaching guests back. 'The club is closed for the night. Back away!'

He cordoned off the entrance using the gold rope and positioned queue barriers to stop entry. He then hung a sign 'Shut for refurbishment'. As he was fiddling with the barrier, Harper sidestepped behind him and snuck in through the entrance door. The small and gloomy lobby area had an alcove with a small desk where punters could hand in lost property. She hid behind the makeshift desk and listened.

Once the doorman had shut and bolted the door, she heard him walk across the central area of the club towards the back of the room. Slowly, she rose and peered over the desk to see who was visible – no one. *Where the hell are they?* She thought. Then she spotted the office door ajar and the lights on inside, so she strained to hear. Sure enough, she heard voices.

A sudden movement caught her unawares. Teddy appeared from behind the bar. He had a tray with a few shot glasses and a bottle of Grey Goose under his arm. He seemed unperturbed. His quick swaggering walk showed he was confident in himself and in a good place. In fact, he seemed excited about something.

She wondered if she had got it all wrong. Maybe the Russian mob weren't going to kill him. Perhaps he was in with them deeper than she had anticipated. But she thought she knew him better than he did himself. He didn't seem to have acquired that sixth sense or even a gut instinct that something was not right. But she did, and, right now, her initial thought was plaguing her.

His flash fresh-from-the-showroom car wasn't something that Teddy had saved up for. It seemed to her that it was probably an impulse purchase. A splash the cash item.

Her thoughts turned to the Russians' sister, Katria. They must realise she was still missing. Would they suspect Teddy? If so, it would surely make sense for them to do away with him. Her heart raced. 'Oh, Teddy, come on, man, have a reality check, will you?' she said to herself, as she watched from her hiding place. A thought occurred to her. No one knew where she was.

She hurriedly texted Michel – **I will ring – don't speak – listen.**

She rang and he immediately answered the call and remained silent.

Suddenly, Harper was drawn to two men who walked into the main room past the bar. One was tall with a ponytail. He wore dark jeans and a black roll-neck jumper. The other man with him was even bigger with grey bristly hair and a square jaw; he was wearing black trousers and also sporting a black roll-neck jumper, although it appeared a tad too tight, clearly demonstrating his huge defined chest. His movements were controlled like a soldier. *Perhaps he was*, she thought.

'Ah, Mr Ryder, I am so glad you came.'

The ponytail man's smile was false – a little over the top – as he turned to the taller man.

'Casper, take the tray from him.'

Casper chuckled. 'Best vodka. Yes?' He took the bottle, and like Teddy, he placed it under his arm and then removed the tray.

'Take it to the office, Casper.'

Teddy was fidgeting, but he politely held out his hand. 'Good to see you, Yuri. So what's the new building you have for me since the old one is now a pile of rubble?' He laughed. 'The plans are complete and I'm ready to start building the twenty-eight flats.' He rubbed his hands together, his face beaming.

So this tall Russian with a smooth voice and sleek approach was Yuri. So far, Katria was telling the truth.

All she needed to do was to get the man alone, hold a knife to his neck, and demand to know what he knew about her sister's whereabouts. She inwardly sighed, knowing that it would never be that easy. For a start, she didn't have a knife. She had gone in completely unprepared, with no weapon and no plan.

Teddy looked at the office. 'Shall we go inside?'

Yuri chuckled. 'I don't think we need to do business together. You see, Mr Ryder, I like a very smooth operation. I like my business to run like, how you say, clockwork, but, you see, you have too much baggage that doesn't seem to want to go away.'

She could see Teddy looking dumbfounded, but that was him all over. He was clueless, a money-grabbing bungling puppet, and Yuri was the man holding all of his strings. She sighed to herself. *Oh, Teddy, what the fuck have you done?*

Teddy's face crumpled, his face ashen. 'What d'ya mean, Yuri?' he asked, looking thoroughly at a loss.

'Your ex-girlfriend, this Harper.'

She glared at Teddy, her eyes squinting to see the detail of his reaction.

'Look, I know Stan Nikki doesn't like his files being touched, and I know Harper is much the bloody same. She had the club running shipshape, and I suppose she clashed with Stan. Anyway, there will be no more headbutting, and I'll find her another job. Or we could maybe come to another arrangement with our business advisor stroke accountant. I am not sure I feel one hundred per cent comfortable with him, if you know what I mean.' He winked.

Harper knew then that Teddy had no idea the Russians believed she had killed the two guards who took her out of the club.

Yuri shook his head and laughed. 'No, Mr Ryder, you don't understand. Maybe when Stan Nikki arrives, he should explain.'

‘Explain what, mate?’

Yuri waved his hands contemptuously. ‘Never mind for now. More importantly, this Harper – your ex-girlfriend, I believe – has threatened our business.’

‘*What?* She couldn’t do that. She’s only been back five minutes since the death of some friend of hers.’

Yuri tilted his head. ‘You seem unaware of her ability,’ he replied, as Casper came back from the office.

‘You’ve lost me, mate.’

‘She’s killed two of my men, two of my best men.’

‘Fuck off. Don’t be silly. My Harper? What, kill two Russian guards? Well, I hate to tell ya, but you’ve got that all wrong, mate. Who do you think she is? Fucking Rambo’s daughter?’

‘This is no laughing matter. She is dangerous, and she knows too much.’

‘What about?’

‘My *business,* Mr Ryder.’

‘Listen, she ain’t as straight as you think. If she knew you were doing dodgy stuff, she’d keep her nose out of it. She served time herself, you know, and she ain’t no grass.’

‘And you, Mr Ryder, know too much as well, and I don’t like it that way.’

Harper felt her tongue glued to the roof of her mouth. She clocked Yuri slide his hand to the back of his trousers and under his jumper.

Oh no, no. She jumped up from behind the desk, leaving her phone on the top, and yelled, ‘Stop!’

Yuri instantly pointed the gun at her. He was quick; she would give him that.

Stepping forward into the light, she slowly raised her hands. ‘Look, Yuri. Is that your name?’

'Harper, babe, what the hell are you doing here? I thought you were at the gym,' said Teddy, in astonishment.

She glanced at him. 'You are such a knobhead, Teddy – a right fucking greedy money-grabbing dipshit.'

'Oi, Harper, don't get rude with me. What's the matter with you? And I told you not to come to work tonight, so why are you here, and where's your gym bag?'

Harper glanced back at Yuri. It was written across his face. He saw Teddy for what he was – a flash bastard without an ounce of intelligence. And it was almost laughable to see Teddy standing there, almost in denial, even though a gun was being pointed in their direction.

'I changed my mind, Teddy. I thought it would be better to come to the club tonight, to get a few shifts in. A good thing too, wouldn't ya say?'

'Shut it!' bellowed Yuri. 'You are Harper Kane. Yes?'

Harper stared at him. 'Yep, that's me.' Inside, her heart was beating so fast that she had to swallow to stop herself from being sick.

'Oi, Yuri, what the fuck are ya doing? Put the gun away, mate. This is only me missus, well, ex-missus, but ya know what I mean.'

Harper wanted to roll her eyes. So Teddy actually was that thick.

'Is this Harper?' asked Casper, with his nose screwed up.

Yuri nodded. 'This is the one.'

'So she is the woman who killed the two men?'

Yuri slowly nodded. 'Yes, this is the very woman.'

Teddy rubbed the back of his neck. 'Oh, leave it out, will ya. Harper – kill two of your men? Not even I'm capable of that.'

'No, Teddy Ryder, you are not capable at all. Yet you expect your son – *our* son – to be, though, don't you. You can't stand the idea that he might be gay, so you have a little girl come to the house to sleep with him, you cruel cunt.'

Teddy, again dismissing the gun being pointed at him, looked at her sheepishly. 'I was . . . oh fuck it. When he told me, I was shocked. In fact, that night, I was high on cocaine, so I might have overreacted. But that's all, Harps.'

'Oh, I see,' she replied, sarcastically. 'So you don't mind if our boy is gay, then.'

'Well, it's not ideal, but—'

'You are a disgusting human being. You knew all about those girls that Cody chained up. And you used the information to blackmail him.' She assumed that all the time she was arguing with Teddy, Yuri wouldn't use the gun. And, hopefully, someone would come to the bloody rescue.

Suddenly, Teddy's eyes were out on stalks. 'You what? No, you've got that all wrong, Harps.'

'Don't you Harps me. And for the record, the answer is no, Teddy, I didn't get it wrong. You knew that Cody or Taboo, my cousin, killed those girls.'

'I . . . er . . . I didn't know the extent. I only knew bits.'

'You're a vile man, Teddy Ryder.'

There was silence as Teddy bowed his head in shame. 'I just wanted to build an empire for you and me and our Eddie.'

'You, *build* an empire? Don't make me laugh. You forced Vadim to leave the country. You didn't even have the guts to fight him one-on-one, did ya? Oh no, you had to mow him down before he would sign the club over to you. You're a fucking coward!' She shook her head in utter disappointment. 'But I can see now that it wasn't just you who did all the dirty work.' Her eyes locked on those of Yuri and Casper, in disgust. 'I reckon it was this pair of cunts who you paid to get rid of Vadim. Because it seems to me, Teddy, that they run this show, not you.'

Yuri laughed as Casper clapped. 'That was so good! It was like watching one of your soap dramas on the television. But now is reality time, and you two have messed up a situation for me.'

'Yes, yes, yes, and now we die. I get it, Yuri,' snapped Harper. 'I can die. I will be out of your life, but if you have any honour inside of you, then please answer one question for me.' Her heart was now beating so fast, she thought she would collapse.

Yuri turned to face her square on. He smiled and licked his lips. 'I do have respect for you. I like a strongheaded, tough woman. Maybe in another life, you would have been my ideal woman. You're beautiful, you're smart, and you have the guts to kill two of my best men. So I will answer your question. But then, you die.'

Harper nodded. 'Thank you. Now, tell me this. What have you done with my sister? I want to know if she is alive.'

Yuri looked at Casper and then at Harper. 'I'm sorry. Who is your sister?'

'Please don't play games. You have my sister, or you've killed her, but please do me the honour of telling me before I go to the grave.'

'No, really, Harper, I do not know who your sister is.'

'Her name is Charley.'

Yuri shook his head. 'No, sorry, I don't know a Charley.'

'What the hell are you banging on about, Harper? Why would Yuri know where Charley is? Are you on some kinda drug?'

'Shut up, Teddy, you silly prick!'

CHAPTER THIRTY-THREE

Holding the gun in his right hand, Yuri glared at Harper. He then crossed his arms over his chest. 'And should I know this sister of yours?' he said, with an offhand expression.

Being backed into a corner and poked with a stick was usually the point at which Harper would lose all self-control and launch an attack, irrelevant to the circumstances. However, his last words 'this sister of yours' stopped her in her tracks. A vision of his sister in Terry's kitchen came flooding back to her like the force of a fast train. She smiled. 'Yes, I think you do. And look at me.' She held her arms on either side of her body. 'I am prepared to die for my sister. I'd do anything for her! Would you do the same for yours?'

Yuri suddenly unfolded his arms and pointed the gun in her face. 'I don't have a sister.'

'Oh no? So who is Katria, then?'

Casper looked uneasy and shot a concerned look at Yuri. 'What is she talking about? How would she—'

'Casper, get me a drink.'

Teddy was lost for words; his droopy eyes ping-ponged from Harper to Yuri.

'How do you know about Katria?' asked Casper, ignoring Yuri.

'Casper!'

Again, ignoring Yuri, he stared at Harper. 'How do you know Katria?'

Harper smiled and folded her arms before she began to tap her feet. 'I know a lot about her. In fact, I have just left her.'

'Now you are telling lies. I had respect for you up to this point,' mocked Yuri.

'Where do you think she is, if she is not tied up with a gun to her head?'

'She died in the explosion.'

'You bastard!' said Casper.

'Shut up, Casper. She never liked you anyway.'

Harper smiled. 'She wanted so much to be a part of your family, Yuri. She misses her mother. All she has is you and Daria. She would do anything for you, even the unthinkable.'

'Where is Katria?'

'Not here, mate, clearly, but one word from me and she's a gonna. Sorry, in Queen's English that means she's dead.'

'Shoot her. I don't care. She is nothing to me,' said Yuri, not even blinking.

Harper knew then how cold this man was. But Casper, on the other hand, seemed bothered.

'Wait!' said Casper. 'Prove she is alive.'

'Well, to be honest, Casper, she was alive when I left the place, but after all the torture she is going to endure, she might not be soon.'

Casper's face was burning red. 'Don't you fucking hurt her.'

Harper glared at Yuri. 'I've got a deal for you. You let *my* sister go, and I'll instruct the same for yours. And you know who I mean by my sister. She's the undercover cop who managed to photograph your paperwork and who sent it to me.'

Both Yuri and Casper looked startled. Yuri's mouth fell open. 'You mean *Kristi*? Kristi is your sister? But she cannot be. She is a Russian working for the British police. Yes?'

A quiver of excitement almost took Harper's breath away. 'Is? Did you say *is*?'

Casper nodded. 'Yes, *is*.'

'So she's alive?'

Unexpectedly, Yuri used the gun to smash Casper in the ribs. 'Shut up, you idiot!' he said, in his own language.

Casper coughed and doubled over, his face a deep burgundy from rage.

'She is not your sister. Kristi is Russian.'

'No, she's just fucking good at her job and has obviously mastered the art of rolling her Rs.'

Again, in Russian, Yuri called for his men. Two came from the office and two from the side room that led to the back exit.

'Take them down to the basement.'

Like robots, the four men, all in black, with gigantic frames and popping muscles, grabbed both Teddy and Harper.

Harper didn't even bother to struggle. She was completely overpowered. 'Where is my sister, Yuri?'

He laughed, and a cruel smirk graced his face, but his smile dissipated when Harper screamed, 'Well, fuck you, then! Kill her, Michel! Kill Katria!'

Casper ran at her and grabbed her around the throat. 'Who are you talking to, bitch?'

He let go as Harper tried to catch her breath. 'Michel, an undercover officer, who has gone rogue, is with your sister, and he can hear me.'

Yuri glanced around. 'What are you talking about?'

'My phone is on the desk back there, and he can hear everything I am saying.'

Yuri nodded to one of the guards to fetch the phone.

Harper smiled at Casper. 'Clearly, she means a lot to you. Do you want her alive?'

'If you fucking kill her, I will slowly remove every one of your teeth.'

'Then tell me where my sister is.'

Yuri glanced at Harper's phone and laughed. 'Very good, yes, and this Michel will hear your screams.'

He lifted his chin, nodded at the biggest of the four men, and again spoke in Russian.

The guard instantly gripped her around the throat and began to squeeze. She ripped at his hands, tearing at his flesh, while her pulse pumped like hot oil through her veins. She could hear Teddy screaming for the man to stop, but then his pleadings became less audible, until there was silence, as if her ears were blocked and her vision narrowed. Feeling one of her bones cracking as she hit the floor, she gasped as if she was being held underwater. On all fours, she desperately tried to breathe in as much air as possible. Her lungs burned, and her head hurt, but at least she was still alive.

'Now, tell me where my sister is, Harper, since Casper is keen to keep her alive. Or I will have my guard use his teeth to take out your windpipe.'

Harper, having almost died, was unaware of a new person in the vicinity.

'What is going on!' bellowed a lordly voice.

Harper blinked to clear her vision. There in front of her dressed in a long navy-blue Crombie and a pair of black leather gloves in his hand was Andrew Mercer. She knew it was him because he had silver hair and a glass eye. Beside him was Stan Nikki, the midget, with a cocky sneer on his face and cloaked in ill-informed confidence.

'So we meet again, Harper Kane,' said Nikki, before he ran up to her and kicked her in the ribs. Once again, the force wasn't enough to make her scream.

'Woah, Stan, mate. What the fuck are ya doing? Leave off!' bellowed Teddy, as he tried without success to shake off the two guards who were holding his arms as though each one was being held in a vice. 'Get off me.' He looked at each guard in turn. 'I thought me and you two were mates.'

‘Shut your insignificant mouth, Ryder,’ said Nikki. ‘They aren’t your mates, you dumb piece of shit.’ He chuckled. ‘Mates? What, a few beers and a fight in an alleyway with Vadim, and you think you’ve got a couple of pals. Christ.’ He shook his head. ‘You really are an oaf.’

‘What’s going on here?’ asked Teddy, as the guard tightened his grip on him. ‘Andrew, would you shed some bloody light here?’

Andrew shrugged. ‘I am as much in the dark as you. I was called to a meeting.’

‘So was I,’ said Teddy, looking at Yuri.

Harper could see they were confused by how they all glanced at each other.

But it was Teddy who piped up. ‘Your bloke, Yuri, told me I was to meet you and discuss a new project worth a quarter of a million pounds.’

Yuri jumped back. ‘What the fuck is going on here? I had no one call you. You just turned up and arranged drinks for us.’

‘Well, some cunt with a Russian accent spoke to me.’

Harper focused on Yuri. He glanced uneasily around at his guards. Distrust clouded his eyes, and she could tell he appeared worried.

‘Casper, what’s going on and where the fuck is my brother?’ His accent cut through the air.

Casper shrugged his shoulders. ‘I don’t know.’

He looked at Nikki. ‘Was it you who called the meeting? Did we do something wrong? Is there a problem?’

‘No, Yuri, I didn’t call a meeting, but, clearly, there is a problem. You assured me that this operation would run smoothly. I gave you everything you needed to complete what I started, yet you stand here like a clown. You blew up the building without removing my chemicals. You cost me money.’ His eyes were dark, and his jaw stubbornly locked to the side as he stamped his foot like a spoilt child.

Harper, however, was more surprised by Yuri's reaction when he clasped his hands together, virtually begging forgiveness. 'Stan, I am sorry, but it was not my fault. Look, we can take the girls away, get rid of them, and no one will know. I can replace the chemicals. It is not a problem!'

'You fool! As I entered the club, I overheard you talking to some Michel or other on the phone. This Michel has Katria; he is listening to our conversation right now. Give me that bloody phone.'

Casper handed it to him and stepped back as if he too feared the midget's backlash.

Nikki put the phone to his ear and inclined his head. 'Hmmm, I can hear you driving, Michel. So, if you truly have Katria, put her on the phone.'

Harper felt her heart drop into her stomach. *Why the hell was he in a car?*

Nikki grinned and put the call on speakerphone. 'Speak, Michel, so that we can all hear you before I put a bullet through Harper's head. I am itching to do it, too.'

Before Michel could say a word, Harper butted in. 'What is it with me, hey? Why the fuck do you hate me so much when I don't even know you?'

Nikki waved his hand dismissively. 'Shut up, Harper Kane.'

'No, come on, you mouthy prick, tell me. You seem to be running the show here. You, I assume, are the big boss. Though God know how, you little runt! So, go on, tell me. Why am I such a threat to you?'

'I said, shut the fuck up.' He suddenly pulled out a gun and stomped towards her. 'One more word, and you will have a hole through your head.'

Harper bit her lip as she stared down the barrel of his gun, believing he would do it as well.

'Take her out to the back room and tie her up. I want to have some time alone with just her and my knife.'

The two guards gripped Harper tighter and dragged her to the back room while Teddy struggled to free himself. 'Leave it out, Stan, mate. She's an innocent in all of this.'

Nikki turned around and looked Teddy up and down. 'You really are a fucking useless piece of shit. I should never have got you to buy the club and the old hospital. What was I fucking thinking?' He shook his head dramatically.

'Never mind about that. Where is Katria?' said Mercer, nervously. 'Ask that man on the phone where she is. I have to know that she and my child are okay.'

Something inside Casper snapped as he suddenly ran at the ex-commissioner. With one punch, he floored him. 'You don't deserve her, you perverted creep!' he screamed, as Andrew went down so heavily that the back of his head hit the floor.

Yuri pulled Casper away. 'No, don't be stupid. Leave him. We must not fight among ourselves, and we need to get away from here soon. Where the fuck is Daria?'

The two guards entered the back room holding Harper; one pushed her down onto one of the chairs and the other looked inside the cabinets for something to tie her up.

While they were distracted, she noticed someone in the shadows hiding beside the tall freezer. She wasn't sure if her eyes were deceiving her, but she was convinced she could see a woman's leg. A sudden movement as the woman quickly leaned out to take a look prompted Harper to get her brain into gear. She needed to create a distraction. With all her strength, she leaped up and threw her arms around one guard's neck while kneeing him hard between the legs. As he groaned in pain and doubled over, the other guard, who had been searching inside the cabinets, snatched Harper around the throat and savagely forced her against the wall.

‘No escape, this time, Harper Kane. You killed my friend last time, but today, you die,’ was all he said, before his face paled and his eyes widened in shock. He let go of his grip and plummeted to the floor like a sack of hot shit, leaving a clear view of the woman with the bare legs.

Without even breaking a sweat, she went over to the other guard and plunged a knife into his neck as well.

As soon as the woman removed her knife and turned around, Harper wanted to run to her and squeeze her so tightly. However, a brief smile from her sister Charley was all she needed to save her hug and stay in control. She couldn’t believe that her little sister was so fast and dangerous. She had always thought that she was the tough nut in the family. The difference was that Charley was precise and acted like a trained soldier, and she certainly didn’t take prisoners. Charley then pulled a gun from the back of her shorts and handed Harper the knife. ‘In case’ was all she said, before Nikki bowled into the back room.

Harper gritted her teeth and flared her nostrils. The man was as arrogant as fuck and ready to give her a hard time.

Clearly expecting to find Harper bound to a chair, he stopped dead in his tracks. His startled eyes scanned the room as he spotted the two dead guards.

Then his eyes rested on the two women.

Harper momentarily revelled in his horror as she stood proudly next to her gun-wielding no-nonsense sister. She felt honoured, relieved, and euphoric all at once.

She didn’t see him slyly attempt to retrieve his gun. But in the time it took most people to blink, Charley raised her gun to his head and laughed. ‘No, you don’t.’

‘Fucking shoot me, then!’ he screeched like a girl, sounding once more like the spoilt brat he was.

Yuri and Casper, hearing Nikki’s high-pitched voice, hurried into the room but stopped dead when they saw Charley with a gun in her hand and Harper gripping a knife.

'Oh fuck,' said Yuri, but he wasn't looking at Charley or Harper. He was looking over their shoulders.

'Oh yeah, Yuri, *oh fuck*,' came the deep, gravelly voice.

Harper felt her skin become alive. That voice had always made her heart beat faster and her skin tingle with excitement.

Charley momentarily pivoted but lowered her gun when she heard his name.

'Vadim?' said Nikki, his face turning grey with shock. 'Why are you back? I thought you were sick.'

Vadim slipped between the two women with his gun in his hand and pointed it at Nikki's face. Two of the largest men Harper had ever seen hurried around them and grabbed Yuri and Casper, wrestling them to the ground. Even Casper, built like a brick shithouse, was no match for these men. In a second, Vadim's men had them face down and their hands securely tied.

The two men restraining Teddy tried to flee through the club's main entrance, but with all the commotion and shouting, Harper assumed that Vadim had more men present at the front who had secured Yuri's two guards, preventing them from escaping.

Teddy was like a headless chicken. He ran to the back room and stopped, now eyeing the carnage. His eyes flitted around the room, trying to take it all in, and Harper knew by his perplexed expression that he didn't know whose side he was on.

However, Nikki's eyes were glued to Vadim; clearly, he was more afraid of the man than anyone.

'Yes, Stanislav Nikitin, since it was all your idea to have me beaten up, you thought I would die, didn't you? But Ryder never actually finished me off. Mind you, he almost did, and yes, I thought he had left me disabled. You thought you'd brainwash the Russian mob, Yuri, and his idiot brother Daria and manipulate this man Andrew Mercer to be your face of respectability as co-owner of this club. Well, you clearly got it wrong. Manipulation, yes, Stanislav, you're good. We know that. But picking the right people to work with' – he chuckled – 'has never been your strong point. And neither, it seems, is your dress sense.'

Harper was gobsmacked. So the midget was a stinking Russian.

'You were always so very jealous of me, Stanislav.' He sneered at him, looking him up and down with so much hate. 'You came a long time ago with fake papers to my office, trying to convince me that my father had left half his inheritance to you. And, yes, you are clever. You perfected the English language very well. But you know nothing about the matters of the heart. I knew my father would never have left you a thing. You were his bastard, the biggest drunken mistake he'd ever made.' He huffed. 'You took after your mother. She was a greedy gold digger. I shouldn't be surprised if you weren't even my father's son but the result of your mother's whoring.'

Nikitin's face was tight with rage. But Vadim wasn't perturbed. His deep angry tone was one Harper had never heard before. She had seen him lose his temper in the past, but this was on a whole other level.

'I should have known that you would exact revenge.' He growled. 'I hated you as a kid, and I hate you now. If you had been kind as a child, I would have looked out for you, even possibly cared for you, but you hated everything and everyone I cared about.' He pointed the gun as if pointing a finger. 'You killed my best friend. You hurt my mother and me.' He paused. 'I hear that you have upset Harper. But no more. You should have stayed down in the depths of the chemistry labs where you belonged. You were good at that. At least, I guess you were until you became so greedy.'

Looking at Nikitin, Harper realised she was facing pure evil. A true blackness shrouded him like the little vile demon he was. He wasn't listening to Vadim any longer; he was fixed on her, and blatantly, he gripped his gun. Before he had a chance to shoot her, a loud bang rang in her ears.

Vadim had shot him in the head.

His brains sprayed up the wall as he fell back like a wooden soldier.

'What the fuck! Shit me!' yelled out Teddy.

Teddy wasn't bothered one bit about the demise of who he assumed was his business partner. It was his thousand-pound suit that he was concerned about, which was now coated in what looked like red lumpy vomit mixed with Cherryade. He was so grossed out that he dry-heaved. 'What the fuck!' he said, before he dry-heaved again.

Charley was about to go after Andrew Mercer, who was now on his feet and ready to slip out unnoticed, when Verity arrived.

Seeing her face had Harper gunning for a fight. She hated the woman, and there she was wearing a police flak jacket and pretending she wasn't a part of all of this.

But Charley's reaction was what surprised her the most. 'A bit late, Verity, aren't you? The top boss and two Russian guards are dead.' She pointed her thumb over her shoulder.

Verity winked. 'All self-defence?'

Charley grinned. 'Of course.'

'Oi, you bitch! What are ya doing with my keys?' Harper yelled, when she clocked her club keys in a clear bag in Verity's hand.

But as Harper ran at Verity, Michel grabbed her by the waist and pulled her back. 'No, Harper, she's one of the good guys. Apparently. Terry found the keys in Katria's pocket. I called her when Katria finally admitted Verity was innocent.'

Harper stopped and looked at Charley. She could see that her face was changing. The serious deadpan expression softened, and, instantly, her shoulders relaxed.

Michel wasted no time throwing his arms around his wife and allowing the floods of tears to pour down his face.

Harper watched as her sister squeezed his cheeks and kissed him. 'We got 'em, Michel. We got 'em.'

'Well, not quite you and me,' he said, flicking his head at Harper.

Feeling a little embarrassed, Harper uncharacteristically looked down at the floor.

But Charley went over to her sister and hugged her tight, whispering in her ear, 'You were always there for me, Harper, weren't you? You never gave up on us. But you can't fight our battles, not anymore. We're grown women now.'

'I couldn't stand it. I didn't know if you were dead or alive.' Harper looked at the state of her sister's face and arms. 'And if you *were* alive, what they were doing to you locked away somewhere.'

'These bruises look worse than what they are. Daria, Yuri's brother, attempted to get information out of me about the tablet. I sent them on a wild goose chase to our holiday home in France to buy time. But he had orders from Yuri not to kill me. Yuri had some sick idea that he and I would be a couple, the fucking idiot. Anyway, I think apart from me being a potential useful tool, his fantasy helped keep me alive. And these bruises will heal, unlike the injuries sustained by my colleague. They fucking killed him after a week. At least I lasted ten days.'

'Oh my god, Charley, you are one hard woman. How did you escape?'

'A little friend of ours helped me. A courageous little girl, that one.'

'Oh my God, you mean Yalina?'

Charley nodded. 'Yes, she's outside. She's safe.'

Suddenly, a rush of officers came flooding in, all wearing flak jackets and holding guns.

Verity called out for them to search the building for the girls.

From nowhere, Vadim approached. 'I know where they are.' He pointed to the floor.

'What do you mean?' asked Verity.

‘They are in the basement. Stanislav knew this building had a huge void underground. It spans the width and length of the club. It was originally going to be an underground club, but I left it as it was. So the place is already equipped with extractor fans for his dirty business.’

Verity tilted her head. ‘Sex trafficking, you mean?’

Vadim shook his head. ‘No, Stanislav was a chemist. He would have used the girls to work in his meths lab. But he probably used them as prostitutes before he had this place equipped.’

Verity called the officers to check out the basement.

Vadim pointed to the office. ‘Access is through there into the flat, and by the front door, there is another smaller door that leads down to the basement.’

‘How did you know this was Stanislav’s intention?’ Verity asked, in an accusing tone.

‘Because I recently heard he blew up a building near Moscow. Ten girls died. They were making a methamphetamine lab. He wasn’t known to the police in this country, so he wanted my club. It would have been perfect for his moneymaking scheme.’

‘Thank you . . . Er, excuse me.’ She focused her eyes on Casper, who was being handcuffed by an armed officer.

‘So,’ Verity said to Casper. ‘Katria was dating someone else as well as my father. I thought I had seen her with another man, who was clearly *not* my father. Well, since you will be arrested for the murders of Hulou and Dominica as well as the human trafficking of minors, you can write to each other in prison. If, of course, you want to write to her considering I guess she used you, and . . .’ She stopped and looked at her father.

Holding her head high, Verity stared at the man with a glass eye, who was once full of confidence and pride and a man who everyone aspired to, including herself. But not now.

‘I am arresting you . . .’

‘Verity, I am sorry. Listen, I’ll call my lawyer and have this mix-up sorted in a minute.’

She shook her head. ‘Not this time, Father. Not this time. That man, over there, Vadim, he is here with none other than Interpol. This is an international crime. And even though the photo of a contract that Michel just showed me was blurred, I could still recognise your signature. You can’t get out of this now. You are going away for a long time’

‘*What?*’

‘Yes, Father.’ She shook her head, ashamed of him. ‘You and Katria both used me. You both had me believe that Michel and Charley had gone rogue. Do you have any idea how much torment you have caused your own people? Not the disgusting Russian mob, but us, the good guys. Michel would have been arrested for Peter’s murder, but it was either you or Katria. Either way, we’ll get to the truth.’

‘No wait, stop a minute. Verity, please let me explain.’

‘One question, Father, why?’

He lowered his head. ‘For you, my sweetheart.’

‘Oh, shut up. The least you can do is to be honest.’

‘Everything I gave you growing up came at a price – our home, your education, the holidays.’

‘What? But you inherited vast sums of money and the house from Grandfather.’

He suddenly looked down. ‘No, I didn’t. I made the money the best way I knew how.’

‘Poker at the gentlemen’s club?’

He nodded. ‘I was in debt. You must understand, Verity, I am a highly regarded member of society. I couldn’t lose it all. I couldn’t tarnish your good name—’

She held up her hand to stop him from saying anything else. ‘You mean your good name, don’t you? Christ, is that all you’ve ever really cared about? Well, I don't need to know any more. I have heard enough. You simply confirmed my suspicions. Andrew Mercer, I am arresting you for. . .'

Harper didn't listen to the string of offences. She merely watched as the ex-commissioner was escorted away from the club. His head was so low in shame, it almost appeared to roll off his shoulders. But, she realised, at least he would still live a life of some description. She reckoned that Yuri would have disposed of him at some point. He was clearly a risk to his organisation.

Harper suddenly felt alone, with all the officers and paramedics running around the club. Everyone had a role. Except she didn't, not now. Her job was done, so it seemed.

She was in the middle of what seemed like a merry-go-round until she felt an arm around her shoulders.

'Sis, you're okay, and thank fuck for that. I wasn't sure if using me teeth, tits, and tan were enough to distract the Russian guards, but thank fuck I did. At least it gave our Charley a way in. Well, blimey, if I wasn't in the middle of a siege, I would have poured myself a drink and taken in the eye candy.' She pointed to the armed officers checking over the club.

Harper was suddenly laughing and crying simultaneously. 'You came for me, Erin. You came to help.'

'Yeah, I know I was a bit late in the day, but I do love ya, Sis, and it was about time I womaned up. Talking of which, Muvver's outside. She came, an' all, but she said her new hairdo and red lipstick wouldn't be enough of a distraction, so she was the lookout for Charley.'

When Erin clocked Vadim directing officers, she whispered, 'He came back for you, Harper. For you, love. That's your man, not Teddy.'

Harper looked over, and at the same time, Vadim glanced her way. He did what he often did and winked. A tear tickled her nose, but she stared back with a gentle smile, feeling the wings of a million butterflies in her stomach. She was so distracted, she didn't even notice Teddy being taken away in cuffs.

Outside was like a scene from an American cop movie. There were ambulances, police cars, and vans taking up the entire road. Harper was thrilled to see the young girls being led away from the club, each with a warm blanket around their shoulders and holding a hot drink.

'That's Yalina,' whispered Charley, who knew that Yalina had never actually formally met Harper. The tall pretty teenager was comforting two younger-looking girls.

As Harper approached Yalina, she looked up at her and smiled. 'I think I can guess who you are. It's Harper, isn't it?'

Without saying a word, Harper wrapped her arms around the girl and kissed the top of her head. 'You brave, brave girl. You saved the others, Yalina. You did it.'

CHAPTER THIRTY-FOUR

Six months later

Immediately after she climbed out of her car, Harper felt the warmth of the sun on her bare shoulders. She stared at the club and smiled at the sign: Bling Palace. It actually looked beautiful. Desiree had got her way and stuck with the new name.

A burst of nostalgic emotion poked Harper in the chest, making her reflect on The Click. She would miss the place, but too many ghosts were there to haunt her. The good times couldn't outweigh the bad – not after the horrific events that had taken place over time.

A gentle kiss on her neck made her body tingle. 'I don't think I have ever been so happy,' she whispered.

'This is our life now, and tonight, my queen, we will celebrate.'

'Oh, Vadim.' She stared at her hand. 'Yes, tonight the champagne will be flowing. I cannot wait to tell everyone. But you know I have to do this one thing before we can start afresh, don't ya?'

'Yes, I know,' he replied, as he stared into her eyes and eased a loose strand of hair away from her ear. 'I love you, Harper Kane.'

Smiling, she blushed and tilted her head down. 'You know that's the only time anyone has said those words to me with sincerity behind them.'

He kissed her cheek, not wanting to smudge her delicately applied lipstick. He then looked at her hands. 'Beautiful nails.'

'Always, for you, Vadim, always.'

‘Go on, Harper. Eddie is waiting for you. I will be back tonight for the grand opening with the new doormen, and I have personally vetted them.’

Harper nodded. She was so proud of Vadim. With the help from Michel, he had set up his own security firm, taking on doormen, guards, and bodyguards. He had also covered other security aspects, like guarding demolition sites and protecting abandoned buildings, which belonged to local authorities. He had engaged in training programmes to help the men identify certain potential crimes, like serious drugs, and, more importantly, trafficking. His life was now in the UK, with her and Eddie, and she couldn’t wish for anything more.

***

The last-minute banging and crashing to get the club ready for the opening compelled Harper to get herself into her management role to ensure the work was completed on time. Inside, it was a hive of activity. While Roxy was filling the shelves, Dax passed her the bottles; thinking no one was looking, he gave her a quick kiss and a pinch of her backside. Seeing them together put a smile on her face. She had grown attached to Dax since meeting him in person six months ago. Away from his brother Byron, Dax was a different person. He still liked to wear his surfer shorts and have his hair long, but he had stopped smoking the wacky baccy and concentrated on what was best for business. And what made her respect him even more was that he hadn’t attempted to change his mother’s mind over the will. The club was hers and her sisters. Of course, she would change that one day to include him when the time came. He knew that the club would make a mint and would only have gone to rack and ruin if it had been left to Byron and himself to run, so he was happy with his wages and working in the new cocktail bar, under Harper’s supervision.

Harper eyed Desiree buzzing around; she was looking pristine as usual in her Chanel tweed suit.

And there, with tool belts around their middles and nails and screws between their teeth, were the workmen who were adding the finishing safety measures for the pole dancing stage. She had offered all the dancers from The Click a job, and all of them had jumped at the chance.

'Harper!' yelled Terry.

Her eyes looked in his direction; even he was pitching in, with a tool belt around his waist.

'Your mother is still at the hairdresser's. Bloody hell, she's like a cat on hot bricks, and I wouldn't mind, but look at your aunt, ol' Desiree, as cool as a cucumber, reading a magazine. Charley and your mum will take it in turns to come. Baby Delores has colic, bless her, so you know Charley – she don't want to leave her for too long.'

Harper smiled and put her arms around him. 'It's gonna be the best night ever, eh, Tel?'

'I should coco. Footballers and all sorts are gracing us with their presence. It's gonna be a right blinder, my girl.' He sighed. 'If only I could get this poxy drill to work. Oh, fuck it.' He placed the drill on the stage and put his arm around her shoulders. 'Come and see the extension. I know when Desiree gave Eddie the nod to throw together a few plans for the room, she never actually expected to be carrying them out. But your Eddie has come up trumps with the design. Close your eyes, Harper.'

She placed her hands over her eyes and allowed Terry to guide her before he said, 'Ta-da! Open them.'

She pulled her hands away and marvelled at what she saw. Slowly, she turned around and gazed in utter shock, soaking in every fine detail. She stopped when she saw Eddie. His face beamed with pent-up excitement.

'Do you like how it looks, Mum?'

Harper was speechless and tears streamed from her eyes. 'What, all of this was *your* doing?'

He nodded. 'Yeah, all down to me. I thought I would tone down the bling from the main part of the club and introduce a calming feel. You know, soft velvets, fewer crystals, mood lighting, an area that quietens the minds and allows conversation and . . .'

'What you really mean is you want it to be classy.'

He smiled. 'Yeah, that's exactly what I want, although I think Aunt Dez loves the bling in the main bar.'

'You are a bloody artistic genius.' She laughed and looked at Terry. 'I can't believe he's my son.' She turned back to Eddie and pinched his cheek. 'And I thought your career was all sorted out. In marine biology, wasn't it?'

Eddie shook his head. 'No, Mum. I think I was searching for Teddy's affection – his attention, I mean – and so when we went to Egypt, I had that, and I suppose I linked it to diving and, in my head, it was a future career, where I assumed I would be at my happiest, but . . .' He waved his hand, showing the room. 'I think this is my calling. In design, whether it be clubs or clothes or anything like that.'

Harper hugged him, kissing the top of his head before smelling his hair as she always did.

'You, my baby, will be whatever you want to be, and this has blown me away. It's stunning. Anyway, are you ready?'

Eddie nodded. 'Yeah, Mum, I suppose I am. But it has to be the only time until I *am* ready. I'm not going to be at his beck and call ever again. You do know that, don't you, Mum?'

Harper kissed him again. 'I know, Son. Okay, let's do this.'

***

Harper shuddered as she entered the visiting room. The sounds of the metal doors banging and clanging, and the keys jangling were enough to put her on edge. Even though this was a male prison, the sounds and smells were like those she had experienced when she'd been banged up.

As soon as a warden called the names Kane and Ryder, Eddie looked at his mother. 'That's us, then.'

Harper slowly stood up and followed the prison officer to the visiting room. The layout was also much the same as the prison where she'd served her time. It had a tuck shop area and equally spaced tables and chairs screwed to the floor. She felt uneasy setting foot inside the room, but it was time she spoke to him.

As the door at the back of the room opened, the prisoners hurried in, joining their families or friends.

When Teddy appeared, she had to look twice. He was how she remembered him the very first day he came to visit her in prison. Then, he was full of hugs and tears and sorrow when he had to leave her behind. Of course, as time went by, and with each visit, he changed. At the time, she had refused to believe it. She'd hung on in the hope he would be there for her and also for what she thought at the time was love.

That was until that fateful day. It would be forever cast in her memory. Teddy had brought her baby, her three-year-old toddler, Eddie, to see her for the last time. Teddy was in a suit that day, smelling of Hugo Boss, and his wild waves had been cut to suit the new trendy styles. He'd told her he was stepping out of her life and into a new one. So, in effect, he was leaving her alone to get on with it. And he did it in style. Walking out of the visiting room, for the final time, in his Italian leather shoes and posing in that trademark cocky swagger of his, she recalled Eddie waving so sweetly as his father carried him out of the visiting room.

Today, though, there was no swagger, no neatly cut hairstyle. His natural waves flicked in all directions, his skin was pale, and his eyes lacked that confident glint.

'Harper, I'm so glad you came.' He sat down and slid his hand across the table for her to hold.

But she pulled it away. 'Teddy, don't.'

He looked at Eddie and smiled. 'All right, Son?'

Eddie nodded. 'Shall I get some food, a tea, Teddy, I mean Dad?'

'Yeah, good idea, Son.'

As soon as Eddie got up from his chair, Teddy turned to Harper. 'Babe, I have no one. I have nothing. I miss you. I—'

'Yeah, I know just how that fucking feels.'

'Oh, I see. It's like that, is it? You've done all of this to get your own back. Because I stopped visiting you in prison, and I stopped you seeing Eddie, now it's payback. Is that right?'

'You never knew me at all, did you, Teddy? I'm not that kind of woman. I'm not you. And I didn't put you in here. You did that all by yourself. You tried to kill Vadim because all you could see was the amount of money shoved under your beak and the promises of plenty more from the most unscrupulous Russians on the planet. And because you couldn't bear the thought of Vadim and me having any feelings for each other, jealousy turned your insides out, didn't it?'

Teddy didn't interrupt her; he simply shook his head in denial.

'You couldn't stand to think of me being happy with anyone other than you. It was fine for you to live your best life with my sister while I was inside because you knew where I was and what I was doing. But then I came out and had something going with Vadim.' She sighed and shook her head. 'You revelled in the idea that you thought you had broken the man. But you didn't break Vadim, Teddy. Although you almost broke me. But you didn't stop there, though, did you? I think you loved to see me weak with heartache because, in your small brain, you conjured up a fantasy of being my knight in shining armour. You could scoop me up from the pit of grief and offer me a flash home, diamond earrings, and dine me in fancy restaurants. But what was worse – if anything could be – was that you completely ditched your moral compass the day you decided to work for the Russian mob.' She shook her head. 'Human trafficking of young girls? You disgust me, Teddy. You really do.'

Vehemently, he shook his head. 'Not human trafficking. No, I didn't know anything about that. Sure, I knew about the meth labs, yeah, but not the kids.'

Harper bit the inside of her lip. 'Not the kids? No? So how did you manage to get your hands on Yalina, a kid who you brought to your home and paid for her to have sex with . . .' She stopped, looked around her, and lowered her voice. 'With our fourteen-year-old son, for fuck's sake? Didn't you think that was odd? She is a *child*. They *both* are! What the fuck was the matter with you?'

He lowered his face in shame. 'All I've ever wanted was you and me and a decent life. I fucked up, I know, but my intentions were good.'

Harper leaned back on the hard plastic chair, shaking her head in disbelief. 'Your intentions were good? Really, Teddy? Were they good when you had a hand in Paddy's murder? You couldn't just let me be happy. You were a fucking greedy, cocky, narcissist who honestly believed in your warped, sick mind you could have it all.'

His eyes were suddenly wide as his head shot up. '*What?* No, I never!'

She grinned. She knew Teddy only too well, and his look told her he'd had a part to play in Paddy's murder.

'I spoke to the policemen who arrested his actual killer, and you gave Paddy's killer a tip-off, didn't ya?'

The mere storm in his eyes told her she was right. 'You looked up the man who Paddy served time over, and you gave him my address. You knew he would want to kill Paddy.'

He stared back, now defeated and silent.

'Ya know what, Teddy? I felt guilty when Paddy died. I went to his grave day in, day out. I knew you were there watching, and I hated you with all my being. You took my son, you took Vadim, and then you took Paddy, and so I detest you. I was going to get you one day. Then Hatty, Paddy's sister, told me that the police had his killer in custody, so I doubted my feelings. I had been cruel to think that you would have killed Paddy.'

Teddy folded his arms, his eyes pools of sadness, but those puppy-dog eyes didn't wash with her now.

'I tortured myself by constantly going over the facts until I couldn't stand the not knowing. I had to know the truth, so, as I say, a few weeks ago, I managed to get to speak to the coppers who arrested his killer. They told me that someone had tipped the perpetrator off to where Paddy was that morning. And the only fucker who knew where he was that day was you, Teddy Ryder. Because you had been following me all the time like some sick-minded stalker.'

Eddie approaching the table with his arms full, had Teddy snapping out of his stare. 'Thanks, Son.'

As Teddy took the chocolate bars, he looked back at Harper, clearly stumped for words.

'I'm going to the ladies' room. You two can talk.'

Eddie nodded and waited for his mother to leave the table.

'So how is school?' asked Teddy, not knowing how to speak after the conversation he'd had with Harper.

'I've changed schools.'

'What?'

'Didn't you read my letter?'

'What? Oh yeah, sorry, of course. So how's the new school?'

'Don't bother with small talk, Teddy. We both know that I was mainly a bargaining tool for you.'

'No, Son. Don't be stupid. I love you. I always have. You're my boy.'

'You told many lies to keep Mum and me apart.' His eyes filled up as he looked around. 'I remember a room like this one. I remember Mum sitting at the table, again like this. You were walking away, and when I looked over your shoulder, my mum was smiling and crying all at the same time. I have never forgotten that expression on her face. I can still see the pain she held behind her eyes. I knew you did that to her and to me. You denied my mother until it suited you, and then you wanted her to live with us like you had done nothing wrong.'

'No, it wasn't like that. I was doing it all for you. I wanted the best for you.'

The moment he saw his mother heading their way, Eddie stood up and said, 'Goodbye, Teddy.'

The overhead strip lights reflected off something on Harper's left hand.

Teddy looked as though he was taking his last breath. He couldn't believe what he was seeing. There, now, in full view was the most enormous diamond ring on her finger. He glanced in horror and leaped from his seat to grab Harper's hand. '*Who?*' he demanded, before two officers physically dragged him back to his chair and forced him to sit down.

Harper didn't answer. She slid her hand around her son's waist and walked towards the door.

Eddie glanced back at his father. There was no pain on his father's face. There was no goodbye smile either. But there was anger and frustration. Eddie shook his head in disgust. His father was behaving like a spoilt child in not getting his own way.

'Harper, don't walk away. Please. You can't leave me here like this, alone to rot!'

Under her breath, she mumbled, '*But you left me to rot, Teddy Ryder. You left me.*'

Other books by Kerry Barnes

Ruthless

Ruby's Palace

Raw Justice

***

Cruel secrets

Wicked Lies

Ugly Truth

Raising A Gangster

***

The Hunted

The Rules

The Choice

***

Voice of Reason

Voice of Rage

***

Deceit

***

Outcast

***

Trusted

Taboo